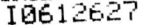

EPERTASE

UNTAMED

DOUGLAS R. BROWN

Epertase Publishing

UNTAMED

Book Two in the *Werepets Unleashed* series

Douglas R. Brown
Published by Epertase Publishing
Copyright © 2023 Douglas R. Brown

Copyright ©2023 by Douglas R. Brown
ISBN: 978-1-7368820-7-8
Edited by Rebecca Brown
Cover art by Steve Murphy

Visit Douglas R. Brown on the Web at
www.epertasepublishing.com

BOOKS BY THE AUTHOR

THE LIGHT OF EPERTASE BOOK ONE
LEGENDS REBORN
THE LIGHT OF EPERTASE BOOK TWO
A KINGDOM'S FALL
THE LIGHT OF EPERTASE BOOK THREE
THE RISE OF CRIDON

TAMED

DEATH OF THE GRINDERFISH

A FIREFIGHTER CHRISTMAS CAROL AND
OTHER STORIES

A WICKED LINE

.

To the love of my life, I dedicate the *Untamed*. For thirty years you have been my world. I love you, Angie. Now and forever.

UNTAMED

IN THE YEAR 10,000 B.C.E., THE DOG
WAS DOMESTICATED BY MAN.

12,000 YEARS LATER, THE
WEREWOLVES GOT THEIR TURN.

AND NOW IT'S TIME TO HUNT THEM.

SPORT

PROLOGUE

Curtis couldn't catch his breath. He'd been running through a strange jungle all night, and for the life of him couldn't remember how he'd gotten there. His right shoulder had gone numb and he couldn't lift his arm anymore after taking a bullet when he'd last stopped for a rest.

As a werg, he could see in the dark and run faster than those bastards chasing him, even with his one dead arm. It was probably the only reason he was still alive. There were at least three of them. From what he could tell, two men and a woman. When they got too close he could smell their gunpowder.

After finally losing their scent, he leaned against a tree for another rest and evaluated his wounded shoulder. At least the bleeding had slowed.

His heart pounded into his skull as he gasped for air, a high-pitched sound accompanying every labored breath. Why were they trying to kill him? Where was he?

Exhausted, he staggered away from the tree and caught another scent, this one of meat and blood. He couldn't remember the last time he'd eaten. Maybe that was why he was so weak.

He locked on to the fresh scent, momentarily forgetting the chase, and followed it to another tree. A small animal carcass, maybe a squirrel, dangled from a rope. He licked his dry lips and looked around. Somewhere deep down he might have realized it could be a trap, but his thoughts were a fuzzy mess.

He moved forward, stepping onto a small pile of leaves. Something clanked at his feet an instant before flesh-ripping pain rocketed up his leg. His eyes darted down to the jaws of a trap clamped around his shin, metal teeth embedded in his bone. He yanked his leg back, but a chain fastened to the trap went taut with a jolt and doubled his pain. He grabbed the metal jaws, ignoring the agony it caused, and thrashed and pulled until his good arm felt made of lead and his lungs couldn't suck in air fast enough. He lunged for his lower leg, about to gnaw it off.

"There you are."

Curtis spun around with his teeth bared.

A lone man stood holding a rifle and wearing an evil grin. "You did real good outlasting the others. You gave me quite the chase."

The leaves rustled to the man's left, and another man stepped out of the brush. "This one's mine, Gary."

"Heh. Not this time, Carson. I got to him first. These are my points."

"We were both tracking him. It was my bullet that wounded him and slowed him down."

"Yeah, but then you lost him," Gary snapped. "I found his trail." His voice rose. "You were just following *me*."

Carson held up his hands. "Okay, okay, okay. Calm down. How 'bout we share these points? Does that sound okay?"

Gary made a strained face and then nodded.

"Good," Carson said. "Let's hurry before Jody finds us. She's too close to me on points as it is. I can't afford to share this one with her."

Gary snickered and shook his head. "You two have got to be the most competitive couple I've ever met."

Carson snorted. "Probably. But that's why I love her so much." He tilted his head as he looked at Curtis. "You think Mr. Salvatore will be mad about the damage from the trap?"

Gary leaned forward for a better view. "Nah. It's not too bad. They can stitch it up and hide it."

"Yeah, you're probably right. So, are you taking the shot, or am I?"

Gary grinned again. "If you don't mind, I'd love to." As Carson stepped back to watch, Gary lifted his rifle.

Curtis lunged at them in a rage, but the trap stopped him just out of reach. He growled and snapped his teeth. Gary's rifle bounced slightly.

Curtis barely heard the pop over the roar of his own bloodlust, but he felt the impact to his chest and his back hitting the ground.

The two men approached cautiously and hovered over him as he lay frozen and helpless. It wasn't that he didn't want to kill them; he just couldn't find any strength to move. A burning pain filled his throat even as a chill rushed through his body.

The two men stood over him and watched as the night faded into absolute blackness. He heard their voices in the dark.

"He still looks good enough, don't you think?" Gary asked.

"Yeah. Mr. Salvatore will be pleased," Carson answered. "This one'll be the perfect display for his foyer."

Gary grunted. "That Italian bastard's one sick puppy, huh?"

"Heh. I guess. This was the toughest hunt we've had this year. Pietro really put us in handcuffs not letting us use explosives."

"What? Did you wanna blow the hell out of him?"

"I don't know. Maybe. I didn't bring grenades for nothing."

They were quiet for a moment before Carson said, "Hey, have you seen his new pets yet? Those winged thingies?"

"Oh yeah. I've heard they're even more violent than these wergs."

"That's what I've heard, too."

Someone nudged Curtis with his foot.

"It looks like he's about done," Gary said. "I'll call for the cart. Why don't you finish it? I hate watching them suffer so much."

"You old softie." Something cold and sharp touched Curtis's neck. "They'll sew this up, too, right?"

Curtis didn't hear an answer. Blood poured over his fur around his neck. What little air he had been getting into his lungs disappeared, replaced by gurgling emptiness. He fought desperately to get it back. He didn't want to die.

The two men laughed and joked, their voices growing distant like they were moving toward the opposite end of a long tunnel.

"That'll do it," Gary said. He said something else, but Curtis was beyond hearing.

WERG RESCUE

1

Christine stood in full werg form beside a six-foot-tall fence topped with razor wire on Chicago's south side. She scanned the neighboring buildings with her night vision. There was no one around, but she needed to hurry. Morning was approaching fast.

She effortlessly jumped over the razor wire with a duffel bag of clothes over her shoulder. She shifted back to human form and quickly got dressed.

The trail she'd been following had led her to a warehouse for decorative brick and concrete items not affected by temperature extremes. It was designed without bay doors on either end to allow truck drivers easy access. Christine stepped inside.

The dull orange glow of dawn through the windows near the high ceiling painted three-foot-wide slivers of light on the concrete floor. Christine stepped into one of the slivers.

The slight breeze shifted, bringing the scent of her prey wafting past. She needed to be extra careful now. He had probably already caught her scent too.

This particular werg had been some rich brat's toy and had so far avoided the Dog Catchers. That wasn't their official title, of course, but it was easier to say than the mouthful that was the Federal Bureau of Werg Registration and Welfare.

The warehouse was silent save for two distinct sounds. One was a steady drip from the leaky roof in one aisle between stacks of bricks, remnants of an earlier storm. And the other was the sound of her unsteady breaths. She held perfectly still. This was always the scariest part of the hunt. Nervous anticipation kept her head on a swivel. Her heart beat at twice the speed of a clock's second hand.

And then a beast on all fours exploded through the puddle in the aisle. He was magnificent. If he had been hunting average prey, it would already be too late.

But Christine wasn't average prey. She dropped her duffel bag and stood her ground.

He dipped in and out of each sliver of sunlight, grunting as he ran. Bloodlust filled his eyes. She could already smell the rotten meat on his breath.

Once locked in, he attacked head-on, indicating he wasn't any more clever than the average pampered werepet. Her eyes shot left and then back to the charging beast.

The last thing she wanted was to fight him, but it was looking like she might have to. He was within twenty feet when she let the whites of her eyes drown in inky black and her nails lengthen into claws.

"Damn it, Aiden," she whispered. "Where are you?" The beast pounced from a few feet away. She dove from his path, still holding on to her mostly human form. He hit the floor, surprised at her speed, and scrambled to recover for his next attack. And then a tranquilizer dart punched into the side of his neck.

Christine scrambled out of reach as he rose to his feet and roared. The echo reverberating through the warehouse could awaken the gods. He wobbled as she scooted away.

Aiden burst from one of the shadowy aisles, slung a metal net over the disoriented and pissed off werg, and dove onto the werg's back.

The beast flailed, his strength rapidly fading thanks to the dart's highly diluted form of Carfentanil. A slightly stronger dose would have brought down an elephant. The werg thrashed beneath the net, his movements rapidly growing sluggish. Aiden rode him to the ground.

Once the werg finally went limp, Aiden's wide eyes shot to Christine. "Are you all right?"

She stood up and dusted herself off. "I'm fine. What the hell were you waiting for?"

He climbed off the sleeping werg. "I couldn't get a clean shot. He was faster than I'd expected. When the wind shifted, I lost his scent and—"

She waved off his excuses. "I thought I'd have to fight him."

"I know. I'm sorry." He gave her a sly grin. "You could have handled him, though."

Christine rolled her eyes. "Yeah, probably."

He pulled off the net and tossed it aside so he could roll the unconscious werg over, exposing the back of his furry neck. "You got the stuff?"

Christine grabbed her duffel bag and slid it to him.

He fished out a medical kit. "We have to act fast. This one sometimes runs in a dangerous pack. We might need to bail in a hurry. Keep your eyes peeled and your nose sharp." He nodded at the werg. "Unless you're ready to try it?"

Christine considered briefly, but then shook her head. "I'll watch one more time. Maybe the next one." It wasn't that she was timid with medical procedures—she was a paramedic after all—but this was basically backroom surgery, and one wrong move could paralyze the poor guy for life. She held a flashlight for Aiden instead.

Aiden spread the werg's skin apart with two fingers and wiggled the barbed tip of the Carfentanil dart free like he was removing a fishing hook. Then he used a scalpel to slice open the skin on the back of the neck.

Christine watched closely as Aiden described each precise cut before removing the bloody WereHouse microchip and dropping it to the floor. He shoved a bandage over the fresh wound. They would finish cleaning it up after the werg shifted back to human. It usually didn't take long after removing the chip.

While they waited, Aiden caught her eye.

"What?"

He shook his head. "Nothing." He leaned in and gave her a peck on the lips.

She playfully pushed him away. "We don't have time for that."

He continued to smile. "You're always so serious."

She shrugged and shook her head. "Here. Help me get him on his back."

They rolled him over as the fur on his face sucked into his pores and his snout started to shrink. It was likely his first shift to human in quite some time. He'd be disoriented when he woke up. As his shift continued, a rail-thin, twenty-something man with red hair, freckles, and pockmarks slowly replaced the powerful beast.

Christine turned his head and removed the gauze. Aiden pinched the surgical site shut while she stretched Steri-Strips across the wound. She applied a fresh bandage. With the wound covered, she retrieved a syringe of Narcan. Though the shift back to human would have burned off some of the Carfentanil, it was a strong enough dose that it could still suppress his breathing. Plus, they didn't want to leave him sleeping unprotected in a dark warehouse for the next several hours. He shivered and pulled his knees to his chest as he began to come around. Aiden dressed him in an extra set of clothes from the duffel bag while Christine pushed Narcan into the vein on the inside of his elbow.

He moaned as he slowly came to. His eyes fluttered. Then he sat up like lightning had struck him.

Aiden placed a firm hand on his shoulder. "Take it easy, pal. Everything's all right now."

The young man's eyes darted around the warehouse, the speed of his breathing like a snare drum. "Wh-wh-where am I?"

Christine knelt in front of him until she captured his panic-stricken gaze. She saw the terror in his dilated pupils. His reaction was no different than her many patients who'd had anxiety attacks over the years. She gave him a soothing smile. "You have to try and calm down. I know it's hard," she said in a calm, comforting tone. "Focus on your breathing. In through your nose, out through your mouth." She demonstrated with her own slow, steady breaths.

His breathing slowly eased as the tension in his face melted away.

"You're doing good," she said softly.

"What happened?" he asked when the worst of the anxiety attack was over.

"You were a werepet," Aiden answered bluntly. He rarely sugarcoated the details.

"I-I-I don't understand."

"It's okay," Christine said. "Tell us your name?"

"S-Sy."

"What was the last thing you remember?"

"I-I-I don't know. A black van following me, I think. I ..."

Christine touched his hand. "You're gonna be okay, Sy."

Sy reached for the back of his neck, but Aiden brushed his hand away. "Don't touch that. It's gonna be sore back there for a bit. That's where the chip was."

"Chip?"

"Yeah. To keep you a werg, the WereHouse surgically implanted a microchip into your neck. I know you have a shit-ton of questions, but you were running with a pretty rough pack of wild wergs, and we can't stick around here."

As if on cue, a wolf-like howl sounded outside, followed closely a second one from the opposite direction.

Aiden shot a nervous look at Christine. "I don't have enough tranqs to help them all. We need to get moving."

She nodded. "Can you stand, Sy?"

He climbed to his feet and wobbled. Aiden steadied him.

Christine slung her duffel bag over her shoulder and Aiden snatched his from where he'd stashed it. He rolled up the net and stuffed it in.

She sniffed the air. "They're getting close from the west."

"I know. I smell them, too. You get Sy to safety. I'll lead them away and meet you at the hotel."

She scowled.

He sighed. "I'll be fine. This is what I do, remember?"

She reluctantly agreed and took Sy's hand. "Come on." Together they ran toward one end of the warehouse while Aiden headed for the other.

She led Sy toward the entrance gate where a flatbed truck had stopped outside, its engine running and the driver standing at the facility's keypad.

"Perfect," Christine said. By the time they reached the gate, the trucker had swung it open and was back in his cab. Christine passed through as though she belonged there.

The trucker furrowed his brow when he noticed her.

She waved and shouted over the engine's rumble, "Early start this morning, huh?"

He was confused, but since she obviously wasn't stealing anything—bricks would be tough to hide—he didn't question her.

She led Sy to the nearest bus stop where she left him with an envelope of cash and a prepared letter better explaining everything that had happened to him.

With Sy safely on the next bus, she returned to the hotel as planned and waited for Aiden. It was still hard for her to believe she was helping to free werepets with the very man who had tried to kill her when they first met. And it was even more unbelievable that he had won her heart.

As morning passed into afternoon, she grew concerned, nearly wearing out a path in the carpet with her pacing. She was on the verge of going to look for him when the door rattled and opened.

"Where have you been?" she shouted.

Aiden went to the foot of the bed, sat down, and rubbed his forehead. "Those fuckers tracked me for hours. I was lucky to lose them without a fight." He glanced up at her with a shy grin.

"Why are you looking at me like that?" she asked.

"You were worried."

She scoffed. "No I wasn't."

"Yes, you were." He took her hand.

She playfully pulled it away. "No. I wasn't."

His grin broadened. "I can't believe this. The rough and tough firefighter extraordinaire Christine Alt was worried about little ol' me." He pressed his forearm dramatically to his forehead. "I think I'm gonna faint."

"Stop it. You're being ridiculous."

He let out a groan and fell dramatically to his back.

She sat next to him. "You're impossible, you know." She shook his shoulder. "Now, get up. I'm hungry."

He didn't move, his eyes clenched shut.

She shook him again.

He still didn't move.

"Okay. You asked for it." She pressed the knuckle of her middle finger to his sternum and gave him what paramedics called a sternal rub. Whenever someone faked being unconscious, which was way more common than one would think, a sternal rub would force them to react. She was very good at them.

Aiden grimaced and swatted her hand. "Ouch. Stop it."

Christine sat back. "Did you forget what I do for a living?"

"No, but I didn't expect you to grind my sternum into my spine." He sat up and lifted his shirt in search of a bruise.

She rolled her eyes and smacked his shoulder. "Stop it. I barely touched you."

He leaned in for a kiss.

There was something strong yet gentle about Aiden's touch. She loved kissing him.

After eventually pulling away, she said, "I wish I didn't have to work tomorrow. It'd be nice to stay another night." She went to the mirror above the dresser and tussled with her hair. "Thoughts on dinner?"

"Some place nice?"

She crinkled her nose. "I'd rather someplace fun."

He stepped behind her and put his arm around her chest. She leaned into him. "I saw a bowling alley arcade not far from here. I bet they have food. We can bowl and play some games."

Her eyes widened. "That would be great. I owe you an air hockey beatdown after our last game."

"You're welcome to try. Though I figured you'd want to go somewhere nicer considering the date."

She gave him a sly smile. "And what's so important about today?"

"Three months ago today, I found the stones to officially ask you out and you said ... maybe."

She chuckled. "Don't act like you suddenly found the courage out of nowhere. I was giving off some pretty strong signals." She grabbed her makeup bag, kissed his cheek, and started for the bathroom. "It was three months ago tomorrow, by the way. But nice try."

They ate at the bar of the bowling alley restaurant. She ordered a Cobb salad, and he ordered ribs. Unable to resist, she snuck a rib off his plate. She still didn't like meat all that much, but sometimes her cravings got the better of her.

After they finished eating, Aiden set a skinny, black, rectangular box with a red bow on the bar. "I probably shouldn't give this to you until tomorrow, but here you go."

Her forehead creased. "Aiden. You shouldn't have gotten me anything."

He brushed off her protest with a wave. "Go on. Open it."

Hardly able to contain herself, she slid the ribbon off and pried open the top. Inside was a thin, gold necklace. She lifted it from the box. "Aiden, it's beautiful."

"You like it?"

She tried it on. "Of course. But you shouldn't have."

"Why not?"

"It looks expensive."

He scoffed. "Don't worry about that. I made plenty of money working for Bernard. He may have been a prick, but he paid me obscenely well."

Christine bristled internally at the mention of the man who had unleashed the werg virus on the world and turned her whole life upside-down. She really didn't want to think about Bernard Henderson right now.

"Well, I love it. Thank you." She kissed Aiden.

After dinner, she got her revenge at the air hockey table and, though he wanted a rematch, she quit while she was ahead.

They played a couple of other games and gave their winning tickets to a little boy playing nearby. On their way out, she pulled Aiden into a photo booth and slid the curtain closed. After feeding money into the machine, she sat on his lap and directed his face to the screen as the timer counted down from three.

"Smile," she said.

They made different faces for each of the four flashes, including an overly serious one and a goofy one that gave them both the giggles.

They climbed out and she grabbed the photo strip as soon as it dropped into the slot. "Perfect," she said as she playfully held it where he couldn't see.

"Come on, Chris. Let me see."

She flashed it at him and then yanked it away before he could grab it.

"Chris, that's a terrible picture. Let's do another one."

She shook her head. "No way. I said it's perfect."

"But I look like I'm having a baby."

She snorted. "Too bad. I'm keeping it. In fact, I'm gonna hang it on my fridge so you see it every time you're over."

He groaned.

As they were making their way hand-in-hand to the car, she noticed some commotion near the back of the parking lot where a van had stopped. Several uniformed men hoisted an unconscious werg into the back. She pointed it out. "Look," she whispered.

"Dog Catchers," Aiden growled.

A chill ran through her body. Dog Catchers always made her nervous, despite Senator Wooten's pledge to leave her and Aiden be. She didn't completely trust the crooked politician.

Aiden clenched his jaw and shook his head. "I recognize that werg. He ran in that pack with Sy. I had him as a future rescue. I need to work faster."

Christine squeezed his hand. "You're doing everything you can."

"It's not enough."

JERICHO

2

Jericho Bennet sat at the bar of a local dive, sipping at his second Jack and Coke of the evening. Though he tried to hide his trembling from the cute bartender, covering up the shakes was getting harder and harder these days.

She didn't act as though she'd noticed. "You from around here?" she asked with a playful smile. She couldn't be older than twenty-three.

"Yeah." Jericho tapped his empty glass. "If you don't mind."

She poured another. When she set it down, she leaned in with her elbows on the bar. "I haven't seen you in here before."

Jericho picked up on her flirty tone. "First time. Nice place." He sipped at his drink.

She smirked. "It's okay, I guess. You single?"

Jericho gave a warm smile. "Darlin', I'm probably twice your age."

She bit her lower lip. "I won't tell."

He chuckled. Though tempting, he hadn't dated anyone since his wife had left him two years back. "I'm not lookin' for any company right now."

"No?" She brushed his hand with a finger. "You sure?"

It surprised him how good a woman's touch made him feel after two years without. He nodded, fully aware that he would kick himself when he woke up alone in the morning.

She made a pouty face. "Suit yourself." Then she wiped the bar top with a dry rag and moved on to another customer.

As Jericho finished his drink, he kept his eye on a group of three men and four women hootin' it up at the corner table. They'd been at it all night. The man in the center of the action, who never seemed to buy his own drink and always had a woman in his lap, was the one he'd followed there. Young, handsome, and confident. All Jericho knew of him was that his name was Adam and he was a fighter with a special gift. It was that gift which most interested Jericho. He just needed to get him alone without causing a stir.

By midnight, Jericho had traded his Jack and Cokes for water. He hoped to go to the bathroom at the same time as Adam, but the little prick had the bladder of an elephant. What Jericho wouldn't give to be twenty-something again.

Just when Jericho's bladder had him dancing in his seat, Adam pushed the young lady off his lap and stood up.

"I gotta put out a fire," he said loud enough for the whole bar to hear.

Jericho sighed. *Finally*. He threw thirty bucks on the bar, thanked the pretty bartender, and made his way to the men's room. He was already mid-piss by the time Adam opened the door.

The squirrely loudmouth stepped up to the only other urinal beside Jericho. Despite only coming up to Jericho's shoulder, he stood tall and proud. "Ahhh," he groaned. He glanced over and gave a nod. "Sometimes taking a leak can be better than sex, am I right?"

Jericho quietly stared at the newspaper on the wall above the urinal and finished his business. Standing next to someone while holding your prick wasn't the best time to start up a conversation. Especially not one as serious as what he had planned. He zipped his fly and went to the sink.

Adam finished and stepped beside him. But instead of washing his hands, he flicked his bangs away from his eyes and primped in the mirror like a high schooler on a date. He turned to leave.

"Your name's Adam, right?"

The young punk hesitated with his hand on the door handle. Without looking back, he said, "You sellin' insurance or some shit, boomer? I'm not interested."

"I know your secret."

Adam's eyes narrowed. "I don't know you, pal. But you're skating on thin ground."

Thin ground? What, is this guy an idiot? "Just hear me out. I know where you were earlier tonight, and I know what you can do."

"And what can I do?" Adam subtly clenching his fists at his side wasn't lost on Jericho. Someone pushed the door from outside and Adam pushed back. "Piss off. It's occupied." The guy on the other side gave up and moved on. Adam stepped away from the door. "I don't know who you are, but if you know what I can do, then you know how dangerous it is to make me mad. So, you'd better git on with it."

Jericho held up his hands in surrender. "I'm not here to make you angry. I just need some help."

The whites of Adam's eyes flashed to black for a split second. He took a deep, calming breath. "How'd you hear about me?"

"I've been lookin' for somebody who can do what you can do for a while now. A friend told me about the Dog Park. I went there tonight to check it out, but couldn't get in. Then I saw you leavin' with your friends and a bunch of rich snobs were congratulatin' you on your fight. I put two and two together and followed you here."

"You followed me?"

Jericho nodded. "But just to talk."

Adam relaxed his fists and rubbed his chin. "Hmph. You talk to anyone else about me?"

Jericho shook his head. "Nah, man. I swear."

Adam checked his watch. "I don't wanna talk about this in here. Meet me in the alley behind the bar in twenty minutes. And don't say shit to anyone else. If I even smell someone else with you or think you've talked to anyone, I'll gut you like a bird. You understand?"

Jericho nodded.

Adam glared back at him as he flung open the door. Like flipping a switch, he dropped his serious demeanor and slipped back into the jovial partygoer. "You all better not be drinkin' without me," he shouted.

Jericho left the bathroom and headed for the exit without making eye contact with anyone. Once outside, he paced in front of a Dumpster behind the bar for the next hour and a half.

Last call was at 2:00. It was 2:15 when he decided the kid had blown him off.

But then a shadowy figure appeared at the end of the alley and stood like a statue in the darkness. It was skinny enough to be Adam.

Jericho waited, half expecting a Wild West whistle to announce a quick draw. The figure stepped forward, moving into a cone of light. It was indeed Adam. He stopped a few feet away.

Jericho extended his hand. "Thanks for coming."

Adam ignored it. "Are you a pig?" His face fell into a scowl. "Or maybe you're one of the Dog Catchers."

"Dog Catchers? You mean the feds?"

"Yeah."

Jericho shook his head. "Doc says I have Parkinson's Disease. Early stages."

"And?"

Jericho held up his trembling hand. "See this? It's only gonna get worse."

Adam rolled his eyes. "This ain't Dr. Phil. Tell your problems to someone else. Besides, a lot of people live with diseases like that."

"But we might not have to anymore. I saw on 60 Minutes that scientists are lookin' at the werg virus for all kinds of interestin' things."

"Like what kinds of things?"

"Different cures and such."

"Oh, let me guess. Parkinson's was on that list?"

Jericho nodded. "And I found an online forum where some dude said gettin' infected cured his MS."

"That still doesn't tell me what this has to do with me."

"I want your help. I know you've got the virus."

"Heh. You do, do ya?"

Jericho nodded.

Adam tapped his chin for a couple of seconds. "Tell me, Jericho. What do you do?"

"Construction. MMA as a hobby."

"And you'd be willing to become one of those monsters for a chance to cure your disease?"

"I would. I have things I still need to do, and I can't do them if my body turns eighty before I'm even fifty."

"Like what kinds of things?"

"The personal kind."

Adam didn't press. "Well, you've come to the wrong guy, pal." He turned to leave.

"Wait," Jericho shouted. He softened his tone. "Please."

Adam paused. "I'm listening."

"If you help me, I'd owe you bigtime."

Adam eyed him from head to toe. "Construction, huh?"

Jericho nodded.

"And you're a fighter?"

"Was."

Adam rubbed his chin. Then he held out his open hand. "Give me your license."

"My license?"

"You heard me."

Jericho reluctantly removed his license from his wallet. For all he knew, Adam was an identity thief and he was handing him a jackpot.

Adam snatched it and stuffed it into his back pocket. As he backed away, he said, "You'll hear from us soon. Don't speak to anyone else. We'll be watching." Then he disappeared from the mouth of the alley.

A heavy-handed pounding on Jericho's front door woke him with a start. His clock read 5:57AM. He'd barely gotten to sleep around 4:00. He heard muffled voices in the hallway outside. His eyes went to the closet where he kept his shotgun as he swung his feet off the couch.

"Open the door, Jericho. It's Adam." The pounding on the door resumed.

"Okay, okay," Jericho answered. "Stop. You're gonna wake the neighbors." He rubbed his forehead and went to the door. When he opened it, Adam and two other guys barged in, slamming the door shut behind them.

"Good morning," Adam said. He sauntered across the living room, taking it all in. He stopped at Jericho's trophy case and picked one up. "First place at the Arnold Classic Black Belt Division, 1998." He glanced back. "Impressive." He replaced the trophy on the shelf and pulled a dark hood from his inside jacket pocket.

"What's that for?" Jericho asked.

Adam smiled. "If you want special favors, you've gotta meet the boss. And to meet the boss, you've got to wear a hood. That's just how it is."

"Can I put on a coat and some shoes first?"

"Of course."

Jericho slipped on his shoes and coat. He had no idea what he was getting into or who all these people were, but he'd gone this far. There was no stopping now.

Adam slipped the hood over Jericho's head. "See, that wasn't so bad, was it?"

The three men escorted Jericho from his apartment and shoved him head-first into the back seat of a running vehicle. One of the men crowded in beside him while the other two got into the front. The car started moving.

No one spoke for at least an hour before the paved road turned bumpy and rough with rocks peppering the underside of the car.

The stress of his situation gave the Parkinson's an excuse to make his head bob slightly despite his best efforts to stop it. At least the motion of the car masked it from the others. He didn't want them to know they were getting to him.

Eventually, the car stopped and the doors opened. The men helped Jericho out.

The increased ache in his joints told him rain was on the way. A lifetime of contact sports had given him unwanted rain-forecasting superpowers. Maybe it had also given him the Parkinson's. Hell, he'd had five confirmed concussions between playing running back in college and fighting pro MMA.

He limped after Adam and the others to where the gravel turned to grass. Once they stopped, one of the men gently pressed on his shoulder, guiding him to his sore knees.

The hood was ripped from his head. Though the sun was only just rising and the sky was overcast with dark, angry clouds, it was still brighter than under the hood. He squinted and strained to focus. It took longer for his eyes to adjust than when he was younger. On top of all his other aches and pains, he probably needed glasses. If this was his forties, he'd be the walking dead by the time fifty rolled around.

Adam stood facing the porch of an old, two-story farmhouse with his back to Jericho. The two other men now stood flanking him. They both looked young like Adam.

One of them smirked. "Check him out, Adam. He's trembling. He must be scared."

Jericho scoffed. "I've got Parkinson's and it's fifty degrees out, dumbass."

Eventually, the front door of the farmhouse swung open and a man wearing an ankle-length, blood-red monk's robe with an oversized hood stepped onto the porch. A decorative golden rope was tied around his waist. Only the bottom half of his face showed under the shadow of the hood and Jericho could tell he too was a younger man, chin smooth and delicate.

The man walked down the three porch steps with his palms pressed together like he was praying. "Your name is Jericho?"

Jericho nodded. What kind of cult had he stumbled onto? He considered standing up because his knees were killing him, but he didn't want to risk angering the strange man. "It is."

The man grinned. "My name's Slater." Just as he said it, a wolf howled somewhere behind the house.

Jericho grinned back. He *was* in the right place. Slater gestured for Jericho to stand up. The two men flanking him helped him to his feet.

Jericho took in more of his surroundings. There was the start of what appeared to be an airport runway poking from a hangar behind the house and some heavy construction equipment off to the side.

"Why have you come here, Jericho?" Slater asked.

"I think you know."

Slater shrugged. "Yeah. Parkinson's, huh?"

"That's right."

"And you think I can help you?"

"I know you can."

Slater studied him for a second. "Even if I could, why would I?"

Jericho hated talking himself up, but he had to sell himself. There were things he still needed to do, and getting his Parkinson's under control was the first step. "Because I'm loyal. I'm upfront and tell it like it is, so you'll never worry about what I'm thinkin'. And most important, I don't gossip. Your secret, if you choose to share it with me, will always be safe."

Slater chuckled. "Tell me, Jericho. What's your family life like?"

That seemed an odd question. Jericho shook his head. "Nothin' that would concern you."

"Well, I disagree. We need to know everything about you before we would ever consider letting you stay in our little club here. Tell me, why did your wife leave you?"

Jericho cocked his head, surprised by the question.

Slater sighed. "If you're keeping secrets already ..." He flicked his hand. "Take him away."

Jericho panicked. "Okay, okay, okay. Wait."

Slater fixed him with a stern glare. "Honesty from here on out would serve you well. Lie to us and you'll help us dig a hole in the middle of the woods, if you know what I mean. Ain't that right, Trey."

One of the guys beside Jericho opened his eyes wide and traded unreadable looks with Adam.

It sounded more like bluster than a legitimate threat. Just the same, Jericho figured he'd best play along. He shrugged. "Okay."

"Now, tell me why your wife left you."

"We'd been married for fifteen years when she fell for a guy I trained with."

"MMA, right?"

"Yeah."

"Like that UFC stuff?"

Jericho nodded. "Kinda. Not competitively anymore. Actual fightin' for money or belts is a young man's game. I just train for the love of it now. And teach."

"And what'd you do about your ex-training partner?"

Jericho's eyes narrowed. "What do you mean?"

"He stole your wife, right?"

"Yeah."

"What'd you do to him?"

"I didn't do nothin'."

"Why not?"

"It was as much her choice as it was his."

Slater studied him. "And you didn't want to hurt them?"

"Pussy," Adam muttered under his breath.

Jericho side-eyed him. "I wouldn't wanna be with someone who didn't wanna be with me anymore."

Slater shrugged. "And yet, here you are."

Jericho nodded. "Here I am." They locked eyes for a few uncomfortable seconds before Slater clapped his hands.

"Adam said you do construction, too."

"That's right." Jericho eyed a bulldozer parked near the side of the house.

"Interesting. Do you have any children, Jericho?"

Jericho shook his head.

"Parents?"

"Dead."

"You got a job?"

"Did. I quit three days ago. I'm all in."

Slater scratched his head. "And you think I have what you're looking for?"

"I don't think it anymore. I know it."

Slater chewed his lower lip for a second. He shook his head. "We need fighters here. Not people who let their wives and best friends walk all over them." He flicked his hand at Trey.

Trey hesitated. "Sir?"

Slater groaned. "Just get him out of here.

When Trey reached for Jericho's arm, Jericho punched him in the mouth, dropping him. Then Jericho spun toward the other man, who put up his fists.

Adam stood by and watched, amused.

"Wait a second," Slater interrupted. "Stand down, Cole."

The young man sighed as he lowered his fists.

Slater peeled back his hood, revealing long, blond hair pulled into a ponytail with the sides shaved. A tattoo of three bloody claw marks decorated one side of his head above his ear. He pulled the band from his ponytail, letting his hair fall over the tattoo. "Maybe you do have a little fight in you after all." He glanced at Adam. "Did everything else check out?

Adam nodded. "Nothing in his background says he's ever been in law enforcement."

Slater bobbed his head. "Jericho, I like your spunk."

"As I said, I'm all in." This was the moment of truth.

Slater studied him. "Why don't you hang around for a while and we'll see what happens? Maybe we could make use of some of your skills around here."

Jericho grinned.

Slater extended his hand. "It's nice to meet you. I trust my men disposed of your cell phone already?"

"I don't know. I was under a hood."

"We took care of it," Adam answered.

"Good." Slater rested a hand on Jericho's shoulder, and it felt weightier than his size suggested. "I'm sure you understand our need to remain off the grid, don't you?"

"I do."

Slater didn't need to spell out how illegal harboring unregistered wergs was now. With werepets being released into the wild by owners who had suddenly developed consciences once they'd learned what their pets truly were, the government was struggling to get a handle on things. Werewolves everywhere, both chipped and unchipped, had become a growing threat to society. At least a hundred people had already been killed by wild ones, according to the national news, and that was only in the US. Who knew how many more had been infected.

"There're some rules here," Slater continued. "First, you earn your keep. Second, you stay off the grid. If you do go out, you don't tell anyone about this place and don't leave any digital footprints. You know, credit cards, speeding tickets. That kind of thing. As you can already tell, I make all the decisions and my decisions are final. Got it?"

Jericho nodded.

"I can't stress this enough. If you go to the city, blend in. Do not, and I repeat, *do not* let anyone know what we are."

"Easy enough. So, when does it happen for me?"

Slater held up a hand. "Patience. You earn your way for a bit and then we'll see. Cole will take you back to your place after the work's done today to pick up anything you might need. Clothes, cash, that kind of thing. You'll put your thirty days' notice in for your lease so no one comes looking for you. If you work out here, we have a person who can make you new legal documents like driver's licenses and passports and such."

"What do you mean make them? Like forgery?"

"How else do you think we stay off the grid? Sylvia can pretty much make any kind of document. She's got all the software and is quite talented."

"Okay. I get the driver's license, but why a passport?"

"In case we need to take my plane somewhere. We've been known to enjoy a weekend up in Canada on occasion. Lots of hunting grounds up there. You ever seen a moose in person?"

"Can't say that I have."

"They're quite impressive. And durable."

Jericho didn't have any intention to stay with Slater's group forever, but being off the grid wasn't the worst idea in the short term.

A loud siren blared and a red strobe light flashed from the second story just below the eaves.

All eyes went to the strobe.

"What's goin' on?" Jericho asked.

Slater shrugged. "Probably nothing. Perimeter alarm. Likely tripped by a deer or something. Adam will take care of it."

Adam disappeared around the back of the hangar just before a beastly roar echoed from that direction.

Slater grinned and clapped his hands. "How 'bout I show you around?"

Jericho extended his hand toward Trey, who now stood gingerly touching his bloody lip. "Sorry 'bout that, brother."

Trey regarded Jericho's hand briefly before shaking it.

As Slater started walking, he pointed to some open land and more construction equipment behind his house. "We're getting ready to build an apartment building. We could use your expertise."

"Just give me the tools."

As they rounded the side of the house, Jericho got a better view of the runway and the hangar it stretched from. "Who's got a plane?"

Slater puffed out his chest. "I do. Everything here is mine. Does that surprise you?"

"You seem pretty young to have your own plane."

"Heh. I'm almost thirty. I made a lot of money in stocks before I left it all to start this place."

Slater led him to an outbuilding and gave him supplies to set up a tent near the construction site. "You can sleep out here or inside the hangar."

"Where's everyone else sleep?"

"They sleep in my house. You haven't earned that privilege."

Jericho nodded. "The tent will be fine."

"Cole will help you get situated. We start work in an hour." He strutted back to his house.

THE FARM

3

Over the past few months of living on the farm, Jericho had settled in pretty well. He'd quickly proved his worth by heading up the construction of the apartment building behind the main house. His construction knowledge, combined with Slater's seemingly bottomless well of cash and everyone's hard work, had seen the completion ahead of schedule. The finished project consisted of two stories with ten apartments on each floor, a cafeteria, weight room, laundry room, and half-court basketball gymnasium.

Nearly everyone in Slater's motley crew had managed to impress him. Trey had taken to drywall work like a natural while Cole enjoyed framing the most. Cole was the more confident and outspoken of the two. Jericho often noticed Trey giving Cole subtle glances in search of approval after completing various tasks or attempting a joke. The two often spent a lot of time messing around on and off the worksite and it was obvious they had become close. Adam had some electrical skills he'd learned from his uncle when he was younger, and Jake was willing to learn anything.

Jake was a shy eighteen-year-old who had been a member of the group for less than a month. He had stumbled across Slater's property while walking along the lane after his stepdad had kicked him out. He'd offered to help with the apartment construction in exchange for a place to stay and never left. Slater took to him right away, perhaps because he was so quiet and nonthreatening.

Slater hardly lifted a finger, instead fashioning himself a foreman when he actually showed up on site.

There were two other farm residents who'd helped as well. Sylvia was a motherly older lady and the resident document forger. She had a high-pitched voice that sounded like someone talking to their pets and gave Jericho a school lunch lady vibe. And then there was free-spirited Jess. She was a pretty, petite woman in her early twenties with a purple mohawk and more piercings in her face and ears than Jericho could count. She had an obvious crush on Adam and showered him with affection while he only returned it when it suited him.

Jericho was still waiting to be given the werg virus and hardly a day passed that he didn't ask Slater about it. He was starting to wonder if Slater ever planned to follow through. He was running out of patience. He still had things he wanted to do in life that didn't involve living in a commune.

He wouldn't have stayed past day three had he believed any of the others truly bought into Slater's nonsense. Other than Sylvia, they were young and impressionable, but Slater wasn't as charismatic as he believed he was. They basically played along to keep him happy.

Another of Slater's goofy "mandatory" weekly meetings was scheduled for later that night. Jericho intended to skip as usual. They were cheesy fraternity-type affairs where Slater mostly bragged about his own greatness before discussing any issues that might have arisen during the previous week. The over-the-top production was more than Jericho could tolerate. Maybe his repeated absences were why Slater kept putting off giving him what he wanted.

That evening, he ate dinner in the cafeteria at his normal table along with Cole, Jake, and Trey while Adam, Jess, Sylvia, and Slater sat at a different table. Community dinner was another mandatory activity, but that was one Jericho enjoyed.

After finishing Sylvia's famous chicken Marsala, Slater made his way over, leaned into Jericho's ear, and whispered, "Come to the meeting tonight. It'll be to your benefit." Then he carried his plate to the sink and left. He never washed his own dishes.

At 8:55 that evening, Jericho dressed in the required dark slacks, white shirt, and tie, and headed to the cafeteria where the meetings were held. It was all very culty.

Jericho was at the doors to the cafeteria by nine, as per Slater's rules. No one would be let in if they were late. The only light in the place came from dozens of candles lining a path to a stage full of blazing torches.

The fire hazard drove Jericho nuts. But no matter how many times he'd bitched about it, Slater always ignored him.

Slater stood on the stage between two of the torches wearing his stupid robe with the golden rope belt. He held a microphone. "Jericho," he said in an excited, high-pitched voice. The rest of the group turned around in their chairs to look at Jericho.

"What's goin' on?" he asked.

Slater gestured to a single chair beside him on the stage. "Come on up. Have a seat."

Jericho hated being the center of attention. He groaned and marched to the stage with all eyes locked on him. He stood looking at the chair.

"Go ahead," Slater said. "Have a seat. It's okay."

What kind of happy horseshit is this? Jericho sat down facing the others. They were smiling. He held his hands on his lap to hide the shaking. Maybe it was time to increase his meds.

Slater began his typical spiel about how great it was to live on his farm as he paced the front of the stage. He took credit for the successful construction of the apartment building and laid out plans for the future creation of what he called "the church" where these "stupid meetings" (Jericho's words, not his) would eventually take place.

Jericho fidgeted in his seat.

After about twenty minutes of Slater's ramblings, the wannabe Jim Jones stepped behind Jericho and lowered his hood.

"Tonight's your night, Jericho," he announced. "I have decided you've earned the right to receive our gift."

The tension left Jericho's shoulders with a sigh. It was about time. He looked down at his trembling hands, imagining a life without the shakes, and it made putting up with all of Slater's bullshit suddenly worthwhile. "Awesome. So, how do we do this? Do you inject me with some tainted blood or something?"

Slater chuckled. "Not quite. Go ahead and put your hands behind the chair, please."

Jericho glanced back at him. "What for?"

Slater gave a warm smile. "Go ahead. It's okay."

"Wait a second. Tell me what's gonna happen first."

Slater's jovial demeanor hardened. "You came here for a gift, didn't ya?"

"Of course."

"Then put your hands behind your back."

"Why?"

"Because I said so. This is what you wanted, and this is how it has to happen. Now, do as I say. You only get one chance at this."

Jericho closed his eyes and took a deep breath. Then he reluctantly put his hands behind his back. His stomach tingled and his face warmed as if his blood pressure was rising.

Slater slapped a pair of handcuffs on his wrists, intertwining his hands with the slats of the chair back. Jericho's breathing doubled when the cold metal touched his skin. Up until now, it hadn't felt real because he'd always had a chance to change his mind, but the handcuffs really brought it home.

His eyes darted around the room. Everyone looked on encouragingly. Jess even smiled and mouthed, "It's all right."

Jericho's heart pounded through his chest. When Slater put his hands on his shoulders, he flinched at his touch.

"Relax," Slater crooned.

It was easy for him to say.

Slater walked to the front of the stage. "I have decided Adam will be the one who cures you of your disease." He waved Adam forward.

Adam made eye contact with Jericho and winked. "It'll only hurt for a minute, buddy," he whispered as he took off his tie.

Hurt?

Adam took off his shirt, and a few seconds later he was as naked as God had made him. The whites of his eyes blackened.

Jericho couldn't catch his breath and his fingers tingled. He'd never had an anxiety attack before, but imagined this was what it felt like.

Adam dropped his head back and released a deep, beastly roar that echoed through the cafeteria and into Jericho's chest. His fingers elongated, his black-as-night fingernails growing into daggers. His head jerked to the side. His mouth and nose pushed out from his face, and he grew two feet taller in an instant. Coarse, wild hair sprouted from his every pore.

Jericho had never witnessed a transformation. It was horrifying beyond anything in his wildest imagination. For the first time, he had second thoughts.

Every snap and crack and pop of Adam's bones sent shockwaves through Jericho's soul. The agony on Adam's face was almost too hard to watch. Jericho twisted his wrists in the cuffs, his skin scraping raw against the metal.

When Adam's shift was complete, his devilish eyes locked on to Jericho's terrified gaze.

Slater leaned in and whispered, "Everyone feels like you do at this moment. Be strong and embrace your new birth." He backed away and stood proudly to the side, rubbing his hands together.

A low snarl left Adam's mouth as he moved closer, his heavy steps thudding on the stage.

Jericho stiffened and pushed the chair backward, his eyes wide as saucers. "Wait, wait, wait," he cried as Adam leaned in, his breath hot and wet on Jericho's face. Jericho turned his head to the side.

Adam clamped on to Jericho's shoulder with flesh-piercing teeth, sending a jolt of fire through his body.

Jericho grunted as the pain reached his brain. Adam fed on his blood like a vampire for a few seconds before jerking his head away as though the taste of meat was too tempting.

Slater pressed a gauze pad to Jericho's gushing wound. The blood held it in place. When he undid the handcuffs, Jericho shoved a hand to the dressing.

Adam stepped off to the side, shifted back to human form, and redressed. He gave Jericho a nod. "Sorry about that, pal."

Slater's grin couldn't have been any broader when he held the microphone to his lips again. "That concludes this evening's meeting."

Jericho was stunned, trying to process everything that had just happened.

Slater turned off the mic and set it aside as the others formed a line at the base of the stage. He offered his hand to Jericho. "Congratulations. We'll help you adjust to your new gift and teach you how to control it over the coming days. For tonight, though, go to your apartment and get some rest. You might be a little nauseous. Don't worry. That's normal."

Jericho hesitantly shook his hand. Slater left via the back of the stage. Jericho stood up and timidly walked down the steps. He was almost in a daze, trying to process everything that had just happened.

Each member of the group congratulated him and patted his back as he passed. Sylvia peeked under the dressing and smiled. "It'll be fine, sweetie."

Unsure of how he felt about all of this, Jericho made his way back to his apartment, suddenly exhausted. He vomited three times before he crashed on the bed and slept for the next twenty hours.

PIZZA NIGHT

4

It had been almost a year since Christine and Aiden had brought down the WereHouse, and almost seven months since they had rescued Sy. She had stopped going with Aiden on missions shortly after that, settling back into her life as a firefighter. She had burned most of her vacation leave, which made spontaneous trips around the country difficult. Aiden still asked her to help with any local werepet rescues, but she felt she was only slowing him down. He had become even more obsessed with saving as many as he could before the Dog Catchers could find them.

Christine had just gotten back from an afternoon EMS call when an announcement came over the PA that it was time to make pizzas. Firefighter tradition dictated Saturday was family night, Christine's favorite night to work. The firefighters made homemade pizzas for their spouses and kids. Few things better broke up a twenty-four-hour shift than seeing your family and watching children laughing and playing around the trucks.

Christine sauntered into the kitchen from the bay to help. "Hey, guys, did you see it started snowing?" She loved when it snowed.

Willie, the official firehouse cook, wannabe weatherman, and local fun-sucker answered, "Don't get your hopes up, Chris. It's just gonna be flurries today."

She crinkled her nose at him. "You suck, Willie."

He shrugged. "I try."

The kitchen had a long, stainless-steel island where Willie rolled the dough. His flour-covered apron read *Firefighters answer the call ... For dinner*. Sweat streaked his forehead and a drop hung precariously from the end of his nose.

Christine grabbed a paper towel and dabbed his face like he was a surgeon performing a heart transplant. "Willie, I'd prefer my pizza without sweat, if you don't mind."

"Flavoring," he quipped.

Christine gagged as she threw the wet towel in the trash. The next time sweat formed on his forehead, he wiped it away with his sleeve. It wasn't ideal, but better than the alternative.

She took a pan of flattened dough to one of the two long tables and set it next to a rookie named Anthony who everyone had started calling Junior because he was only twenty and his dad had been on the job for years at another station. When Anthony argued that he wasn't a junior because his dad had a different first name, that tiny bit of protest was enough to make the nickname stick, likely for the rest of his career. This was Anthony's second Saturday at Station 22.

Eight stainless steel bowls sat in the center of the table, each with a different topping. Christine grabbed the one with sauce first and spread it on the dough.

Then the cheese. "Hey Junior, pass the mushrooms," she said.

Their lieutenant, Alex, entered the kitchen next. "Where's the anchovies?" he asked as he clapped his hands. The mention of anchovies sucked the air from the room.

"Seriously, Lieu?" a firefighter named Dave asked. Dave had transferred into the station earlier in the year. "Are you really going to use anchovies again?"

With an evil grin, Alex answered, "Of course. Anchovies are gooood."

"In the pantry, Lieu," Willie said.

Christine glared at him. "Why do you keep buying them? You can't just tell him you forgot? It ruins one of the pizzas."

Willie shrugged.

Alex crammed himself in between Junior and Christine and playfully nudged her. Nothing made him happier than ruining a pizza with anchovies. He opened the can and took an exaggerated sniff.

Christine made a pained face as Alex lifted an anchovy from the can and let it drip onto Christine's previously perfect vegetarian pizza.

"Really, Lieu?" she groaned. Disgusted, she abandoned her almost finished pizza. "I guess this one's yours now."

His smile never faltered. "Thanks."

The kitchen door swung open and her former medic partner Billy popped in. He worked a nine-to-five position at headquarters now, but still stopped in for pizza on Saturdays.

Christine's face brightened when she saw him. "Hey, Billy."

"Hey, cougar." He bounced his eyebrows at her.

She groaned.

Though he'd gotten a prosthetic hand after losing one in the fight with Bernard at the WereHouse, he rarely wore it. When Christine asked him why, he'd replied, "I'm not gonna hide who I am just to look how other people consider normal." Then he added, "Plus, it's an icebreaker with chicks." Same old Billy.

"What's the brass got you doing nowadays?" she asked.

His shoulders slumped. "Building inspections," he groaned.

"That sounds ... fun?"

"Yeah. Fun." He couldn't have laid on the sarcasm any thicker if he tried.

Willie put the pizzas in the oven, seven altogether, including Alex's anchovy monstrosity that stunk up the entire room.

The crew wiped down the island and tables and pulled out the plates as families started to arrive. Mick's wife and two kids showed up first.

When Mick's son, Devin, saw Willie, he ran to him. "Hey, Willie?" Devin held out his closed hand.

"Hey, homeslice. Whatchu got there?"

"A Matchbox car."

Willie swiped it and held it up for a better look. "Well, I'll be. That's a nifty toy. What is that? An ambulance?"

Devin giggled. "No, silly. It's a ladder truck."

"Oh." Willie handed it back.

"You wanna play tag, Willie?" Devin looked ready to burst with excitement. All the kids loved Willie.

Willie rubbed the back of his neck. "Uhh. I'd love to, but I'm pretty busy right now. How 'bout after dinner?"

Devin bobbed his head.

Christine grinned and checked her phone for the tenth time. She had been anxiously waiting to hear from Aiden. He was set to return from a hunt in Northeastern Ohio at any moment. Shortly after Willie's wife arrived, Aiden texted that he was there. She excused herself, grabbed her jacket, and raced outside to greet him as he got out of his car.

She met him with a passionate kiss in the parking lot. "How was the hunt?" she asked as they walked to the station door.

"Flawless. I freed two former pets this time."

"Really? Two? That's great."

"One had been a pet for nearly six years."

"Wow."

"He said he was from Florida. The other guy was from Cleveland, but farther east than where I found him."

She didn't realize she was staring until he stopped and gave her a funny look. "Why are you looking at me like that?"

She shied away. "I'm just proud of you."

"Why?"

"Helping all these people all the time."

"It's the least I can do after everything I've done to them in the past."

She opened the station door. As they walked through the bay, she asked, "Are you staying at my place tonight or yours?"

"Mine. I'm heading down to Kentucky tomorrow and need to get things ready. I'll be gone before you even get home in the morning."

"Why're you going out again so soon?"

"I've heard of something I need to look into right away."

"Oh?"

"There's an albino werg that's been spotted going through Dumpsters and I'm hoping to get to it before the Dog Catchers get wind." He got out his phone and pulled up a photo. "This was taken two nights ago." It was a remarkably clear picture of a werg standing under a streetlight. "Do you see anything odd in this pic?"

"Yeah. I've never seen an albino."

"Besides that."

Christine studied the picture. Her eyes widened. "Is that a …?"

Aiden nodded. "Yep. A female. And I'm wondering if she has a chip."

"A chip? How?"

"I'm not sure."

"But I thought the WereHouse didn't do females."

"They didn't."

"I don't understand."

"Remember, the chips don't tame the wergs. It was the WereHouse's torture that did that. The chips just kept them from shifting into humans and kept them confused. Someone out there might be experimenting. I'm going to see what I can figure out."

"Should I take some time off and go with you?"

"Nah. I'll be fine. I'll let you know what I learn."

Christine led him to the kitchen door, but Aiden tugged her hand before they went inside. "What?" she asked.

"I've had a lot of time to think on my hunts and I was wondering something."

"Okay?"

"I was wondering … well …" He looked away.

She leaned into his view and giggled. She found it adorable when he suddenly got shy. "What is it?"

"I was just wondering if … I think it's kind of ridiculous us both …"

"Go on."

"I mean … Keeping clothes at my place and yours seems silly since I spend most of my time with you when I'm in town …" He looked away again.

Panic crawled up from her stomach as she realized what he was getting at. She shook her head. "Aiden? Don't …"

"Why not?"

Now it was her turn to look away.

"Chris, listen to me." He gently steered her head back and took a deep breath. He held her hand. "I just thought it might be nice. But we don't have to move in together if you're not ready."

"Well, I'm not," she snapped. The thought of moving their relationship forward gave her incredible anxiety. In the past, she'd always managed to sabotage her relationships when they started to progress too quickly.

"I don't understand you. Every time I think things are going well, you push me away. Why?"

She squirmed, feeling suddenly attacked. Her face flushed and she nervously rubbed her cheek. She didn't want to talk about it right now. "Maybe I'm just not ready." Her tone was angrier than she'd intended.

"Okay, okay. Jeesh. I'm sorry I even brought it up." He let loose her hand.

She cocked her head. "What? So now *you're* mad?"

"No."

"You sound like it."

"It's just that—"

"What?"

"Why do you have to be like that?"

"Like what? You brought it up."

"I wouldn't have if I knew it was going to upset you so much."

Even as she searched for a winning argument, she hated that she was getting so angry when he was trying to do something nice. She just couldn't help it. "Why did you have to bring this up now while I'm at work?"

"I didn't mean to upset you, Chris. I just really care about you."

They stared at each other, both waiting for the other to say something else until Billy opened the kitchen door. "You guys standing out here all night or coming in?"

Christine headed into the kitchen while Aiden stood motionless. She glanced back with a sigh. "I'm sorry, Aiden. Let's eat. We'll talk more about it later."

He lowered his head and followed her.

After dinner, Aiden mingled with the others as if nothing was bothering him. He was good at compartmentalizing his emotions. Billy stood beside Christine. "When are you gonna get rid of that guy?"

"What do you mean?" For a second, she wondered if Billy had suddenly matured and recognized the tension she and Aiden had brewing. Maybe he saw in Aiden what Christine subconsciously pushed away from. Maybe—

"You know, so we can hook up. I've always wanted to be with a cougar." He grinned.

She was shocked to realize she'd actually missed his openly sexist, and at times harassing, comments. He was just lucky they had the kind of friendship they did and she wasn't offended. She rolled her eyes. "You're too much."

He held up his stump. "It's the missing hand, isn't it?"

"Billy, trust me when I say this. You had zero chance of ever getting any of this, with or without a missing hand." She gestured to her own figure as if she were modeling lingerie.

He laughed and gave her a hug.

When she turned back to Aiden, she caught him sneaking a piece of anchovy pizza and groaned.

The flash of the kitchen television screen caught her eye. The news was on, the anchorwoman reporting another police shooting involving a werewolf in the small town of Heath, Ohio. These things were becoming all too common. A wild werg had broken into a house for food and killed a man who was trying to protect his wife. Alex turned up the volume.

"… When officers arrived on the scene, they had to use their new werg protocol, which includes silver bullets and flash grenades, to subdue the beast. They are still trying to determine the werg's human identity …"

Aiden sadly glanced at Christine. As hard as he'd been working to find former werepets and free them of their microchips, he still wasn't moving fast enough. It was too big a job for one person.

As people began to leave after dinner, Christine walked with Aiden to his car. He started to climb in without saying anything.

"Hey," she said before he closed the door.

He looked up.

"I'm sorry. I didn't mean to upset you. You know how I get sometimes."

"I know."

She leaned in for a kiss.

He gave her his cheek. "I'll see ya when I get back." He reached for the door to close it.

She stepped back.

He paused and looked up at her. "Not every man is like your dad, Chris."

His words hit her so hard she staggered.

He yanked the door shut, started the car, and pulled away. She watched his taillights, already regretting not saying more. She vowed to make it up to him when he got back.

By Sunday evening, Aiden had made it to a diner in the small country town of Sadieville, Kentucky, north of Lexington. Nine patrons quickly huddled around after hearing Aiden ask about the werg sightings.

"The old cemetery outside of town," one older man said. "That's where it's been seen most recently. Usually around dusk."

Aiden nodded. A cemetery would be a good hunting ground for smaller game. "Is there a forest near the cemetery?"

"Yeah," a woman replied. "I live near there and it tore up my chicken coop last week. Who'd you say you were with again?"

"Werg Registration and Welfare, ma'am," he lied, hoping they didn't ask for a badge.

Her eyes widened. "Didn't think you'd get here so fast. I only told the Sherriff about my chickens yesterday."

Shit. If the Sherriff knew, the real Dog Catchers might be on their way.

Another woman eagerly showed him a shaky cellphone video of the stunning, all-white albino sniffing around her back deck late one night. "I barely got my dogs inside before it showed up," she said. "Ain't that right, Fred?" The man beside her nodded.

On the small screen, Aiden could make out the werg's milky fur matted with dried blood around her snout and hands.

"Looks like it's been snacking on some deer," Fred chuckled.

Aiden hoped a deer was all she'd been snacking on. If a wild werg tasted human flesh, it would become one of the deadliest creatures alive. That thought prompted him to ask, "Has anyone been reported missing recently?"

The room turned somber at the thought.

"I don't think so," Fred answered.

"Good. She probably hasn't hurt anyone yet, but I'd keep my distance if I were you."

"She?" Fred asked.

"We think so. We won't know for sure until we catch her."

"I never knew there were girl werewolves."

"Occasionally one slips through." Aiden thanked them for their help before getting directions to the cemetery, paying his bill, and leaving.

The sun was setting and the werg would likely be getting ready for a nighttime hunt. With the imminent threat of the Dog Catchers looming, Aiden needed to be quick. He cursed the day the Werewolf Oversight Committee had called for the formation of the new federal agency.

As if on cue, Aiden passed an outdated political sign supporting the former Senator Wooten's presidential campaign. It read *Elect Senator Michael Wooten to shield our nation from Wergs, Waste, and War*. The bastard had used his position as head of the WOC to ride the fall of the WereHouse all the way to a landslide victory in the presidential election. Aiden rolled his eyes.

Ever since Bernard's business had collapsed, wergs had been turning up everywhere. From rogue pets locked in their beastly states to unscrupulous people willingly taking on the curse, the world had lost its collective mind.

It was fully dark when Aiden pulled off the road across from the cemetery entrance. He checked that his tranquilizer gun was locked and loaded with a Carfentanil dart before holstering it on his hip. With a silver blade and two flash grenades next to his dart gun, an AR-15 strapped to his chest, and a duffel bag slung over his shoulder, he climbed out of his car. He'd started carrying the AR and silver blade for use as a last resort after an especially close call in Philly had forced him to reevaluate his vow to never hurt another werg. He hurried across the street near the cemetery entrance and pressed his back to one of the stone pillars beside the iron gate.

He scaled the fence and quickly caught a very distinct scent. Pheromones from a female werg. He was in the right place.

He lowered his rifle to his hip, the strap holding it at just the right position for a quick grab, and pulled his dart gun from its holster. Locked on to her scent, he stalked downwind from grave marker to grave marker until he saw movement at the entrance of a mausoleum.

It was her. She was chewing on something crunchy like a bone. He picked up a rock, held the dart gun close to his chest, took a deep breath, and tossed the rock over the mausoleum. The crunching stopped and the sniffing started. After a few seconds, she stepped outside, scenting the breeze. She was more stunning than any picture or video could do justice.

Aiden extended his dart gun. By nothing short of bad luck, she stepped behind a mausoleum pillar. *Damn it.* He knelt behind a grave marker and used the top to steady his aim. He just needed her to step into the open again. "Pssst," he hissed.

Curious, she peeked around the pillar.

Perfect.

He squeezed the trigger, sending a red feathered dart into her exposed chest just below her right collarbone. She yelped and swatted at it, but its barbed tip held it in place.

She dropped to all fours and retreated. Knowing she wouldn't get far, Aiden nonchalantly stood up and holstered his gun. All that was left was tracking her to wherever she eventually fell and freeing her of her curse. He trailed her scent until he saw her again near a tall angel statue.

She wobbled and fell against it, knocking it over and breaking the angel's head free against a concrete slab. She scurried back to her feet, drunkenly tumbling over another tombstone. This time she didn't recover as quickly.

Just a few more seconds and ...

A waft of unnatural scents froze him in his tracks. Sweat. Metal. Gunpowder. Someone else was hunting that night. But who? Dog Catchers? A new brand of rogue hunter? Farmers pissed about their missing livestock? Whoever it was, things had just gotten more dangerous.

He raced to her side and pulled her behind a headstone. Her confused eyes followed his movements, glinting green in the moonlight, and she lunged lazily at his neck with her teeth. But the potent Carfentanil was doing its job.

"I'm here to help you," he whispered.

She stared at him as her head lolled to the slab. He rested a gentle hand on her shoulder as her breathing turned deep and laborious.

Staying on high alert, he rolled her over to expose the back of her neck and parted the fur, hoping to not find a scar. To his horror, there was one.

He slung his duffel bag to the ground. "When you wake up, you'll remember what it's like to be human," he whispered. "I'm sorry for what I have to do." He put a flashlight between his teeth, got out a scalpel, and went to work. Delicately, he cut out the chip and held it in the flashlight beam for a better look. He wiped the blood away with his thumb and revealed the letters WH. But that didn't make sense. Either Bernard had lied about never using female wergs as pets, which was unlikely, or someone else had entered the game. He grimaced and smashed the chip with the pommel of his knife.

He sniffed the air again. Whoever had joined the hunt was getting closer.

The albino's werewolf snout receded, and her white fur sucked back into her skin. Her claws shrank into human fingernails while the rest of her body morphed into a naked young woman. She was pale with short, spiky white hair.

He hurriedly covered her wound. Then he pulled out some winter clothes from his backpack and began the arduous task of dressing an unconscious person. As he stuffed her into a sweatshirt, something on her lower back caught his eye. He paused for a closer look. It was a three-inch-tall brand that said PET. His stomach sank. He knew the WereHouse had never branded their wergs.

He dug out a syringe of Narcan and injected it into her upper arm. Kneeling next to the tombstone, he watched for the other hunters as he waited for her to wake up.

After a couple minutes, her eyes blasted open as if she'd seen the end of the world. She scrambled to her rear, ready to scream.

He shoved his hand over her mouth. "Shhhh. It's all right. I'm here to help."

Her eyes were wide and terrified.

"You're free now," he whispered, holding her with a steady gaze. "Don't scream." He slowly lowered his hand from her mouth.

"Wh-wh-who are you?" she asked.

"My name's Aiden Talik. I've been tracking you."

She reached for the back of her neck with a wince and Aiden gently guided her hand away.

"I had to remove the chip," he said.

"What do you mean? What chip?"

"Have you ever seen a werepet?"

She shook her head. "I know what they are, though."

"That's what happened to you."

She gasped and lifted a hand to her mouth.

He gave her an envelope containing a little cash and the same form letter he gave to all the former werepets. "This will explain everything. I wish I could tell you more, but there's no time. There're others out here hunting you right now."

"Hunting me? Who?"

"I don't know." Aiden scanned the gravestones, his hand on his rifle. "What's your name?"

"Selena. Wh-where am I?"

"In a cemetery."

"No, I see that. I mean, what city?"

"Sadieville, Kentucky. What's the last thing you remember?"

She shook her head.

"Do you remember being kidnapped?"

Her face twisted. "I was visiting friends in Indianapolis. We got separated."

"When?"

She squinted as she worked it out in her head. "I think January. It was right after my birthday."

"What year?"

She drew back like it was an odd question.

"What year, Selena?"

"2012."

He lost his breath. It wasn't Bernard. Someone else had joined the game.

"Everything's so fuzzy."

"It's gonna be like that for a while. You may never fully get the memory back of your time as a pet."

Whoever was tracking them stopped at the broken angel statue. A man said, "That way."

"Stay hidden," Aiden whispered.

He started to stand, but she clutched his arm. "Take me with you. Help me."

"I can't. I need to lead them away. It's your only chance."

She nodded, gazing at him with increasingly wet eyes.

He gave her a comforting smile. "I know it's a lot to take in. If I don't make it outta here tonight, go find a firefighter named Christine Alt in Columbus, Ohio. Tell her what happened to me. She'll help you and explain everything. Can you do that?"

She nodded.

"After I lead them away, run. And don't look back."

She still held his gaze.

"You're strong, Selena. You'll be okay."

He put on his game face, squeezed the pistol grip of his AR, and prepared for a fight. His hands were already sweaty. He whispered, "Good luck," and crept to another row of graves where shadows were moving in the moonlight. He sat with his back pressed to the stone. His breaths hovered in the chilly air.

"This way," someone shouted.

His back rode up the gravestone and he craned his neck to see over it. There were four of them, spread apart and armed to the teeth. They didn't look like farmers.

Just as his finger found the trigger guard of his AR-15, one of the hunters shouted, "Aiden Talik, we only want you."

Aiden lost his breath. *Me?*

"You've been a tough one to find. Come out willingly and we'll leave the albino alone."

"I don't know you," Aiden shouted.

The man chuckled. "Well, we know all about you. We've been watching Snowflake. We knew you wouldn't be able to resist coming for her."

It sickened Aiden to hear the pet name they'd given her. He saw a brief flash of his own werepet he had named Rufus when he was a stupid kid. He would never truly be free of his own sins. But this wasn't the time for self-recrimination. He hoped Selena had gotten a good enough start. He grabbed a flash grenade from his belt and pulled the pin.

"What do you say, Aiden?" the man shouted. "Come along peacefully?"

"Sure," Aiden shouted back. He heaved the flash grenade and dashed toward a nearby tree. As he ducked behind it, a blue-feathered dart struck the bark near his head. His flash grenade popped. He lifted his rifle and strafed the hunters with bullets. They dove for cover as chunks of headstones exploded in the air.

Aiden hid again, plastering his back to the tree. He'd hardly caught his breath before a smoking canister landed beside him. It popped and released a fruity aerosol agent. He knew from his experience working for the WereHouse that sleeping gas was designed to be deployed indoors and wasn't very effective on wergs out in the open. It dissipated too quickly. Humans on the other hand …

He shoved a handkerchief over his mouth and nose and tied it bandit-style around his head. He held his breath and got ready to run, but when he stuck his head out another dart whiffed past his cheek.

A second canister popped and fizzed nearby. The hunters had already flanked him. He wobbled, the handkerchief not enough to filter out the gas.

The only way to fight the drug's effects was to shift. It was probably exactly what they wanted, but it was the only thing that might keep him awake long enough to escape. He tossed his duffel bag aside, dropped his gun, and roared at the moon. The color drained from the world. His fingers bent and snapped. The pain of his bones twisting was as agonizing as always. His head dropped back, and his shoulders clunked awkwardly forward. His face stretched as though made of putty filled with a million raw nerves. His nose and mouth protruded from his face. His chest jutted outward and his ribs shifted. He yowled.

They surrounded him. When he lifted his head again, he saw with rage and smelled with bloodlust. They were skilled. To lead them away from Selena, he'd have to engage one of them and give himself enough space to flee. He'd have to be fast. He waited for one of them to get closer and then bolted like a gunshot around the tree. He slashed the man's chest, his claws meeting a bulletproof vest instead of flesh. The impact knocked the man hard against a gravestone. It was enough to give Aiden a chance.

But the sleeping gas had slowed him, and a dart struck him from behind. He dropped to all fours to flee. The other hunters charged. He stumbled toward the mausoleum, hoping to find enough cover to figure out his next move. He misjudged the distance and crashed into the side.

"Where are you going, Aiden?" one of the hunters taunted.

Aiden fell to his rear as the world spun. Maybe shifting back to human form would burn off the drugs in his system and allow him a chance to get away and regroup. The color returned to the world, but everything was still blurry.

His transformation burned through enough of the drugs to keep him awake, but his arms and legs felt like Jell-O. He looked past the four approaching hunters to where Selena hid behind a stone cross, watching with a hand held over her mouth. The hunters hadn't seen her.

A face with a thick, dark beard and dark features loomed into Aiden's view. The man's eyebrows bounced and he smiled. "Hey, Aiden. How ya been?"

Aiden didn't recognize him.

"Relax, buddy. You don't know me, but I worked in the Jacksonville chapter back when we were on the same team." He knelt and patted Aiden's shoulder. "You're gonna make the company a pretty penny, my friend. You've been requested personally." He turned to the others. "Let's get him to the Underground."

Aiden closed his eyes.

STRAINED

6

Christine and her EMS crew marched toward a shithole of a house. The front door was cracked open and it was dark inside. An old tube TV sat on the front porch, the grass and straw of a bird's nest poking from a fist-sized hole in the broken screen. A wooden bench swing hung from a rusty chain, one end resting on the warped wooden porch.

Christine's medic partner, Mick, shoved the door open with a flashlight. "Fire Department," he called out before stepping inside. The carpet had been removed, leaving a sticky hardwood floor covered in stains. A cockroach scurried away from his feet. He directed his flashlight beam to a couch where two children slept on opposite ends. The TV played an old eighties slasher film with a guy in a hockey mask. It was three in the morning.

"Hey," a man called from the hallway. Mick shot his light toward him. The man was shirtless, rail-thin with sunken cheeks, and pockmarks covering his skin.

Festering sores ran up both of his arms in various degrees of healing and seeping.

"Track marks," Christine whispered.

Mick nodded.

"Watch your feet," she said to the approaching engine crew guys. "There might be needles on the floor." She paused. "Or bedbugs."

"She's in the bathtub," the man cried. "You gotta help her."

As he led them down the hall, an ammonia stench punched Christine in the face and she covered her nose.

A woman was in the drained bathtub, soaking wet and only wearing a white T-shirt covered in vomit down the front. She wasn't breathing.

"What'd she take?" Christine snapped.

"Nothing," the man answered. "I mean, I don't know."

"Bullshit. Just tell us what you guys usually use. Heroin? Meth?"

"I don't know. She was gettin' clean."

"What's she normally take, then? We're not the police. We just need to know so we can help."

Mick pushed the bathroom door open and squeezed past Christine. He lifted the patient's head for a better look at her face. "Hey, Chris. It's Sharon again."

"Oh. Then it's heroin." Christine crowded into the small bathroom and searched for a pulse. She found a weak one. "We need to get her where there's more room to work."

Willie and Dave squeezed past and reached into the tub while Christine carried the emergency kits back to the front room. As she passed the junkie in the hall, she asked, "Why's she so wet?"

"I-I-I threw her in the tub and turned the water on. I-I-I thought it would help."

Christine rolled her eyes. "That only works in the movies. Don't do that next time." It was one of her biggest peeves as it just made everything slippery and harder to work with. Yet the general public always seemed to think it helped. "The good news is she's more likely to drown than die of an overdose this time." She probably shouldn't have been so flippant, but she was tired of sugarcoating it. Especially while working her third overdose of the shift.

Mick joined her in the front room while Willie and Dave dragged Sharon out. Christine had already drawn up the Narcan by the time they pulled Sharon into the living room. Junior pressed a mask tight to Sharon's face and squeezed the bag attached to it. Despite being a rookie, he'd already had plenty of experience with druggies and had quickly learned how to deal with overdoses.

Christine sprayed the Narcan into Sharon's nostrils. "Just breathe for her until the Narcan kicks in."

Junior nodded.

While Mick searched for a vein in Sharon's right arm, Christine glanced at the couch to see two sets of wide eyes staring back. She smiled warmly at the two children who couldn't have been older than five or six. "Hi."

They waved shyly.

The junkie rushed over. "Is she gonna be okay?"

"Probably. This time, anyway. Why don't you take these kids somewhere else? They don't need to see this." Children watching adult nightmares was another of her peeves. She was developing a lot of them.

The junkie snapped his fingers and waved the kids to the back bedroom. "Get the fuck outta here," he shouted as they ran past.

Christine bit her tongue.

The front door opened and two police officers stepped inside. "Hey, Chris," one said. "Whatcha got?"

"Hey, Brian. It's Sharon again. Probably heroin."

Brian and his partner stood and watched; there was little more they could do. Police were always sent on unconscious people calls just in case the scene got violent.

Christine gave Sharon a sternal rub. Sometimes overdose patients liked to stay asleep even after the Narcan kicked in. Sharon's eyes blasted open and she gasped. She pulled the mask from her face and scooted backward to the couch, her eyes still wide as coasters.

"Damn it," Mick said, holding the IV catheter, which was no longer in her vein. "She yanked it out before I could get it secured." He retrieved a bandage and shoved it against Sharon's bleeding arm. "Calm down, Sharon. You know the routine."

"I didn't do nothing." She pulled her knees to her chest. She was shivering.

"I know you didn't," Mick answered. "Just like the last five times we've run on you." He looked to the junkie. "Get her a blanket and a change of clothes."

The junkie stood motionless. "I-I don't really know her. She don't live here. None of her clothes are here."

"You at least got a T-shirt and some sweats you can let her borrow? I mean, she almost died in your bathroom."

"I'll look." He disappeared into the hall.

Christine went to stand next to Brian while Mick dealt with Sharon. "Busy night?"

Brian grunted. "Always is." He hesitated.

Christine tilted her head. "What's up?"

He rubbed the back of his neck. "I, uh, saw your dad again tonight."

Christine's shoulders drooped. "Oh. Where this time?"

"At the corner of High and Williams. He's got a new sign."

"Damn."

"I thought he was staying with you?"

"Nah. He did for a bit, but he said he didn't want to be a burden anymore and left. Something's eating at him, but I couldn't get him to talk about it. Plus, he started drinking again."

"Ah, shoot. I'm sorry. I know how it is. My dad was an alcoholic, too."

"Yeah. Thanks."

"You want me to go over and see if he'll take a ride to rehab again? At least so he can get a couple hours of good sleep?"

Christine touched his shoulder. "I don't think so. Thanks, though. I appreciate it. I'll check on him when I get off duty. What time is it?"

"Three."

She nodded. "Yeah. There's no use talking to him right now. He'll be pretty shitfaced."

"Let me know if you need anything."

She nodded again.

Brian gestured toward Sharon. "Are you guys taking her to the hospital?"

Sharon was already shaking her head, her eyes clearing.

"Knowing her, probably not," Christine sighed.

"Okay. If you're good here, we're gonna take off. Good luck with your dad."

"Thanks again, Brian.

By the time she got back to Sharon, the junkie had returned with a T-shirt and a pair of red sweatpants with cigarette burns in the legs. Christine tried to convince her to go to the hospital, but she adamantly refused. There was nothing else Christine could do except make sure Sharon signed a refusal of transport on Mick's computer. That was crucial since she'd likely be high again and could die before Christine even reached the truck.

"Keep an eye on her," Christine told the junkie, but she didn't put much faith in him.

Before they left, she thought about the kids and wished there was something she could do about their terrible lot in life. She'd send an email to child services through the proper channels when she got back to the station, but she knew not much would be done. The system was overwhelmed. Too much bureaucracy and hand-tying court rulings made it impossible to accomplish anything substantial.

The rest of the night was pretty mild, giving Christine a few hours of much needed sleep. After roll call, she changed into civilian clothes and headed for Williams and High. Before she turned onto High Street, she saw Steven sleeping on a bus stop bench.

She pulled into a CVS parking lot and sat behind the wheel for a few minutes, debating what she would say. Everything she'd said in the past had only started new arguments.

Finally, she dragged herself out of the car. Steven slept with his back to her. He stunk terribly of BO and booze. She pinched her nose and gave his shoulder a nudge.

He groaned.

"Hey, Steve. Wake up." She nudged him harder and considered a sternal rub.

He stretched and rolled over. It had been a while since she'd seen him. His full beard had grown back. Three red, inflamed, jagged lacerations were carved into his cheek, too old for stitches to do any good. He rubbed his face and sat up. "Oh. Hey, Chris." He licked his lips.

"What happened to your face? Are you fighting again?"

He looked away.

"What am I gonna do with you, Steve?"

He rubbed his temples. His breath was as deadly as his BO. "Don't worry about me. I'm a big boy." He still didn't look at her.

She touched his hand. It was ice cold. "Come on. Let's go get cleaned up."

He pulled away. "I don't need your charity."

"It's not charity. You need to eat and get warmed up. And your face is probably infected. I might still have some antibiotics at home that I didn't finish after my root canal."

"And what about Aiden? Will he be there?"

"He's out on a hunt. Don't worry about him. He's not mad at you."

"But I punched him."

"You were drunk. He understands. He's over it. Come on." She reached for his hand again, and this time he didn't pull away. But he didn't get up either. He lifted his eyes to hers. "I'm sorry for everything, Chris."

"Yeah, yeah. You always are." He had apologized at least two dozen times since he'd come back into her life, and she didn't believe him this time any more than the last twenty. She had learned long ago not to count on him for anything.

"Really." His eyes fixed her with a half-drunk, half-somber gaze. "I'm more of a monster than you could ever imagine."

"I don't know. I've got a pretty good imagination. Now, come on."

Neither spoke during the ride. At her condo, he showered while she made pancakes. Some of the clothes she had bought for him during his last stay were still in the spare room. She put his nasty ones in the washer.

He came downstairs almost sparkling, though he hadn't shaved. "Very refreshing. Thank you."

She nodded and set a plate of pancakes on the table. "I made your favorite. Blueberry."

He pulled up a seat.

While she washed the griddle, he plowed into the pancake stack like he hadn't eaten in days, which he might not have.

"Why are you fighting for all those rich people again?" she asked with her back to him.

"To make money."

"There's plenty of ways to make money that are a lot safer. Hell, I'd give you money just to stop drinking."

"I like the competition."

"You *like* it?"

"I guess 'like' isn't really the right word. More like it lets me release the beast and get rid of some of my pent-up anger."

"Who are you so angry at?"

He gave her a crooked look. Then he lowered his head and mumbled, "Myself, I guess."

She turned from the stove and softened her tone. "Why?"

"You wouldn't understand."

"Try me."

"Let's just say I've done things I'm not proud of."

"Like what?"

He shoveled another forkful into his mouth. "Forget it."

"I'm not going to forget it. Talk to me, Steve."

"Hmph." He took a drink of orange juice and held up the glass. "This would be a lot better with vodka."

She groaned. "It might help if you talked about it."

He set the glass on the table. "Oh, you mean like therapy. Maybe I'll pull up a couch and we can talk about my feelings. Maybe I'll have a breakthrough and the therapist won't call the Dog Catchers and report me as an unregistered werg. Wow. I think you're really on to something. Maybe I could join a circus after, and people could point and stare. If they don't put me in the electric chair firs—" He clamped his mouth shut.

Her eyes widened. "Electric chair? Why?"

"I don't wanna talk about it."

"What did you do?"

He lifted another fork of pancakes to his mouth.

"Did you kill someone?"

He froze before lowering the fork to his plate. "Just forget it, Chris." He wiped his mouth and tossed the napkin on the table.

"Was it during a fight? You can't—"

"I'm done with this conversation."

"Who did you kill?"

He pushed away from the table and stood up. "Don't. Worry. About. It."

"Steve, tell me. Please."

He turned away with his head bowed.

"Steve?"

After a few seconds, he glared at her over his shoulder. "Let's just say the world is better without the WereHouse and the people who ran it."

Christine covered her mouth. "Bernard?"

He didn't answer.

She stared at him, stunned. "That was you? On the freeway?" She touched his shoulder.

He shrugged off her hand. "I've said enough."

The reports of how Bernard Henderson had been murdered were horrifying. He had been slaughtered in his limo on the freeway in broad daylight. Her mind raced. On the one hand, she had been disgusted by how brutally he was killed, but on the other, she was relieved she didn't have to watch for him over her shoulder. She didn't know how to react. Steven was a lot of things, but she'd never imagined he was a cold-blooded killer.

And then another thought hit her. In the weeks after Bernard's death, three other WereHouse board members who had been placed under house arrest during the investigation had been viciously mauled in their homes. "And the board members ..." She couldn't finish the question, a part of her not wanting the answer.

"I'm not saying anything else."

But he'd said enough. Her stomach turned.

Steven went to the pantry and yanked it open.

Christine stood motionless. "What are you looking for?"

"You got any Jack?" he asked without looking back.

"Steve, wait."

He opened the cupboard under the sink.

She put her hands on her hips. "Now, why would I have whiskey in there?"

"To hide it."

"From who? I'm not the alcoholic."

He flinched as if her words had struck a nerve. She wished she could call them back.

She took a calming breath. "Listen. I don't want to argue. Let's go in the other room and talk."

He paused, still facing the cabinets. His shoulders slouched. "You're right. I don't wanna fight either. I'm sorry."

If she never heard the word sorry from his lips again, it would be too soon. "You know, sometimes when someone says they're sorry enough times, it loses its meaning."

He nodded and turned to face her. "You're right again. I'm sor—" He winced. "I mean, I understand."

She took his hands and looked into his eyes. "Let's go get some help again. You were doing good before."

He shook his head. "I don't need rehab. I just need a drink to get myself straight."

"That only makes things worse."

"For me it makes things better."

"You haven't drank anything yet today, right?"

"Not yet."

"Then this would be a perfect day to start over. I'll help you again." She pulled out his chair. "Sit back down and finish your pancakes."

He hesitated.

"Please, Steve. For me."

He reluctantly sat down.

"The first thing we need to do is get that wound cleaned up. It's probably infected." She went to the corner cabinet where she kept a small basket of meds and pulled out a prescription bottle. "Here they are. They should still be good." She squinted at the tiny writing on the side and cringed when she saw the expiration date. "Well, they expired a couple months ago but they should still work. You're not allergic to penicillin, are you?" She tossed the bottle to him.

He shook his head and read the label. "Amoxicillin."

"Take one now and follow the instructions. If your face doesn't start getting better in the next couple days, we'll get you to an Urgent Care. Okay?"

He stuck one in his mouth and chased it down with the last gulp of orange juice. "You know shifting helps fight infections?"

"Yeah, yeah. But it can't hurt to takes some meds, too. I'll get my first aid kit and we'll clean that up a bit. I'll be right back."

He nodded again.

She snatched her phone and called Willie on her way upstairs.

"Y'ello," he answered on the second ring.

"Willie, you got the number for our Employee Assistance Program? I need to talk to someone about addiction again."

"Your dad back around?"

"Yeah."

"A'ight. Let me look for it. I'll text it to you."

"Thanks."

"Good luck."

She grabbed her first aid kit from the bathroom and hurried back to the kitchen where she found Steven's chair empty.

The first aid kit dangled from her limp hand.

A note scribbled on a napkin sat beneath the pill bottle beside his plate.

Thank you for caring and trying to help. I wish I could be the father you deserve but I know now that I can't. I know I've said it too much already, but I really am sorry. When I get back on my feet someday, I'll pay you for the booze.

Christine turned toward the living room where her antique liquor cabinet stood. The door was cocked open.

She was almost too sad to be angry. After so many letdowns, it was her fault for letting herself think this time might be any different. No more. This was the last time she would try to help him.

She plopped onto the kitchen chair, shoved her face in her hands, and had a good cry.

THE ISLAND: ARRIVAL

7

Aiden woke up curled in a ball in a 3x3 dog cage, unable to straighten his cramped legs. He was groggy and his head throbbed like a blood vessel had burst behind his temples. He wondered how long he'd been out. Sweat soaked his clothes and hair. It felt like he was inside a closed car on a summer day. His mouth was desert dry. The air was heavy with the strong smell of jet fuel. The cage floor vibrated on a wooden pallet. A few dim fluorescent lights did little to illuminate his surroundings.

He was in the cargo hold of an airplane, surrounded by crates strapped to pallets. The deafening roar of the engines painfully echoed through the metal walls.

His lower back stung and he reached around to touch a sensitive, blistering sore. It was in the same place he'd seen Selena's brand. He wondered what it said. It was too long to be PET. He couldn't twist himself around for a look because something sharp pressed into his neck. The bastards had put him in a metal collar of some sort. Until he could figure out how to get it off, shifting was not an option.

The plane shuddered as it began its descent, eventually landing with a series of jolts and squealing tires. The vibration nearly rattled his teeth loose. When the plane stopped, everything went quiet for a good hour before the rear cargo door hissed and lowered. The muffled chatter of men outside replaced the silence. The sunlight hurt his eyes.

A forklift ascended the ramp, lifted one of the pallets, and carried it from the plane out of sight. Then it returned. Trip after trip, the forklift transported pallets until Aiden's cage was the only one left.

The forklift operator grinned at him when he made eye contact. He lifted Aiden's cage and carried it down the ramp to the runway where a half-dozen men dressed like soldiers had gathered, each holding a rifle.

"Is this the Underground?" Aiden asked the closest soldier.

The soldier snorted. "You've already been through the Underground, man. You slept through it." He banged on the cage and shouted, "You know where this one goes."

The forklift driver hauled Aiden's cage past a hangar to a bumpy dirt path that led toward the back of a one-story, strip mall-style block building. As the forklift rounded the corner to the front, Aiden saw that the building was a row of cells facing a sprawling field bordered by a distant jungle.

Aiden looked into the second cell as the forklift carried him past. A man hung inside, naked from the waist down. He had used his pants to make the noose.

The forklift operator stopped and shook his head. He keyed his radio. "Cell two has another Code One. Send someone down to clean up."

After someone answered, "Copy," the forklift started again.

Though the next cell was empty, each of the three after it held wergs. They stared at Aiden with wide, terrified eyes. The second cell from the end held a man wearing the same kind of razor collar as Aiden. He watched Aiden pass with a haunted expression. Then he looked away.

The final cell was open. The driver pulled to a stop, lowered the cage, and turned off the engine. A man with a rifle rounded the corner and stopped beside Aiden. He smelled of hand lotion.

The forklift operator unfastened the cage door and backed away. Aiden glared at him with disdain.

The man with the rifle nodded toward the cell. "Go on."

The forklift operator jammed a cattle prod between the slats, giving Aiden a jolt. The two men laughed.

"Now do you get the idea?" the one with the gun said. "We can do this the nice way or the hard way."

Aiden considered the hard way, but he needed to save his strength to fight back when the time was right. He crawled out and stood up, his cramped legs almost sending him back to the ground.

The guard with the gun kept his distance. "Go on, dog," he said, gesturing toward the cell.

Aiden marched inside and the iron bars slammed closed behind him.

"Good dog."

The forklift operator climbed back into the cab and the man with the gun hitched a ride on the forks. A puff of black smoke accompanied the engine's rev as they pulled away.

Aiden pressed his forehead to the bars and stared out over the field. Two white-tailed deer grazed at the distant edge of the jungle. At least he had a nice view.

A pair of skinny arms poked through the bars of the cell next to him. "Hey," Aiden called out.

"Hey."

"What's your name?"

"Sammy."

"I'm Aiden. Any idea where we are?"

"They call it the Island."

"Who are they?"

"Our handlers."

Handlers? What the actual fuck? "How long have you been here?"

"About a week."

"Where'd they get you?"

"I was a pit fighter back in the states. A place called the Dog Park. They jumped me right after a fight."

"Columbus?"

"Nah. Chicago."

Aiden knew about the Dog Park. The high class gambling establishment was where his father had first gotten the idea to buy him a werepet. But he didn't know it was still in business, or that there was more than one. "So you're a werg?"

"Um-hm. I assume you are, too?"

Aiden saw no reason to lie. "Yeah." He studied his cell in search of vulnerabilities he could exploit to break out.

"I'm starving," Sammy whined. "All I've eaten in the last week was a squirrel I caught yesterday. There's not much meat on squirrel bones."

A tornado siren drowned out whatever Sammy said next. Aiden waited for it to finish before asking what it was for.

"The wake-up call," Sammy answered. "They'll be here soon. We should probably stop talking."

Aiden reached through the bars toward Sammy's cell and shook his hand. "It was good meeting you, Sammy. Stay strong."

"You too, Aiden. Good luck."

Aiden backed away from the bars. A horse trough sat by the side wall with a thin layer of slime blanketing the water. Though he was thirsty, he didn't want to risk getting the runs.

Less than ten minutes later, three men dressed in tan camo tactical vests and cargo pants with the legs tucked into black boots arrived at Aiden's cell. The man in front wore mirrored sunglasses and chewed on a toothpick. He looked like the bad guy from every cheesy eighties action TV series. *The A-Team* came to mind.

"Good morning, Aiden. My name's Murdock. I'm your new handler."

Aiden nearly snorted. Murdock's voice was higher pitched than expected, which made it even funnier. "Where's Hannibal and Mr. T?"

Murdock sneered. He was probably too young to get the reference. "Are you ready to meet the boss?"

Aiden shrugged. "That depends." He nodded toward Murdock's AR-15. "Do I get one of those?"

Murdock shook his head. "I think you'll be a fun one to break."

"Yeah? And you're gonna be a fun one to kill."

Murdock chuckled. "So, here's the deal, Aiden. You let us escort you willingly or …" He tapped a dart gun on his hip. "We'll drag your unconscious ass. Your choice."

Aiden was tired of being drugged. He nodded reluctantly.

"Turn around, back against the bars, and put your hands behind you."

Murdock's two flunkies reached in and bound his hands with a zip tie. Then they opened the cell door.

"Let's go, tough guy," Murdock said.

They escorted Aiden around the side of the building toward a hill with a humongous three-story house at the top. They crossed a small pedestrian bridge to a stone staircase leading up to the house. To the right was a pole barn with a large overhead door next to a smaller man door. Beyond it was a row of army barracks. A handler stood stretching in the doorway of one of them.

Aiden glanced back to the cells where four armed guards patrolled the roof. He had yet to spot any vulnerability he could exploit.

Murdock stopped at the top of the stairs. A sign above the front door said WereHunt, Inc., which he supposed explained the WH on Selena's chip.

The doors opened to reveal a butler standing in the entryway. "Mr. Salvatore is just returning from an off-island business meeting and will be arriving shortly. He ordered a meal prepared and directed me to have you take our guest to the dining area." He stepped aside and extended his hand.

Murdock gave Aiden a shove, prodding him through the foyer to a large dining room with a banquet table in the center. Murdock's two flunkies stood on either side of the door with their backs to the wall while Murdock pulled out a chair and forced Aiden to sit. He cut the zip tie from Aiden's wrists.

The butler disappeared through a different door and then returned with a pitcher of water and a glass. "Sir?"

Aiden snatched the glass almost before the butler was done pouring and downed it in seconds. He asked for another. The butler looked to Murdock, who gave a nod.

Aiden downed the second glass almost as quickly as the first. The butler withdrew and the minutes ticked by. Though Aiden tried to get Murdock to talk, the man sat at the table and waited in silence.

Eventually, the double doors swung open and a man entered, flanked by two hideous-looking creatures that came up to his waist. They were puke-green, hunched over with their knuckles on the floor, and stank of sulfur. Their bat-like wings draped down their backs, and their pointed ears perked when they saw Aiden. They sniffed the air with two slits at the ends of their short, flattened, pig-like snouts. One of them curled its upper lip, revealing grizzly-like fangs.

The man rested his hand on its head. "Eaaasy," he whispered. "This is our guest."

The creature reached up with a three-fingered hand tipped with talons and gently took the man's hand and held it.

The man smiled. "Ciao, Aiden. I'm Pietro Salvatore." Though he had an Italian accent, his English was pretty good. His jet-black hair matched his goatee—immaculately groomed with nearly every strand perfectly in place. Aiden had seen thousand-dollar haircuts that weren't as flawless. Pietro leaned toward a mirror on the wall and fixed an imaginary stray hair. Then he brushed his goatee with his finger and thumb, took a second look at himself, and turned back. "What do you think of my pets?"

Aiden shrugged. "They're ugly. And they stink. What are they?"

Pietro walked past him, still holding the creature's hand while the other one followed. At the head of the table, they stood on either side of his chair. "I don't really know what they are, technically. A previously undiscovered species, perhaps. We've been calling them gargollas, for lack of a better name."

"Gargollas?" Aiden frowned. "Oh. Gargoyles?"

Pietro smiled. "Si." He sat down, unfolded a napkin, and draped it over his lap. "Like the statues on churches."

"Yeah, I get it."

"We found them in the jungle not far from where Bernard Henderson first found the werewolves all those years back." He made the sign of the cross in front of his chest. "Bernard was looking at them as a new line of pets before he had his unfortunate accident."

"Couldn't have happened to a nicer guy."

Pietro's shoulders fell. "Oh, Aiden. I hate to hear you say that. Bernard thought the world of you. You were like a son to him." He paused and lines creased his forehead. "You didn't have anything to do with what happened to him, did you?"

"I wish."

"I'm sure you do. I'd love to find who killed him and bring them here. Poor Bernie." He chuckled. "You know, he really hated when people called him that."

"If he liked me so much, why'd you bring me here? I didn't kill him."

"Maybe not. But he told me how you betrayed him and how hurt he was by it. That's why I sent a team to find you."

The butler returned with two plates and set one in front of Pietro and the other by Aiden. The slab of meat beside the pile of scrambled eggs looked like an ordinary steak, but the smell told Aiden otherwise.

Pietro sniffed it and closed his eyes. "Mmmm," he moaned as he took a bite. He licked his lips and his eyes practically rolled back into his head. "Delizioso." He held a napkin over his mouth as he chewed. After swallowing, he placed it neatly back on his lap. "Give it a try, Aiden."

"No thanks. I'm not one for cannibalism, pretty boy."

Pietro snorted. "Call it what you will. And you can call me Pietro, Mr. Salvatore, or sir, if it pleases you."

"Why thank you, pretty boy. You can call me Your Highness, My Liege, or Your Greatness if you'd like. And I'm not buying the werewolf meat for breakfast scare tactic."

Pietro took another bite and chased it with a sip of water. He dabbed his lips with his napkin. "I like you, Aiden. Do you know how long my company has been in business on this island?"

"I couldn't give a shit."

"Ten years now. I came on shortly after Bernard had his first hunt here and we hit it off splendidly. Eventually, he tapped me to run it. That's when we came up with the name WereHunt, Inc. Pretty good, huh? You get it? WereHouse. WereHunt."

"Yeah, yeah. You're a real genius. Is that where you got the chips?"

Pietro tilted his head. "Why, yes. You're quite clever. We didn't have a choice. It turns out rich people sometimes lose their taste for hunting when their prey suddenly becomes human again."

"I bet. Enough with the games. Why don't we just get on with it? What do you think I'm going to do for you? Shift so you can put a chip in me? Not likely."

Pietro smiled again and pushed away from the table. He wiped his mouth with the napkin one final time, set it beside his plate, and sauntered around to stand behind Aiden. "That's exactly what you're going to do, friend."

Aiden smirked. "I'm not your friend. And we'll see."

"Si, lo faremo."

"I don't speak Italian."

"No, I don't suppose you do."

"So, what now?" Aiden asked.

Pietro put a firm hand on his shoulder, causing his gargoyles to perk up. He leaned close and whispered through clenched teeth, "I'm going to let my clients hunt you, skin you, feast on your flesh, and then mount your fucking head above their fireplace for what you did to the WereHouse and my friend Bernard." He shoved Aiden's head forward. "Now eat. It's the last meal I'm going to give you. Capisci?"

"I'd rather starve."

"You could at least eat the eggs."

Aiden didn't trust anything Pietro offered. For all he knew, there was some sort of werewolf-shifting drug in them. He pulled his napkin from under his plastic utensils and covered his plate.

Pietro sighed. "Very well. You can watch me, then." He plopped back into his chair and continued eating, outrageously savoring each bite while Aiden glared through him with dagger eyes. Pietro finished, got up, motioned for Murdock to take Aiden away, and took his gargoyles from the room.

After locking Aiden back in his cell, Murdock shouted, "See you tomorrow, Sammy." Then he laughed as he walked away.

Christine hadn't heard from Aiden since he'd left for Kentucky. Though their last conversation had ended in an argument, it wasn't like him not to check in. It had been three days and she was getting concerned. She spent the fourth day after work calling his phone, but every call went straight to voice mail.

She couldn't completely dismiss the possibility that she had screwed everything up and that he was finished with their relationship. Maybe it was more irrational thinking, but it didn't make it any less real to her. She'd half expected him to leave her at some point anyway.

By the evening, her concern had turned to outright worry. Even if he was ending things, it wasn't like him to do so without telling her. She decided if she didn't hear from him by the next morning, she'd drive to Kentucky and start her own search. In the meantime, she needed to blow off some steam.

She drove out of town to a secluded wooded area and parked by a seldom travelled dirt road. It was one of her favorite spots to get in a run because she could be completely alone. The property was owned by a family who didn't allow hunters to use their land, making it the perfect place to get exercise without getting shot. She put her keys with her clothes in a duffel bag, set it in her trunk, and started for the trees.

It was a brisk day. She shivered until she welcomed the werg blood and fur that kept her warm in all but the bitterest environments. Because shifting was so painful, she had learned to do it fast to minimize the agony. She quickly caught the scent of a deer and smiled. What was better than a chase to get the juices flowing?

She tracked the scent to a stream where several deer were drinking. She crouched and stalked them downwind. The deer continued lapping up the water, hardly lifting their heads to check for predators. Christine moved closer. A lioness would be proud of her skill.

One of them lifted its head and twitched its ears. Christine froze, but she was too close and the deer locked eyes with her. The chase was on. Though her hunting skills were improving, the deer had millions of years of practice.

They bolted.

Christine gave chase, locking on to the trailing one. It zigged and zagged, and she mimicked its every move. When it leaped over a felled tree, she cleared the obstacle just as effortlessly and closed the gap.

Her pursuit was flawless. She didn't want to hurt it, only to touch it to prove she was better. The creature darted left suddenly. Christine followed. She felt its fear. She'd just reached out for its tail when it surprised her by darting right, narrowly missing a tree. She dove into a Hail Mary lunge, missing its hindquarters by inches, and tumbled into a bed of dead leaves.

She lay motionless on her back, sucking in lungfuls of wonderful air. There was nothing more exhilarating than those brief moments during a chase when all the worries and stresses of the world were cast from her mind.

But, as intoxicating as it was, all good things eventually had to end. Her mind drifted back to Aiden and how she had let him leave angry. He treated her so well that she hated herself for not embracing him like she should. Why did she always push the good ones away? Thanks to a semester of psychology in college, she knew she had abandonment issues stemming from her dad's departure when she was little, blah-blah-blah. But knowing didn't help her right now.

She sat up, the bliss of her chase a million years in the past. She rolled to all fours, dropped her head back, and howled. If there were any other animals lurking nearby, she'd just let them know it wasn't safe to let down their guard. From somewhere in the distance, a coyote answered with a howl of his own.

Respect.

Christine took the long walk back to her car, stopping briefly at the stream for a drink. After shifting back to human form and getting dressed, she checked her cell phone for any missed calls. Though she didn't expect to find one, her heart still sank to see the blank notification screen. With her mind on Aiden, she drove back to her condo, arriving around midnight.

When she turned into her parking spot, her headlights landed on a strange woman sitting on her stoop. The woman stood up. She had short, spikey white hair and pale skin that almost glowed in the dark. Her whole body practically vibrated with nerves.

Christine climbed out. "Can I help you?"

"Is your name Christine Alt?"

"Who's asking?"

"My name's Selena. I need to talk to you."

"I'm listening." Christine surveyed the parking lot in case it was a robbery. Selena started toward her, but Christine held up her hand. "You can talk from there."

Selena stopped. "It's about a friend of yours. I think he said his name was Aiden."

A pit opened in Christine's stomach. "What about him?"

"Last Sunday night, he helped me change from a werepet. He—"

"I know what he does." A million questions flooded her. "Where is he now?"

"I don't know."

Christine fumbled for her house key. As she stepped around the woman, Selena extended her hand for a shake. Christine ignored it and unlocked her door. "Come in."

Selena followed her inside.

Christine spun to face her before the door had even closed. "Where's Aiden?" she snapped.

"That's why I'm here." Selena showed her the back of her neck. "He cut out a microchip from my—"

"I know about the chips. Now, where is he?"

"I don't know. After he freed me, he was attacked."

"By who?"

"I don't know."

Christine's heart sank. "Is he alive?" The words were out almost before her brain could consider the worst possible answer.

"He was when I last saw him."

"What'd they do?"

"They drugged him and put him in a van."

"And you just watched?"

"There was nothing I could do. They had guns."

"Did they say anything? Think hard."

Selena's brow furrowed. Then her eyes brightened. "They said something about an underground."

"You mean they buried him?" Christine choked on her own words.

Selena shook her head. "I-I don't think so. They said it more like it was a place. Like *the* Underground."

"How'd you know to find me?"

"He told me to find you if anything happened to him."

Christine's brain spun. "Is that all you can think of?"

Selena nodded. "I'm sorry."

All Christine had were two words: The Underground. Who did she know who operated in the underbelly of the werg community and might be able to help? As she racked her brain, a single name came to mind, and it turned her stomach. Her head bowed. If there was anyone she didn't want help from, it was him.

Damn it, Steven.

She lifted her eyes back to Selena. "You should leave now. Thank you for finding me." She started to escort her to the door, but Selena resisted. "What?"

"Where will I go? I don't even know what happened to me."

"Did he give you a letter?"

"Yeah?"

"Did you read it?"

"Well, yeah."

"Then you know everything I know."

"But I don't know where to go now."

Christine shrugged. She wasn't a babysitter. "Go home."

"I-I can't. I've got no way to get there. I don't have any money. I spent everything he gave me just to get here."

"Where're you from?"

"Chicago."

Christine huffed. She didn't have time for this. She went to her desk and dug out an envelope of cash, one of Aiden's emergency stashes. "This should get you a cab to the airport and a flight home."

Selena reluctantly took it.

"Are we good now?"

Selena balked.

Christine cocked her hip. "What else?"

"Aiden said I was a werewolf."

"You are."

"I don't want to be one."

"You've got no choice."

"How do I live with that?"

Christine was trying to be patient. "The next time you change—"

"Change?" Selena's eyes widened. "I'm never turning into one of those beasts again."

Christine sighed. She tried to remember her own confusion after getting infected. "I'm sorry, Selena. It's gonna happen at some point. If I were you, I'd go somewhere secluded and practice until you get it figured out. Anger sometimes helps bring on the change. Once you get good at it, you'll be able to do it at will. The first time will be very confusing. Try and focus on who you are, and it'll come to you. You'll work it out. I wish I could help more, but I can't. I'm sorry."

Selena nodded, but she didn't look too sure. Christine gently nudged her toward the door and called for a cab. She apologized again and left her on the porch. Selena gave her a slight wave as Christine pulled away.

DRUG DEN

9

Christine drove around the south end for hours looking for Steven. Two separate homeless gentlemen said they thought they'd seen him at one place or another, but both of those leads came up empty.

After spending the night searching, she turned into yet another dark alley just before sunrise. Two men stood near a privacy fence at the opposite end, and one of them was Steven.

She shoved the car in park and hopped out. "There you are," she shouted.

Steven gave his friend some kind of street handshake and said, "I better take this."

His friend wandered off.

"What's up, Chris?" Steven belched a nasty wet one she could smell from several feet away. "I heard you been looking for me tonight."

"Where the hell have you been?"

"Down by the Scioto River. Some guys had a bonfire until your friends from the fire department showed up and put it out." He removed a bottle from his raincoat and took a swig. "Were you working yesterday?"

"No. Why?"

"The medics went on a guy I know. He died and I was wondering if you knew any details."

She shook her head. "I'm sorry."

"Don't be. I never liked him much. He stole my shoes one time."

"Who was it? One of our regulars?"

"Maybe. We called him Smells-like-he's-dead Fred." He smirked. "I guess he really smells dead now, huh?"

She gave him a horrified look. "That's a terrible thing to say."

His smirk faded. "Yeah, I suppose so. I was just kidding."

"How'd he die?"

Steven shrugged. "Probably drugs. He recently got into heroin."

"Oh."

Steven put the bottle back in his oversized pocket. "If you're here to give me an earful, don't waste your time. I already know I'm a piece of shit."

"I'm not here for that. I need your help." She couldn't believe what she was saying.

"What's wrong?"

"Someone's taken Aiden."

"What do you mean?"

"Some people tracked him down on one of his hunts, drugged him, and threw him in a van."

"Government guys?"

"I don't know. I don't think so, though. I thought maybe you could help."

"Me?"

"Yeah. The last thing they said was that they were taking him to some place called the Underground."

His face blanched and he appeared to sober up suddenly.

"Steeeven? What do you know?"

"Nothing good, Chris."

"Tell me."

He balked at first, but she pressed, interrogating him with her eyes.

"I've just recently heard of it."

"And what is it?"

"I'm not sure. A real nasty place from what I hear. People who go there don't come back."

"Where is it?"

"I have no idea. I'm sorry. I've just heard bits and pieces."

"Steven, please. How can I find this place?"

"I swear I don't know." Either he was telling the truth or he was a better liar than she realized.

She turned away, her mind racing. "How did *you* hear about it, then?"

"Some smackhead was running his mouth a few weeks ago."

"Who?"

"Just some other homeless druggie."

"Where is he?"

"I don't think he'll be much help. He's pretty whacked outta his mind twenty-four-seven nowadays."

"I have to try. Where's he stay?"

"It's not a good idea."

She raised her voice. "Just tell me, damn it. You owe me that much."

He sighed. "Okay. I'll tell you. But I think you're stepping into something you shouldn't."

"*Now* you're worried about me?"

His head fell forward.

She knew she'd really hurt him, but she didn't care. "Just tell me."

He nodded. "I hear he's been holed up in that old, abandoned school on Fourth. It's a drug den now, mostly for people like us who have given up."

"What's his name?"

"Nicolas."

"How will I know him when I see him?"

"Please don't go there, Chris. It's a terrible place."

"I'm going," she snapped. "There's nothing you can say to stop me. Just tell me what I need to know."

Steven visibly deflated under her piercing glare. "He's got a huge birthmark covering the side of his face."

She turned to her car.

"Wait. You can't go alone."

"I don't need babysat."

"I know you don't. But the people there will cut your throat for a dollar. Most of them are old werepets who couldn't deal with life after their owners set them free. They've got nothin' to lose. At least let me go with you."

"You're too drunk."

"I'm not. Really. Here. I'll tell you what. I'll shift. It'll burn off some of the alcohol. I'll be straight enough by the time we get there. It's the least I can do." He took off his coat.

Despite letting her down more times than she could count, he was right that it was best to have someone along. She reluctantly nodded and then climbed into her car.

Steven crouched behind the car, undressed, and shifted. Two seconds later, he shifted back and redressed. He climbed in the passenger side.

Though his shift might have burned off some of the alcohol as intended, it didn't help his breath. Christine gave him a piece of gum.

They pulled into the parking lot of the abandoned one-story elementary school ten minutes later. Most of the windows were boarded over. Gang graffiti covered the brick face in bulbous, cartoon-like letters. A set of glass double doors split the building in half and led to the lobby. One of the doors was shattered but still holding together, like the tempered glass of a broken windshield.

A woman slept beside the door, curled in a ball. Her lips had a bluish tint, and her fingers were pale and almost waxy. Christine stopped and checked her for a pulse. She had a faint one. Her skin was like ice.

Steven covered her with his coat while Christine called 9-1-1 and requested a medic truck to respond on a hypothermic patient and possible OD. After she hung up, she told Steven, "They'll be here in a few minutes. Stay with her until they get here."

"Shouldn't *you* stay with her? You're the paramedic."

"There's nothing I can do without equipment. Just make sure she keeps breathing."

He obviously wasn't happy about hanging back, but he didn't argue further. "Shout if you need me."

"I'll be fine." She entered the dark lobby. It was smoky and smelled of burning wood. The only light came from the dim moonlight filtering through a hole in the roof and a small warming fire next to the west hallway. That explained the smoke. She covered her mouth with the inside of her elbow and made a mental note to contact Fire Prevention about getting the place shut down ASAP.

She stopped by a man who was half asleep beside the fire and shook him. "Hey, buddy."

He looked up with droopy, vacant eyes. A scarf covered his mouth and nose.

"Do you know someone named Nicolas?"

His muffled voice was hoarse and weak. "Hey, baby. You got any scratch?"

She shook her head. "Not today. Where's Nicolas?"

He pulled off his coat blanket as if he was going to get up. "Maybe you didn't hear me. I said, give me some money." The whites of his eyes turned black.

Christine showed the blacks of her own eyes in return and put a firm hand on his shoulder. "You don't wanna do that, buddy."

He studied her as if weighing the risk. Then he relaxed, pulled his coat back up around him, and settled back down.

It was the right call.

She gave it one more try. "Nicolas?"

He closed his eyes, uninterested. She pulled his scarf down. No birthmark.

A werg stumbled out of the hallway, swayed, and bounced off the wall. A tourniquet was stuck to the matted fur of his upper arm. The fur on his chest was thin and patchy. Though wergs normally had thick chests and skinny waists, this one was extra emaciated. He ignored her as he stumbled past.

"Nicolas?"

He didn't react. He continued across the lobby to the east hall.

There was no easy way to go about what she needed to do. She stepped into the west hallway where people and wergs lay scattered all over. One man was helping a werg shoot up as she approached.

"Hey."

He looked up. He didn't have a birthmark either.

She nodded to his werg friend. "Is his name Nicolas?"

The man shook his head.

"Do you know a Nicolas?"

He shook his head again. He was probably lying. After shooting up his friend, he used the same needle on himself.

She watched as his distant expression turned to ecstasy and felt sorry for him. She turned her attention back to the hall. "Nicolas," she shouted in hopes of a miracle. No one responded. She would have to check every damn room and every damn face. The first door she tried was unlocked, so she pushed it open.

A naked woman lay on a heavily stained mattress on the floor. A werg was crawling onto the bed near her feet. He paused and looked up.

The woman sluggishly turned her head. "Who are you?" she slurred. Her eyes were cold and empty.

Christine looked away. "Is his name Nicolas?"

"We're busy in here. Now, beat it, bitch. Unless you want to join us."

No thanks.

Christine backed out and pulled the door closed. She glanced at the lobby where red and white lights flickered across the room. The medics had arrived. If nothing else, maybe she had helped one person tonight.

As she headed for the next room, red graffiti caught her eye on the wall next to the door across the hall. It was almost too dark to read, but she could just make out the letters spelling *The WergHouse*. It was a fitting name since this place wouldn't exist without Bernard and his evil WereHouse.

Christine tried three more rooms with no luck. She was about to open the next door when a rail-thin tweaker shouted, "Hey." Though his stringy brown hair covered half of his face, she saw the hint of a purplish birthmark behind it.

"Nicolas?"

He stopped short, regarding her from head to toe. "Who da fuck wants ta know?"

"I'm not the police. I just need to talk to you for a second."

He picked at a festering sore on his arm. "I don't know you."

"I need to know who's kidnapping wergs. I need to know what the Underground is."

"What makes you think I know anything?" His hand moved to his bare chest and scratched it raw.

"Someone who knows you said you know about the Underground."

"They're wrong."

Christine felt desperation crawling up her throat, threatening to choke her. "Please, help me."

He glared back. "Whatchu got for me?"

"What do you mean?"

"You got any smack?"

She shook her head.

"What about cash? Surely a pretty lady like you's got some cash."

She shook her head again, even as she remembered the twenty in her pocket.

He slid a pocketknife from his back pocket and opened it. "How 'bout now?"

A tiny pocketknife wasn't going to intimidate her. She blackened her eyes and stared him down.

He returned the gesture. "We can do it that way, too, lady."

She felt suddenly exhausted. "Just tell me what I need and I'll leave."

He gave her a creepy grin. "You help me, I help you."

"I can't give you drug money. I'm sorry."

He opened his mouth to say something else just as Steven shouted his name from the lobby.

Nicolas flinched and spun toward him, lowering the knife. "Stevie? Is that you?"

Steven stormed down the hall. "What are you doing with that knife?"

"N-nothing, man. I-I-I didn't know she was with you." He folded the knife and shoved it back into his pocket. "Honest."

Steven stepped beside Christine. "Tell her whatever she wants to know."

Nicolas nervously dug at his arm again. "You got a smoke, Stevie?"

Steven shook his head.

"I just needed some money, man." His voice had turned whiney. "I'm in bad way. I just need a bump."

Steven glanced at Christine. "You got any cash?"

She recoiled. "What?"

"Trust me. It'll be much easier if you just give him a couple bucks."

Nicolas's eyes brightened. "Yeah, yeah. Just a couple bucks."

Christine was stunned that Steven would ask such a thing. "I can't enable his habit. That's just not right."

"He's already a lost cause, Chris."

She gaped at him. "I can't believe you'd say that."

"Listen. If you want to find Aiden, you need to know what he knows. If you give him a couple bucks, he's more likely to help. If it bothers you that bad, you can find him later and try to help him. But right now ..."

She shook her head. "I just can't."

"Then give it to me. I'll do it."

Though it was essentially the same as giving it to Nicolas herself, it felt like a loophole she could live with for the moment. She reluctantly handed Steven the twenty.

He wadded it up and tossed it at Nicolas's feet. The junkie dropped to his knees and snatched it up. "What do ya wanna know?"

"Who's kidnapping wergs?"

He looked to the graffitied wall in search of something. When he saw what he was looking for, he pointed.

Christine directed her phone flashlight at the wall to reveal a giant WH painted in red. She balked. "The WereHouse? That's impossible."

He shook his head. "Not the WereHouse. WereHunt. They've taken over."

A man wearing a long coat stepped out of a room farther down the hall as if he was the junkie whisperer. Nicolas's attention quickly shifted to him, and he held up a finger.

"Give me a sec, doll."

Before Christine could protest, he had already hurried to the man and handed over the twenty. The man gave him a baggie before disappearing into another room.

Nicolas sat against the wall and got out a spoon and a lighter.

Christine rushed to him. "I need to know where the Underground is."

As he shot up, he said, "Honey, I got no idea." His eyes quickly glazed over and his shoulders slumped.

Christine's heart sank. She was losing her chance. She shook him. "Who would know?"

He didn't answer.

"Tell me, damn it."

"I don't know, man," he slurred.

She never should have let him stick that needle in his arm. If only she had some Narcan. Her eyes lit up. "Steven, is the medic still here?"

He shook his head.

"Damn it."

Nicolas's head drooped forward.

Christine gave him a sternal rub that brought him around a little. "Wake up. Who would know where the Underground is?"

He gave her a blissful smile. "Maxine," he mumbled dreamily. His head flopped forward again.

She yanked his chin up. "Maxine who?" she cried. "Where is she?"

Whatever he said next was incoherent gibberish. Then he started drooling. It was useless.

"No, no, no. Wake up, goddamnit." She slapped him, but he was too far gone. She fumbled with her phone.

"Who're you calling?" Steven asked.

"9-1-1. I'll pump him full of so much Narcan he won't be able to get high again for a month."

Steven covered her phone and gently lowered her hand before she could push the final number. "You don't need to do that."

Christine shot daggers through him with her glare. "What do you mean? I need to know where to find this Maxine."

He shook his head. "You don't need him for that."

She was losing patience fast. "Why not?"

He lowered his head. "Because I know who she is."

Christine waited on edge. "Well? Are you gonna tell me?"

He sighed. "She runs the fighting pits. You know, where I fight sometimes."

Christine marched toward the door. "Come on."

"What do you mean?"

She spun back. "You know where the fighting pits are. You can show me."

"Maxine won't be of any help."

"Sure, she will. I'll beat it out of her if I have to."

"She'll have you killed. Or throw you into the pits with some champion fighter, which would be the same thing."

"You've been there. You've survived."

"That's 'cause I know my place. I've fought there, but that's it. And never at the highest level."

"I have to find Aiden. That's all that matters."

"Even if she would help you, she's not there right now."

"How do you know?"

"Because the fights are only held Thursday through Saturday. During the rest of the week, it's a regular factory with regular workers."

She squeezed her fists in frustration. "Today's Thursday. Is she there today?"

"Probably not until after dark."

"Then we'll go tonight."

"You won't make it within five feet of her. They'll kill you."

"Then go with me. *Help me*. I'm not stopping until I find Aiden."

He grimaced. And though it obviously pained him, he nodded. He knew her determination.

"We'll go to my place and get some sleep. Then we'll go. Okay?"

He nodded again.

As they headed for the lobby, she nudged him with her elbow. "I could have taken him, you know. If he would've shifted."

"Who?"

"Nicolas."

Steven smiled. "I'm sure you could have."

TENSION ON THE FARM

10

Jericho had been spending more and more time away from the compound and was close to leaving altogether. With the Parkinson's disease seemingly in remission, he was ready to pursue something far more important to him. And for that, he needed money, which meant he needed to get back to work. He had looked into a couple jobs and was ready to reenter society as a normal person, or at least a normal secret werg person. He was sick of being off the grid.

He planned to tell Slater he was leaving soon. He did not expect it to go over well. But today was not the day, so he headed to the gym as usual.

The gymnasium was Jericho's favorite part of the apartment building. He used it mostly to run the judo and jiu-jitsu classes. Almost everyone except Slater attended.

But today neither Adam nor Jess had shown up. Jericho had heard the two were having a bit of a lover's spat, which was nothing new. If it was anything like their last quarrel, it wouldn't amount to much.

Jericho was heading to his apartment for a shower after finishing the evening class when Jess stormed down the hall toward him. Her eyes were red and puffy.

"You okay, Jess?"

She sniffled and nodded. "He's just a jerk sometimes."

"What'd he do, now?"

"Same old shit. He wants to go fight in the pits again. I swear, if he had his way, he'd already be dead."

"He's young. He's got a lot of testosterone. Sometimes you just have to let him get it out."

"If he doesn't die first."

"It's kind of a guy thing. I fought a lot when I was younger, too."

"But you weren't a werg back then. It's a lot more dangerous now than when two men slugged it out with boxing gloves."

"Point taken. When is he goin'?"

"Tonight. I've already told Slater. That's why we're arguing. He hates when Slater knows everything he's doing. I swear, if he goes, I'm done with him forever."

Jericho had heard that before. "I'll go talk to him."

"It won't do no good. You know how stubborn he is."

"Where is he now?"

"Slater called him to his office." She started for the stairs.

"Where're you goin'?"

"To blow off some steam in the woods."

"I think that's a good idea."

She smiled and thanked him.

He skipped the shower and went straight to Slater's office. The door was closed and he could hear shouting inside.

"How many times do I have to tell you that you're not going to the Dog Park?"

"You don't own me. I'll go wherever I want."

"Damn it, Adam. It's too dangerous. You know that. I need you here."

There was a clattering sound and then something shattered on the hardwood floor. "You're so uptight."

"I'm uptight because I don't want my best friend to die needlessly?"

"I'm not gonna die. I'm better than all those guys."

Jericho took a deep breath before knocking.

"Go away," Slater shouted.

He cracked the door open and peeked inside.

Slater rolled his eyes. "Great. It's you."

"Can I come in?"

Slater threw his hands in the air. "Might as well. You're another one who doesn't listen."

Jericho closed the door behind him.

Slater went to his closet for a dustpan and broom. "Maybe he'll listen to *you*, Jericho. Everyone else seems to."

Jericho tossed up his hands. "What'd I do?"

Slater swept broken glass into the dustpan and said nothing.

Jericho turned to Adam. "What's goin' on?"

"I'm fightin' in the pits tonight."

As Slater dumped the broken figurine in the trash, he shouted, "No he's not."

Adam's face reddened. "Yes I am," he shouted back.

Jericho waved his hands, trying to cool the temperature of the room. "Okay, okay. Everyone, calm down."

Slater glared at Adam. "Why do you do this? It's bad enough you brought this one here after the last time you went." He jerked his head toward Jericho.

Jericho felt like he had just taken more undeserved shrapnel. "What the hell?"

Slater side-eyed him. "As if you don't know."

Jericho drew back. "What'd I do? Seriously. Tell me."

Slater groaned. "Oh, you know. Ever since you got here, you've undermined me at every step."

Jericho pointed to himself. "Me? When do I ever undermine you?"

"Every time I turn around. You skip my weekly meetings. Give your little karate lessons. Throw out your wisdom like you're some kind of sage or self-righteous know-it-all. Everyone is always like Jericho this and Jericho that. I get sick of hearing it."

Jericho started to argue, but realized they were getting too far off topic. He tried to bring it back around. "Adam, listen. How 'bout you don't go tonight, and we talk about this later with leveler heads?"

Adam shook his head. "It's already been forever since the last time. I'm going tonight. Period."

Slater scoffed. "See, Jericho. You can't tell him anything."

And just like that, Jericho was back on Slater's team. The flip-flopping was enough to make his head spin. "Adam, you're upsettin' everyone."

"Everyone? Oh, I suppose you've talked to Jess, huh?"

"She's worried about you. Just like Slater."

"Too bad. I'm going." His determination appeared unflappable.

"Why do you want to fight for all those rich people, anyways?"

Adam rubbed his finger and thumb together.

Jericho didn't believe that it was all about money. He knew Slater gave him plenty. Arguing further would be useless. He gave Slater an I-give-up look.

Slater's face reddened like his head was about to pop. He gritted his teeth and then closed his eyes and sighed. "There's no talking you out of this, huh?"

"Not a chance." Adam marched to the door. "By the way, Jake's going with me to watch." He slipped out before Slater could argue.

Slater breathed in deep, angry breaths. He glared at Jericho. "You can leave now, too."

When Jericho stepped into the hall, Adam was leaning against the wall at the other end. He wore the biggest grin. "I love to rile him up like that."

"He seems pretty pissed this time."

Adam snorted. "You know we have a lot of arguments like that. They always blow over. He just needs to sleep it off."

"I guess." Jericho hesitated. He'd wanted to check out the Dog Park since the night he'd met Adam. Martial arts had always been his life, after all, and he was never opposed to watching a good fight. "Hey? You mind if I tag along tonight?"

"What for? I don't need a babysitter."

"I know. But I'd like to check it out. Sounds interesting."

"Be my guest." He paused. "You ever think about fighting there?"

Jericho couldn't shake his head fast enough. "My fightin' days are long behind me. Trainin' and teachin's all I do now."

"But you'd be good at it. Plus, first timers get five G's to win."

"About that. Be honest, Adam. It's not really the money, is it?"

Adam gave him a sly smile. "Sure it is. It's all about the Franklins."

"Hold up for a minute. I've always wanted to ask you. Why do you do that?"

"Do what?"

"You know. Screw up every damn saying. You know that it's the Benjamins, not the Franklins."

He shrugged. "It's just my thing, man. It's fun to see how long it takes someone to call me out on it. How long have you been here? You're one of the slower ones."

"It's more annoyin' than anything."

Adam grinned again. "Even better. I started doing it as a kid and it just kinda stuck like paste."

Jericho's shoulders slumped.

Adam grinned even wider and headed for the exit.

"Hey," Jericho called after him. "Do me a favor."

Adam turned back. "What?"

"Make up with Jess before you go. I told her I'd talk to you."

He groaned.

"I'm serious, Adam. Just smooth things over. She's a nice girl and she really likes you.

"Ugh." His eyes rolled. "I guess."

"Tell her I'll be with you watchin' your back. That'll make her feel a little better."

Adam nodded. "We leave at eight. Meet me outside. We're taking the pickup."

****

Jake was already at the front of the truck when Jericho arrived at eight.

"How'd Adam talk *you* into taggin' along tonight?" Jericho asked. He found it odd that Jake had agreed to go since he was fairly timid and never showed any interest in violence.

"He said it'd be good for me. Toughen me up a bit."

"Hmph. Is that what you want?"

Jake shrugged. "It's whatever."

Adam approached with his arm around Jess. He kissed her and said, "Catch ya later, babe."

Her longing gaze as he bounced down the stairs could inspire artists for centuries, and yet he didn't see any of it. They climbed into the truck. He didn't even look back as they pulled away.

During the drive, Adam said, "I go by Viper when I fight, just so you know. I'm fighting Scab in the first match."

"Are you nervous?" Jake asked.

"Nah. I'm happy to start off the show. The early bird gets the seed, am I right?" He gave Jericho a sly wink.

Jericho smirked. "Yeah, Adam. That's exactly it."

The closer they got to the factory-turned-fighting-pits, the less Adam spoke. By the time they pulled into the parking lot, his game face was on.

"There's a doorman," Jericho said. "How do we get in?"

"Tell him that Benson sent you," Adam answered.

"Who's Benson?"

"He's nobody. It's this week's code. I'll come see you after the fights. When wergs win, we're allowed to mingle with the rich snobs. It's like we're rock stars."

He started to walk toward the back of the building where the entrance for fighters was located.

"What if it's not the right code?" Jericho called after him.

Turning to walk backward, Adam shrugged and smirked. "Then you'd better run."

A stretched limo arrived and dropped off a couple at the front door. By the looks of them, Jericho was woefully underdressed. Apparently, blue jeans and a Lynyrd Skynyrd concert tee under a faux leather jacket wasn't the proper attire. Luckily, the "Benson sent us" code worked and security didn't stop him and Jake at the door.

They settled in with the crowd around the center of three concrete pits. By the time the first fight was set to begin, the factory floor was packed and buzzing with electricity. Gun to his head, Jericho would admit to feeling the excitement. It reminded him of his own competition days.

Women who looked like swimsuit models passed out goggles and cheap rain ponchos. Jericho recognized one of them as Adam's lap ornament from the bar where he'd first met him. He thought of Jess and shook his head as he shrugged into his poncho.

When it was time for the first fight, Adam entered the arena, a purple streak freshly painted down his furry back in an obvious nod to Jess's mohawk. Another beast entered the ring from the other aisle.

A small group chanted, "Vi-per, Vi-per," when Adam's name was announced, and Jericho was impressed he had built a mini following. He hammed it up to the crowd until they drowned out the few people chanting Scab's name. Jericho worried he was too cocky and not focused enough for the fight.

The brief calm before show time made the hairs on Jericho's arms stand up. An air horn kicked off the action. Adam charged and ducked a sloppy wayward blow. He lunged with his teeth at Scab's throat. The roars and screeches were deafening. Jericho held his breath for the entire violent but brief fight until Adam stood victorious and barely winded over his opponent, who cowered bleeding on the floor. Adam hadn't been lying when he'd said he was good. The crowd was electric, and when Adam thrust his arms up in victory it only made them cheer louder. Two guards entered the ring and whisked Adam away.

Scab was hauled off on a stretcher while staff cleaned up the bloody mess. Adam had said on the drive over that if the loser survived, he'd never be allowed to fight again, which apparently was worse than dying for some of them.

By the time the next fight was scheduled to start, Adam had shifted back to human form, showered and dressed, and joined Jericho and Jake ringside. Tuxedo-wearing men repeatedly approached him for autographs like they were meeting a star athlete. Jericho wondered if werg autographs were a status symbol of some kind. Adam wore the smile of a champion as he counted his money. "Well?" he shouted over the noise of the crowd.

Jake was all eyes and teeth. "That was amazing. You were awesome."

Adam blew on his knuckles and rubbed them on his chest in a cocky display. "I was, wasn't I?"

Jericho patted his back. "Good job, Adam."

A group of young men shouted Adam's name. Jericho recognized them as Adam's friends from the bar. Adam turned and shouted, "Gimme a minute."

Then he said to Jericho and Jake, "We're headed to the bar, if you wanna come."

Jericho would prefer not to go barhopping, but left it up to Jake.

"I think I'd rather watch another fight," Jake answered.

Adam clapped his hands. "Suit yourself. Tell Slater I'll be home tomorrow if all goes well with the ladies." He waggled his eyebrows and joined his friends.

Jericho and Jake settled in for the next fight.

THE DOG PARK

11

When Christine opened her eyes, it was six in the evening. She sat up and rubbed her temples, surprised to have slept so soundly, especially on her old couch. She got up with a groan, rubbed her stiff back, and headed upstairs to check on Steven. His door was locked.

She decided to let him sleep while she went back downstairs for a bite to eat. She made two sandwiches, grabbed some chips, and retrieved two bottles of water. She sat at the table and took a bite of her sandwich as she played through possible scenarios of her meeting with Maxine. Her sandwich was nearly finished when she lifted the bottle of water to her lips and caught a glimpse of the open liquor cabinet beside the couch. *Oh no. He must have picked the lock.* She was stunned that she hadn't heard him do it. Her stomach sank.

She raced upstairs and pounded on Steven's door, but he didn't answer. How could she have been so stupid to still have alcohol in the house? She had been so exhausted when they got home, she hadn't thought of hiding it.

She ran her fingers along the top of the door trim and found the brass prong key. She jammed it into the keyhole, wiggled it, and flung the door open.

Steven was on the floor, face-down in a semi-dried puddle of vomit. An empty bottle of vodka lay next to his outstretched hand.

She shook him and shouted, "Steven."

He moaned and smacked his lips, but didn't wake up.

She shook him again. "Damn it, Steven. Wake up." She rolled him to his side and gave him the mother of all sternal rubs, but he barely flinched.

She'd seen him this wasted before and knew nothing short of a tornado was going to wake him up. Maybe not even that. Devastated, she fell back on her heels. "How could you do this when you knew how much I needed you tonight?" She wanted to be furious, but she didn't have the energy anymore. She had to face the fact that he couldn't or wouldn't ever change.

After sitting next to him for a few minutes, she dragged herself downstairs, grabbed a pad of paper, a pen, and the plate of food, and took it to his room. She set the plate on a chair and wrote a note.

Once again, I couldn't count on you to be there when I needed you most. I've gone to the factory by myself. When I get home, I want you gone. I never want to see you again.

That last part broke her heart the most. A tear landed on the paper. She wiped it away, signed the note, and set it next to the sandwich. As she stared at his drunk, limp, worthless body, she resolved to never cry for him again. Then she went downstairs to the liquor cabinet, dumped every last bottle in the kitchen sink, and left them on the counter for him to see.

Thankfully, Steven had told her where the factory was located on their drive to her place. It was a half-hour outside of town. She crossed a bridge that spanned a creek and drove down a long, secluded lane before she finally reached the factory-turned-spectacle.

Limos, Porsches, Lamborghinis, and every other kind of expensive car filled the parking lot. She parked her beat-up Ford Taurus beside a vintage Corvette and headed for the front door. A large man in a black suit guarded the entrance. "What's the word?" he asked as she approached.

She panicked. "I'm ... uh ... meeting someone here."

"Without the right code, ma'am, you're not meeting anyone in here."

"But you don't understand. I need to speak to someone. I—"

Before she could finish, a distinguished-looking older gentleman in a tuxedo got out of a metallic-blue Maserati. "Is there a problem here?"

The doorman straightened. "No, sir. This young lady doesn't have the password and I was just sending her on her way."

The older man looked Christine up and down with creepy eyes. "A little underdressed tonight, aren't you ...?"

"Christine," she offered.

"Of course. Christine." He turned back to the doorman. "Christine is with me tonight."

The doorman nodded and stepped aside. "Whatever you say, Mister McNeil."

Mr. McNeil extended his elbow. "Shall we?"

Christine hooked her arm through his. "We shall, Mr. McNeil."

"Please, call me Bradley. Mr. McNeil was my father." He chuckled, and Christine forced a laugh in return. If hanging on this creep's arm all evening got her closer to finding Aiden, then it was worth it.

He raised his free hand over his shoulder and clicked a key fob. The headlights of his Maserati flashed, and the horn beeped. "What do you think of the ride, babe?"

"It's very nice."

"Just got it yesterday. I think I'm in love." As they walked into the hall, he asked, "First time to the Dog Park?"

She politely nodded.

"You're in for a real treat."

They entered a large room with betting booths lining the farthest wall. Lines from each booth stretched deep into the crowd. Signs above the booths declared a minimum bet of $100,000.

Three huge pits were dug into the floor in the center of the factory, surrounded by block half-walls. Bradley pointed to the middle one. "That's where the fights will be tonight." He took a piece of paper from his inside pocket and unfolded it. "Let's see how lucky you are. Pick a dog for the first fight."

Christine nearly crawled out of her skin. Picking a dog was a disgusting way to frame it. With barely a glance, she pointed to a random name.

"Viper it is. I'll go put in the bet and meet you back here."

She nodded with a fake smile. Once he reached the betting line, she melted into the crowd, hoping to lose him in the excitement. Not knowing anything about Maxine put her at a disadvantage. All she could do was ask around, and that was going to take some time.

She tapped the shoulder of a man chatting with an older woman wearing a sparkly, floor-length evening gown. The couple scoffed at Christine's blue jeans and twenty-five-dollar Target jacket.

"May I help you?" the man asked.

"Yeah. I'm looking for Maxine. Do you know her?"

He furrowed his brow and turned back to his date. She asked three more people and got the same annoyed response before Bradley tracked her down.

"There you are. I've been looking all over for you. The first fight's about to start."

Christine fake-smiled again. "I wouldn't miss it for the world."

Bradley led her through the crowd to a reserved spot near the center pit. Models passed out goggles and ponchos.

"What's this for?" she asked.

"To keep their tainted blood off you."

Two separate aisles led to opposing doors that both opened simultaneously. Two beasts stalked down the aisles and entered the ring with deadly eyes locked on each other.

An announcer made his way to the center of the pit. He introduced the light brownish werg as Scab. A brand on Scab's back said PITS, and Christine had an uneasy feeling that he hadn't done that to himself. Then the announcer pointed to a silver beast with a purple streak painted down his back who he introduced as Viper. Viper didn't have any brands that she could see.

Bradley nudged her with his elbow. "That one's yours. I've got five-hundred big ones on him, so I hope you picked well."

A small group chanted, "Vi-per. Vi-per," and she wondered what Steven's fighting name was. Probably Drunk or Worthless or something in that vein.

When the announcer left the ring, the crowd hushed. An air horn blared, nearly causing Christine to jump out of her skin.

The two wergs collided in a howling ball of fur and claws. Flesh ripped as both creatures strove for that elusive bite to the throat. Bradley ducked and flinched with every blow as if he were in the ring.

The entire fight lasted less than a minute with Viper standing victorious. Christine wanted to shove a dressing over Scab's bleeding throat, but restrained her paramedic urges. As the handlers dragged him from the ring, she wondered what would happen to him next, imagining it wouldn't be good.

Bradley threw his fists in the air with a yowl. Then he grabbed Christine's shoulders and planted a kiss on her lips. She recoiled. Caught up in the excitement, he snatched her hand and guided it to the front of his pants.

She yanked it back.

He leered at her. "Shy, huh? I like that. We'll save it for the car."

She'd sooner treat him like Viper had just treated Scab than touch his shriveled prick again. With another fake smile to keep the peace, she touched his chin and guided his eyes back to the pit, reminding herself it was all for Aiden. She dragged the back of her hand across her lips, hoping to remove even the most microscopic remnants of Bradley. She wished she had sandpaper.

The cleanup crew was still mopping up the blood puddles in the ring. She let her eyes rove over the spectators, looking for an excuse to get away. The first man she had questioned about Maxine caught her eye. He was on the opposite side of the ring, and he was pointing her out to a man in a black suit with an earpiece.

Christine leaned into Bradley's ear. "I've gotta go to the ladies' room. I'll be back before the next fight."

"Better hurry."

She weaved through the crowd toward the restroom, but two more men in black suits cut her off at the entrance. "Miss?" one of them said. He took her arm. "The boss would like a word."

They escorted her down a long hallway and up a set of stairs to a steel door with a keypad beside it. One of them typed in a code before the door clanked open. He marched her through while his partner stood guard outside.

Christine faced a large desk with a massive picture window behind it that overlooked the parking lot. Another window on the side wall revealed a tree line at the back of the property. A vibrant lounge area with a bar sat off to the right, and a large TV on the wall showed a live feed of the fight floor. Several men and women drank at the bar.

An older woman in an all-white pants suit with her grey hair pulled into a bun stood with the group. Designer eyeglasses rested on her overly sculpted nose. She excused herself and approached Christine, picking up two glasses from the bar on her way.

"And what is your name, my dear?"

"Christine."

"May I call you Chris?"

Christine shrugged. "Sure."

"Well, Chris, my name is Maxine. And yes, you may call me Max. I run this place."

Perfect.

"A little birdie told me you have been inquiring about me?"

"I have."

"May I ask why? I don't believe we've ever met." She offered one of the glasses and Christine politely declined. She set it on the armrest of a chair.

Christine decided to be blunt. "I'm looking for a place called the Underground and I understand you might be able to help."

The mention of the Underground instantly darkened the feel of the room. Maxine studied her with curious, narrow eyes. "Never heard of it. Now, if you don't mind, I have guests waiting." She nodded to the guard. "Marcus here will escort you back downstairs."

The guard politely touched Christine's shoulder. "Right this way, ma'am." His voice was deep and gruff.

Christine shrugged off his hand. "Ma'am, just give me a minute, please."

Maxine tapped her chin. "Let's say I knew something about this Underground place, which I don't. What makes you think I'd tell you anything?"

Christine stalled, scanning the room for any clue she might be able to swipe and maybe escape through that big window. "I'm just looking for someone I care deeply about, and then I'll be out of your hair. Please, help me." She noticed a folder on the desk labeled with the day's date and wondered if that could be helpful. It was a longshot.

Maxine chuckled. "You might be in a bit over your head here, my dear." She flicked her wrist. "You can leave now."

"What if I fought downstairs in the pits?" Christine blurted. It was more of a bluff, but she had nothing else to bargain with and she would do whatever it took to find Aiden. She blackened the whites of her eyes as proof of what she could do. There was no use holding anything back.

Maxine's eyes widened and she smiled. "Oh. That is lovely. I wonder … escaped pet?" She shook her head. "No, I don't think so. You're too feisty for that. Tell me, where did you acquire the virus?"

"It's a long story. Now, what do I have to do to get information on the Underground?"

"I do like your spunk. I'll tell you what. Go down there and fight tonight and we'll talk."

Christine shook her head. "No deal. Not tonight. But if you give me the information I need to find my friend, I'll come back another night."

Maxine snorted. "That's not how it's going to work." She paced to the other side of her desk and rubbed her hands together. "Fight tonight, and if you win against my champion, I'll take you to the Underground myself."

It had become painfully obvious that the only way to get answers was to take Maxine where she didn't feel so safe and secure and force them out of her. Christine allowed her transformation to build just beneath the surface.

Maxine nodded to Marcus. "I'm done here. You can take her downstairs now. Get her ready to fight."

Christine glanced over her shoulder as Marcus removed his suit coat. His eyes turned black.

Maxine grinned. "You're not the only one around here with that ability." She turned to gaze out the big window.

If Marcus thought just the threat of changing would be enough, he was greatly mistaken. Christine sprang, shifting in midflight. She was fully transformed by the time she shot past Marcus and sliced his femoral artery with her claws. He clutched his half-transformed leg and fell to his rear. She slammed the door closed before the other guard could react.

Nervous panic filled the lounge as the guests scattered to the farthest edges of the room. Maxine's face paled. Christine smelled her fear.

Maxine pressed an alarm button on the underside of her desk. Christine heaved a couch at the door as the keypad chirped and it started to open. She pounced, wrapping her arms around Maxine.

The couch slid across the floor as the door was forced open and four armed guards poured into the room. Christine retreated to the window with Maxine held tight against her chest.

"Let her go," one of the guards shouted, gun in hand.

But Christine still needed answers. As the guards advanced, she spun, squeezed Maxine even tighter, and jumped through the window. Glass went everywhere. The deafening *rat-tat-tat* of gunfire filled the room. A bullet hissed past her ear as she plunged toward the pavement. Maxine screamed all the way down. Their momentum carried them into the side of a brand-new blue Maserati, caving in the door and shattering the side windows.

Two guards charged through the factory's front entrance, cutting her off from her Taurus. Her best bet was the forest she'd seen from the office window.

When Maxine tried to wriggle out of her grip, Christine repositioned and pinned her arms to her sides. The guards opened fire from the upstairs window, peppering the Maserati's roof and hood. Maxine screamed for them to stop, but she must not have been as important as she thought she was. Christine carried her in a serpentine pattern to the forest, dodging more bullets.

She didn't slow until she approached the creek near the bridge she had crossed to get to the factory. Her speed had bought her a few minutes. She threw Maxine to the ground, covering her white suit in mud.

"What are you going to do?" Maxine cried.

Christine pulled her by the wrists into the brisk current beneath the bridge and shoved her face underwater. She held her for a few seconds before pulling her back out by her hair.

Maxine gagged and choked and shivered.

Christine shifted back to human form. "Where's the Underground?" she screamed, standing naked and also shivering in the knee-high water.

Maxine wiped the water from her face, trying to recover. Christine shoved her head underwater again for a few seconds and then pulled her back out.

"Stop, stop, stop. Please," Maxine sobbed.

"Where's the Underground?"

"They'll kill me if I tell you."

The color drained from Christine's sight again. "*I'll* kill you if you don't." She shoved Maxine's head back toward the water.

"Okay, okay. I'll tell you."

Christine clenched her fists and her teeth.

Maxine closed her eyes and whispered, "Detroit."

"The address?"

"I don't know the address."

Christine shoved her under again for a few more seconds.

Maxine's eyes blasted wide when Christine pulled her from the water again. "I-I-I swear. I don't know the address. But I can tell you where it is."

"You'd better get talking."

"There's an old, abandoned factory on Detroit's east side called the Packard factory. It's a famous one. You can find the address easily."

Christine sneered. "If you're lying to me, I'll come back and find you and—"

"I'm not lying. I swear."

Christine hauled her out of the stream and scanned the woods. She caught the scent of another werg. "Give me your clothes."

"Wh-what?"

"Your clothes. Give 'em to me."

Maxine balked, her lips already bluish and quivering from the cold.

Christine grabbed the front of her blouse and tore at the buttons.

Maxine pulled away. "Okay," she cried. "I'll do it." She slowly stripped to her bra and panties.

Christine quickly dressed in the cold, wet clothes as she scanned the trees for pursuers. They were getting close. She shot one last glare at Maxine before climbing the hill to the road at the edge of the bridge.

HIDING

12

Christine darted across the road and hid behind the concrete parapet of the guardrail on the other side. A set of pickup truck headlights raced toward the bridge from the factory. She peeked over the rail to see Maxine standing half-naked on the berm on the opposite side of the road. A werg heeled on all fours beside her. The pickup truck reached the bridge.

The werg sniffed the air, his soulless black eyes going straight to where Christine hid. Maxine pointed and growled, "Get 'er."

Single-minded and locked on its target, the werg exploded blindly into the street as the pickup sped across the bridge. Maxine started to shout and the werg whipped his head around. Too late. The headlights swallowed him. Tires squealed. The truck slammed into his side. Metal twisted like taffy and glass shattered. The truck jolted and bounced and then rolled to a stop in a shallow ditch beside the road. The werg landed with a thud near Maxine.

Christine ran to the driver's door. There were two men in the cab. Stunned, the passenger rubbed a knot on his forehead.

The werg struggled to all fours and shook away the cobwebs. Christine panicked. "You gotta help me," she cried.

The driver was a young man in his late teens. He gave her an uncertain look as he shifted into Park and turned the key, choking the stalled engine back to life.

"They're gonna kill me," she shouted, grasping his arm through the broken window.

The driver looked to his friend. "What should we do, Jericho?"

The passenger, Jericho, glanced over his shoulder to where the werg was rising to his feet and locked eyes with him.

"Please," Christine begged.

Jericho grimaced. "Get in the back."

His friend's face blanched. "Jericho, what're you doing?"

Christine didn't wait for him to change his mind. She climbed into the bed. The driver gunned the engine, the truck's ass end sliding in the grass until it caught the pavement and lunged forward. Christine slid hard against the tailgate. She pulled herself up enough to see the werg giving chase at a full gallop.

"Go, go, go," she screamed to the driver.

Jericho slid the cab's back window open and shouted, "Hold on." The engine revved and the truck slowly pulled ahead. The werg eventually gave up and dropped off the side of the road.

Christine scurried to the back window. "Thank you."

"We're not in the clear yet." Jericho pointed ahead.

Two cars had stopped nose to nose across the road, blocking it. A woman and two men wearing SWAT-style uniforms took cover with assault rifles behind the cars.

"Shit," Jericho shouted.

"What do I do?" the driver screamed.

"Ram 'em, Jake."

"*What*?"

"They don't look friendly. Ram 'em." Jericho reached behind his seat and pulled out a shotgun. He lowered his window and climbed onto the door like an action movie hero.

The wannabe cops opened fire, bullets peppering the windshield. Jake's side mirror was blasted away. Jericho sent a clap of thunder through the cab and the shotgun's recoil nearly knocked him from the car. He recovered and jerked the forearm slide back to chamber another shell. His next blast sent one of the men sprawling across the car's hood. The man's bulletproof vest did its job. He dropped from the hood and scrambled off the road, clutching his chest.

More bullets riddled the windshield. Jake grunted.

"*Jaaake*." Jericho ducked back into the cab and grabbed the wheel.

Jake looked at him, terrified. "Jericho?" he whispered. He slumped against the driver's side window, his foot still on the accelerator.

"Hold on," Jericho screamed.

Christine curled up close to the cab beneath the back window and covered her head with her arms.

The truck plowed into the cars and bucked violently. The force nearly flattened Christine against the cab. The truck coasted into the ditch, this time dead for good. Steam hissed from under the shredded hood.

Christine shook away the fuzz and pulled herself to the cab window again. Her shoulder had taken the brunt of the impact. Jericho groaned as he picked himself up off the floorboard. He felt Jake's neck for a pulse. "Stay with us, Jake." He found his shotgun and reached for the door handle. A hail of gunfire peppered the truck again. Jericho leaped out.

One of the fake SWAT guys shouted, "Get down," as the concussion of Jericho's shotgun punched the air. The enemy gunfire momentarily halted.

Christine climbed over the side of the truck and pulled Jericho's sleeve. "We've gotta run," she cried.

Jericho's eyes locked on Jake. "I can't leave him."

"We have to. His only chance is if *they* treat him. He'll die with us for sure."

Jericho looked to the enemy again. One of them took aim with an automatic rifle from the cover of the crashed vehicles. "Look out." He shoved Christine aside and fired another shot.

Christine spun in time to see the man dive behind the car and a hole blasted out of the front fender near where he had been standing.

Jericho rounded the truck to the driver's door. "Shift, Jake." Before he could open the door, another barrage of gunfire sent him scrambling for cover in the ditch on the opposite side of the road. Christine followed.

The driver's door swung open. Jake tumbled out, only half transformed, his distorted werg limbs still popping and cracking.

"Hey, Boss," one of the men shouted. "Look. This one's a werg, too."

"Get him. We'll cover you."

"Shit." Jericho scanned the field beyond the ditch and then looked back to Jake as two men approached him, guns raised. He'd just started to lift his shotgun when a barrage of gunfire pinned him back down.

When the gunfire paused, Christine peeked over the ditch to see the men dragging Jake back to their vehicles.

"They've got him."

Jericho thrust the shotgun muzzle over the ditch and fired off a blind shot into the air. The enemy scrambled for cover.

"Come on," he whispered. "Stay down."

As they ran along the ditch with their heads ducked below the road, the woman shouted, "Hey, Boss. You want us to chase them?"

"No. Let's get outta here. One of Maxine's stupid security guards called in the Dog Catchers."

"Why'd she let them do that? We could have handled this."

"I know. But it's too late now. They'll be here any second."

Christine and Jericho climbed out of the ditch and raced through a field toward a distant housing development. They crept through a back yard and stopped at the side of the house. The upstairs light was on.

The faint *whoop, whoop, whoop* of a helicopter announced the Dog Catchers' pending arrival.

"Shit," Jericho hissed. "How'd they get here so fast? We gotta hide." He pointed to a Dumpster beside the skeleton of a house under construction. "There."

"No. They'll find us there. We need to get inside one of these houses."

"Right. Which one?"

She scanned the neighborhood and then pointed to a house with no cars in the driveway and no lights on inside. The mailbox was overflowing. "That one."

They crossed the street and ran to the back of the house. The door was locked. Jericho slammed his shoulder into it. Though it took three tries, the bolt lock finally splintered the jamb. He poked his head inside. "Looks clear."

Almost as soon as they got inside, a helicopter buzzed the neighborhood. They waited until it passed, and then Jericho fiddled with the busted door to keep it closed. Though it wasn't secure, it would look normal enough from the outside.

Christine sneaked down the hall and quietly checked the bedrooms to assure that the homeowners were really gone and not dead or just lazy.

Both bedrooms were unoccupied, tidy with beds made. A third door led to a laundry room, and she made a mental note to return if she had time to do something about Maxine's filthy, wet clothes. She joined Jericho in the front room where he watched the street through a gap in the blinds.

The helicopter circled low overhead, its spotlight dancing over the ground. Two blacked-out SUVs drove slowly into the neighborhood, stopping only to speak to the nosier residents standing on their porches.

Jericho lifted the shotgun and chambered another shell. Then he let the blinds close, set his shotgun on the dining room table, and went to the refrigerator. "Thirsty?" He grabbed a Gatorade bottle and took a swig.

She nodded. "Whatever's there."

He tossed her a bottled water.

"You think they'll go door to door?" she asked.

"Maybe." He didn't volunteer a solution as he sat at the table. "What's your name?"

"Christine."

"I'm Jericho. Nice to meet you. You should go find something dry to change into. We might be stuck here for a while."

She went back to the laundry room, disrobed, and wrapped herself in a blanket she found folded on the washer. With Maxine's clothes in the dryer, she returned to the table and sat down.

"Thank you for helping me, Jericho."

"Of course." He took another swig. "Though I've gotta ask. What the hell did you get me into tonight?"

"It's a looong story."

"I'm not goin' anywhere. Not right away, at least."

She had no idea if he was trustworthy, but her instincts said he was. Besides, she didn't have much more to lose. "Were you at the fights?"

He nodded.

"I went there to try and find a friend who's gone missing."

"And you thought he might be fightin'?"

"Not exactly. He was taken to a place called the Underground. I heard the lady who ran the fighting pits might know where that was."

"Oh. What'd she say?"

"She said it was in Detroit. I have to get there as soon as possible."

He listened and bobbed his head.

She couldn't tell if he knew more than he let on or not. "Have you heard of it?"

"Just rumors." He took another drink.

A loudspeaker crackled outside, followed by a man's amplified voice. "Citizens, there is no need to panic. A rogue werg has gotten loose and is somewhere in this neighborhood. She and her accomplice are considered extremely dangerous. If you see anyone suspicious or any wergs whatsoever, inform us immediately. If you harbor either of these fugitives, you will be in direct violation of the Werg Registration Act, and you will be punished to the fullest extent of the law."

The loudspeaker announcement faded as the SUVs turned onto a side street. The helicopter continued circling overhead.

Jericho went to the couch and propped his feet up with a groan. "We're gonna have to hunker down for a bit, I guess. Might as well get some rest."

"You can sleep?"

He shrugged. "I can try."

"Aren't you worried about your friend?"

"Of course. But I can't do anything about it right now." He tipped his head back and closed his eyes. "Get some sleep, Christine. We'll figure this out in the mornin'."

THE ISLAND: TORTURE

13

Aiden sat alone in his cell as those bastards took Sammy for a round of torture. He gave in to his thirst and drank from the stale water trough. The slime on top still made him gag, but barring a good rainfall, he'd die of thirst without it.

When Murdock's flunkies finally escorted Sammy past Aiden's cell, they practically carried him. Blood stained the front of his shirt. He could barely lift his head enough for Aiden to see his black eye and swollen cheek.

Murdock shoved Sammy into his cell and shot a glare at Aiden. "Your time's coming, dog."

Aiden gave him the finger.

After Murdock and the others left, Aiden loudly whispered, "Sammy?"

"Yeah?"

"You did good. You made it another day."

"I think they broke me this time, Aiden." His hoarse voice was full of abject despair.

"No. No, they didn't. You're still here. That means you're strong."

Sammy groaned as he sat with his back to their common wall. "I don't know." He coughed, and it sounded like he threw up a little.

They sat quietly for a while before Sammy broke the silence. "Hey, Aiden?"

"What's up, pal?"

"You up for talking?"

"If you are."

"I need to get my mind off what's coming tomorrow. They said they're gonna waterboard the shit outta me."

Aiden cringed. He'd heard how bad waterboarding could be. "What do you wanna talk about?"

"I don't care. Anything."

"Okay." Aiden thought about it for a second. "Where you from?"

"Chicago. South side."

"Do you still have family there?"

"Nah. I was raised by my grandma after my mom died when I was six. Then my grandma got cancer."

"Ah, man, that sucks. Not many breaks, huh?"

"Heh. I guess not. We didn't have any money, so I started selling drugs when I was fifteen. Nothing hard like smack or anything, just pot and some of my grandma's pain pills here and there. On my eighteenth birthday, I got caught with a fresh batch. Man, it was the worst time for them to pull me over. They charged me with dealing. I did a couple years in the clink for that one.

"When I got out, my grandma had died and I kinda went through some things. I couldn't get a job and I didn't wanna sell drugs anymore, so I basically just

lived around until the WereHouse grabbed me and …
well, you probably know the rest."

"Yeah, I get it." But something didn't make sense.
"You don't have a chip, do you?"

"Nah. I never got one. Before they got around to it,
someone attacked the WereHouse and set us all free."

Aiden chuckled. "No shit?"

"Why's that funny?"

"You're not gonna believe this, but that was me."

"What do you mean?"

"I helped take down the WereHouse. I was there that
night setting the wergs free."

"Seriously?"

"Yeah."

Sammy snorted, followed by a painful cough. "Man,
it's a small world. I guess I owe you a giant thank you."

"Nah. You don't owe me anything. I just wish it
turned out better for you. How'd these people find
you?"

"Heh. Now *you're* not gonna believe this. For maybe
the first time in a long time, I decided to do the right
thing. I registered under the new Werg Registration
Act. I guess not all the registration offices are
completely legit. Three days later, some men tracked
me down and brought me here. Who's the idiot now?"

"Nonsense. You were just doing what you thought
was right."

"I guess. What about you? Did you register, too?"

"Nope. I don't have much use for government.
Whoever came for me did it in retaliation for what I did
to the WereHouse. Apparently, Bernard Henderson had
some friends."

Sammy didn't say anything for a minute. Then he
volunteered, "I have a daughter."

"Oh yeah?"

"Yeah. Her name's Destiny. She's seven. I got her mom pregos when I was seventeen."

"When was the last time you saw her?"

"I-I-I haven't." His voice wobbled. "Me and her mom had a falling out before she was born. Then I went to prison. I've always wanted to patch things up just to see her, but it never worked out. By the time I got out of jail, her mom was married, and I didn't figure they needed some ex-con sniffin' around. I've made a lot of mistakes, man."

"Haven't we all?" Aiden had never truly forgiven himself for all the werepets he had put down. He wondered how many fathers he'd stopped from ever seeing their kids again.

"What about you, Aiden? You got any kids?"

"Nah. Never really worked out for me. Would have liked to, though."

"But you have someone who'll miss you when you're gone, right?"

He thought about Christine and their last argument. "I guess."

"Wife?"

"Nah. Girlfriend."

"Well, at least you've got someone. I don't got nobody."

"You have a daughter."

"That I've never seen."

"That doesn't mean you can't still make things right. As long as you're alive, you can mend fences. Hell, my girlfriend hadn't seen her dad in a couple decades, and he showed up out of the blue to see her one day."

"No kiddin'? How'd that turn out?"

Aiden balked, realizing he hadn't thought it through. "Uh … Pretty good," he lied. There was no reason to kill all of Sammy's hope.

"So, what's her name?"

"Who?"

"Your girl, man."

"Oh." Aiden hesitated, a lifetime of keeping secrets holding him back.

"It's all right if you don't wanna tell me. It's none of my business."

After what Sammy had been through and how honest he'd been, Aiden thought he deserved an answer. "Christine."

"Christine, huh? I bet she's a real looker."

Aiden snorted. "Why would you think that?"

"Because I've never met a Christine who wasn't either good lookin' or batshit crazy. Or both." He chuckled, bringing on another coughing fit.

Aiden grinned. "Yeah, she's pretty. And tough as nails. She's a firefighter in Columbus."

"Georgia?"

"Nah. Ohio."

"A firefighter, huh? You gonna marry her?"

Aiden rubbed the back of his neck. Christine hadn't exactly been open to his previous attempts to advance their relationship. Marriage seemed a bridge too far. "We'll see."

"Well, I hope you get to see her again someday."

"There's no hope about it. I know I will, Sammy. And you'll get to meet Destiny, too. You'll get that chance to make things right as long as you hold out a bit longer. I promise."

"I don't see how."

"I'm going to help you. I was one of the best werg hunters in the world. Once I get to the jungle, things will be a lot different. I've just gotta figure out how to get there without the damn chip so I can think clearly."

"I wish I had your confidence."

Aiden lowered his head. "Yeah," he mumbled, also wishing he had as much confidence as he portrayed.

"How will you get there? Do you have a plan?"

"First, I'm going to …" A sudden realization hit him and he froze.

"Aiden?" Sammy called.

Aiden scooted to the trough and trailed his fingers under the rim. "Be quiet for a minute."

"What's wrong?"

"Don't say anything else, Sammy. They might have bugged our cells. We've already said too much."

"Oh shit. I never thought of that."

Sammy sat quietly while Aiden searched every dark crevice of the cell. He didn't find any bugs, but that didn't mean there weren't any. He had to be more careful.

Neither man said anything else, and Aiden ended the day with push-ups and jumping jacks to keep the blood flowing.

He sat by the bars, watching the moon rise above the trees. As he looked out over the potential freedom of the field, he wondered if zoo animals felt the same way he did. It was after midnight before he finally went to sleep.

The next morning started with the usual tornado siren before Murdock and his men came for Sammy again. This time they had to drag him out.

Aiden pressed his forehead between the bars and shouted, "Be strong, Sammy."

But from the look of his bowed head, Sammy had already given up.

It was only two hours later when Murdock returned with a captive werg on a leash and put him into Sammy's cell. Murdock's cocky strut and toothy smile infuriated Aiden. He stopped just out of reach of Aiden's cell. "I can't wait till they kill that little prick."

"I can't wait until I kill you," Aiden growled.

Murdock snickered. "Try and get some sleep tonight. It's your turn under the knife tomorrow."

After he left, Aiden ran to his and Sammy's adjoining wall. "Sammy," he shouted.

Sammy grunted.

"I'm gonna get you out of here, Sammy. I know how to remove the chips. Just be strong for a few more days. If they send you to the jungle, hide. I know it's hard for you to think right now, but concentrate on what I'm saying. Whatever you do, you have to hide. Don't engage them. And don't be tempted by whatever bait they use." Aiden pressed his forehead to the wall. "I'm gonna make sure you see your daughter again."

Then he turned and let his back ride the wall until he sat on the floor. He pulled his knees close to his chest. The day faded into night. Though he was exhausted, he didn't sleep.

ON THE RUN

14

Jericho was looking through the blinds next to the front door again when Christine woke up. It was daytime.

"Hey," she said.

"Shhh." He glanced over at her. "You were right. They're goin' door to door."

She sat up with a start. "What?"

"They're coming our way. Just be cool. I'll talk to them. I'll tell them I live here."

"What if they traced your truck and know who you are?"

"It wasn't mine." He flicked his hand at her. "Now, hide."

Christine hurried into the hall where she could still see the door.

Jericho took a deep breath and opened it. He pretended not to see the men coming up the walk as he pried the stack of mail from the box. "Oh?" he said as if startled. "Good morning."

"Good morning, sir," one of the men answered.

Jericho briefly studied the top envelope and set the mail on a small table beside the door. "What's goin' on, guys?"

Christine watched from the hall, catching little glimpses of the men through the gap between the door and the frame on the hinge side. Both men wore dark suits and sunglasses. One of them carried a rifle and the other flashed some credentials.

"I'm Agent Thompson. We need to speak with you, Mister …"

"You can call me Carl," Jericho said without missing a beat.

"May we come in, sir?"

"Well, Mister Thompson, do you have a warrant?"

"We don't need a warrant, sir."

"How the hell do you not need a warrant? Aren't we still in the United States?"

"When there's a public health emergency, we have greater authority under the law. Do you own this house, sir?"

"Yes."

"Is your last name …" He looked at a clipboard. "Clayton?"

Jericho smiled. "Clay*born*."

Christine sighed. *Good catch, Jericho.*

Thompson nodded. "Right. Clayborn. Sorry about that. Are you alone this morning?"

"Unfortunately."

"The neighbor said a family of three lives here and that they were on vacation." When he said "vacation" he stuck his foot in the doorframe.

Jericho glanced down. "Now who told you that? Phil down the way?" He pointed generally down the street.

"It's not important who told us, sir."

"Yeah, it was probably Phil. He's always up in everyone's business. What Phil didn't know was that my wife and kid went to see the in-laws in Pittsburgh. They've been gone all week. I've been using the time to catch up on some work." He cocked his head. "What's the Dog Catchers want with us? No one around here owned any pet werewolves that I know of."

"We've had a couple go rogue in the area and we need to find them."

"No shit? Well, there're no wergs anywhere in here."

Jericho started to push the door against the agent's foot, but Thompson leaned into it. "One of the suspects was wearing a similar color shirt as you're wearing. Are you sure there's nothing else you want to tell us?"

Jericho was slick on his feet. "You're not gonna believe this, but in a crazy scheme to make money, a lot of companies made navy blue shirts. But if you think I'm lying, come on in out of the cold and have a look around."

Snidely, Thompson asked, "Even without a warrant?"

Jericho smirked. "You wanna come in, too, Mr. …?"

"Agent Harris," the other man answered. "And I think I'll stay right here."

"Suit yourself."

Christine sneaked into the back bedroom and quietly pushed the door almost shut. She glanced at the bedroom window that led to the back yard, wondering if Jericho wanted her to run. The return of the helicopter squashed that idea. She watched through the gap in the door as Agent Thompson started down the hall, gun drawn. He pushed open the first door on his left, flipped on the light, and disappeared inside. When he came back out, he headed straight for Christine's room.

She grabbed a menorah from the dresser and hid behind the door as Agent Thompson eased it open, his gun barrel poking into the room first. Christine lifted the menorah over her head.

Then a scuffle broke out in the front room, and he turned toward it.

Christine ripped the door open and bashed the back of his head with the base of the menorah. He dropped without a sound, unconscious and bleeding.

She raced to the front room where Jericho was dragging Agent Harris's limp body in from the porch. Her eyes went wide. "Did you kill him?"

He shook his head. "I just choked him out. We don't have long, though. He'll come to in a few seconds."

Christine dropped the menorah, snatched one of Harris's wrists, and helped Jericho drag him the rest of the way inside. As she slammed the front door, she saw an SUV stop in front of the driveway and several heavily armed agents climb out.

"They saw us," she cried.

Jericho grabbed his shotgun from the table, Harris's rifle, and a set of keys from the counter. "I found a car in the garage while you were asleep." He pulled Christine toward a door off the kitchen.

The front window shattered and a canister landed on the carpet. Though Christine never would have dreamed a few years ago that she'd know what a flash grenade looked like, experience was a harsh teacher. The blast popped her ears. She managed to close her eyes before the flash. Jericho didn't.

She ripped open the door to the garage where a cherry-red '69 Mustang sat facing a closed overhead door. She grabbed Jericho's hand and guided him into the garage as a hail of bullets shredded the front door.

Someone shouted, "Hold your fire. Harris and Thompson are in there."

Christine ripped the driver's door open and shoved Jericho inside.

Still blinded, he threw the shotgun on the passenger floorboard and crawled over the center console, blinking frantically. She climbed behind the wheel and jammed the keys into the ignition. A garage door opener hung on the visor. She pushed it.

As the door rose and the Mustang roared to life, Jericho climbed onto the passenger door and held the stolen rifle across the roof.

"Can you even see?" Christine shouted.

"Not really."

Christine stepped on the gas, exploding from the garage as agents dove for cover. An SUV blocked part of the driveway. Jericho blindly popped off a series of shots above their heads.

"Hold on," Christine shouted.

Jericho dropped back into his seat as she closed her eyes and plowed into the ass end of the SUV. It spun away. The Mustang jerked and rocked. Christine bounced against the steering wheel, recovered, and floored it.

Bullets riddled the side of the Mustang as agents raced to their crashed SUV. The helicopter banked around and gave chase. Jericho stuck Harris's rifle out the window and opened fire.

The helicopter's spotlight shattered, raining sparks all over the road. The copter jolted left, smoke pouring from its tail rotor, and retreated to the field behind the development for an emergency landing.

Christine gunned it. Repeated checks of the rearview mirror assured her the agents hadn't regrouped quickly enough to catch the stolen muscle car.

Jericho checked the magazine of the rifle. "I'm out. He tossed the gun into the back seat and checked the shotgun. "Only one shell left. Everyone in the country will be looking for this car soon. We need to ditch it fast."

"Where?"

"A place I've been stayin'."

"What kind of place?"

"A compound of sorts."

"Like a cult?"

He snorted. "Actually, yeah. In a way. But not like the Branch Davidians or Jonestown or anything. It's just a place where people like me can stay under the radar. The guy who runs it is a little wacky. His name's Slater. But before we get there, I need to know somethin'."

"Anything."

"The Dog Catchers said we're wergs even though they didn't know who I was."

"And?"

"Does that mean you're a ... you know?"

Yeah, she knew.

Her inner argument over whether to come clean or thread together some bullshit answer was brief. He had already done so much for her. "I am." It felt good to tell someone her secret.

"That's what I figured. You'll fit in good where we're goin'. Though, I have to warn you things might get a little tense at first."

"Oh?"

"Slater doesn't take to outsiders easily, and he's already pissed at me. The news about Jake isn't gonna help."

She winced. With everything else going on, she'd almost forgotten about the young man who'd been shot for trying to help her.

Jericho directed her to a country road. They drove for miles before turning down a lane that led to a turnaround. Christine pulled to a stop at an old country farmhouse in front of a much more modern apartment building.

Jericho climbed out and waved to the young man approaching from the house. "Hey, Cole."

Cole caressed the car's damaged front corner. "What'd you do to her?"

"We had to smash it up a bit."

Cole dragged his eyes over the rest of the car. "Whose is it?"

"Borrowed. Can you get Slater?"

"Sure." Cole headed to the house, his eyes lingering on the Mustang.

Jericho motioned for Christine to get out of the car.

While they waited for Slater, another guy approached from around the side of the house. Jericho introduced him as Trey. Trey also ran his hand over the car. Christine wondered if it was a guy thing.

A man wearing a long, hooded robe stepped onto the front porch with Cole next to him. Jericho leaned into Christine's ear and whispered, "That's Slater. I told you he was a bit squirrelly. Just play along."

"Jericho," Slater shouted. "Where have you been? We've been worried sick."

"We ran into some trouble at the fights and had to hole up for a bit."

"Adam came home this morning and said he'd heard there was some commotion after he'd left."

"We barely escaped before the Dog Catchers showed up."

Slater looked past him to the car. "Where's Jake?"

"Those bastards from the Dog Park shot him."

Slater paled. "What? Is he …?"

"He was alive when they took him."

"Took him? Where?"

"I don't know."

Slater's face twisted. "So, he may or may not be alive, and he may or may not have been taken somewhere, but you don't know where?"

"That sounds about right."

His eyes darkened. "This is your fault."

Jericho shook his head. "Bullshit. It's no one's fault. Throwin' blame around isn't gonna help right now."

Slater's lips moved as he mimicked Jericho like a child. Jericho rubbed his forehead in frustration.

"And how do you propose we find out if Jake's still alive?" Slater demanded.

"I don't know. Maybe we can check the hospitals. They may have taken him to one."

Slater turned to Trey. "Go get the burner phone and make some calls."

Trey rushed into the house.

Slater's eyes drifted back to the Mustang. "Where's my truck?"

Jericho gave him a thumbs down. "They shot it up, man. That's when Jake got hit. I'm sorry."

Slater groaned and side-eyed Christine. "You might as well tell me who this is now."

"She's a friend."

"Why's she here?"

"We needed a quick getaway. She helped me escape."

"*She* helped *you*?"

"You heard me."

Slater scowled. "What's your name, honey?"

"Christine, sir."

"Why did you come here, Christine?"

"I need help. Jericho said you might be—"

"Jericho doesn't run this place."

Jericho's jaw clenched.

"I understand that, sir," Christine replied, looking uncertainly from Slater to Jericho and back.

"My compound isn't for strangers."

Jericho held up a hand. "I told her she could stay here for a couple days. She has nowhere else to go."

Slater's eyes blasted wide. "W-w-what?"

"She needs help."

"But ... Uh ... I ... You know the rules, Jericho. I approve any new arrivals before they come here."

"Okay. This one'll be a little different, then."

"No."

"What if we took a vote?"

"Y-y-you already know how that'll go," Slater stuttered. "They-They always side with you."

Jericho clapped his hands. "I don't know what to say. She's stayin' at least for today. We can figure out what's next later."

He started to turn away, but Slater shouted, "Stop."

Jericho glanced back. "What?"

"Uh ... Whose car is this?"

Jericho pressed his lips together and winced. "Oh yeah. About that. I had to borrow it. Can you get rid of it? The Dog Catchers'll be all over it soon."

"What do you mean 'get rid of it'? How am I supposed to do that?"

"I don't know—"

Cole cleared his throat. "I'll do it."

Jericho smiled gratefully. "Thanks, Cole. Is that all right, Slater? Let Cole do it?"

"I guess."

"I really am sorry about Jake. I did everything I could. We were outgunned and I couldn't get to him."

Slater sneered. "This is my place, Jericho."

"I know."

"You need to remember that."

"I do."

"All right, then."

Christine hurried to Slater and extended her hand. "Thank you for letting me stay for a bit, sir. I'll be out of your hair before you know it."

Slater stared at her awkwardly and then turned and huffed into the house.

Christine joined Jericho and whispered, "He hates me."

"Yeah, well. Not just you. Let's get out of the firin' line." Jericho led her around the house and into the lobby of the apartment building. "I'll show you where you'll stay tonight. We're off the grid, so you won't be able to have any electronic devices. Is that okay?"

She nodded. Her phone was in her car at the factory anyway.

He led her to the second floor and opened the third door on the right. "It's fully furnished. Just think of it like a hotel room."

She stopped in the doorway and turned back. "Jericho?"

"Yeah?"

"I can't stay here long. I need to find my friend. I need to get to Detroit."

"There's nothing we can do today. I'll ask around and see if anyone knows anything about this Underground place, and then we'll take it from there. Deal?"

She nodded. "One more thing."

"Yeah?"

"I need to go home and get some things." She gestured at Maxine's filthy, rumpled suit. She was in desperate need of clean clothes. And underwear.

"I don't think it's a good idea. If the Dog Catchers found your car, they'll definitely be watching your place. For now, get some rest. I'll bring you something to eat in a little bit."

She sighed and nodded.

"There's a pen and paper in the kitchen drawer. Put together a list of things you need. Clothing sizes, toiletries, that kind of thing. I'll get it for you."

"I should call work and let them know I won't be in for a while. They're probably worried already since today was my workday and I'm officially AWOL."

"Slater keeps burner phones at the house. I'll get one."

"Thank you."

"Of course. I'll be back for that list in a bit." He smiled and left.

Christine grabbed the legal pad and jotted down a few basics. She was tempted to add "Ride to Detroit," but decided to see how things played out first.

FITTING IN

15

Christine tossed and turned all night, unable to get her mind off Aiden and what might be happening to him. A nightmarish vision of him hanging from a gallows haunted her every time she closed her eyes. She finally sat up and swung her legs off the side of the bed.

With her elbows on her knees, she rubbed her temples and tried to gather her thoughts. Her eyelids were still heavy. She stretched with a tired groan, went to the window, and parted the blinds. The early morning sun peeked over the forest.

To her right was a vast open field broken by an airplane runway that stretched past where she could see beyond the corner of the apartment building. She pressed her cheek to the window and saw the front of a hangar.

She closed the blinds. Jericho had gotten everything she'd asked for, including soap, shampoo, and conditioner. He'd even brought a bouquet of flowers to, as he put it, "Warm up the place a bit." Her lips turned up in an unexpected smile when she passed them on her way to the bathroom for a shower.

The hot water soothed her tired muscles, and she briefly considered staying in the shower all day. But that was ridiculous.

She dressed in the clothes Jericho had purchased, dried her hair, and put it in a ponytail. Ready for the day, she unlocked her front door and poked her head into the hall.

A young woman with a purple mohawk and enough metal studs in her ears and nose to short circuit a metal detector walked toward her carrying a gym bag. She was fit, wearing tight yoga pants and a sports bra, and smiled when she saw Christine. "Hi," she said in a bubbly voice. "You must be Christine."

Christine nodded.

"I'm Jess. Coming to class?"

Confused, Christine shook her head.

"No worries. I love to get the juices flowing first thing in the morning, and Jericho's classes really do the trick."

"He'll be there?"

"Of course. He's the one teaching."

"On second thought, maybe I will tag along. Do you mind?"

"Not at all. You ready?"

Christine presented herself like she was modeling her new outfit. "Am I okay to wear this?"

Jess looked her over and giggled. "Almost." She reached for the back of Christine's leg and ripped off an orange clearance sticker. They shared a laugh.

As they walked, Christine said, "You already heard I was here, huh?"

"Um-hm. We're a small community. Like, teeny-tiny. News travels fast."

"What else have you heard?"

"I heard you and Jericho got Jake hurt and pissed off Slater something fierce."

"About that. I didn't mean to. I just—"

Jess waved off her explanation. "Don't worry about it. Slater said Jake's gonna be fine."

Christine started. "He did?"

Jess nodded.

That made no sense. Either Trey had tracked Jake down at a local hospital or, more likely, Slater had lied about it. She decided to let it slide until she could ask Jericho about it later.

Jess added, "Even if Jake wasn't shot, Slater would still be pissed. He's a douchebag. He and Jericho have been butting heads ever since Jericho got here."

"But Slater runs this place, right?"

"I guess. He funds everything. He was a Wall Street kinda guy before he bought this land. Most of us just play along with his weirdness, but Jericho is always pushing his buttons."

Jess led her to a set of double doors on the first floor that opened into a half-court basketball gymnasium. Jericho stood on a mat in the middle of the floor with Cole and Trey. When he saw Christine and Jess, he smiled and waved them over.

"Since you were late again this morning, Jess, you get to be the uke."

Jess groaned.

Christine whispered, "What's an uke?"

Deflating like a grounded teenager, Jess answered, "It's Japanese. It means to receive. As in, I'm about to be a crash test dummy in his demonstration."

Jericho grinned. "As we continue learnin' some judo, we see how judo stand-up can lead right into our jiu-jitsu on the ground. You can't use our skills on the ground if you never get there."

Jess dressed in a white, long-sleeve top she called a gi and tied a white belt around her waist. "What are we practicing today?"

"Harai goshi," Jericho answered in his best attempt at a Japanese accent.

"Ugh. I hate getting thrown."

"Just remember how to fall properly, okay?" Jericho gripped the lapel of her gi and the sleeve beneath her opposite elbow. Using some fancy footwork, he spun away, sending her for a ride over his hip. Her legs whipped up and around and slammed into the padded mat with a loud bang.

Christine cringed, convinced Jess was now crippled. Using Jess's momentum, Jericho landed behind her and wrapped his arms around her neck. She gave his elbow three rapid taps, and he immediately released her. She bounced back up and rubbed the back of her neck. A throw like that would have sent Christine straight into a wheelchair. Or the morgue.

"That choke is called a rear naked choke. Here, watch it again."

To Jess's obvious chagrin, Jericho whipped her in the air and squeezed her neck until she tapped his arm again.

Trey and Cole partnered up while Jess observed. The sound of Trey's body slapping the mat startled Christine each time, but he repeatedly got back up, unfazed.

"Would you like to try?" Jericho asked.

Christine shook her head emphatically.

"Come on. It's fun. I promise you won't hurt me."
Before Christine could protest, he had already faced her
and lifted her hand to his lapel. "Hold on right here."

She gingerly gripped the fabric. It was course and
thick and sturdy.

He squeezed her hand. "Harder. Really grab hold."
He positioned her other hand on the fabric hanging
from his elbow. Since she wasn't wearing a gi, he held
her arm and sweatshirt. "Now, step just like this." He
stepped forward, pivoted his body, and gave a slight
tug, lifting her a few inches off the ground. He lowered
her feet back to the mat. "Just like that, but when *you*
do it, you do it fast so it whips me over your hip. Got
it?"

"Not at all."

He chuckled. "Sure, you do. Just give it a try."

"I have no idea what I'm doing."

"That's all right."

"It's your funeral."

"That's a risk I'm willing to take."

He walked her through her foot positioning and then
gave her the go-ahead. Mimicking the technique he'd
shown her, she effortlessly hurled him over her hip and
slammed him into the mat with a loud slap.

She let go, amazed at how light he was and how
easily she had thrown him. "On my gosh," she cried.
"Are you all right?"

He feigned an injured back and groaned.

"I'm so sorry."

He laughed. Then he helped position her arms
around his neck to show her how to finish the throw
with the choke. "Now breathe in deeply and squeeze,"
he said.

As soon as she did it, he tapped her arm. She immediately let go, worried she'd hurt him again.

He bounced to his feet. "You're a natural. If I didn't know the proper way to land, you might have actually hurt me."

Christine wouldn't readily admit it, but it was kind of fun.

"You wanna try again?"

"Not right now. I need to speak with you for a minute."

"Okay." He waved at Cole, who wore a blue belt instead of white. "Work on arm bars until I get back."

Cole acknowledged him with a wave.

Jericho walked with Christine to an empty spot in the gym. Before she could say anything, a young, handsome man strutted in. When he caught Jess's eye, she smiled and waved. He nodded back. He already wore a gi with a blue belt like Cole's.

"Who's turn?" he shouted.

Trey raised his hand. The two men slapped hands and then started wrestling.

"That's Adam," Jericho said. "He's Slater's top guy. He was at the Dog Park the other night, too. He fought under the name Viper."

"Oh." She remembered making that prick Bradley McNeil a lot of money by picking Viper.

Jericho wiped a bead of sweat from his forehead with his gi sleeve. "So, what's up?"

"Did you find out anything about the Underground?"

"Actually, yeah. Adam said a guy named Curtis used to live here before he just up and disappeared one day. They thought the Dog Catchers got him, but Adam did some diggin' and found someone who saw the guys who took him. They were some sort of mercenary unit, and they talked about sending him to a place called the Underground."

"Any idea what it is?"

"Not really. Adam thinks some of the guys he's fought in the pits came from there. The extra vicious ones he's never seen as humans."

"Then that's where I need to go right away."

"It might be tough. Slater's not about to give us a car after we lost his truck. He's still pretty pissed."

"What if I talk to him? Smooth things over."

"You could try, I guess. Probably won't do any good, though."

"Where is he?"

Jericho checked his watch. "Probably meditatin' on the roof."

"If he won't give me a car, will you help me get to the airport?"

"I don't think goin' to the airport would be a good idea. If the feds are looking for you now, they'll be monitorin' flights. You won't get past the main gates."

"Then I'll hitchhike."

"Why don't you see what Slater says first and then we'll go from there?"

Christine agreed and then asked for directions to the roof. She turned to leave and hesitated. "Hey, Jericho. Did Slater say anything about Jake being fine?"

"Not that I've heard. Why?"

"Oh. Nothing. Just something Jess said. I probably misheard her. Don't worry about it." She made her way to the second floor where a ladder led to an open hatch in the roof. She climbed up.

Slater sat at the far edge with his back to her. He wore his red robe with the hood up. One look at the view on that peaceful, brisk early morning told Christine exactly why he chose the roof to meditate.

"What do you want, Christine?" he said without looking back.

She decided to lay the respect on thick. "Sir, I was wondering if we could chat for a minute."

"Can't it wait?"

"Actually, no, sir. It can't."

He lowered his hood and glanced back at her. His shoulders slouched. "What is it, then?"

"I feel like we got off on the wrong foot and I'd like to remedy that." She quickly added, "Sir."

He groaned and stood up. His oversized sleeves dropped over his hands as he gestured her closer. She stepped to the roof's edge beside him.

He walked to a bag lying beside his yoga mat, got out a bottle of water, and took a long swallow. He wiped his mouth with his sleeve. "What can I do for you?"

"First, let me thank you for allowing me to stay last night. I am so appreciative of your generosity."

He straightened a bit.

"This is a wonderful place you've built—"

"Mostly by myself," he interjected.

"I can tell. You are a master for sure."

"Jericho helped with the apartment building, I guess, but that's just 'cause I was so busy."

"Oh, I'm sure."

"What can I *really* do for you, Christine?" His tone seemed more inviting this time.

"I want to apologize for all the tension when I got here. I didn't know it was going to be like that."

"And?"

"I'm just sorry, is all."

"Apology accepted. That Jericho's nothing but trouble sometimes. Is there anything else?"

"Yes, actually. Have you ever heard of a place called the Underground?"

"Of course, I have. What about it?"

"My boyfriend has been taken there. I need to go find him."

"And? What's stopping you?"

"Well, I need a car an—"

He shook his head emphatically. "Nope, nope, nope. Stop right there. I'm not helping you. I don't know what you're up to, but no way, no how."

"But ..."

He continued shaking his head. "End of discussion. If you want to go there, start walking, honey."

"I just need a car fo—"

"Nope."

"What about the Mustang?"

"Already gone."

"So, you won't help me at all?"

"I gave you a place to stay last night."

"And I appreciate that."

He sighed and looked to the sky. "Do you know why this place exists and why I don't want you here?"

How would I know that? She shook her head.

"I worked at a stock brokerage firm for a few years and made a lot of money. But I felt like there was more for me in this world. You're not going to believe this, but when I was younger, I got picked on in school."

"I don't believe that for a minute." It took a conscious effort not to roll her eyes. If there was anyone most likely to be picked on in school, Slater was it.

"No, really. The kids thought I was odd. And maybe I was a little odd at times. I never fought back, though.

I was too weak. I figured I'd show them by getting rich one day. I expected to be the next Bill Gates. But even as I started making money, I didn't feel any better.

"At my ten-year reunion, no one cared that I arrived in a limo and had my own personal driver."

Christine didn't care either. All she cared about was finding Aiden. "Slater, I should probably go. I—"

"Just hear me out."

She bit her tongue.

"I wanted to be strong, but money doesn't make you strong. Sure, I could pay to have a bodyguard and boss people around, but that wasn't enough. I realized that night of the reunion that nothing I did mattered. And it wasn't any better at the office, either. When they say people grow up and mature, they're lying. Those guys were just like the kids at school. Do you know what I did about it?"

Christine contemplated going over the edge of the roof. "Nope."

"I bought a werepet. While the other guys were buying Beamers and Ferraris, I bought the most powerful beast on land." He puffed out his chest proudly. "Everyone took notice then. Suddenly, I had friends wanting to come to my place and check it out. These guys were so tough at work, but they were too afraid of their wives to get their own werepets. That stupid dog became my best friend.

"And then the news came out that the WereHouse had been shut down and my best friend was actually a human. I couldn't believe it."

His story was finally starting to interest her. "What'd you do?"

"I found a black market doctor who figured out how the werepets were kept in a permanent werg state. They had special microchips implanted and—"

"I know about the chips."

He cocked his head. "Right. Anyway, I had his chip cut out and freed him from his curse to go back to his family." He paused, a nostalgic look on his face as if he was remembering his old friend. "After that, I decided to help former werepets. I quit my job, sold everything I had, and bought this place. Adam was the first one I brought here. I even asked him to infect me too so I could have more in common with my new friends." He smiled.

"Why are you telling me all this?"

"Because I want you to understand why I'd rather let your friend die than to risk this place and the people I've helped here being discovered. That's why we're off the grid. And that's why no one, not you, not Jericho, not God himself, is going to risk that." The whites of his eyes blackened briefly.

"But what about Jake? What if the people who took him are the same ones who took Curtis?"

Slater's face froze and his forehead creased. "Who told you about Curtis?"

"Jericho."

He sneered. "Curtis knew the risks. And so did Jake."

"But if he's there, we—"

"The answer's no. As much as I'd like to help Jake, we're safe here. He shouldn't have gone to the fights. And you should leave as soon as possible."

"Why?"

"Because I don't trust you."

"I understand that. I wish I had more time to earn your trust, but I don't. I need to get to the Underground before it's too late for my friend."

"Well, you'll have to do it without us. I don't want you here, Christine. I just don't know how to get rid of you without that damn Jericho ..." He shook his head. "He's become too popular here, so I'm stuck. I never should have let him into the group. He's like a cancer. Everyone seems to love him, and I can't for the life of me figure out why." He glared at her. "I don't care if you run and tell him I said that, either."

"Slater, I don't want anything to happen to you or your place. I didn't ask to be in this position and—"

"Neither did I."

"What if they come for you next?"

"They won't."

"How do you know?"

He gritted his teeth before taking a deep, calming breath. "They just won't. We're careful. We're off the grid."

It was obvious the two were on entirely different planets. She decided her best bet was to stop talking.

Slater sat down on his blanket and pulled his hood up. "You're dismissed."

Christine glowered at the back of his head before storming to the hatch where Adam was pulling himself onto the roof. He was sweating and still wearing his gi.

"Excuse me," he said. "I didn't realize Slater had company." He playfully bit his lower lip as he looked her up and down. "You must be Christine." He offered his hand.

She took it. "I am."

He lifted her hand to his mouth and gave it a gentle kiss. "My name's Adam."

She politely retracted her hand. "I've heard."

He glanced past her at Slater. "I hear you got off to a rocky start with ol' grouchy over there. Did you two smooth things out?"

"I don't think so. He doesn't like me much."

"Eh. Don't worry about it. Slater's a good guy. He's just a little odd."

"I suppose."

"I owe him my life, actually. He's the one who freed me." He turned his head and showed her the puckered scar on the back of his neck. "I had a chip in my neck and—"

"Yeah, I know about the chips." Everyone wanted to explain the damn chips.

"Oh, right. Slater said I used to be some asshole's pet. I was the first one he brought here."

"Yeah. He just told me."

"He did?"

Before she could answer, Slater shouted, "Adam, is that you?"

"Yep."

"Come over here."

Adam rolled his eyes and smiled. "It was nice meeting you, Christine. Maybe we can meet up later and have a couple drinks."

There was no way that was happening. "Maybe."

Adam hurried over to Slater. Before Christine climbed down the hatch, she heard him say, "We need to go find Jake."

Slater dropped him a crooked look. "You, too?"

"He's our friend, and I'm not gonna swallow your bullshit like the others did. We didn't know where they took Curtis until it was too late, but we know where they'll take Jake. We can—"

Slater opened his mouth to argue then caught a glimpse of Christine listening. He shouted, "I said you are dismissed. Now, leave." He waited until Christine climbed down the hatch to continue.

She ran into Jericho in the hallway heading to his apartment.

"What'd he say?" he asked.

"You were right. He's no help. Thanks for everything you've done for me." She tried to march past him, but he stopped her.

"What're you doin'?"

"I'm leaving."

"What?"

"I have to go, Jericho. I need to find Aiden. I can't sit back and do nothing."

"How 'bout I talk to him?"

"You already said it wouldn't do any good."

"Maybe not. But at least let me try. If you give me a chance and I can't convince him to give us a car—"

"Us?"

He squared his shoulders. "Of course. I'm part of the reason they captured Jake. I'm goin' with you. If he's alive and they've taken him to this Underground, I need to do everything I can to find him. If Slater won't give us a car, I'll get one. We'll leave tonight either way. Deal?"

She nodded. If it wouldn't be so inappropriate, she'd hug the guts right out of him. "Thank you, Jericho."

He smiled. "Of course."

It was bright and early when Murdock and his flunkies came for Aiden. With the razor collar around his neck and his hands bound, they led him to a pole barn they called "the Garage."

The inside was immaculate with stainless-steel walls and tile floors sloped slightly toward a drain in the center. The smell of bleach was almost overwhelming. The glistening countertops along the far wall screamed sterility.

A metal table sat next to a high-back dentist chair that was bolted to the floor in the center near the drain. Murdock gestured toward it. "Take a seat."

Aiden sat down awkwardly, his hands still bound behind his back. Murdock strapped a NASCAR-style safety harness across his chest and locked it tight. He pressed Aiden's head to the cold metal headrest and wrapped a leather strap across his forehead. "I recommend you shift sooner rather than later."

"I recommend you pound sand."

Murdock blew him a kiss.

Three other men were in the room. Two were handlers. The third, dressed in a doctor's lab coat, was busy fiddling with surgical instruments on a metal tray. Someone else entered and Aiden instantly recognized his scent.

"Glad you could join us, pretty boy," he called out.

Pietro leisurely crossed the room with his hands clasped together at his waist. His suit was perfectly pressed and flawless. "Aiden. Buongiorno. Are you hungry?"

Of course he was hungry. He quietly seethed in his chair.

Pietro nodded toward Murdock. "Why don't you get Aiden a little snack? We want him focused today so he makes the right decision."

Murdock went to a small refrigerator. From Aiden's position, he could see inside when the door opened. There was an apple on the top shelf and multiple shelves of drug vials. Murdock grabbed the apple and closed the door. He carried it over and held it to Aiden's lips. Though anger and pride made Aiden want to ignore it, he desperately needed the nutrition. He took a bite.

Pietro stood patiently and waited for Aiden to devour the apple to its core. Aiden would have eaten that too if Murdock hadn't pulled it away.

"Do you feel better?" Pietro asked.

The apple hadn't made a dent in Aiden's hunger, but he refused to answer.

Pietro waved Murdock aside. "So, Aiden. I have some good news."

Aiden lifted his eyes. "Yeah? And what's that?"

"We've got a major hunt coming up and we'd love for you to attend."

Somehow, Aiden didn't think he meant as an honored guest. "Hmph. Why me?"

Pietro pressed his lips into a thin line. Then he licked them. "You were one of Bernard's finest rogue hunters. We here at WereHunt, Inc. owe quite a debt to my old friend. If it wasn't for him and his funding, I'm convinced we would have never gotten this operation off the ground." He clapped his hands. "Now, enough of that. How about we get started?" He snapped his fingers twice and held out his open hand. Murdock handed him an electronic tablet and a stylus. He tapped the screen as he spoke. "You see, Aiden. Normally we'd take a few weeks to really break you down with some truly imaginative techniques. It's part of the fun of running this place. But unfortunately, with such an important hunt scheduled, time is not our friend." He swiped across the screen and tapped it a dozen more times and then turned it for Aiden to see.

It was a picture of Christine's fire department ID photo. Aiden's heart skipped a beat.

"Do you know this woman?" Pietro asked.

With panic welling up on the inside, Aiden fought to keep a stoic expression. He took a subtle, calming breath. "Never seen her before."

Pietro cocked his head. "Really? Now, that's not what I've heard. I think maybe you do know her. In fact, I think you might even be touching her naughty parts on occasion." Pietro searched Aiden's face for a crack in his armor.

Aiden stared back, an emotionless mask firmly in place.

Pietro studied him. After what felt like a lifetime of awkward silence, he clapped his hands again. "Very well. Here's what we're going to do. Instead of cutting off your body parts or waterboarding you or whatever else we come up with, we will simply do those nasty things to poor Miss Alt."

Aiden swallowed hard. "And why should I care what you do to some stranger?"

"Maybe you don't. But we'll be sure to record everything so you can see the results of your stubbornness. Or we could set up a live feed. How would that be?"

Aiden wanted to kill him. Through clenched teeth, he answered, "I said. I. Don't. Know. Her."

"Well, then. I guess you're off the hook." He tapped his chin. "I actually met this girl once, you know?"

Aiden glared back.

"I was attending a dinner with Bernard last year and this pretty young lady was his date, if I remember correctly."

"What's this have to do with me?"

Pietro circled Aiden's chair as he talked. "That was one crazy night. Some nasty werg showed up and busted the whole place up. I was lucky to get out of there in one piece. I ..." His eyes widened. "Wait a minute ..." He rubbed his chin. "That was you, wasn't it?"

Of course it was me, you imbecile. "I don't know what you're talking about. I don't know about any dinner parties. And I don't know who that woman is."

"If you're dating this woman and—"

"I said I'm not dating her."

Pietro rolled his eyes. "Yeah, yeah. How about we cut the charade now? Here's what I'm offering. You shift for us"—his face hardened and he spoke through his teeth—"and I won't murder that young woman in a very nasty way. I'm done playing games."

Aiden was nearly as furious at himself as he was at Pietro. He should have known from the start that the cells were bugged. He thought about poor Sammy and how much information about his daughter he had divulged during their conversation. Was that how they'd finally broken him, too? He had to push those thoughts away and do what he could to protect Christine. It didn't sound like Pietro knew how crucial she had been to Bernard's downfall. He needed to keep it that way, and to do that, he needed to shift and hope the chip didn't work as intended. He swallowed hard and nodded.

Pietro smiled. "Eccellente. I just knew we could work something out."

"And you won't hurt that woman if I do this?"

"Why, Aiden, I am a man of my word. Not a hair on her pretty little head will be touched." He crossed his heart.

Aiden didn't believe him, but he was in a box with few options. "Let's get on with it."

"Very good."

Murdock and the other handlers untied Aiden's hands and unbuckled the harness. They took him to the stainless-steel table and ordered him to lie face down on it. Before removing his collar, the handlers readied their tranquilizer guns.

Aiden climbed up and pressed his bare chest to the cold steel. They extended his arms and secured them to the table.

Pietro rested his hand on Aiden's shoulder. "Unfortunately, we can't sedate you because it might cause you to shift back before we're ready. I'm sure you understand." He called over the lab coat-wearing man. "He's all yours, Doc."

Aiden considered making his last stand right then and there, but it would be next to impossible to shift, escape his restraints, and disarm Murdock and the other handlers before they successfully tranquilized him. Not to mention what they would then do to Christine.

Pietro patted Aiden and backed away. "You can shift anytime now, my friend."

The only way Aiden figured he could maintain even a speck of consciousness when the doctor inserted the chip was to focus on the things that made him want to be a man. As the color drained from his vision, he concentrated on who he was and what was at stake if he mentally lost control. When his fingers twisted and snapped, he thought about helping Sammy get back to his daughter. When the fur covered him from head to toe, he remembered rescuing former werepets and how good it felt to do something meaningful with his life. As he stifled a roar, he thought about Christine waiting for him to return.

And then he stopped fighting. His snout grew from his face and the muscles in his legs swelled and elongated.

He was barely through his bone-cracking change when the doctor picked up a scalpel. With every slice and prod, Aiden tried to think of the life he was building with Christine. The pain was excruciating, but every time he started fantasizing about eating the bastards' hearts, he pulled himself back again.

A bloody scalpel landed on a sterile tray. The doctor delicately picked up a new microchip with surgical tweezers and went back to work. Whatever he did next electrified Aiden's nervous system, sending jolts of agony down his spine like he had clutched a high voltage line with his bare hands. The pain was blinding and didn't lessen until after he felt multiple clunks of a staple gun against his neck.

The doctor finally stepped back. No one spoke.

A low buzz rose in Aiden's head. He tried to remember what he had been thinking about before the pain began, but his mind had gone blank.

A familiar scent tickled his nose. A man's scent. Aiden knew he didn't like the man because ... because ... There was something crucial that he was supposed to remember, but he couldn't think what it was. He only wanted blood and to satisfy his terrible hunger.

The man approached and said, "You did magnifico, Aiden."

Aiden. That's right. That's my name.

"You belong to WereHunt now, don't you, Aiden?"

Aiden nodded, still trying to figure out why he hated this man so much. What was his name? Peter? No. Pietro.

Pietro nodded to the others. "How about we let Aiden up and see how he does."

Something told Aiden he had a purpose—that he wasn't always so confused—but nothing made sense.

When the restraints loosened around his wrists, he pulled his arms out of them, free at last. The straps around his ankles loosened next and he sprang from the table, thirsty for blood.

Pietro backed away with his hands held up in surrender. Aiden swept the room with his cold, colorless gaze.

And then a popping sound preceded a needle slamming into his neck. He staggered, suddenly drunk, and dropped to his knees as the floor spun.

Pietro stepped beside him. "You are going to be a great one for the hunters to chase. Grazie, Aiden."

DETROIT

17

While waiting for Jericho to talk to Slater, Christine wandered the grounds, ending up near the hangar. She decided to take a peek inside. It was mostly empty except for a small plane in the center, a rolled-up tarp near it, a forklift, a bunch of crates, and the biggest toolbox she'd ever seen.

As she walked past the plane, she dragged her fingers along the wing. Lost in fantasies of flying to Detroit and rescuing Aiden, she didn't hear someone else enter the hangar.

"Hey," Adam shouted, almost giving her a heart attack.

She spun toward him.

"What are you doing out here?" he asked as he crossed the floor.

"I-I was just looking around."

"Did Slater say you could mess with his plane?"

"I wasn't messing with it."

He marched past her and examined where she had been touching.

"Really. I was just looking."

He patted the wing proudly. "Piper."

She blinked. "Excuse me?"

"The plane. It's a Piper Cherokee six-seater."

"Oh. Right."

"You ever been in one?"

She shook her head. "The only time I've ever flown was to Vegas, and that was in a commercial plane."

"Vegas, huh? I've been there a few times. The city that never sleeps."

She started to tell him that was New York City's motto, but decided it wasn't important.

"Maybe I can take you up in her sometime." He looked her up and down. "You know, like a date."

"I thought you were with Jess?"

"I am." He gave her a cocksure grin. "Until I'm not, if you know what I mean."

He suddenly reminded her of her ex-boyfriend Roger. She would have been tempted to punch him if she didn't need something from him now. She followed him around the plane to the single propeller on the front. "I didn't know you're a pilot. Have you been to Detroit?"

"Detroit?" He smirked. "Nah. Never been."

He knew. He had already talked to Slater, and she'd just said too much. She had to find Jericho and figure out how to get Adam on their side.

Adam went on about places he'd flown—Alberta, Canada and Miami, Florida—while she searched for the right moment to excuse herself. The more he rattled on, the more she realized there wasn't going to be one. She'd have to cut him off mid-ramble. "Hey, Adam. Any idea where Jericho is right now?"

He shrugged. "It's not my day to babysit, but he might be getting ready for dinner in the cafeteria."

Perfect. "Thank you."

"I didn't do anything."

"No, I mean for showing me the plane. I'd love to take you up on your offer to go for a ride someday."

He bowed. "It would be my honor, milady."

She curtsied back. "I'll see you at dinner?"

"I'll be there in a few."

She excused herself and headed for the cafeteria where Jericho was already standing in the chow line behind Trey and Cole. Slater and Jess were sitting at a table with a space reserved between them for Adam.

Christine got in line behind Jericho. "Did you know Slater has a plane and Adam can fly it?"

"Of course. What of it?"

She looked around furtively. "I was just thinking maybe he would give us a ride to Detroit. He seems to be more of a free spirit than Slater."

Jericho grinned. "Listen, Christine. Adam's an all right guy, but he's Slater's best friend. You'd have to expect anything you ask him will get right back to Slater. I don't know that he'll be much help."

"What about you? Can *you* fly the plane?"

Jericho shook his head. "Only Adam and Slater can fly it. And while Adam would be more likely to help than Slater, I still don't think he'll go behind Slater's back." He was at the front of the chow line now and filled his plate.

Christine trailed after him, filling her own plate with spaghetti, sauce, and a piece of garlic bread. Then she followed the guys to an empty table.

Adam burst into the cafeteria like the king and strolled to Slater's side. He leaned in and whispered something that caused Slater's face to darken.

He glared at Christine. Adam straightened and sauntered over, nodding politely at Jericho. He put both fists on the table across from her and loomed over her. He gave her a death stare. She wilted under it.

Loud enough for the whole room to hear, he said, "I know what you were doing at Slater's plane—"

"I wasn't doing anything," she protested.

"Slater already gave you an answer. I'm not taking you to Detroit. If you wanna stay here, you will not go behind Slater's back ever again. Is that understood?" He glanced back at Slater for approval.

Christine nodded. "I-I'm sorry."

Then, to her shock, he leaned closer and whispered, "Meet me out front at midnight. I'll get you a car." He stood up again, snatched Christine's garlic bread off her plate, and stormed over to the food table. After filling his own plate and returning to Slater's table, he gave Jess a kiss and sat down like the whole scene hadn't happened.

Christine leaned close to Jericho and whispered, "What the hell just happened?"

"I think he wants to help."

She discreetly smiled as she ate her spaghetti.

Adam was waiting beside a running BMW when Christine arrived in front of Slater's house ten minutes before midnight.

"Sorry to be so dramatic at dinner," he said. "I had to sell it."

"I don't understand. Why are you helping us?"

"For Jake. I wanted to take the plane and fly you there, but there's no way I can swing that. So, I got you the next best thing. This time of night, you can get to Detroit in less than four hours."

"You should go with us."

He crinkled his nose. "I'd love to, but I can't. I know Slater is a strange bird, but he did save my life. I owe him *some* loyalty. Be careful. He loves this car."

"Of course. I can't thank you enough, Adam."

He tossed her the keys and winked as Jericho made his way around the house. He gave him a bro hug. "Make sure you find Jake."

Jericho nodded.

Christine gave Jericho the keys and climbed into the passenger's seat. "What do you think Slater will do when he finds out we took his car?"

Jericho cringed. "Have an aneurysm, probably."

She snorted. "No, really."

"There's not much he *can* do at this point. But when we get back, I'm sure I'll get a stern talkin'-to." He couldn't hold back a grin.

They pulled out and headed for the freeway.

They didn't talk much at first, but Jericho eventually broke the silence. "So. What's your story?"

"What do you mean?"

"How'd you get tied up in all this?"

"Oh God, where do I start?" She decided the medic run where she was infected was as good a place as any.

Over the next hour, she told him everything up to their meeting at the Dog Park.

"You've had a crazy life, Christine."

"I guess." Her fingers were cold, and she shivered. They reached for the heater at the same time and his fingers brushed the back of her hand.

He flipped the heater fan on high. "You're freezing. Here."

She held her hand above the vent. "Have you ever been married?"

He didn't answer right away, and she was immediately sorry for prying. But then he said, "Once. Not anymore."

Sensing she'd picked a sensitive topic, she asked if he had any kids. Most people liked talking about their kids.

He shook his head. "I wanted children, but my wife wasn't able."

"It's not too late. You could still have kids one day."

He scoffed. "Christine, I'm gettin' to be an old man."

"You're not old."

"I didn't think so either, but then one day I looked for my car keys for ten whole minutes when they were in my hand all along."

She playfully smacked his arm and giggled. "Stop it. We all do stuff like that."

He was easy to talk to and the hours passed like minutes. He told her about his construction career and getting into martial arts. "Have you ever heard of the Gracie family?" he asked with a grin.

She shook her head.

"They're basically the royal family of Brazilian jiu-jitsu."

"Okay?"

"Back in my twenties, I was in the same tournament as one of the Gracie brothers. We met in the semifinals, and I put up a good fight. But then he caught me in a submission with only a few seconds left and I had to tap. He told me afterwards that I almost had him. To me, that was as good as a win. I thought I must've been gettin' pretty good. That's when I decided I should pursue teachin' after I retired from fightin'." His smile faded and he shook his head a little. "What about you? Firefighter, huh?"

She told him about her academy days and some of the more insane runs she had taken over the years. By the time they reached Detroit, she felt like she had reconnected with a long-lost best friend. He was funny, sweet, and kind, and she was thankful to have met him.

As they entered the city, the conversation died and Jericho put on a serious game face. They reached a stretch of old, out-of-commission railroad tracks in a bad end of town just before sunrise. The tracks ran past a sprawling complex of broken-down buildings inside a six-foot chain-link fence with multiple holes cut in it. The compound covered an entire city block. The broken second-floor window of one building had black charring around the frame. The roof of another had collapsed, leaving a mess of concrete and rusted metal debris.

Jericho pulled off the side of the road and parked half on the sidewalk. They got out and listened to the low whistle of the wind. Christine half expected tumbleweed to come rolling down the street. "It doesn't look like there's anyone around."

"Could you have been given bad info?" Jericho asked.

Christine immediately imagined what she would do to Maxine if that bitch had lied, which seemed more probable the more she thought about it. "Let's look around."

They passed the shell of a burned-out car. She noticed an enclosed pedestrian bridge that crossed the road from the third floor of one building outside the fence to the third floor of one inside. Predawn light glinted off the broken windows.

Just as Christine was about to write it off as another abandoned structure, Jericho pointed. "Look."

A figure dressed like a soldier walked past one of the windows on the bridge.

They shared a look and set off across the street, hugging the buildings as they made their ways toward the door beneath the bridge. Before they reached it, a set of headlights turned onto the road in the distance.

Jericho pulled Christine between two buildings to wait for it to pass. But instead of passing, the van stopped at the front door.

The driver got out and opened the sliding door. A woman climbed from the back with a rifle. They were dressed like soldiers, too.

The woman jerked a man with his hands bound behind his back and a black hood over his head out of the sliding side door. They escorted him inside.

Jericho grunted. "I'd say we're definitely in the right place, wouldn't you?"

"I'd say so."

"Did you recognize them?"

She nodded. "They're the ones who took Jake."

"Let's make sure no one else is in the van."

They jogged over and peeked inside. It was empty with the keys still in the ignition.

"Whoever they are, they're not worried about someone stealing their van," Jericho whispered.

They sneaked into the building and followed the small group into the stairwell, creeping silently at a safe distance. The men entered a door on the third floor. Christine and Jericho pressed their backs to the wall beside it.

"Hey, Killzone," someone said.

"Hey, Cornell," someone else replied with a gritty voice.

Jericho gave Christine a look and mouthed, "Killzone?"

She shrugged.

"Got another one, I see," Cornell said.

"That's right," Killzone answered.

"Got the paperwork finished?"

"Of course."

"Leave it on the desk. You know where to go. Rory will have your check." Cornell's all-business tone turned overly friendly. "Hi, Jasper."

"Hey," a woman answered in a flat, uninterested tone.

Jericho motioned Christine away from the door and whispered, "I've got an idea. You be my prisoner."

Christine shook her head. "That'll never work. It's just a movie cliché."

"You have anything better?"

She didn't.

"Then put your hands behind your back, prisoner." He smiled. "We don't have any rope or zip ties, so you'll just have to pretend."

"What if it doesn't work?"

He gave her a pained look. "Then we'll have to shift and fight our way out."

She wiped her suddenly clammy hands on her pants and then clasped them behind her back.

Once Cornell was alone in the room and Killzone and his friends were all the way across the pedestrian bridge, Jericho whispered, "Be cool." He nudged her through the doorway.

A man sat at a desk with a rifle leaning against it. He was balding with glasses. He lifted his eyes from his paperwork and tugged the glasses lower on his nose.

"Hey, Cornell," Jericho said as though they were old friends.

Cornell's forehead crinkled. "Who are you?"

"It's me. Big Daddy."

Christine almost blew everything with an uncontrolled snort, but she caught it before it escaped.

Cornell studied him with narrowing eyes. "Is this a joke?"

"Nah, man. I got one for ya. And let me tell you, this bitch is feisty."

Cornell's puzzled gaze didn't waver. "I've never met you before."

"Sure, you have. I'm usually with Killzone. In fact, he should already be here by now. Have you seen him?"

"Uh ... He was ... Um ... You just missed him."

"Oh, cool. I've been meanin' to talk to him. Is he underground already?"

"Uh ... Yeah. But ..."

"Perfect. I'll go find him."

"Hold on. Do you have the paperwork?"

Jericho patted his pockets and then grimaced. "Shit. I left it in the truck. No sweat. I'll get it to you after I talk to Killzone."

Cornell put one hand on the rifle and picked up a walkie-talkie from his desk.

Christine panicked on the inside. Jericho gave her a nervous glance, which didn't help her confidence.

"Let me just verify with the boss." Cornell lifted the walkie to his mouth. "Hey, Rory, you there?"

"Go ahead."

"We got a—"

Jericho launched himself across the desk, grabbing Cornell so hard and fast that the rifle fell and the walkie slid across the floor. Jericho hip-tossed Cornell to his back and wrapped his arms around his neck. Cornell thrashed briefly, but Jericho was too strong. Within seconds, Cornell's arms fell limp. Another second after that, the rest of his body did the same.

"Don't kill him," Christine blurted out.

Jericho released him, allowing his body to sprawl on the floor. "I didn't kill him. Find somethin' to tie him up."

Within a few seconds, Cornell's eyes fluttered and he started to come around. Jericho pinned him to the ground while Christine searched the desk. "What about the cord from this lamp?"

"That'll do."

After hog-tying Cornell's hands and feet, Jericho dragged him on his belly to a closet with the door half hanging off. He stuffed Cornell inside and propped the door across the opening.

"Cornell?" Rory called from the walkie.

Jericho snatched it and shattered it against the wall.

"I guess we're done talking?" Christine said dryly.

"I guess so. Let's go." He took Cornell's gun, and they ran across the pedestrian bridge into another room where voices filled the stairwell. "Play it cool."

Christine shoved her hands behind her back again as three soldiers poured out of the stairwell with guns drawn.

Jericho held Cornell's gun up in surrender. "What's up, guys?"

"Who are you?" the man in front shouted.

"Freelance werg hunter, sir. Bringing in my catch."

"Where's Cornell?"

Jericho nodded toward the bridge. "Where he's supposed to be, I'd guess. That's where he was when we passed through. His walkie wasn't workin'."

Like idiots, the soldiers charged across the bridge. Christine couldn't believe it had worked.

Jericho grabbed her arm. "Game time." They barreled down several flights of stairs and past the ground level to a closed door at the bottom.

Christine cracked the door open and peeked out into a massive underground complex stretching as far as she could see. A row of cages held wergs along the wall to the left and an office behind a screen was to the right. Killzone and the woman called Jasper stood there with their prisoner, talking to someone dressed like a civilian behind the screen, presumably Rory.

"What should we do?" she whispered.

Jericho glanced up the stairs. "We don't have much time before those guards find Cornell and come back. I guess just act like we belong here for as long as we can." He pushed the door open and stepped out.

And then one of the guards reached the landing above them and shouted, "*Intruderrrrs.*"

All eyes darted Christine and Jericho's way.

Jericho clenched his stolen rifle. "Here we go," he whispered. He flipped off the safety.

THE KILLING ZONE

18

Christine forgot to breathe. Killzone locked eyes with Jericho. In seemingly slow motion, he drew his weapon and squeezed off a shot. The bullet buzzed Jericho's ear and slammed into the wall next to her head. The guards scattered. Rory ducked behind his desk within the caged office. The wergs cowered on their cage floors.

Jericho ran for one of the concrete pillars in the center of the complex as he unloaded a burst of semiautomatic gunfire. A guard fell, his Kevlar vest ineffective against lucky headshots. Jericho dragged his body behind the pillar as other guards fled past where Jasper and Killzone took flanking positions behind more concrete columns. He stripped off the man's vest and put it on.

Christine covered her ears and fell back into the stairwell. From the floor, she kicked the metal door closed as bullets filled it with dents.

The guards on the landing above took cover up the stairs around the corner. Christine had two choices:

attack or die. She charged the landing, hoping to catch them off guard. As she cleared the stairs, the color drained from the world and her clothes burst apart.

A gun barrel jutted around the corner. She hugged the block wall as wild bullets sailed wide. She swatted the weapon away, her claws tearing into the gunman's arm. He yowled and retreated. Christine smelled blood and wanted more.

Someone shouted, "Silver, silver, silver."

She rounded the corner. One man fled up the stairs while the other dropped the magazine from his rifle. She threw him headfirst into the wall before he could insert his silver bullet magazine and left him unconscious on the landing to chase his buddy.

In the room attached to the pedestrian bridge, the other guard stopped. His magazine hit the floor, but he had no time to reload. He hurled his empty weapon at her as if that would help. When she was almost on top of him, he drew a silver-bladed knife.

He drove the blade toward her throat. She juked left and swatted his arm. The knife slid across the floor as his blood sprayed the wall.

Cornell appeared at the bridge entrance with a tranquilizer gun. Christine grabbed the guard and spun, tossing him into the path of the dart as Cornell squeezed the trigger. It stuck in the guard's ass cheek. His eyes went wide.

Cornell backed into the pedestrian bridge, already slinging open his dart gun and fumbling to load a second dart. Christine closed the distance in a flash, grasped his throat, and lifted him off his feet. She snarled in his face and hurled him through one of the few intact windows. A glance outside found him wailing on the street, both legs twisted at unnatural angles.

Christine sprinted back downstairs and nudged the door open to see Jericho still pinned down behind the pillar. The ground was littered with empty casings and spent flash grenades.

She burst out of the doorway and sprinted toward the caged office. Killzone turned his attention to her, giving Jericho a chance to attack. Jasper fired as soon as he broke cover. A round struck his stolen Kevlar vest, sending him spinning to the ground.

Christine launched herself into the screened office window, her momentum collapsing the divider. She landed behind a solid metal desk and looked back to check on Jericho.

He held a hand to his chest as he scrambled behind another pillar. He waved frantically. "Get the guy that was in there," he shouted. Then he tossed his empty weapon aside, stripped off the Kevlar vest, and turned his eyes coal-black. He roared as his snout grew away from his face.

Jasper yelled, "Get to her. I'll cover you." She opened fire on the pillar as Killzone charged the office, gun raised.

Christine ducked behind the desk as bullets shredded the wall where she had been standing. When Killzone reached the office, he ducked behind the wall on the other side. She could hear his heavy breathing. She lifted her head enough to see over the desk.

Jericho retrieved the Kevlar vest and held it like a shield between him and Jasper as he sprinted toward Killzone. He was an impressive beast, tall and muscular with dark fur only broken by a patch of light grey on his chin. One bullet grazed his side, but he didn't slow.

Killzone spun away from the office and aimed his rifle at Jericho. He had him dead to rights.

Christine leaped onto the desk and swatted Killzone's back. Her claws met Kevlar, but she had struck hard enough to knock him off balance and send his bullets wide. By the time he recovered, Jericho was there, dropping the makeshift shield and plowing into him, slamming both of them into the wall.

Jasper redirected her fire onto Christine, sending her diving back behind the desk. Jericho lifted his bloody snout and roared.

Jasper cried out for Killzone as Jericho jerked the mercenary's limp body into her line of fire. She let off the trigger and Jericho charged, using Killzone as a shield this time. Jasper retreated and he gave chase.

Christine caught a fresh scent at the back of the office. She followed it through a door, down a hallway, and into what looked like a break room. The scent led to a closet. She ripped the door from the hinges.

A man cowered on the ground, his hands in front of his face. "What do you want with me?"

She snarled inches from his face. The smell of fresh piss filled the closet. He would be an easy one to break. She yanked him from the floor and slammed him against the wall as he wailed like a scream queen in a horror flick.

She shifted back to human form. "Give me your coat."

He couldn't take it off fast enough.

She put it on and zipped it up. It hung to her mid-thigh. "My friend was brought here within the last week. I wanna know where he is."

"If he was brought here more than a day or two ago, he's already gone."

"Gone where?"

"I don't know."

"Where do you send them?"

"It could be any of several places."

She grabbed his shirt and leaned close enough for him to feel her breath. "Don't make me shift again."

He looked away. "Some of 'em are sent to the Dog Parks to fight. Others become pets."

"Where'd you send my friend?"

"I-I-I don't know. I'd have to see my logbooks."

"Where are they?"

He pointed back down the hall to the office.

She jerked him out of the break room. "Show me."

Jericho was standing next to the desk in human form wearing a guard's bloody uniform. His eye was swollen almost closed, and he was covered in cuts and scratches. He cocked his head. "Do you smell piss?"

She gestured at Rory.

"Oh."

"Where's Jasper?"

"She got away."

"And the other guards?"

"Still out there. We ain't got much time."

Rory pulled out a logbook from a desk drawer. Christine snatched it away and shoved him to his knees. She rifled through it until she found two pages dated from the last week. Three-quarters down, she found Aiden's name. Her knees went weak. A line of dots followed his name to the words *The Island*.

"What's the Island?"

He shook his head. "I-I-I don't know."

"Bullshit." She grabbed his throat. "I'm done fucking around. What is it?" she screamed.

He squeezed his eyes shut and blurted out, "A place to hunt wergs for sport." Then he flinched and put his arms over his face in anticipation of a beating.

Christine's stomach clenched. It was like someone had knocked the wind out of her. "Hunt? What do you mean? Like deer?" She dreaded his answer.

He nodded behind his arms.

Images of Aiden being slaughtered like a trophy animal almost made her vomit. The room felt suddenly cramped and the walls were closing in. Her face went hot and she staggered, catching herself on the edge of the desk.

"Are you all right?" Jericho reached for her arm. She pulled away. "It doesn't mean it's too late. Just because he was taken there doesn't mean they've already hunted him. We can still find him."

She slid down into the office chair to catch her breath.

Jericho grabbed Rory and slammed him into the wall. "Where's the Island?" he screamed.

"Near Costa Rica."

"What's its name?"

"Please, don't make me tell you."

Jericho punched the wall beside his head.

Rory winced. "It-it's called Sandalio."

"Show me on a map."

"It's not on a map."

"What?"

"Important people want to keep it a secret. You won't find it in a GPS or on a map."

"Then how do I find it?"

"It's east of the Corn Islands. The locals know where it is. If you ask around, they'll tell you."

With Rory's shirt bunched up in his fist, Jericho snatched the logbook and shoved it against his chest. "They brought my friend here a few days ago, too. His name's Jake. He was shot. Where is he now? And if you say the Island, I'm gonna kill you."

Rory's hands trembled as he took the book and opened it. His quivering finger followed the dots after Jake's name. "He's still in our infirmary."

Jericho gripped his arm. "Take me to him." As he shoved Rory toward the door, he glanced back at Christine. "You comin'?"

She noticed a ring of padlock keys on the desk and thought of the captive wergs. She grabbed the keys and shook them in Rory's face. "Are these for the cages?" Rory nodded. "I'm going to free them. I'll meet you at the stairs."

Jericho grunted and dragged Rory through the hall.

Christine took a few more seconds to gather herself before climbing over the desk and through the window. The main part of the complex looked like a warzone, bodies strewn everywhere and bullet holes pockmarking nearly every block wall. Killzone lay in a puddle of blood next to a pillar, his windpipe slashed open.

She ran to the cowering wergs in the cages. Though they were timid and fearful, she approached slowly and cautiously. One by one, she freed them, wishing she had the equipment and time to cut out their chips. She shooed the wergs up the stairs and then waited for Jericho.

He soon appeared in Rory's office with Jake's arm draped over his shoulders. Jake was shirtless with a heavy trauma dressing on his chest and a bulky silver collar around his neck. Jericho also clutched an IV bag that ran into Jake's arm.

"There were more guards back there," he shouted. "They're coming."

She held the door as he practically carried Jake past. They raced up the stairs and across the pedestrian bridge. Christine slowed to glance out the windows. Killzone's van still idled in the street and the freed wergs were already meandering around it, curiously sniffing the doors and tires. There was no sign of Cornell.

She caught up to Jericho and Jake as they hurried down the stairs and out onto the street.

"Shit." Jericho nodded toward Slater's Beamer in the distance. A blacked-out SUV had stopped beside it and three men were investigating. "We'll have to take the van."

Christine shooed the curious wergs away and slid the side door open. Jericho lifted Jake inside. She climbed in beside him, took the IV bag, and hung it from a jutting piece of metal near the top of the door. Jericho climbed into the driver's seat. The SUV started toward them. A dozen guards ran across the bridge above.

Jericho blasted the horn, causing the wergs to scatter, and whipped the van into a U-turn. Christine watched through the tinted back windows as the SUV driver laid on their horn and slowed down to maneuver around the wandering beasts. The guards poured out of the entrance. Jericho spun the wheel to the left and gunned it.

A few more turns later and they appeared to be in the clear. Eventually, they passed a sign pointing toward downtown. Christine told him to follow it, figuring that would be the best place to find a hospital.

She examined Jake as best she could. The collar around his neck had a razor edge like the one Bernard had made her wear. It smelled of silver. "How do you feel?" she asked.

"It hurts." His voice sounded tired and sore.

"Okay. Don't try and say anything else. Just rest. Let me see if I can get this collar off." She pulled the stolen keys from Rory's coat pocket and tried several of the smaller ones before finding one that fit. She tossed the collar to the back of the van and sat with Jake as he dozed on and off until they found a hospital.

Jericho pulled into the drive-up ambulance entrance where two paramedics were unloading a patient on a stretcher from their rig. He followed them up the ER ramp and slipped in the door before it closed. A few minutes later, he returned with a wheelchair. Christine helped him lift Jake into it.

"Listen, buddy," Jericho said, kneeling down to look Jake in the eye. "I'm sorry I have to leave you here, but they'll get you fixed up. It's too dangerous for you *and* us if we stay."

Jake nodded.

Jericho pushed him to the closed ambulance entrance and waited for the paramedics to return with their empty stretcher. Shivering, Christine climbed into the passenger seat to wait and turned the heater on full blast. After a few minutes, Jericho hurried back to the van.

"We gotta get outta here. They told me to wait for the police since Jake's been shot, so I bailed."

Two security guards exited the ambulance entrance as Jericho sped from the lot. After a few random turns, they followed signs to the nearest freeway.

"Once we make some distance, we'll stop and get some clothes and supplies," Jericho said, glancing at Christine's bare legs.

"Should we call someone? Tell them what's going on in that old factory?"

He shook his head. "Odds are they've already cleaned it out and moved. Hell, it's probably on fire by now."

"Do you think they'll track Slater's car back to the farm?"

"Nah. Slater's so paranoid he has a fake license plate. If they track it or his VIN, they'll end up in Cleveland at some mom-and-pop dealership."

"What about the police and our fingerprints?"

"Nothin' we can do about 'em now."

"Should we go back to Slater's, then?"

Jericho tapped the steering wheel, deep in thought. "I guess that's where we have to go. We need to regroup." He bit his lower lip and took a deep breath in through his nose.

"What is it?" she asked.

He let the breath out with a sigh. "Where else are we gonna get a plane and a pilot to get to the island?"

Her eyes widened. "Are you serious? You're going to help me get to Sandalio?"

"Of course."

"Slater'll never help us."

Jericho shrugged. "Probably not. But Adam might after everything we've learned. He'll appreciate what we did for Jake."

"Will we need passports?"

His face creased. "Probably." He tapped the steering wheel again. "Sylvia can make 'em."

"Make 'em?"

"You know, fake ones."

"But that's illegal."

"You wanna save your boyfriend, don't you?"

"Of course."

"Then we need fake passports."

"Oh. Right."

"We'll need to make one for Aiden, too. Do you have any pictures of him?"

She deflated. "In my phone. Which is in my car. At the Dog Park."

"Damn. Any other pictures?"

She thought for a minute and then remembered the silly photo booth pictures they had taken together at the bowling alley. "I've got the perfect ones. They're on my fridge at my condo."

"Shit. That's no good either. We can't go there, not if the Dog Catchers are lookin' for you."

Her eyes lit up. "I've got an idea. What if I had one of the guys from the firehouse do a well-check on me and snag it? The Dog Catchers wouldn't hassle a firefighter checking in on his friend, would they?"

"They might."

"Then I'll have Willie do it. If they stop him, he'll talk them into such circles their heads will spin. I'll have him drop it off at a vacant house in our fire district. I just need a phone."

"Sounds good. I'll get us a burner when I get new clothes."

After a few miles, he pulled off the freeway at a Walmart. Christine stayed in the car. When he returned, he had clothes, a duffel bag, snacks, and a burner phone. Christine called Willie and told him the plan, emphasizing the critical need for secrecy.

"I won't even tell God," Willie promised.

It was late afternoon by the time Jericho and Christine arrived in the south end of Columbus. The photo strip was already in the vacant house's mailbox. She was going to hug the hell out of Willie the next time she saw him.

LUCK RUNS OUT

19

Christine and Jericho arrived at Slater's farm just before dinner. They saw Sylvia outside and Jericho called her over.

"Where have you been?" she exclaimed. "Slater's livid."

"Yeah, I figured. I'll talk to him. Can you do me a favor?"

"Sure."

"I need two passports and I need 'em quick."

"You already have one."

"Not for me."

"Why? What's up?"

"It's a long story. How fast can you have 'em ready?"

"I'd need photos."

Christine handed over the strip. "Will this work?"

Sylvia looked it over for a second. "I think so. With a little Photoshop help. If you need them quick, I can repurpose a couple we've already made. Give me a couple hours?"

"Perfect." Jericho smiled. "Thank you, Syl."

She smiled back and headed for Slater's front door just as Slater barreled past her.

"You've got some nerve," he shouted. "Who do you think you are, Jericho?"

"We found Jake, no thanks to you," Jericho snapped.

Slater froze. "You found him? Where is he?"

"We took him to a hospital."

"Is he all right?"

"I don't know. We couldn't stick around. But he's alive."

"There was a doctor at the Underground who stabilized him before we got there," Christine offered.

Slater scowled at her. "I didn't ask you shit." He turned back to Jericho. "Where's my car?"

Jericho glanced back at the van. "I got you an upgrade."

"Cut the shit, Jericho. It's not funny."

"I know. I'm sorry. Listen, Slater. There's a lot goin' on that you don't know about. Let me just exp—"

"I don't get you, Jericho. After everything we've done for you—"

"It's just a car, man. We—"

"It's not just the car. You go against everything I say. You're a cancer here and you're gonna get us all captured. Or worse."

"Why? Because I question some of your crazy ideas? I don't get *you* sometimes."

"You're not supposed to get me. Maybe you're just not smart enough to fully grasp what I'm trying to do here. Why did you even come back?"

"What do you mean? We found out where they take the missing wergs."

"Yeah. The Underground. We've heard of it."

"No. The Underground is just a pit stop. There's a company still sellin' 'em, and not just as pets either. They're sendin' 'em to the fightin' pits and to an island near Costa Rica to be—"

"And why would I care?"

"Because that's where they took your friend Curtis. That's where they were gonna take Jake. And that's where they'll take you, if they find you."

Slater angrily chewed on his lower lip. "And what good does knowing about it do?"

"That's where they took Christine's friend. He's there right now."

Slater's jaw dropped. "Ohhh, I see. And you thought maybe you could use my plane to get there?"

Christine couldn't bite her tongue. "Slater, we can save a bunch of people if you just help us get there and—"

Without looking at her, Slater held his hand up in her face. "I don't think I was talking to you."

She swatted it away. "But—"

"But nothing."

If it wasn't obvious before, it was now. Slater was a lost cause. "What if Adam took us?" she asked.

His eyes narrowed. "Are you insane? Not only do you need a crazy, impossible favor, you also expect me to expose myself and everyone here to the very people hunting us? Now, that's some Kool-Aid-drinking level of devotion I'm not even remotely interested in giving you. What did you think, Christine? You could come here, shake your ass around at Jericho, and everyone would drop everything to do what you want?"

Jericho lifted his hands. "Wait a minute, Slater. Let's not start insultin' anyo—"

"Shut up, Jericho. She may have gotten you under her spell, but—"

Jericho straightened. "Don't tell me to shut up."

The space between them heated. Slater must have found some courage while they were gone because he stepped nose-to-nose with Jericho. His eyes flashed black.

Jericho curled his upper lip. "Don't push me, Slater. I've been plenty respectful of you."

"And when were you respectful? When you brought me a piece of shit van in place of my Beamer that you stole? Or when you sneaked out and jeopardized this whole place? You should leave. Both of you."

Christine crowded between them with her hand on Jericho's thick chest. "All right, you two. Calm down. Slater, please listen to me. What would you do for someone you truly cared about? What would you do for Adam? Anything, right? That's all I'm trying to do for someone I care about."

Slater's eyes shifted from Jericho to her. "If they took your friend to Sandalio to be hunted, he's already dead. I bet his head is hanging on someone's wall right now."

Christine's shoulders dropped along with her stomach. She staggered backward. How could anyone say something so callous?

Slater glowered at her. "The answer is no. My plane's not going anywhere. Get your stuff and be gone by morning." He whirled around and stormed into the house.

Christine wobbled like she'd been hit in the face with a baseball bat. In the excitement, she hadn't let the true possibility of Aiden's death set in.

Jericho reached for her shoulder. "Chris?"

She backed away, shaking her head. "He's right."

"No. No, he's not. Nothin's for sure until it's for sure."

She wanted to cry and scream and fight the world all at once. The color drained from her vision.

"Christine? What are you doin'?"

She needed to be alone to think. She released a furious roar.

"Christine? Don't shift. We can talk."

But it was too late. She dropped to all fours as her clothes ripped and her bones twisted and snapped. The last thing she heard as she dashed for the forest was Jericho yelling for her to wait.

She ran as fast as she'd ever run and didn't stop until she reached an old bike trail leading to the main road to Slater's compound. She collapsed to her rear on the path and returned to her human form.

Alone, naked, and cold, she sat with her knees pulled to her chest, picturing Aiden's body lying broken and bloody at the feet of some cruel hunter celebrating his kill. It tore out her heart to know their last conversation was an argument, that she'd pushed him away like she had every other man in her life that got too close. She buried her face in her hands and had the good, strong cry that she had needed for days. Maybe Slater was right. Maybe Aiden had given a good fight, but the odds were too stacked against him. She had been foolish to think she could find him in time. And worse than all of it was that she'd never truly know for sure what had happened to him. She would forever wonder if there was more she could have done.

When she finally lifted her head, Jericho was standing not far away. He held the duffel bag full of extra clothes from Walmart. Compassion weighed heavily in his eyes. He gave her the bag and turned away so she could dress. Once she finished, he sat beside her and put his arm around her shoulders. She leaned on his chest.

He held her close, resting his cheek on the top of her head. "We'll get through this," he whispered, caressing her shoulder. He didn't say anything else—he didn't have to—and held her until she ran out of tears.

After sitting quietly fort a while with her fingers growing numb from the cold, she said, "We should probably head back."

He nodded and helped her up. They had just started back for Slater's when Jericho stopped suddenly.

"What is it?" she asked.

"I just realized somethin'."

"What?"

"I was runnin' through what Slater said and somethin' doesn't add up."

"What do you mean?"

"When I told him about the Island, I never said the name Sandalio. And I didn't tell him what they did there either. He already knew."

She pulled back. "You're right. But how?"

He shook his head. "I don't know." The confused wrinkles in his forehead turned tense. "We need to ask him. I ..." His eyes lifted past her to the main road at the end of the path.

She followed his gaze to see a line of black government SUVs speeding toward the compound. What looked like an armored school bus brought up the rear.

Jericho's face paled. "Shit. The Dog Catchers found us. We've gotta help the others."

He grabbed her hand, and they ran toward the compound. Three-quarters of the way there, Slater's tornado siren shattered the quiet evening, followed immediately by a terrifying explosion.

They reached the field adjacent to the property. Three SUVs and half a dozen agents dressed like soldiers and carrying weapons stormed Slater's house. Another half-dozen charged the apartment building, setting off flash grenades inside.

Christine covered her mouth. *Oh God.*

Jess crashed through a second-floor window, shifting into full werg form in the air before landing beside two agents. She tore through them in seconds, leaving them bloody and groaning on the ground. Then a flash grenade went off beside her.

The explosion disoriented her enough for an agent to fire a dart. She spun away and Christine saw the fear in her face. It was a devastating look that would haunt her forever. Two more agents swarmed her with a net.

"Come on," Jericho shouted, and took off across the field toward the airplane hangar.

More agents exited the front of the apartment building, dragging another unconscious werg slowly shifting to human form in their net. It was Cole. She hoped his shift burned enough of the sedative away to keep him breathing. Jess, too. Or at least that those bastards would treat them with Narcan if needed.

Jericho and Christine ducked around the airplane hangar and followed the wall closer to the rear of Slater's house. Two agents marched Trey toward the armored bus, a razor collar around his human neck.

A naked man covered in blood ran toward Christine from the apartments. When he passed through a security light, she saw that it was Adam. He slowed as he approached without a shred of modesty. With his head on a swivel, he whispered, "We're taking the plane and getting outta here."

Christine nodded furiously. That was a great idea.

"We just need to find Slater first."

She didn't like that part as much.

"He might be in his panic room."

From what Christine knew of Slater, hiding while his people were being hunted sounded like something he would do. Together, the three snuck along the side of Slater's house and poked their heads around the front corner.

The armored bus had parked behind the SUVs and agents loaded Cole, Trey, and Jess into it. Two more agents escorted Slater from his house, his wrists zip-tied behind his back. They stopped in front of a woman in a dark suit.

Adam's eyes turned black and he tensed to spring around the corner, but he froze when Slater shouted, "Why are you doing this, Evelyn? We had a deal."

The woman, Evelyn, scoffed. "You broke the deal."

Her words hit Adam like a bomb. He staggered and clutched his chest. "What? No."

Slater groveled. "Wha—How? We didn't do anything wrong."

"You mean besides harboring a fugitive?"

"We aren't harboring anybody."

She gave him a disgusted glance. "Really? Are you telling me a woman named Christine Alt hasn't been here?"

"She was, b-b-but not anymore. I made her leave."

"You attacked our facility in Detroit, killed a bunch of our men, and took one of our subjects. A man named Jake."

"That wasn't me. Someone stole my car."

"You've gotten awfully sloppy, Mr. Slater. We don't feel you can be trusted anymore." Another agent approached Slater carrying a razor collar. Evelyn smiled. "We need to meet with the boss. You know the routine."

Slater's defeated gaze drifted over the house and fell on the corner where Christine, Adam, and Jericho hid. Adam locked eyes with him.

Oh no.

Sadness washed over Slater's face. He mouthed, "Adam." But instead of selling them out like Christine fully expected, the whites of his eyes turned black.

"What are you doing, Slater?" Evelyn shouted as she backed away.

Slater's shift was lightning fast. He whipped his hands forward, flinging the severed zip tie into the air. Evelyn screamed and retreated behind an SUV. Slater attacked the collar-carrying agent first as the others took cover. The armored bus puffed diesel smoke from its stacks and started a three-point-turn to leave.

While Slater fought, ducking around the vehicles for cover, Adam turned his back to his friend. "I need to preheat the plane. Where's Sylvia? I didn't see her on the bus."

"She was makin' us passports," Jericho answered.

"Then she must be in the panic room. Why was she making you passports?"

"We figured out where Christine's friend is and it's near Costa Rica. We were hopin' you might help us get there."

Adam's face twisted. "Let's get somewhere safe first and take it from there. All right?"

Christine nodded. It was the best they could hope for under the circumstances.

"I need to get my passport from my apartment," Jericho said.

"Okay. You two go get that and meet me in the hangar. We'll go find Silvia in the house after." He jogged back to the hangar.

Christine and Jericho raced to the back entrance of the apartment building where two agents stood guard at the door. Another flash grenade popped somewhere on the second floor.

"Wait here," Jericho whispered.

Christine grabbed his arm. "No. They'll catch you."

"No, they won't." He gave her a fake smile and gently pulled away. "I'll be all right."

He used the shadows to close the distance undetected. By the time they saw him, it was too late. He performed some fancy judo move to incapacitate one agent and then pounced on the other.

With both of them down and out, Christine joined him and they slipped inside. They found the stairs to the second floor and waited in the stairwell for two agents to kick open an apartment door, toss in a flash grenade, and rush in after it.

"Now," Jericho whispered. They rushed to Jericho's ransacked apartment and hid inside seconds before the two agents moved to the next door down. He grabbed his passport, driver's license, and some cash. After the agents left, he led Christine back downstairs. The two agents Jericho had taken out were gone.

Jericho and Christine hurried to the hangar door where they heard two men arguing inside. Christine slowly pushed the door open. Two dead agents in their underwear were sprawled on the hangar floor.

Near the plane, Slater lay on his back with Adam on his knees straddling his chest. They both wore the agents' clothes. Adam squeezed his fists, barely holding back.

"I swear, Adam," Slater cried. "I only made a deal to protect us. They promised to leave us alone if we didn't cause any problems."

"And look where that got us," Adam shouted. "Why didn't you tell me about the deal?"

"I was afraid you'd leave."

Adam slammed his fist into the concrete beside Slater's head. He leaned back, staring up at the rafters in anguish. Tears streaked his cheeks. He moved to the side, freeing Slater from his weight. "I can't believe you did this."

"I swear, Adam. Please. I only wanted you to be safe. Let me make it up to you," Slater sobbed.

"They've got our friends now because of you."

Slater sat up. "I know. But I'll get 'em back. I swear."

Adam shook his head. "I don't trust you anymore."

Slater grabbed his hand with both hands. "Please, Adam. I swear. I would never hurt you. My true loyalty is forever with you."

In obvious pain, Adam said, "If you help our friends, then we can talk. Until then, you're dead to me."

Slater nodded feverishly. "I will. I will. I promise."

Adam glanced at Christine and Jericho, stood up, wiped his eyes, and waved them over.

Slater got up and jogged toward the hangar opening at the opposite end. He was fully shifted by the time he disappeared outside.

"He'll never catch them," Christine said.

"He knows what he's doing. If they're headed toward the freeway, there's a shortcut through the forest. If he's fast enough, he can cut them off. Let's go find Sylvia."

The three hurried back to the side of Slater's house and peeked around front again. Several agents dragged the wounded to the remaining SUVs where Evelyn was shouting orders. "Two of you stand guard here. Send two more men around back. No one gets in or out of this house until the cleanup crew arrives."

"Yes, ma'am," the agents answered.

Evelyn climbed into one of the SUVs and it pulled away. Most of the others followed.

Adam drew Christine and Jericho close. "You two take out the men in the front. I'll deal with the guys in the back."

Jericho nodded. "Be careful."

Adam hurried to the back, stripping off the stolen clothes and shifting as he ran.

Jericho took off his shirt. "Wait here. I'll handle these two."

"Try not to kill them."

He nodded. Then he took off his pants and shifted.

A burst of gunfire exploded around back, followed by screams. The two agents in the front bolted around the opposite side of the house.

Jericho gave chase, catching up to them before they made it to the back. Christine gathered his clothes and followed. By the time she reached him, the two disarmed agents huddled next to a propane tank that fed the house. One of them held his hand over a nasty laceration on his thigh that was gushing blood.

She tossed Jericho his clothes and pointed at the uninjured agent. "Tie yourself to the piping from that tank."

The agent took a handful of zip ties from his belt and fastened himself to the iron piping.

"Now zip-tie his free arm to it." She gestured to the bleeding agent. When he finished, she knelt beside them and disarmed them of their backup weapons and silver knives. "I'm going to help you," she told the injured man. "Don't do anything stupid or I'll let you bleed out. It looks like he got an artery."

The agent's fearful eyes widened.

She glanced back at Jericho, back in human form and fully dressed. "Find me a strong stick or something. I need a tourniquet." She removed the agent's belt and wrapped it around his leg just above the wound. "This might hurt," she warned, and yanked it tight. She jammed the buckle's prong through the belt to make a new hole.

Jericho returned with a thin metal baluster from the front porch railing. "Will this work?'

"Yeah." Christine shoved the baluster between the agent's leg and belt and turned it until the bleeding stopped. The agent winced in pain. She guided his free hand to the baluster. "Hold this tight and don't let it unwind. Wait for your friends. I'm sure they'll be here soon. Good luck."

She and Jericho left the men tied to the tank and raced to the front door.

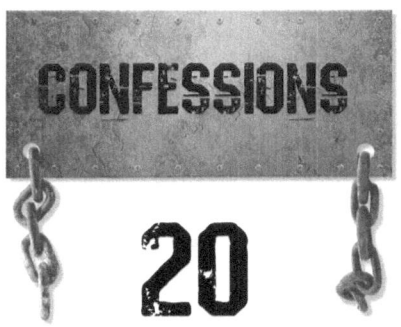

CONFESSIONS

20

Adam stood in the front room of Slater's house with Sylvia beside him. He wore a fresh set of clothes and held a partially open duffel bag overflowing with cash. He called it Slater's emergency get-out-of-town-in-a-flash cash.

Sylvia handed Christine a manila folder. "I repurposed Jake's passport for that Aiden guy and Jess's for you. I hope you don't mind that your new names are Sasha and Stetson."

"Stetson?" Jericho echoed.

She shrugged. "That's the name Jake wanted. Don't ask me why."

Christine turned to Adam. "How long do you think we have?"

"Not long. They'll send in their cleanup crew soon." He started to say something else, but stopped. "You hear that?"

Christine listened close and heard the faint rev of a diesel engine. They rushed to the window to see the armored bus returning. It sped toward the house with Trey at the wheel.

They met the bus out front.

Trey was frantic as he climbed out. "They shot him with silver," he shouted.

Before Adam could ask who, Cole carried Slater's limp, naked body from the bus. Sylvia gasped and covered her mouth.

"Oh shit," Adam breathed. "Get him inside."

"They'll be here any minute," Jericho argued. "We can't stay here."

Adam shouted, "I know."

As Trey went past, Christine saw a bullet hole in Slater's chest and heard a faint sizzling. She turned to Jericho. "Is there a first-aid kit anywhere on the grounds?"

"In the apartments."

"Get it." Her internal clock was screaming at her to get to the plane, but Slater would die if they didn't help him first.

Trey laid Slater on the couch and Adam knelt beside him. When he looked back at Christine, his eyes were red and puffy. "Help him," he whispered.

Christine pushed past him and rolled Slater to his side in search of an exit wound. She found an inflamed and swollen hematoma near his spine and examined the swelling with her finger. There was a hard lump in the center. She wiggled it. "I think the bullet's right here."

"Then cut it out," Adam snapped.

"I can't cut it out. I'm a medic, not a surgeon."

"He'll die if you don't."

As much as she hated to admit it, he was right. She bit her lip, weighing the consequences if anyone ever discovered what she was about to do. Losing her paramedic certification along with her career was just the beginning of the trouble she'd face. But she also knew the silver would kill Slater in the next couple of minutes if she did nothing. She decided to take a chance.

Jericho arrived with the first-aid kit. Adam leaned into Slater's ear and whispered, "Hold on, buddy."

Christine found a scalpel in the kit. After taking a deep breath, she cut Slater's flesh over the hematoma. Blood oozed around the blade.

Slater groaned.

She spread the laceration apart with her fingers and massaged the lump toward the opening until a smashed bullet fell to the carpet and the sizzling stopped. She shoved a bandage over the wound.

"Will he make it?" Adam cried.

"I don't know. Depends on the damage inside. He needs a hospital. Call 9-1-1."

"We're too far out. It'll take them forever to get here."

"He'll die if he doesn't get into an operating room soon."

Adam grimaced and looked out the window. "What if we flew somewhere safer and called from there? Is he stable enough?"

"I don't know."

"It's our only choice. Leaving him here is a death sentence. That Evelyn chick might just let him die."

Christine bit her lower lip. Damn it, he was right again.

Sobbing, Sylvia went to Slater's side and hugged him. Adam gave her a minute and then touched her shoulder. "We're taking him somewhere to get help,

Syl. The Dog Catchers will be back any second. You've gotta get outta here with the others."

Sylvia nodded, kissed Slater's cheek, and pried herself away from him.

Adam turned to Trey. "Take the van out front and get somewhere safe. Use the back roads I showed you. Go to Slater's safe house. You know the one. I'll find you there when this is all over."

Trey and Cole helped Sylvia and Jess to the van. Adam watched them leave and then turned to Christine. "I'll help you find your friend after we help Slater. Deal?"

She nodded. "I'll do what I can."

Adam gently picked Slater up and headed for the door. Jericho stopped him with a kind hand on his shoulder. They locked eyes.

"Thank you, my friend," Jericho said.

Adam nodded. "In for a quarter, in for a pound. Right?"

"Exactly."

They carried Slater, the money bag, and the first-aid kit to the plane. Jericho sat up front while Adam lifted Slater into the back with Christine. Slater coughed and groaned as he opened his eyes slightly. Adam started for the cockpit, but Slater touched his arm. "Wait," he whispered. "Stay with me for a minute."

"I can't, buddy. We've gotta take off."

"No. I need to tell you something."

"No time. We can talk all you want after we get you some help."

Slater coughed again and gave Adam's arm a feeble squeeze. "It has to be now."

The clock was ticking so loudly in Christine's head that she thought it might burst a vein. She shot a wide-eyed look at Adam.

Adam nodded. "I know. Just give me a minute."

She shoved down the screaming sense of urgency and kept her cool. She took Slater's blood pressure. It was low.

Adam leaned close to his friend.

"Did the others make it?" Slater asked in a weak and tired voice.

"Yeah, buddy. You did good."

Slater's smile was strained. "I'm hurt pretty bad, Adam."

"I know. We're gonna get help. You just have to hold on."

Slater shook his head. "Just listen. What I need to say is going to be hard for you to hear. Remember when I told you how I found you and brought you to my farm?"

"Yeah?" Adam took his hand.

"That was only partially true."

"I don't understand."

"I didn't rescue you from some random family." He paused and winced. "You were *my* werepet. *I* bought you."

Adam let Slater's hand fall. His face twisted. "Yours? You mean *you* were the reason I was tortured?"

Slater closed his eyes and nodded. When he opened them again, they were filled with immense pain. "I didn't know what you were when I purchased you. As soon as I found out …"

Adam bit his quivering lower lip.

"I'm so sorry, Adam. I was too ashamed to tell you before."

Adam turned away. Showing surprising maturity, he immediately turned back, cupped the side of Slater's face, and whispered, "I forgive you. But I need to know everything. What deal did you have with them?"

Slater groaned as another wave of pain washed over him. Once it subsided, he said, "When I first took you to the farm, the Dog Catchers found us. They threatened to take us to the Underground for processing, but I bought a one-on-one video meeting with Evelyn for eighty grand. It was worth every penny. She offered me a deal I couldn't pass up."

"What kind of deal?"

Slater looked away.

Christine glanced nervously out the window. This was taking too long.

"Slater?" Adam asked.

"I … I …"

The creases on Adam's forehead deepened. "It was Curtis, wasn't it?" He was barely able to get the name out.

Slater's silence was his answer.

"So, the Dog Catchers work with the Underground?"

Slater nodded. "It's all connected."

Adam dropped to his rear.

"I didn't want to," Slater cried. "I swear. She said if I gave her wergs whenever she asked and didn't cause any trouble, she would leave us alone. After what I'd done, I owed it to you to protect you no matter what. I had no choice. They would have killed us."

Adam's tortured expression sickened as he put the pieces together. "You gave them Curtis? Who else did you give them?"

"No one."

Adam gritted his teeth. "No one *yet*, you mean. Who was next? Cole? Trey?" His eyes widened. "Jess?"

"I was hoping nobody. The deal was working. They were leaving us alone."

"You were grooming our friends to save your own skin." Adam buried his face in his hands.

"No. Not me. To save you, Adam. It was all to save you." His voice had weakened further.

Adam rubbed his forehead raw. "I can't believe you did this. If you'd just told me, we could have figured something out together. Tell me one more thing. Did you even care what happened to Curtis?"

"Of course. I—"

The perimeter warning siren blasted to life again.

Adam's eyes met Christine's. He touched Slater's shoulder. "We gotta go. We'll work everything out after we get you help." Then he scrambled to the front and fired up the plane. He taxied from the hangar onto the runway and throttled it forward. "Hold on," he shouted as he pulled the stick back. The nose lifted.

Christine watched out the window as they headed for the clouds and a convoy of tactical vehicles sped along the road.

Once the compound was a fading speck of light in the darkness behind them and Adam had leveled the plane, Christine turned back to Slater. He looked different—worse. His gut had distended and his face had paled. His eyes rolled back in his head. She shook him. "Slater?"

He didn't respond.

She shouted his name over the rumble of the plane, causing Adam to glance back. "What's wrong?" he yelled.

She answered him with worried eyes.

He set the autopilot, gave Jericho a brief tutorial of what to watch out for, and climbed into the back. "Slater?" he shouted as he shook his friend.

Christine felt for a pulse on the side of Slater's neck and didn't find one. She pushed Adam aside. "He's bled out into his belly."

"Do something," Adam cried.

She moved her hands to Slater's sternum and began chest compressions. Adam watched with tears filling his eyes.

"How long till we can land?" she shouted.

Adam stared back, stunned.

"How long?"

"I don't know … Twenty more minutes?"

"Shit." She alternated between compressions and breathing into Slater's mouth as sweat poured down her face. Repeated pulse checks came up empty. Without replacing the blood he was losing into his belly, CPR was a wasted effort. But she continued going through the motions for as long as she physically could, more for Adam than for Slater.

She dreaded what she had to do next. She took a deep breath, bowed her head, and stopped.

"What are you doing?" Adam shouted.

She somberly shook her head. "I'm so sorry, Adam. There's nothing more we can do."

"No, no, no," he cried. He grabbed her hands and moved them back to Slater's chest. "Please. Keep doing it."

She continued shaking her head. "I can't, Adam. It won't help. He's lost too much blood."

Adam pulled up his sleeve. "Give him my blood."

"That's not how it works."

"But you have to do something."

Sugar coating the facts would only give Adam false hope and instill uncertainty over whether she had done everything she could. As cold as it seemed, the best thing for him was blunt honesty. "It's over, Adam. He's dead."

His mouth fell open and his lip quivered. "He can't be." He stared at her in disbelief and then fell onto Slater's chest, hugging him as tightly as he could.

Christine touched his back as he sobbed. It was important to let him have this time. She sat with him in silence until he found the strength to pull away. He stared quietly at his friend.

Christine gave him as much time as she could before softly reminding him that the plane needed to land soon. He bobbed his head, caressed his friend's cheek, and then climbed back into the pilot's seat.

Jericho touched his shoulder. "I'm sorry, Adam."

Adam took control of the plane, made the necessary radio communications, lowered the landing gear, and touched down onto a small airport runway.

He carried Slater's body to a bench next to a small office that had a "Closed" sign in the window. Then he sat down and held Slater's head in his lap as he stared off into the distance.

"Is there anything we can do for him?" Jericho asked Christine.

"No. It's best to leave him be for now. It'll help his grieving process."

"What about the body?"

"I don't know. We'll need to see what Adam feels comfortable with."

Adam sat with Slater for nearly an hour while Jericho and Christine quietly waited by the plane. When he finally lowered Slater's head to the bench and stood up, Christine went to him. "Adam?"

He looked at her with vacant eyes.

"What do you want to do with him?"

Adam walked to a payphone on the office wall and dialed 9-1-1. "My friend's been shot," he said in a flat and empty tone. He listened for a second and then said, "He's at the Newark-Heath Airport on a bench by the office. Trace this call." Then he wiped off the receiver with his sleeve, left it dangling, and lifted his eyes. "We should go."

Christine followed him to the plane as he walked like a zombie. After a final look back at his friend, he turned the plane around and throttled along the runway as flashing emergency lights approached from the distance. He didn't speak again until they had to land to refuel.

THE ISLAND: DINNER PREP

21

Aiden woke with a jolt and a sick feeling that someone was watching him. He smelled Murdock before he saw the bastard standing outside his cage holding a cattle prod. Three other handlers stood with him. Aiden scooted to the back of his cell, his neck stinging something awful. Touching it only made it hurt more and reminded him of the room with the doctor and a lot of pain. He strained to remember what had happened or even who he was.

Murdock dragged the prod across the bars, each clank making Aiden flinch. "Morning, dog."

Aiden bared his teeth.

Murdock chuckled. "Feisty. I kind of wish I was going on this hunt. I'd love to have your stuffed carcass in the entryway of my vacation home."

Aiden knew the hunt was important, but his memory was a tangled mess.

Murdock opened the cell door. Two of the three handlers entered with cattle prods extended, while the third remained outside with a dart gun. The handler on the right wore an eyepatch. Two shackles attached to a dog collar dangled from his belt, jingling like wind chimes as he walked.

Aiden's back rode the wall as he pushed to his feet.

The handler on the left smelled like Preparation H. "Take it easy, boy," he whispered, gingerly holding out a muzzle. "Get ready with the prod, Taylor."

When he got close, Aiden swatted the muzzle from his hand. The one-eyed man, Taylor, jammed the cattle prod into his side, sending lightning through his body. Aiden recoiled, heaving angrily. Why were they doing this to him?

Taylor unclipped the collar with the shackles from his belt. "We can do this the easy way or the hard way, big boy."

A primal part deep inside Aiden wanted the hard way. The man's throat was so tempting.

The handler that stank of hemorrhoid medicine retrieved the muzzle. "He's too feisty, Murdock. Why didn't we tranq him first?"

Murdock shrugged. "The boss wants him awake today, Darryl."

Aiden growled.

Taylor lifted the collar toward Aiden's neck, his hands trembling. "Come on, boy. Take it easy."

His fear smelled sweet.

As Taylor stepped to the side, Aiden's eyes flicked past him to the open door. All he had to do was to make it across the field to the jungle and they'd never catch him. The thought briefly took him back to running in a forest with a strangely familiar female werg. While he was lost in fantasies of freedom, Darryl jammed the cattle prod against his left leg, sending another bolt of lightning through his body. His leg gave out and he instantly forgot what he was thinking about.

Taylor lunged with the collar, quickly clamping it around his neck. He lashed out, striking Taylor's Kevlar vest. As Taylor spun away, Aiden caught him with a claw that opened a gusher on his exposed upper arm and knocked him to the ground.

The handler still outside with Murdock nervously lifted his dart gun, but Murdock gently pressed it back down. "Not yet." Then he kicked the cell door closed and the lock clicked.

"What are you doing?" Taylor cried.

Murdock smirked. "Boss wants some of the fight out of him before the big dinner. You guys drew the short straws."

Taylor scooted across the floor with one hand clutching his bleeding arm. He pulled an army-style tourniquet from one of the many pouches on his vest and, using his teeth and his good arm, tightened it around his biceps. When Aiden went in for another swipe, Darryl blasted him again with his prod.

The shackles dangling from Aiden's collar whipped around with his every move. He smelled blood, and it smelled good. He saw an opening and lunged for the bars, jamming his arm between them. Murdock moved just out of reach as Aiden's claws whiffed past his face.

"Woah, big fella." Murdock let out a nervous cackle and nudged the dart-gun-wielding handler with his elbow. "See. That's why you can never let down your guard around these monsters."

More lightning exploded in Aiden's flank and his leg gave out again. He put a hand out to stop his fall.

With one arm dangling, Taylor slapped a shackle around Aiden's wrist and snapped it shut. He lunged desperately and linked the shackle to the collar inches from Aiden's chest. Then he retreated to the bars. "Let me out," he pleaded.

Aiden made a looping swipe with his free arm. Darryl thrust with the prod, sending fire ripping into Aiden's armpit. Instinctively, Aiden tucked his arm to his chest to protect the soft spot.

Darryl dropped the cattle prod and dove at Aiden's free arm, securing his wrist in the other shackle and linking it to the collar in one reckless move.

Winded, with his arm drenched in blood, Taylor staggered to the cell door. "Let us out."

"In a minute," Murdock answered.

Darryl scurried for the cattle prod and zapped Aiden's leg, dropping him to his knees. He fumbled with another set of shackles until they were around Aiden's ankles. "Just one more thing, big fella." He retrieved the discarded muzzle from the corner.

Aiden glared at him defiantly. This shouldn't be happening. None of this felt right.

Darryl lifted the prod, but instead of zapping him with it again, he spun it around and bashed Aiden's face.

Aiden shied away from the blow. When he turned back full of rage, Darryl shoved the muzzle over his snout and cinched the straps tight around his head. He gave it an unnecessary extra yank.

Murdock applauded and unlocked the cell door. "You two did good. The boss will be pleased. Now bring him along." He stopped Taylor and asked, "How bad's your injury?"

"I don't know. My hand is numb."

Murdock examined his arm. "You'd better go have it looked at."

Taylor nodded.

The handler with the dart gun stepped into the cell and holstered his weapon. He grabbed a handful of skin on Aiden's neck and held him still while he brought something that looked like a pair of pliers up to Aiden's head. An audible clunk preceded blistering-sharp pain in his left ear. He recoiled.

"You'll be the red werg for tomorrow's game," the handler said.

That meant nothing to Aiden. After the initial sting faded, his ear felt heavy and numb. The handler fastened a chain to his collar and led him outside.

He could only stutter-step with the shackles around his ankles and it was difficult to keep up. They led him around the building, across a small bridge, up some stairs, and into a mansion. Memories of a conversation with that Pietro guy at a dinner table came rushing back.

A full-sized, taxidermy werg stood on a platform inside. Its fingers were curled, claws extended as if ready to strike, and its lips were pinned up so its teeth were on full display.

Murdock led Aiden into a grand ballroom filled with a dozen round tables decorated with flowery centerpieces and fancy china place settings. Around each table were eight high-backed chairs, each wrapped in ivory fabric tied into large fluffy bows at the back. A long guest of honor table took up the stage at the front.

Waiters dressed to the nines rushed in and out, prepping the tables and adjusting the settings so that every utensil, plate, and napkin was perfectly spaced. Every time one went through the service door, the overwhelming aromas of fruity desserts and buttery vegetables wafted in from the kitchen, making Aiden salivate.

His eyes drifted to the far wall where two other wergs stood hunched over, chains fastening their collars to metal rings in the floor. There was a third space at the end that was empty. He had an idea who it was for.

Murdock walked Aiden past a tuxedoed pianist practicing with a band on a secondary stage. At the end of the row of wergs, he turned Aiden to face the room and jerked him down low enough to clamp the chain to the ring in the floor.

Less than a minute later, he heard two men arguing on the other side of the doors he'd just come through.

"Where is he?" a man shouted.

Aiden caught two distinct scents and recognized them both. One was that bastard Pietro, and the other he couldn't quite place.

"Right this way, President-elect Wooten," Pietro said as the door swung open.

Aiden stared coldly as Wooten stepped into the room. He couldn't remember how he knew this man, but he was certain he hated him. Wooten's shoulders slouched as soon as he saw him.

Pietro pointed. "He's the one on the end, sir."

"I know which one he is," Wooten snapped.

Pietro followed Wooten across the room like a lap dog. Wooten stopped in front of the wergs and shook his head. "Damn it, Aiden," he said somberly.

Aiden glared back.

Wooten turned to Pietro. "Out of every werepet and unchipped werg in the country, you had to capture this one?"

Aiden saw flashes of a fight with strangers in a graveyard.

"He wasn't on the protected werg list," Pietro answered, eyes wide in a parody of innocence.

Wooten glared back. "Don't give me that shit. You know damn well he was."

"I didn't see his name."

Wooten scowled at him. Aiden sensed the rising tension between them. Pietro looked away first.

"How'd you even know who he was?" Wooten asked.

"Bernard talked about him all the time."

Wooten rubbed his forehead. "Fuckin' Bernard."

"Aiden was one of his top hunters until the ungrateful bastard backstabbed him. Bringing him here was the least I could do to honor my old friend's memory."

Wooten lowered his head. "Bernard was a fool who got sloppy. I was already considering getting rid of him and putting someone else in charge when he fucked everything up. He made so many stupid deals and left so many messes for me to deal with." He continued rubbing his temples. "That's why there's a fucking list."

"Non ho visto il suo nome," Pietro mumbled under his breath.

Wooten looked up sharply. "What?"

"I said I didn't see his name."

Wooten's lip curled. "In English from now on, Pietro. You got that? If you ever say another word in Italian in front of me, I'm going to rip off your head."

"Yes, sir."

Wooten glared daggers at him, his jaw working. "Do you know how much of a headache you've given me here?"

Pietro stood quietly.

"This one's girlfriend is a menace. I had a nice little agreement with her that kept her out of my hair after the WereHouse debacle."

"Oh, you mean Christine Alt?"

That name hit Aiden in the chest. He saw a woman's face, blurry at first but quickly coming into focus. As he listened to Wooten and Pietro talk, he strained against the fog to remember more.

"Don't worry," Pietro was saying. We didn't do anything to her. We simply used the threat of hurting her to get him to shift."

Wooten shook his head again. "She's on the list, too."

"Like I said, we didn't do anything to her."

Aiden closed his eyes. He stood in a bowling alley in front of an air hockey table. A puck slipped past his defenses and he looked up to see that same woman's face looking back at him. Her smile filled him with a deep, warm feeling. She was someone he cared for a great deal. An instantaneous slideshow of memories raced through his brain, flickers of the life they were building together, and he realized who she was and what she meant to him. He opened his eyes.

Wooten glanced over his shoulder and said, "I'm sorry about all this, Aiden. You should know I had nothing to do with it."

Aiden barely heard him, his mind rapidly filling in the blanks. Despite his thoughts clearing more and more with every second, the chip tried repeatedly to drown his brain in quicksand. It took all of his concentration just to hold on. But he couldn't lose his sense of self again, no matter what.

He refocused on Wooten with new clarity. He knew what he needed to do. Getting back to *her* was all that mattered.

Wooten glared at Pietro again and put a hand firmly on his shoulder. "If you knew the hell I'll go through now because of you."

"Do you want me to remove his chip and release him, then?"

Aiden liked that idea.

Wooten dragged a hand down his face. "No. It's too late for that. Keep him in the hunt."

Hunt? Aiden remembered now. These bastards were going to hunt him like it was a game. He quietly seethed at the idea. If a hunt was what they wanted, a hunt is what he'd give them.

Wooten continued, "At least now I have an idea of who's been causing so much trouble in the states. Maxine said a strange woman attacked her at the Columbus Dog Park, and then Rory said someone made a mess at the Underground. We had to move those operations and destroy a bunch of stuff. Not to mention the personnel we lost."

"And you think some firefighter bitch did all that?"

"Don't underestimate her. She's quite resilient. She's the one who helped Aiden bring down the WereHouse."

"No shit?"

Wooten nodded.

"I guess my mistake was in not going after her, too, huh?"

Wooten's shoulders slouched. He sighed. "You're not listening. They were both supposed to be off limits." He shook his head. "She won't rest until she finds him. Damn it, I didn't want to have to kill her. I rather admire her tenacity."

Aiden couldn't stop the snarl that escaped his lips. He thrashed at his restraints, desperately wanting Wooten's throat between his teeth more than anything in life. He had to save her.

Wooten and Pietro watched his temper tantrum play out, amused. Perhaps hearing the commotion, Pietro's two pet gargoyles landed on a terrace, stalking through the open French doors. Pietro lifted a calming hand, setting them at ease. They squatted, licked their lips, and tucked their wings to their backs.

Aiden fixated on Christine's smile to fight the rage and the rising static it brought. He took a deep breath. *Focus,* he repeated to himself like a mantra.

Wooten cocked his head. "Pietro?"

"What is it, sir?"

Wooten squinted. "Look at him."

"What about him, sir?"

"I'm not sure. Look at his eyes. They look different all of a sudden. Like they've cleared a bit. It looks like he's ..." He stepped forward, his gaze trained on Aiden's face. "Aiden?" he whispered. "Are you in there?"

Aiden stared at him blankly.

Pietro snorted. "See, sir? His brain's as mushy as all the others. He's got the same chip they all get."

Wooten stood quietly for a few seconds, studying Aiden's face. "I suppose." He sighed. "No matter. He'll be a trophy soon enough either way." His gaze lingered for another second, and then he turned back to Pietro and clapped his hands. "So, I'm taking all the proceeds from this hunt to pay for the damage you've done.

Killing a hero firefighter and keeping it quiet won't be cheap."

"Sir? I don't understand."

"You heard me. I want all of it this time."

"But that's millions of dollars."

"And?"

"It won't even be worth my time to put it on."

Wooten's eyes darkened. "Who's your boss, Pietro?"

"You are, Mr. President-elect."

"Exactly. And I'll take whatever I want. And this time I want it all. You don't have that psychopath Bernard taking your side anymore. There's no room for debate. Is that understood?"

Pietro slouched and bowed his head. "Yes," he mumbled.

"Yes, what?"

"Yes, sir."

Aiden liked seeing the bastard squirm.

Wooten turned his attention to the gargoyles. "You know, I never grow tired of seeing your pets. They are quite magnificent."

"That they are, sir. Have you ever seen them hunt?"

Wooten shook his head.

"We have an extra werg available, if you'd like a show before dinner."

Wooten waved off the offer. "I'm not dressed to be gallivanting in the jungle tonight."

"Oh, you won't have to, sir. They are quite efficient. Their prey won't even make it to the trees. We can watch from the hilltop."

Wooten smiled. "In that case, maybe I *will* take a look."

Aiden lost the thread of the conversation, slipping back into the constantly rising static. As he watched the two men talking, he started to wonder who they were.

"What's your history with Christine?" Pietro asked.

The name snapped Aiden back to himself and he shook away the fuzz. He refocused his thoughts on her.

Wooten answered, "It's not important. Say, why don't we bring our friend Aiden along for the show? I'd like for him to see."

"Uh ... Sir? I don't know if that's such a good idea. I don't trust any of these wergs."

"Nonsense. Your men got him up here just fine." He nodded at Aiden. "You'll be a good boy, won't ya?"

Yeah. I'll be a real good boy, you prick. Just keep showing me around. As soon as I find a way out of this mess, you're the first one I'm coming for.

Even as dreams of violence brought the static rising to the surface, he anchored himself with a memory of sitting next to Christine on the couch in her condo, watching TV. He couldn't remember what they'd been watching, but it didn't matter. He felt the moment, which was all he needed. Just being that close to her was one of the happiest moments of his life. If there was such a thing as The One for him, she was it.

Pietro nervously motioned for Murdock and the other handlers to bring Aiden along. With cattle prods and tranquilizer guns at the ready, they unhooked Aiden's leash from the floor. If he hadn't been wearing a muzzle, he might have tested his luck right then.

The handlers tugged Aiden outside first with Pietro and Wooten trailing them. As they walked, Pietro asked, "Are you joining tomorrow's hunt, sir?"

Aiden had to stop himself from turning his head to stare at the former senator. If Wooten went along for the hunt, then he could save Christine and himself all in one slash of his claws.

To his utter disappointment, Wooten declined. "As much as I'd like to, I have meetings all day. I'll be flying out as soon as tonight's dinner is over."

They climbed a hill where they had a good view of the field that led to the jungle. Pietro used a dog whistle that hurt Aiden's ears to call his pets. The gargoyles swooped down and landed next to him. He spoke into a walkie-talkie. "Get ready to free number four." His posture straightened. "It'll just be a few minutes, sir."

Wooten took in a deep, refreshing breath. "What do you think, Aiden? It's a beautiful day."

It'd be more beautiful without the chains and the muzzle.

Pietro's walkie crackled. "He's ready when you are, sir," a voice on the other end said.

"Set him loose." Pietro turned to Wooten. "Watch closely now. You won't want to miss this."

All eyes went to the field. It was eerily quiet until a single werg burst from a cell and galloped toward the jungle. Pietro snapped his fingers and pointed. His gargoyle pets shot into the air. They moved like falcons as they gained on their prey.

Aiden's eyes widened as he watched the werg run, silently praying for him to run faster. He felt a deep, burning need to break free and help him, and he struggled to fight the urge. It was so hard to think clearly.

The werg was halfway to the jungle when the first gargoyle swooped at him. He spun to face it, baring his teeth and claws. While he was focused on one gargoyle, the other attacked from behind and ripped a chunk of flesh from his side. The werg stiffened and clutched the wound. The diving gargoyle shot past his head and slashed his eyes with its rear claws.

The werg howled in pain and blindly flailed his arms above his head as he took off for the jungle again. He wasn't nearly as fast upright. Aiden felt ill.

The gargoyles swooped again and again, ravaging the helpless werg with their claws until his muted grey fur was soaked in blood. He staggered but continued running. His tormenters circled like vultures. He whirled around, still flailing blindly, but they easily avoided his claws.

Steps away from the jungle, a gargoyle got in a nasty blow and the werg stumbled to his knees. His counterattack was slow and impotent. He'd lost too much blood to last much longer. Aiden strained at his chains, the static rising in his head.

Wooten cleared his throat. "Okay, okay. I get the point. Enough playing."

Pietro's sick grin faded. "Very well, sir." He blew the dog whistle again and the gargoyles' heads whipped around. He slid his thumb across his throat.

After shredding the werg to a bloody mess, the gargoyles grabbed his arms and flapped their wings. He was too weak to fight back. Together, they lifted him high in the air and carried him up toward the sun until they were merely specks in the sky.

Aiden watched the horror play out, his insides twisting and his resolve hardening. These men deserved no mercy and he would give them none.

And then the gargoyles let go.

The werg hit the ground with a thud. Aiden flinched and finally averted his eyes.

Pietro clapped his hands once. "Well?"

Wooten rubbed his chin. "Very impressive." He side-eyed Pietro. "I think I'll take 'em."

Pietro's eyes narrowed. "What do you mean?"

"I said, I think I'll take 'em. They'd make great pets."

"But ... But, sir."

Wooten gave him a cross look. "Is that a problem?"

"But they're ... they're mine."

"Maybe you don't completely understand how this works."

"I do, but don't take my pets. Please. They ... um ... can't go with you."

"Why not?"

"They don't actually belong to me."

"Who do they belong to?"

"It's not who, sir. It's what. They belong to the house. They're guardians of the property."

"They weren't here when you got here."

"Well, no. We had to relocate them and train them to accept this house as their territory."

Wooten clapped his hands. "Perfect. Then you can send your guy to relocate them to my house in the States."

"But that's not fair, sir."

"It's what you get for going behind my back and ignoring the list."

Pietro lowered his head and mumbled, "I didn't see his name."

"We both know you did. I want those gargoyles on my jet tonight. I'm already pissed at you, Pietro. Don't fracture our relationship even further." He started back toward the house and stopped next to Aiden. "Again, I wish it hadn't worked out this way for you and Christine."

Aiden glared through him.

Wooten continued down the hill. Pietro stood looking like he'd just lost a loved one. "Bastardo," he whispered as soon as the other man was out of earshot.

As the handlers dragged Aiden back to the ballroom, he glanced at the dead werg in the field and wished he could have done something to help him. Whoever he was, at least his suffering was over.

THE ISLAND: DINNER

22

The guests started pouring in a few hours after Aiden had been re-chained to the floor in the ballroom. He had spent the time scouring through the flood of memories in an effort to combat the chip's effects, but no matter how hard he tried, a constant low buzz continued to torment him. Thoughts of Christine were the anchors keeping him right.

The men entering wore tuxedos, and the women wore fancy ball gowns. As each guest arrived, they gravitated to the werg captives and studied them with great interest.

Earlier, Murdock had placed signs in front of each werg. One excited gentleman came closer after reading Aiden's sign and regarded him from head to toe. He was a fit, middle-aged man with a Hollywood haircut and a square jaw.

"Ten thousand points, eh? You must be quite special. I look forward to putting silver into your heart tomorrow night."

I look forward to tearing off your arms and shoving them up your ass, Aiden thought.

An older man, grey and balding on top, stepped up. "No chance of that, Congressman." He spoke with a southern twang.

Aiden was disgusted to learn that Wooten wasn't the only high-ranking American politician involved in murder and human trafficking.

The congressman spun around. "Oh, hello, Carson. How many times have I told you to call me Gerald?"

"I know, Gerald. But it's a respect thing." Carson studied Aiden as Gerald had. "Ten thousand points, huh? This one belongs to me or my wife."

"Oh no. I'm getting this one. I promise you that."

"Heh-heh." Carson had a smoker's laugh. "You'd better hope so. If I get him, I take the overall lead and put this year's challenge out of reach. If Jody gets him and I get just one of the other two, there'll be no way for you to catch me."

Gerald rolled his eyes and scanned the room. "Where is the missus, anyways?"

Carson pointed to a table. "Right there." A woman seated at the table waved.

Gerald smiled and waved back. "Is she as sassy as ever?"

"You bet."

He chuckled again. "I'll be sure to say hi before the night's over." Then he shook his head. "I still don't know why they let you two hunt together. It doesn't seem fair."

Carson shrugged. "It's all about the money. And boy, do we have a lot of it." He snickered. "Seriously, though. We're actually at a disadvantage."

Gerald's brow dipped. "How so?"

"The closer we work together, the more we take away from each other's points. They're not transferable, you know. This late in the season, it gets pretty tense on the home front. And you know Jody. She's Michael Jordan competitive."

"I suppose."

Carson turned back to Aiden and eyed him yet again. He pointed at the tag in Aiden's ear. "I'll be taking that tag tomorrow, my red friend."

Aiden couldn't stop the low and menacing growl that bubbled up his throat.

Gerald slapped Carson's back. "Carson, you old coot. You're not getting him, even if I have to shoot ya myself."

After the two men walked off laughing, more spectators came to ogle the wergs. Aiden watched each of them with piercing hate and disdain. He wondered how they would feel if it were their loved ones on display waiting to be slaughtered.

The chatter slowly grew louder as more and more people arrived. When guests stopped trickling in, Wooten approached the stage. He removed the microphone from the stand and examined it until he found the on switch. It made a high-pitched squelch that hurt Aiden's ears.

"Woah." Wooten jerked the microphone away from his mouth. He tapped it a few times to make sure it was working. "Sorry about that. Good evening. I am happy to see each and every one of you here tonight."

"And our large campaign checks, no doubt," Gerald shouted.

The crowd erupted in laughter.

Aiden rolled his eyes.

Wooten smiled. "The election's over, Jerry. We won, remember?" He waited for the renewed laughter to subside before continuing. "But I will come calling again for my future reelection campaign. Wooten 2016. Start saving up now, folks."

The crowd cheered and laughed some more.

"Okay, okay. Enough with the jokes. The reason we are all here tonight is that our good friend Pietro has put together a wonderful event, and I think he deserves a hand."

The crowd applauded again. Pietro took a bow from his seat at the guest-of-honor table. After the applause dwindled, Wooten continued. "As you have no doubt already seen, we have our first ten-thousand-point werg in tomorrow's hunt. One of our three hunters may just put this whole contest away and wrap up the ten million dollars by the end of the week."

Someone in the back of the room shouted, "What makes *that* werg so special?"

Wooten flashed his politician's smile. "He was a rogue hunter back in the WereHouse days. One of the best, actually."

Aiden had spent nearly a year striving to make up for the life he'd lived. To be dragged back to that nasty place by the words of a corrupt politician spoken to his psychopathic friends hurt in a deep and encompassing way. Damn Wooten and Pietro and all the others for doing this to him. As his blood pressure rose, the low buzzing in his head grew louder until it became deafening.

Aiden looked around, suddenly confused. Where was he? What …? *No.* He dragged himself back from the brink. He pictured Christine sleeping next to him after their first night together, and it blasted the fuzziness away with a vengeance.

He lifted newly focused eyes to Wooten. Though he may never truly escape his past, he knew what he needed to do to survive. It wasn't rage and anger that would get him back to Christine, but the skills he'd learned from that horrible past. He couldn't run from the man he had been any longer. It was time to embrace him.

Wooten's speech was winding down. He nodded to each of the three hunters before speaking directly to them. "Jerry. Carson. Jody. I want you to be very careful out there tomorrow. While werg hunts are always dangerous, this one will be especially so. Stay safe out there."

They nodded graciously.

Aiden shifted position, his chains clanking. He was right to warn them. This wouldn't be any ordinary hunt.

Wooten addressed the crowd again. "You are all part of the reason I'm in the position politically that I am today, and we have a lot still to do for our country. When I take office in January, I won't forget any of you. Well … except you, Carson. I'm always trying to forget you."

Everyone laughed again, including Carson.

"Now, enjoy the evening. Make sure to get yourselves a peek at my pet gargoyles in the other room before you leave. They are quite interesting creatures."

A man shouted, "I've already seen 'em … And I want one. How much?"

Wooten grinned. "Let's just say we're working on that." He took a bow and switched off the mic. Pietro met him on stage and shook his hand as if his heart hadn't been torn out less than three hours earlier. Aiden smirked in his muzzle. Under all the posturing, Pietro was a coward.

The band struck up a rendition of "Chattanooga Choo Choo" as waiters streamed in with the first course. Dish after dish was served, each more extravagant than the last. The snobbish guests hardly seemed to notice they were eating a small fortune. Watching them laugh and stuff their faces and dance in celebration of the future murder of three men was disgusting.

When everyone finally began to filter out of the ballroom at some ungodly hour, Gerald made one last trip to inspect the wergs. Aiden took special note of his musky cologne as he drew near. Even if the bastard took a thousand showers before the hunt, he wouldn't be able to wash off enough that Aiden wouldn't recognize him.

"I'll make it quick, old sport," he promised. He pointed to Aiden's heart, winked, and clicked his tongue. "Silver, baby."

Aiden answered with a low rumble.

Gerald smiled. "I like your spirit. I'll see you tomorrow."

Aiden couldn't wait.

Once everyone had left, the werg handlers returned. One at a time, they unchained the other wergs from the floor and took them through the back of the ballroom. Aiden was the last to go.

When they retrieved him, however, they took him through the foyer and out the front door where the partygoers had formed lines along both sides of the walkway. Aiden despised them all. They applauded as the guards led him past and didn't stop until he was at his cell.

Before pushing him in, Murdock pointed to the jungle. "There's your freedom, dog. Good luck."

One of his companions asked, "Why do you even talk to them? You know the chips scramble their brains."

Murdock shrugged. "I talk to my fish sometimes, too. What about it?"

The handlers locked Aiden's wrists to the cell bars and removed the collar and shackle contraption and muzzle. Then they unshackled his ankles and closed the door. Finally, they unlocked his wrists. It felt good to have his hands free again. After they left, he retreated to the trough for a much-needed drink.

That night, multiple private jets left the runway and flew away overhead. Aiden imagined Wooten's was one of them and thought about Christine. *Hold tough, babe. I'm doing everything I can.*

THE ISLAND: THE HUNT

23

Aiden paced his cell during the day leading up to the hunt. He wanted to sleep, but he was afraid the static would take over if he did. By evening, clouds had moved in and low rumbles of thunder following distant flashes of lightning set the eerie mood. The calmness of a brooding storm really got his juices flowing. Though he should have been terrified, he saw tonight as an opportunity to turn the tables. Finally, he'd have a chance to fight.

As night fell, a slight mist descended. The nervous energy from the other two wergs was palpable as they shuffled in their cells. He hoped he could find a way to help them, too.

It was close to midnight when Pietro's tornado siren pierced through the thunder. Aiden's hackles rose. It was time.

A cell door clanked open, quickly followed by a second. The two other wergs shot out, heading for the trees as if freedom had called for them.

Aiden's cell door clanked open last. He stepped out and lifted his eyes to the angry sky. The mist had turned into a light rain that felt good on his face. He opened his mouth and let the pureness wash over his tongue. As the rain wet his fur and flashes of brilliance danced across the clouds, he closed his eyes and took a calming breath. He looked to the empty cell next to his and remembered Sammy. He wondered where he'd gone.

He thought about Christine and hoped she was safe. He closed his eyes and quietly steeled himself for violence.

The tornado siren ceased as suddenly as it had begun. Aiden dropped to all fours and exploded toward the jungle where the other wergs had already scattered. He stopped at the trees and took a last look back. A green flare popped in the sky and illuminated the field as it floated toward the ground under a parachute. Three night vision flashlight beams rounded the side of the cell block and bounced across the field.

The game was on.

Aiden's heart pounded against his sternum. He was as excited as he was scared. He plowed into the forest, not slowing until he'd put enough distance between him and the hunters to catch his breath.

As he slowed to a walk, he caught a waft of raw meat and followed the smell to a tree where a small animal's skinned carcass hung from a rope.

He tilted his head, deathly hungry yet remembering setting traps like these in his WereHouse days. He scanned the ground, quickly finding a small pile of sticks and leaves. He carefully brushed the leaves away to expose a metal chain that led to a post embedded in the dirt. He knew that somewhere nearby would be an orange flag marker that couldn't be seen with werg eyes.

If the jungle was full of traps, running was too dangerous. He was lucky he'd gotten this far without incident. He found a fallen tree resting against the trunk of another, partially hidden by overgrowth. The gap between the fallen tree and the ground was the perfect place to hide. Aiden crawled in and waited.

As the night passed, heavy bursts of rain moved through, gradually turning into a slight drizzle. The thunder became a distant rumble again. The jungle was left wet and sloppy.

Hours must have passed, and still Aiden waited, thoughts of getting back to Christine keeping the static at bay. It was almost a relief when the quiet was shattered by the sudden pop of an explosion far off in the distance, followed by a barrage of gunfire. He kept his sniffer poised, searching for anything unnatural to a jungle. Human sweat. Gunpowder. Gerald's cologne.

As he lay motionless, something moved near his head. He slowly turned to find a praying mantis balancing delicately on a leaf, its front legs probing the air. He watched its every movement, waiting for it to get closer. Though he wasn't keen on eating insects, his belly rumbled and he licked his teeth. The mantis bounced gently on the leaf with her head swiveling and tilting. Aiden barely breathed. When the mantis found a branch and unwittingly stalked closer, he snatched her and shoved her into his mouth. Though it wasn't much, it was something.

And still he waited.

At last, he caught the faint scent he'd been waiting for. He had been right. No amount of scrubbing could hide Gerald's musky smell. The man was a fool. Maybe women in the civilized world liked his cologne, but it was going to get him killed in the jungle. Though the light breeze immediately carried the scent away, it had given Aiden a direction. He watched and waited.

The cologne wasn't the only thing exposing Gerald. Aiden didn't know how experienced he was, but he wasn't good enough to avoid every tiny stick and branch beneath his feet. Even waterlogged, they made sounds if one listened close enough.

A night vision flashlight beam sliced between two trees just before the faint outline of a figure stepped into view. The bastard was nearly invisible, likely wearing orange camouflage. But orange only worked if the prey didn't know what to look for and where to look.

Gerald scanned the trees, as cocky as a professional werg hunter. He lowered his orange poncho's oversized hood from his pith helmet, shut off his flashlight, and flipped down a pair of night vision goggles. Though his actions might indicate that he'd found Aiden's trail, it was yet another mistake on his part since the goggles weren't painted orange. Aiden focused on them.

Gerald tucked the front of the poncho behind a holstered 9MM, also not painted orange. An AR-15 was slung across his chest. Equipped with every high-tech gadget a millionaire could order from his favorite militia weekly publication, he probably thought hunting average wergs was easy.

Unfortunately for him, Aiden wasn't average.

Gerald squatted, picked up a broken twig, and examined it. He surveyed the terrain until his goggles landed on the fallen tree where Aiden hid. He slowly stood up and backed out of sight. Maybe he wasn't a complete idiot.

Aiden's muscles coiled as he waited on edge. Listening. Smelling. Preparing. Time passed at a snail's pace. When he could no longer smell his foe, for the first time his excitement gave way to real concern. Maybe Gerald had lost his trail and moved on. Or maybe he had circled around and—

Something landed in the brush near Aiden's feet. He spun in time to see a flash grenade just before it threw the sun into his eyes. The heat seared his flesh, instantly polluting his nostrils with the rank smell of burnt hair. A crackle of gunfire followed. Aiden sprang from his hideout in a blind panic and slammed into a tree as bullets shredded the bark beside his head. His instinct told him to zig but his experience as a rogue hunter told him to zag. He cut left. Bark sprayed from the tree to his right.

He pressed his back to it and blinked away the afterimage of the flash in time to see Gerald's indistinct figure sprint across the path ahead. Aiden dove as bullets ripped through the tree where he had stood.

Gerald took cover behind another tree, likely expecting Aiden to full-on charge or full-on retreat. He would do neither.

He took stock of his surroundings while Gerald replaced his spent magazine. A dead branch hung on the tree above Aiden's head. He snapped it free and moved to where Gerald would have to expose himself to get a clear shot.

And that's just what the bastard did. When he came around the tree, hands clutching his rifle, Aiden heaved the branch. Gerald recoiled, shielding his face with his weapon.

There was too much distance between them for Aiden to attack head-on, but it gave him a chance to flank Gerald if he moved quickly enough. He dropped to all fours and sprinted toward the carcass trap he had found earlier. Careful of the leaf pile, he ripped the flag free and jammed it into the soft dirt farther away. He sliced his own arm with a claw and smeared blood on a tree. Beyond the hidden trap, he broke a couple of twigs, making sure the path led directly past it. Then he ran to a gully with a creek at the bottom, climbed down, and peered over the embankment.

Gerald quickly discovered his trail. He had discarded his poncho and now had unobstructed access to all his weapons. His every step was methodical and cautious, his head on a constant swivel. He approached the relocated flag and gave it a wide berth, which took him directly to the tree with Aiden's blood. He touched it and then pumped his fist victoriously. Any second now he would find the broken twigs. He just needed to move a few feet to his right.

Aiden lifted his head slightly and pretended to look around. He could almost sense the smug smile on Gerald's face. If only the bastard knew what was coming.

Gerald crouched, checked his rifle, and took a step directly onto the leaf pile. The clank of the steel bear trap only preceded Gerald's bloodcurdling scream by a millisecond. He dropped the rifle and left it dangling by its strap as he grabbed his leg. He thudded to his rear, writhing in pain.

Aiden inhaled the sweet, metallic scent of blood and cleared the bank in a single leap. The hunted had now become the hunter. He was upon his enemy in a flash.

Gerald fumbled for his rifle at the last second and Aiden swatted it from his hand. Gerald tried to scoot out of reach, but the trap was chained to a ring embedded in concrete. He wailed as he fell to his back.

Aiden went in for the kill.

Gerald drew his 9MM and fired off seven sloppy shots. In his adrenaline rush, Aiden didn't feel one of the bullets rip through his side below his ribs. He slashed Gerald's gut, feeling his claws chip the man's spine. Gerald tensed and covered his stomach with one arm.

That's when the pain from the gunshot finally registered in Aiden's brain. He winced and staggered against the tree. The bullet must have been silver judging by the way his skin sizzled. His hand shot to his back in search of an exit wound. Thankfully, he found a cavernous hole. It was a nasty wound, but at least the silver wasn't still in him. Blood soaked his fur all the way down his leg.

He licked his lips, suddenly thirsty again. Dizzy, he shook his head like a dog about to sneeze. He glanced back at Gerald, who gasped for air.

His enemy's eyes slowly glossed over as blood poured from his stomach. He sighed a final breath. His arm dropped from his gut and his hand fell open, revealing a final deadly gift. A grenade rolled from his palm, landing at Aiden's feet.

Oh no.

Aiden dove away as the explosion punched the breath from his lungs. His body hurtled over the embankment into the creek. Everything went dark.

Aiden couldn't breathe. His head was cloudy and felt like it was about to pop. He opened his eyes underwater in a panic. His hands and knees met a rocky creek bed and he pushed away from it, lifting his snout into fresh air. He gasped for breath.

He felt like his body had been run through a wood chipper and his right arm didn't work properly. He tried to recall what had happened, but it was too difficult. He was supposed to remember someone. A name. *Christine.* That was it. She needed him. He focused on her—the only woman he'd truly cared about since losing his mother. Despite the pain ravaging his body, the brain fog slowly receded again.

He struggled to his feet and doubled over in pain. The right side of his body was charred black. The lingering stink of burnt hair and flesh turned his stomach. A broken bone protruded from his forearm. And he was still deathly thirsty.

He tucked his broken arm close to his body and lapped up creek water. Then he waded to shore and shook himself dry. He needed to hide and regroup. The explosion would surely bring the others.

As if the thought had summoned them, he caught another scent beyond the burnt hair and flesh. *Shit.* They were already there. He clambered up the embankment with one working arm.

As soon as he reached the top, a gunshot echoed from the other side of the creek and a bullet grazed his neck.

A frantic look back revealed Carson on the opposite bank with his rifle raised. Jody was crossing the river farther upstream.

"Pin him down," she shouted.

Aiden cleared the embankment as a barrage of gunfire shredded the trees around him. He ducked behind one. When the gunfire let up briefly, he fled on three limbs, his broken arm still held tight against his body.

"There he goes," Carson shouted.

Aiden reached the base of a hill and started up. His feet slid in fresh mud and slick grass. Using his claws, he made it to the top as Carson reached the base. Aiden looked back down the hill to see Carson pointing a strange weapon at him.

A loud *tha-wump* rang out and a projectile whistled toward Aiden. He dove out of the way as the ground exploded behind him.

Holy shit, the fucker has a rocket-propelled grenade.

Aiden fled to the opposite side of the hill and took cover behind a tree stump four feet tall and nearly as wide. He peeked around it, searching for signs of the hunters. His hands trembled and he didn't know if it was from his injuries or fear.

Jody reached the top of the hill first and ducked behind a tree near the crater left by Carson's RPG. Carson joined her seconds later and crouched with a fresh RPG loaded on his shoulder.

Aiden heard another *tha-wump*. With nowhere else to go, he threw himself down the backside of the hill as the tree stump exploded. His good arm gave way in the mud and his shoulder hit the ground, flipping him head over heels. His back struck a large rock, tossing him into a roll. As he tumbled, each impact sent waves of agony through his broken body.

He landed on a felled tree at the bottom, snapping a thick branch and sending pain ripping through his side. He tried unsuccessfully to muffle a yowl.

A broken branch jutted from his gut like a spear pinning him to the trunk. Blood oozed around it. He reached behind his back, braced his good arm on the trunk, and closed his eyes. With a grimace, he pushed himself off the natural spear. The pain was brilliant and vomit-inducing.

He roared, no longer worried about who heard him. Focusing on defense was getting him killed. It was time to go on the offensive.

But first he'd have to do something about the bone sticking out of his forearm. He grabbed his wrist and yanked, causing the bone to slip back under his skin. He barely felt the ungodly pain over the agony in his side.

The heavy breathing of the out-of-shape millionaire and his psychotic wife sounded at the top of the hill above. He couldn't see them past the trees, which he hoped meant they couldn't see him either.

It would take them time to safely climb down the wet, muddy hillside. Aiden pushed to his feet and limped away. He caught the scent of wet dog and blood and followed it to a van-sized boulder. Lying behind it in a puddle of bloody water was the bullet-riddled corpse of a werg with a missing left ear. His ankle was caught in a bear trap. The bastards had killed him without giving him a chance to fight back. Where was the sport in that?

Aiden grimaced, angry at himself for not getting to him faster. He wished he had time to give the poor guy a proper burial. Instead, he vowed to give him proper vengeance. He stepped on one of the trap's jaws, got a good grip on the other and strained until the teeth separated from the dead werg's leg. He continued pulling until the trap locked open and then followed the chain to the buried block of concrete. He dug the block loose and pulled it free.

With his good arm, he swung the concrete into the boulder as hard as he could again and again. On the fourth swing, the concrete crumbled away from the stake. He set the trap aside, lifted the dead werg, and wedged him between the boulder and tree to make it look like he was standing. Then he retrieved the bear trap and circled back, conscious of staying downwind of Carson and Jody's likely approaches. He hid nearby where he could still see his decoy.

Carson was the first to appear. When he spotted the decoy werg, he froze and held up a fist. That gave Aiden an idea of where Jody was, even though he hadn't seen her yet. Carson positioned himself against a tree and held his rifle scope to his eye. He took a deep breath before pulling the trigger. The bullet took off half the dead creature's skull. Carson threw up his hands in celebration. "Did you see that, honey?"

Jody stepped into view to Aiden's left, startling him with how close she had gotten. "Good shot," she shouted back.

It was now or never. Aiden charged, hoping to catch Carson off guard since he was closest.

"Look out," Jody shrieked, and fumbled for her gun.

Carson spun with his weapon raised. Aiden hurled the bear trap at him. Carson flinched. The trap struck his left arm and sprang shut. He shrieked and flailed with his rifle, sending a spray of bullets flying. One of his errant shots struck Aiden just beneath his armpit with a dull thump.

Despite a seeming cannon blast knocking the wind from his lungs, he reached Carson and ripped out the bastard's throat. Then he spun toward Jody before Carson's body hit the ground.

Her rifle lay at her feet. She clutched at a hole in her chest and dropped to her knees. Her face went pale as a circle of blood grew on her shirt. She sat back on her ankles, wobbled, and then collapsed to her side.

Aiden's chest sizzled, a trickle of smoke wafting from the hole. He suddenly couldn't swallow and his wheezing breaths were almost louder than a howl. The bullet must have collapsed one of his lungs. The fur around the wound fell out in clumps, replaced by red welts.

He could feel the bullet burning inside, and all he could think was he had to get it out fast. He dragged his finger along his ribs until he found a gap of missing bone just beneath the hole. With a grimace, he jammed his dagger-like claw into the wound and dug blindly as the world started to spin. The static he had been so successfully fighting rushed back with a vengeance.

He thrust his claw deeper, striking something hard. It might have just been part of his shattered rib, but it was something. He curled his claw around it as his airway closed. He ripped the mass free, along with blood and meat. The pain was as bad as anything he'd ever felt, and something broke loose in his brain.

A blunted piece of bloody silver dropped to the ground. He fell to his back. His vision blurred as he gazed at the treetops. He needed to breathe. Maybe Death had finally found him. He was ready.

As he lay watching the treetops, he vaguely remembered there was a name he was supposed to hold on to, but for the life of him he couldn't get it back. He looked around and wondered where he was.

And then he gasped in a wonderful breath before closing his eyes.

"What the hell happened here?"

The creature squinted, blinded by the brightness of a brand-new day. Strangers milled around, taking in the carnage. One of them smelled familiar, but the creature couldn't remember why.

"I'm sorry, Pietro," one of the men said. "I don't know what happened."

The one called Pietro threw his hands up in the air and mumbled, "Questo è un disastro."

"What?"

"Questo è un disastro."

"I don't speak Italian, sir."

"I said this is a disaster. You realize this sonovabitch just killed a congressman, the head of one of the largest software companies in the world, and her husband."

"I know, sir. But they did sign the waivers."

"Waivers? Who gives a shit about waivers? These are people who are going to be missed. There'll be a lot of questions over this. Which werg is it?"

One of the men checked the creature's ear. "The red one, sir."

"I see that. Which one's the red one?"

"Aiden Talik, sir."

That name meant nothing to the creature.

Pietro rubbed his forehead raw. "I should have known. This is a nightmare. We're gonna have to tell President-elect Wooten right away. He's going to be furious."

"It's a dangerous sport, sir. I'm sure he'll understand."

Pietro glared at him. "Have you *met* Wooten, Murdock?"

Murdock nodded. "Point taken, sir."

The creature groaned as he tried to move. For some reason his entire body hurt something awful.

"He's awake again, sir," Murdock said.

"Put him back to sleep," Pietro snapped.

"Yes, sir." Murdock pulled out a pistol and fired a feathered dart into the creature's neck. "What do you want me to do with him now, sir?"

Pietro sighed. "I don't know, Murdock. Bury him."

"You don't want to display him?"

"Look at him. He's all burnt to shit. He'd make a terrible trophy."

"We could cook him. I haven't had werg meat in a while."

Pietro shook his head. "I don't want any evidence that this one was ever here. Capisce?"

"Whatever you say, sir." Murdock motioned to three other men who were trying to free a battered werg corpse wedged between a boulder and a tree.

The creature imagined himself biting their throats, but when they grasped him under his arms, he couldn't follow through. They dragged him away, chatting to each other.

"This one's a tough bastard, huh?"

"Yeah. And look where that got him."

The creature's eyes blasted open to nothing but darkness and pain. Each shallow breath he took felt hot and sticky. His heart thudded in his chest. Panic filled his gut and rose into his throat. He couldn't think straight, a loud hum reverberating between his ears. He squirmed and one arm bashed into a wall. The other arm ached something fierce and he couldn't remember why. He tried to sit up, but his snout bumped into wooden boards, sending a small shower of dirt between the cracks. Throbbing pain in his side punished him for the effort.

He tried to focus, but his thoughts were twisted and fuzzy. The stink of burnt hair assaulted his nostrils. Flashes of a previous life flickered across the backs of his eyes, and he tried desperately to hold on to them, but they were too fleeting. He remembered a hunter shooting at him. A creek bed. The taste of blood, metallic on his tongue. None of it made any sense. And the rage. God, the rage overflowed from within. It took everything he had to keep from completely surrendering to it.

The air grew thinner with each labored breath. It felt like one lung didn't even work. He pushed the heavy ceiling with all his strength, but it only caused more dirt to fall through the cracks.

The world closed in, or maybe it was just in his mind. He tried to turn over, but there wasn't any room and he only succeeded in pinning his arms tighter to his body.

He tried to roar, but the pain was too intense. What little sound he could make was muffled and almost popped his ears like he was in a …

The man had said, "Bury him." He swallowed acid.

Oh no.

The creature had a split second of calm before an avalanche of terror washed through him. He exploded into a rage, thrashing against his tomb.

Wooden splinters pierced his fingers as he clawed frantically at the ceiling. He ignored the pain. Bulging veins threatened to burst through his temples. He couldn't breathe.

A chunk of wood ripped loose. He dug into the gap and tore away another tiny piece. Each splinter of wood he pulled free caused more dirt to rain onto his chest.

Completely blinded by rage and an instinctual urge to fight until his last breath, he ripped at the wood. Once the ceiling above his face was replaced by an avalanche of smothering dirt, he pushed his head through it, his face breaking free of darkness and into light. He spit out dirt and sucked what little fresh air he could into his good lung.

With his head now free, he dug until he was able to roll onto his back on solid ground. Fortunately, his grave diggers had been lazy.

Every part of his body throbbed. He couldn't make sense of anything. He felt full of hate and anger and wanted to kill, yet he couldn't remember why. All he knew was blood and anger and violence ...

And hunger.

His stomach cinched, nearly doubling him over. He struggled to stand, his aching arm pulled tight to his body, and wondered why he was so broken. Who had hurt him so badly?

He didn't have time to think as a squirrel darted close to him. He pounced without thought, snatched the squirming critter, and sank his teeth into its side. Warm juices flowed over his tongue as he chewed the creature to the bone. He dropped the stripped skeleton, looking for more. It had barely made a dent in his hunger.

It took hours of patient hunting before he spotted a tapir drinking from a stream. He stalked closer, his instincts taking over. Each cautious step had to be perfect, each breath efficient and silent. And yet, even with all his skill, he couldn't defeat luck.

The tapir glanced back, saw him, and took off running. It cut left before darting right. The creature stayed on him, ignoring every scream of pain throughout his body. He wondered how much faster he'd have been if he were whole.

The tapir gave him a helluva chase, but in the end it tried to cut one too many times. The creature swatted its hindquarters, tearing a chunk of muscle from its rear leg. The tapir squealed and fell.

The creature killed the tapir quickly with a bite to its neck. As he stood victorious over his fallen prey, he caught sight of an old jaguar who had taken interest in his kill. He glared back, ready for a fight. The jaguar hesitated, considered the risk, and then lowered his head and moved on.

Once finally full, the creature drank from a stream and then found a small hole at the base of a large rocky protrusion. He dug out the dirt beneath the hole until he could fit inside.

Before crawling into his new den, he marked the surrounding area with piss to warn other predators they weren't welcome. Then he went to sleep.

SANDALIO

25

After spending the night in Fort Myers, Jericho sat with Christine for the Cancun leg of the journey. They mostly talked about trivial things like their favorite movies—*Saving Private Ryan* for him, *The Notebook* for her—with nothing getting too serious until he mentioned his wife in passing.

"Tell me about her," Christine said.

He shrugged. "We had a good marriage for a while. She was the love of my life. Sure, we had our ups and downs, but I'd always felt like she was my soulmate, and we could get through anything together. I was only twenty-five when I met her."

"*How'd* you meet?"

"I was a dishwasher at a nursin' home. She was one of the cooks. We got married two months after our first date."

"Wow. That's fast."

"Yeah. I guess we didn't know any better. But it worked for the most part. We were married for fifteen years."

"What happened?"

"We fell into a rut, and I suppose I stopped payin' attention to her. Probably took her for granted, if I'm bein' honest. She ran off with my good friend."

"That's terrible."

"It was as much my fault as it was hers."

She heard a quiver in his voice, despite his tough exterior. "I bet she's regretting it."

"Heh. Maybe."

"I'm sure of it."

He gave her a look full of kindness and vulnerability that she couldn't help but feel drawn to. When she realized she was staring, she looked away.

"What about you?" he asked. "Ever been married?"

She snorted. "God, no. Not even close."

"Why not?"

"I'm pretty difficult to get close to. If something starts to get serious, I always seem to push it away."

"What about this Aiden guy? You must really care about him to go through all this."

Christine caught herself smiling. "I do. We haven't even known each other for a year, but it feels right."

"A year? Heh. I'd already been married for ten months by that point."

She laughed. "What about after your wife? Did you try to meet anyone else?"

He shook his head. "I decided to focus on myself after some medical setbacks."

"Oh? What kind of setbacks?" She caught herself and quickly added, "I don't mean to pry. It's none of my business."

"No worries. I don't mind talkin' about it. After my wife left me, I noticed some odd things happenin' to my body. I started losing my balance for no reason and couldn't sleep worth a shit. I'd always been a sound sleeper before that. There was a bunch of other little things, too, but I just chalked them up to gettin' older. When I noticed I couldn't keep my hands from shakin', I knew there was somethin' really wrong.

"I finally went to the doc, and he ran some tests. Said I had Parkinson's Disease. I didn't even know what that was. After he explained what was gonna happen to my body, I realized my life was about to change dramatically."

Christine listened quietly. She had dealt with Parkinson's patients many times on the medic and felt sad for the future he was facing. "I haven't noticed your hands shaking or anything."

"I saw a TV program that said the werg virus might be a cure, or at the least slow the disease. That's when I went lookin' for wergs and found Slater's group."

"Oh no. You didn't."

He chuckled. "I did."

"And Slater changed you?"

"Adam, actually. In a way, I owe him my life."

"And you just planned to stay at Slater's forever?"

"Nah. I figured I'd get the werg virus and then move on to somethin' I'd been wantin' to do. I hung around a little longer than I'd planned because I needed to learn how to control my new gift. And I rather liked the others, aside from buttin' heads with Slater. I was plannin' to tell him I was leavin' when I met you."

"What is it that you planned to do?"

He turned away.

She smiled. "What?"

"It's nothin'."

"No, really. What is it?"

"It's just … I've never told anyone other than my ex-wife about it."

She crossed her heart. "I promise, your secret will be safe with me."

He smiled shyly. "I want to start my own dojo for troubled kids."

"Really? That's awesome."

He gave her an unreadable look. "There's more to it."

She nudged him on with a compassionate smile.

"A few years ago, some kid was hangin' around the construction site in the mornin's when he should have been at school. He had a black eye one time, so I got to talkin' to him. His name was Tommy. He said he was bein' bullied. Since I'd never been bullied myself, I gave him some shitty advice about fightin' back. I didn't see him again after that and figured he'd stood up to his bully and all was good. Then, a few weeks later, I found out he'd killed himself …" He breathed deep and turned away. "I couldn't help but feel like I could've done more."

"That's awful. But it wasn't your fault."

"I could've helped him if I wasn't such an idiot tough guy. I didn't realize how bad being bullied could get. I'll live with that failure for the rest of my life."

"You didn't know."

"Yeah, I don't suppose I did. But it doesn't make it any better. I did a lot of soul searchin' after, and that's when I decided to open my own dojo dedicated to teachin' children how to have confidence and stand up for themselves. I wanted to dedicate the rest of my life to makin' that happen. That was right before my wife left me and the first Parkinson's symptoms showed up.

"I couldn't let it stop me. I figured the struggles of being a werg would be worth it if I could help even one kid. Truth be told, that's the real reason I wanted the virus. I didn't care so much about myself anymore."

"When all this is over, I think building a dojo is exactly what you should do."

"That's the plan." He went quiet for a second. Then he glanced over and smiled. "What are you looking at?"

She realized she had been staring again and quickly looked away. She thought of Aiden and felt an instant rush of guilt over having such warm feelings for someone she had just met while he was suffering through who knew what. "We should make some kind of plan for rescuing Aiden," she blurted out.

"Yeah." He seemed like he wanted to say something else but held back.

Instead, they discussed finding someone in Costa Rica who could get them to the island and what to do once they got there. They had to assume it would have at least as much security as the Underground and the Dog Park, if not more. Walking straight in wouldn't be an option, so they would have to rely on stealth and the element of surprise. It wasn't much of a plan, but since they didn't really know what they'd be walking into, they would just have to be flexible.

After two more refueling stops, the three landed in Costa Rica over forty hours after their journey had begun. Adam tucked the bag of cash into a hidden cubby after stuffing a few grand into his pocket. They left the plane carrying backpacks and duffels full of protein bars, water bottles, and spare clothes in case their adventure called for them to shift suddenly.

"Wish we had guns," Adam grumbled.

Christine agreed.

They passed through Customs and a metal detector without incident. Jericho hailed a taxi to take them to the eastern shore where they hoped to charter a boat to Sandalio.

"Does he speak English?" Christine gestured at the driver.

Jericho pinched his finger and thumb together. "A little."

"Do either of you speak Spanish?"

Jericho shook his head.

"I do," Adam volunteered. "Enough, at least."

They climbed into the back seat. During the ride, Adam tossed out the name Sandalio as their final destination to see the driver's reaction.

The driver's jovial mood darkened. He shot a look over his shoulder, heavy concern creasing his forehead. "No, no, no. You no go there. Mucho peligroso."

"I know it's dangerous," Adam answered. "But we have to."

"Asustado."

"Is there anyone who isn't afraid?"

The driver refocused on the road, ignoring Adam's question.

Adam held a fifty over the seat. "Por favor, señor. Help us."

The driver stopped at a light and stared at the cash for a moment. His eyes flicked back to Adam. He took the money. "Si. Te llevaré a un hombre con un barco."

Adam grinned and settled back into the seat.

"What'd he say?" Christine whispered.

"I think he said he'll take us to someone with a boat."

It cost five hundred bucks, but the driver secured them a two-and-a-half-hour boat ride to Sandalio's western shore. The boat captain spoke even less

English than the cab driver. He insisted on waiting until dark to avoid being seen by those who owned the island. Christine had no leverage to argue.

Adam huddled with the captain near the front. Their conversation grew heated. Eventually, the captain sighed, his shoulders drooped, and he nodded. He squeezed past Adam to get a notepad and pencil and hastily drew something.

Adam patted his shoulder and walked to the back of the boat where Jericho and Christine waited. He sat across from them.

"What was that all about?" Jericho asked.

"I told him he had to come back and get us tomorrow. He didn't like that prospect too much."

"How'd you get him to agree?"

"I promised him a thousand more bones when we get back to port."

"And you think he'll actually come back for us?" Christine asked.

"Does a tiger shit in the woods?"

Christine rolled her eyes. "What'd he draw for you?"

"A map. We can't go traipsing around a strange jungle with no clue of where we're headed."

It was good thinking.

The trip to Sandalio went off without a hitch. At the island, the captain ran his boat ashore, climbed out, and held it with a rope. He flicked his wrist and shouted, "Vete. A la mierda."

Christine looked to Adam.

"He's basically telling us to get outta here."

Christine, Adam, and Jericho climbed out. The captain pushed off, clambered aboard, and got the boat turned around in record time.

Adam shouted, "Mañana."

Without looking back, the captain shouted, "Hombre lobo. Hombre lobo." And then he sped into the night.

"What's that mean?" Christine asked.

"It means werewolf."

"Oh."

Adam started up the shore toward the jungle. "I think we've got a few hours of walking." The whites of his eyes darkened to coal black. "You're gonna need your werg eyes to see. Can you do that?"

Christine nodded as the color drained from her sight.

They eventually reached a manmade trail, just like the map showed. Though roughly drawn, it proved to be surprisingly accurate. After traipsing through the jungle for a few hours, they heard voices in the distance and scurried from the path to hide. The voices grew louder as a bouncing flashlight beam approached.

There were two men bitching to each other and carrying something box-like between them. "I can't believe the boss has us out here getting this thing this late at night," one of them said.

"Boss is pissed about losing his pets. Shut up about it already. You know how these things are. They don't stay trapped for long. We need to move fast."

"You think he'll be mad that it's just a baby?"

"He wants babies, dumbass. That's why the cage is so small. But don't tell him we didn't take out the mother or we'll be in the next hunt."

"It's not our fault we couldn't find her. What's it matter, anyway?"

"How should I know? Boss doesn't tell me shit."

As they walked closer, Christine noticed the box-like thing they carried was a cage about the size of a microwave. Inside was a strange animal no bigger than a raccoon.

She glanced at Jericho. He shrugged and held a finger to his lips.

As the men passed, she got a better look at the creature. She'd never seen anything like it—hairless with wide, bulging eyes and puke-green, semi-translucent skin showing its veins. Its bat-like wings were tucked tight to its back. It locked wide eyes on her as the men carried it past, and she hoped it wouldn't give her away.

The men soon disappeared up ahead and Adam stepped out of the brush. Christine and Jericho joined him.

"What the hell was that?" Jericho asked.

"I have no idea." Adam scratched his head. "Some kind of bat, maybe?"

Christine blinked, still trying to process what she'd seen. "Did you guys ever see that 90's Disney cartoon on TV? The one with all the gargoyles?"

Adam's eyes widened. "Oh yeah. But gargoyles aren't real ... Are they?"

Jericho shook his head. "I didn't think so."

Adam shrugged and started off along the path again. "Whatever. Let's go. Early fish gets the worm."

It took the rest of the night, but eventually they arrived at the edge of an open field. The two men carrying the caged creature were already at the other end near a one-story, strip mall-style building with cell doors along the face. Behind it was a large mansion on a hill and a pole barn off to the right.

Adam glanced at Jericho. "I think we've found it."

Jericho nodded. "Now, what's the plan?"

Adam looked to the horizon as a hint of sunlight lit the underside of the clouds. "I think our best bet is to get closer before it gets too light out."

"You mean like right now?"

"No time like the current."

Christine swallowed hard. She wasn't sure she was ready.

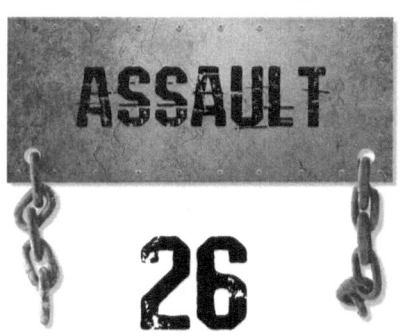

ASSAULT

26

Christine, Jericho, and Adam stood at the edge of the sprawling field, staying hidden within the tree line. Just enough of the sun had risen over the jungle to silhouette the guards patrolling the top of the cell building.

"Snipers," Jericho whispered. "We'll have to deal with them first."

"And how should we do that?" Christine asked. "Circle around?"

Adam shook his head. "That won't work. They'll have every angle covered."

The field grass brushed Christine's knees, giving her another idea. "What if we army crawled?"

Adam shook his head again. "That'd take too long. And they'd still see us before we reached halfway. Maybe if we waited until night again—"

"No," she snapped. "We don't have time. It may already be too late."

Christine and Adam hashed out ideas until she noticed Jericho was being very quiet, standing off by himself with his head bowed. "What's going on, Jericho?"

He lifted his head. "I know what we need to do." There was a heaviness in the way he said it.

"I'm all ears."

"We need a distraction."

"Okay?"

"I'll make one."

"What do you mean?"

"I'll draw their fire so you two can get closer."

Her eyes narrowed. "No way. They're snipers. They'll shoot you."

"Maybe."

"Absolutely not. It's too risky. Think of something else."

"There isn't anything else. It's the only way short of a full-on bull rush to the compound that would get us all killed."

Christine shook her head. "It's suicide."

"Maybe not. It'd take quite a shot from that distance."

Adam squinted at the snipers. "That might actually work."

Christine shot him a glare. "Don't encourage this nonsense." She turned back to Jericho. "Stop. This is ridiculous. We'll think of something else. We'll ..." But he was already taking off his shirt. She grabbed his arm. "No, no, no," she moaned. "I don't want you to do this."

He smiled sadly. "We're wasting time."

She didn't know what to say.

He looked into her eyes. "Before I go, I need you to know something."

"What is it?"

"I care about you, Chris. I—"

"Don't say anything else. What you're feeling's not real. You've only known me for a week."

"I know. But sometimes a person just knows."

She shook her head again. "We're here for Aiden. We—"

He leaned in and pressed his lips to hers.

Every part of her knew she should pull away, but his kiss was gentle and safe and perfect. He touched her neck and she felt his strength and tenderness all at once. She wanted him to tell her everything would be all right, and for the briefest of moments she closed her eyes, unable to resist.

Then she stiffened and pulled away, ashamed she had let it get that far. Though Jericho was someone she could easily develop feelings for in another life, she had to shut him down. "Jericho, this was a mistake. I'm here for Aiden." Even saying his name filled her with incredible guilt. She had to wonder if she was really attracted to Jericho, or if she was once again sabotaging a perfectly good romantic relationship.

Jericho's sad smile returned. The nurturing, caring part of her wanted to comfort him, but Aiden deserved her devotion. She turned away. He finished undressing behind her, shifted, and tore off into the jungle.

"Please, be careful," she whispered without looking back.

"You two lovebirds done?" Adam asked in a cold and cavalier way.

She couldn't imagine a more callous thing to say in the moment. "You can be a real asshole."

He held up his hands in surrender. "Jeesh. Touchy."

She shook her head as she marched past him.

After they made some distance from where Jericho had run, they squatted in the weeds and watched the snipers.

"What now?" she asked.

"We wait till he does his thing, I guess. This ain't rocket surgery."

"We shouldn't have let him do this."

"To get anywhere near that prison, we need a distraction. Jericho's giving us one."

"I know, but ..."

"We all knew we might die here. If you're not willing to risk your life, you'll hesitate. If you hesitate, this will not end well."

He was right, but that didn't make it any less painful. "Should we shift for the run?"

"Not yet. Not unless they see us." He eyed the snipers. "Let's leave the bags here and get ready to motor."

A beefy roar in the distance broke the dawn stillness. One of the snipers lifted binoculars to his eyes. He waved the others over, leaving three of the four corners unprotected.

"Now." Adam charged onto the field. Christine gave chase, her years of keeping up her cardio for the fire department paying dividends.

The sniper lowered his binoculars and braced the butt of his rifle against his shoulder. Christine followed his aim to see Jericho sniffing the ground and pretending to investigate something.

Okay. They see you. You've done your job. Now hide. But he didn't hide. She slowed in the middle of the field as Adam kept running. "What are you doing?" she whispered.

Jericho continued selling it, wandering aimlessly deeper into the field. The sniper steadied his aim.

Christine held her breath. She considered screaming to get their attention, but right at that moment Jericho lifted his head and looked directly at her. He might have smiled.

The sniper's rifle bounced, followed immediately by a devastating boom. She flinched.

Jericho recoiled and dropped into the tall grass.

Christine covered her mouth. Her stomach fell to her feet. "Jericho?" Her knees went weak and she couldn't move. As she watched for any hint that he was still alive, one of the snipers glanced her way and pointed her out to the others.

Adam had reached the cell building and plastered his back to the wall, ripping off his shoes. "Christine," he yelled. "What are you doing? Run."

His voice broke her trance. She shook away her horror and got moving again.

The snipers raced across the roof to line up a shot on her. One of them lifted his rifle. He had her dead to rights.

"Shift, Christine," Adam screamed, seconds before shifting himself. He scaled the side of the building.

She was too far away for shifting to do any good. The world slowed. She locked eyes with the sniper as his finger moved to the trigger. He took a deep breath.

Adam reached the roof, but he was too far away to get to the sniper in time. Just as she braced for the blast, something above the building caught her eye. The sniper lowered his weapon as if he sensed what she had seen. He spun around as a hideous winged creature swooped down from the sky and snatched him from the roof. It lifted him high into the air where more of the gargoyle-like creatures circled and dropped him screaming from the clouds.

Christine put on a burst of speed.

The other snipers panicked and ran for the roof ladder. As they fled, they unwittingly crossed Adam's path and he tore through them like they were made of paper.

Christine finally reached the building just as a warning siren erupted near the mansion. Adam leaned over the edge of the roof and got her attention. He pointed to a row of military-style barracks beyond the pole barn where armed men were pouring from nearly every door. The gargoyles dove for them. Gunfire erupted. A gargoyle took a blast to the chest and crashed to the ground. Others plowed into the men with reckless abandon, ripping and tearing at them.

A gargoyle swooped toward Adam's head.

"Look out," Christine screamed. Adam ducked away from the edge just in time. The gargoyle grabbed empty air. "Adam," she shouted.

After a few nervous seconds, he peeked over the edge of the roof and then took off for the opposite side.

Christine ran along the front of the cells, checking each one for Aiden. With each empty cell, she lost a little more hope. And then she reached the last one and her heart sank. She wanted to sit down and cry.

But there was something else festering deep in her gut besides overwhelming sadness. It was a hot, angry sensation that bubbled up into her chest trying to find an escape. She thought about Aiden and what they had likely done to him, and the sadness was swallowed by rage. No wergs should ever have to face such horrors. She gritted her teeth and surveyed the chaos with a new sense of purpose. She would destroy this place, even if it killed her.

She poked her head around the corner. Some sort of soldier stood at the other end. When he saw her, he shouted, "There's one," and lifted his rifle.

Christine yanked her head back as a hail of bullets blasted the concrete of the building. The gunfire ceased suddenly, replaced by a scream. She peeked around again. A gargoyle tore him to shreds before launching back into the sky.

As Christine crept along the side of the building, she saw a dozen more soldiers thundering across a small bridge to get to the mansion at the top of the hill. The gargoyles strafed their ranks, twisting and swerving as the soldiers opened fire. One took a headshot. Another took a shot to the gut. Both soldiers and gargoyles alike rained from the sky, but the soldiers were losing numbers faster. It was becoming a massacre. They fled back to the barracks to regroup.

Christine crept toward a discarded rifle near the back corner of the cell building, but two gargoyles landed close to it. One of them lifted the rifle and examined it before hurling it into the stream under the bridge.

Christine ducked behind the building as the creatures turned toward her. She held her breath, hoping they hadn't noticed. When they took off again, she sighed in relief and ran toward the mansion.

Once across the bridge, she started up a long run of stairs leading to the front door. A soldier crashed against the stairs beside her, close enough that his blood splattered her cheek. The sound of the impact alone was enough to make her gag. She wiped her face with her sleeve and kept going, watching the sky and ready to shift at a moment's notice.

The gunfire slowed near the barracks. She wondered if the soldiers had made it to cover or if they were dead. With a glance to her right, she saw Adam tearing through two fleeing soldiers near the pole barn while miraculously avoiding gargoyle attacks. When he saw her, he started for the mansion.

The front door swung open and a man stepped onto the porch with a rifle. He didn't see her right away, too focused on Adam closing in. He opened fire. Adam dove to the side as dirt and grass flew into the air around him.

Christine continued up the stairs, praying she got to the man before Adam took a bullet. She was nearly there when he spun toward her. She panicked.

But before he could squeeze the trigger, a gargoyle dove for his head.

"Look out, Murdock," one of the soldiers at the barracks shouted.

Murdock threw his weapon up defensively. The gargoyle knocked the gun away as it sailed past. He fell against the doorframe.

Christine's eyes shot to the rifle at the same moment as his. They both darted for it. She had him beat. But then he changed course and slammed into her instead, sending them both tumbling down the stairs to the first landing.

They both scurried to their feet, her back to the mansion and his to the bridge. She let her eyes go black and he returned the gesture. She glanced over her shoulder at the rifle a little higher up the stairs. She was getting ready to spring for it when he fumbled for his holster and drew a dart gun.

"Don't move," he shouted.

She froze.

Then he whipped the dart gun to the side, aiming for Adam as he stalked closer.

"Stop, Adam," Christine shouted. To be tranquilized now meant death. He snarled, but did as he was told.

"You've only got one dart," Christine said grimly.

"Yeah. Which one of you wants it?" His eyes flicked between Adam, Christine, and the sky. Most of the gargoyles had moved to the barracks, but there were plenty of stragglers like the one that had disarmed him. "Who the fuck are you?" he screamed.

"My name's Christine. I'm looking for—"

Murdock's face twisted. "Christine? As in Christine *Alt*?"

She lost her breath.

His mouth hung open for a second. "You managed to get all the way over here to save your boyfriend? Seriously?"

Oh my God. He knows Aiden. Her heart nearly jumped from her chest. She was about to ask where he was when another werg appeared on the bridge behind Murdock. One of his arms dangled limply with blood staining the fur from his shoulder down to his fingers.

Jericho. Christine sucked in a stuttering breath, unable to believe her eyes. *Keep him talking.* "Where's Aiden?"

Murdock smirked. "I'm afraid you're a few days too late to save your boyfriend. He was part of our last hunt."

His words choked her.

Jericho stepped off the bridge, silent as a lion.

"That doesn't mean he's dead," Christine insisted.

Murdock snorted. "Of course, it does. We're really good at what we do here."

Jericho stalked closer.

"He's dead and buried and ..." A light breeze stirred the air. His cocky smile died. His eyes widened and then blackened again.

Jericho pounced, effortlessly clearing the stairs to the landing.

Murdock spun, shifting in a flash. The two wergs collided and rolled down the stairs, kicking and slashing along the way. Even with one arm, Jericho was a force, landing on top of the other werg.

He struggled, but Jericho slashed his chest. When he bucked, Jericho repositioned and grabbed his throat.

Christine cried, "Don't kill him."

But to her horror, Jericho splayed Murdock's neck open and then stood and watched while his enemy quivered and gurgled on his own blood beneath him.

Jericho looked back over his wounded shoulder. Christine raced to him and threw her arms around him. "I was sure you were dead. Don't ever do anything that stupid again."

He grimaced.

She pulled back and examined his shoulder. A chunk of his collarbone and muscle were missing. She pinched the top of his hand. He didn't react. She'd seen enough injuries in her career to know how bad this one was. But there was no time to treat him now. They were too exposed. She scanned the area for threats and was stunned by what she saw.

Though the majority of the gargoyles appeared to be herding the remaining soldiers toward the jungle, a lone creature shot overhead toward the mansion. It didn't slow as it crashed through an upstairs window. Seconds later, it emerged with the captured baby hugged tight to its hips. It released a blood-curdling screech before launching into the sky and disappearing into the distance.

"We have to finish this," Christine said. She grabbed Jericho's hand on his good arm and led him up the stairs to where Adam waited at the open door. Together, they stepped into the foyer.

WEREHUNT, INC.

27

A staircase to the left led to the second floor. To the right was a stuffed seven-foot-tall werg. Seeing it turned Christine's stomach.

Adam tilted his head and gingerly stepped toward the display. He reached out and touched the stuffed werg's claw.

"Adam?" Christine whispered. "Do you know him?"

His teeth locked together. His chest rose and fell with rage. He sniffed the air and then sprinted past her for the stairs.

A soldier on the second floor tossed a flash grenade down the hardwood steps. As Adam passed, he scooped it up mid-bounce, hurled it back, and turned away before it exploded. He reached the top in three quick strides and disappeared around the corner. Growls and screams echoed back down the stairs.

By the time Christine and Jericho reached the upstairs hallway, two soldiers lay dead at Adam's feet. Christine approached cautiously and reached for his shoulder. He spun and snapped at her hand. She recoiled. "Adam, it's me."

A low, staccato growl rose from his gut as he backed against the wall.

"Was that your friend Curtis?"

He looked away.

She bowed her head. It was a horrible discovery, and her heart broke for him. She decided to give him some space while she and Jericho cleared the rooms. There were four doors down this hall. She pointed to the closest. While Adam stood off by himself, Jericho lowered his good shoulder and barreled through.

A young man inside huddled against the farthest wall with his arms shielding his face. "Please don't hurt me," he cried. He wore a pair of dark slacks and work boots, and his sweat-drenched white T-shirt clung to his skin.

Christine pushed into the room. "Who are you?"

"Please, don't hurt me. I'm a prisoner." He peeked over his arms and she noticed a partially healed black eye.

"What's your name?"

"Sammy," he answered, his voice quivering.

"Why are you in here, Sammy?"

"They shoved me in here when everything went to shit outside."

"If you're a prisoner, where're the guards?"

His finger trembled as he pointed to the doorway. "You just killed them."

"Get up." Christine reached for him. He flinched. She softened her tone. "I'm not gonna hurt you. Come with us. We'll get you out of here."

He reluctantly took her hand. "Who are you? What are you doing here?"

"We came to find my friend. He was brought here to be hunted. His name's Aiden." She turned for the door.

Sammy's next words stopped her cold. "I knew Aiden."

She whirled around. "What?"

"His cell was next to mine. He got here last week."

Oh my God. "Do you know where he is? Someone said he was killed in the last hunt. Is that true?"

Sammy looked away. "I'm really sorry, ma'am."

She almost broke down. Every confirmation of Aiden's death was harder to hear than the one before.

"What's your name?" he asked.

"Christine."

"*You're* Christine?"

Did everyone on this godforsaken island know who she was?

"He talked about you. He said he couldn't wait to get back home to see you."

His every word shattered another piece of her broken heart.

But she had no time to grieve now. The faint odor of smoke was drifting in from the hall. She swallowed hard and wiped tears from her eyes. Years of being a paramedic had taught her how to push aside the bad stuff long enough to do what needed to be done. "Jericho. Check it out."

Jericho bolted from the room, and she and Sammy followed.

Light smoke trickled from beneath the door at the end of the hall. Jericho bashed it open and stood in the doorway. Christine raced past him, her firefighter instincts kicking in. Flames danced above a metal wastebasket next to a wall of security monitors. An empty fire extinguisher lay near the open window. She grabbed a discarded soldier's shirt from the floor and wrapped it around her hands. She held her breath, grabbed the flaming wastebasket near the bottom, and held it away from her body. Moving as quickly as she could, she threw it out the window.

That's when she saw an unfamiliar werg running toward a waiting airplane on a runway in the distance.

"Adam," she shouted.

He ran in from the hallway and joined her at the window. She pointed. He snarled and leaped from the window.

"Go with him, Jericho. Help him stop that werg."

Jericho hesitated.

"I'll be fine. Just go."

He jumped down and joined the chase. Sammy waited in the doorway, looking bewildered.

Christine turned to the wall of monitors, each showing a video feed from a different area of the compound, including two that focused on the runway.

The wall adjacent to the computer screens was stacked from floor to ceiling with a system of drawers. Curious, Christine opened one with the letter K on the face. The drawer was full of external hard drives, each labeled and catalogued by what appeared to be last names.

She took one labeled Krause to a computer tower and plugged it into a USB port. A folder popped up on the computer screen. She double clicked it. A list of video files filled the screen.

"What'd you find?" Sammy asked as he moved to stand behind her.

"I don't know yet."

She chose a random file and clicked it. The screen changed to a video of a man bound to a metal chair in the center of a large room. His wide, terrified eyes danced around in their sockets. A man wearing a lab coat stepped beside him. The choppy, grainy video screamed snuff film.

Christine watched in stunned silence for a moment. "Do you know what we might have just found, Sammy?"

"No," he answered, coming even closer. "What?"

"These could be files of everyone this place has abducted and murdered." She looked at the drawers, stunned at the magnitude of how many there were. "They might have one on Aiden."

Just as she turned back to the video, someone else stepped into view beside the restrained man. The new arrival wore the same clothes as the soldiers she'd been fighting. When he turned toward the camera, Christine tilted her head curiously. "Wait a second. That guy looks just like you, Sa—"

A horrible pain erupted in her lower back. She reached around and felt Sammy's fist wrapped around the hilt of a knife. He pulled his hand away, leaving the blade lodged hilt-deep in her back. She lost her breath and stumbled against the computer tower. She turned to Sammy, her eyes wide with surprise.

He shrugged with a smirk. "Sorry about that, Christine."

"Why, Sammy?"

He chuckled. "My name's not Sammy. You're as gullible as your dead boyfriend was. He told me all about you, and all I had to do was feed him some bullshit about a fake daughter and my boo-hoo tough life."

The room started to spin. She wobbled away from the tower, needing to sit down and catch her breath. But she also knew sitting down meant giving up. She let the color drain from her sight.

Sammy shook his head. "Shift if you'd like. That won't impress me." His eyes turned black.

Christine curled her fingers around the hilt, held her breath, and ripped the blade free. The pain was excruciating. She swallowed, took a breath, and leaped, shifting in the air. The adrenaline rush of changing gave her an added burst of strength.

Sammy shifted almost as quickly as he retreated from her flailing claws. She caught both of his wrists and locked eyes with him. She held his cocky gaze as she stretched his arms outward and kangaroo-kicked him in the gut. He grunted. She dug her claws deep into his stomach and then ripped them free, splatting his innards on the hardwood floor. His cockiness turned to fear an instant before his eyes glazed over. She released his wrists and he dropped in a heap.

Then the pain in her back hit her again. She wobbled and grabbed the back of a desk chair for support. It gave way, tumbling over and throwing her hard to the floor. Her blood pooled around her and she suddenly felt cold. Wanting to see the last moments of her life with her human eyes, she shifted back.

Shivering and naked on the carpet, she watched the monitor with the airplane as the fleeing werg climbed inside and pulled the door closed.

When the pilot engaged the throttle, Adam and Jericho appeared at the bottom edge of the screen. They could only watch as the plane pulled away. She watched the plane speed down the runway toward freedom before it raced off the screen.

She looked for the monitor showing the other end of the runway at the edge of the jungle. The plane appeared on the screen traveling right to left. Another werg exploded onto the runway from the jungle, galloping toward the plane. The front tire lifted from the pavement. The werg leaped onto the left wing. The plane wobbled as it fought for altitude, barely missing the treetops. The door flew open and the unfamiliar werg Jericho and Adam had chased slammed into the werg on the wing. The plane dipped drunkenly to the left and clipped a tree. Locked in a violent struggle, the two wergs rolled over the edge and fell into the jungle.

The plane struck another treetop and cartwheeled into a fireball in the trees.

Christine smiled as she relaxed and pressed her cheek to the cold, hard floor. Her vision blurred. "Aiden," she whispered. She would recognize him anywhere.

WEREGATE

28

"Christine?" **a muffled** voice shouted. "Christine?" It sounded like Jericho.

A blanket draped over her and a firm hand pressed the wound on her back. "Hold on, Chris," Jericho said. "Adam, go find a first-aid kit. A place like this should have somethin'. Hurry."

She needed more than a first-aid kit. "Aiden," she whispered.

"No, Chris. It's me, Jericho."

She was trying to tell him that she had seen Aiden, but she was too weak to clarify.

"You're gonna be all right, Chris. We're gonna get you some help."

She chuckled at the absurdity of finding help on that hellish island and drifted off again.

When she next opened her eyes, she was wearing her spare clothes and was lying on pillows in the monitor room. An IV ran from her left arm to a bag hanging on a nail in the wall. She took a breath and a sharp pain in her lower back threatened to steal it away.

She tried to focus. Adam stood shirtless in human form, leaning against the door frame and picking at one of his nails. A bloody trail led into the hall from where Sammy's body had fallen. Jericho's back was to her as he scoured the hard drive drawers. His injured arm was in a sling. There was a third man who wore a white lab coat sitting in an office chair looking at the monitors.

Adam pulled away from the doorframe and walked across the room to Jericho. "So. What's the deal with you and Christine?"

"What do you mean?" Jericho asked without looking over.

"You kissed her, didn't you?"

"Yeah. What about it?"

"Well, what the hell did you think was gonna happen?"

"Just drop it."

"It seems kinda silly, is all. We're here to rescue her boyfriend. What did you think she was gonna do? Be so overwhelmed by your kiss that we'd just pack up and leave that other dude on the island?"

"I thought I was about to die, okay? I wanted to let her know how I felt. Can we just drop it?"

"Oh yeah. Heh. Great idea. Hey, Chris. I know you're about to find out your boyfriend is dead, but how 'bout I throw my hat in the ring right before I die too? Why lose one boyfriend when you can lose two?"

Jericho groaned. "I can't believe I'm takin' shrapnel from *you*."

"What's that supposed to mean?"

"The way you treat women. You're a dog."

"How do I treat women?"

Jericho side-eyed him. "You've got that poor girl Jess completely obsessed with you and you're out dogging around every weekend."

Adam opened his mouth to argue, but stopped short. After a moment, he said, "I like Jess. She's a good gal."

"Then why don't you respect her?"

"What do you mean? I do respect her."

"Then grow up and start treating her like it."

Adam scoffed, "You're just ... I mean ... Shut up, man." He glanced at Christine, smacked Jericho's shoulder, and pointed to her.

"Hey, Doc," Jericho shouted as he ran over.

The man sitting at the monitors looked over with a swollen, black eye.

Jericho knelt beside her. "Chris, how do you feel?"

"Dizzy," she whispered. "And tired." Her throat hurt to speak.

"The doc says you're gonna make it."

She grimaced. "Who?"

Jericho nodded at the man in the lab coat. "The doctor. He works here on the island. Adam found him and I convinced him to help."

Jericho's knuckles were red and swollen. He tucked his hand behind his leg when he realized she'd noticed. "He thinks the knife missed your kidney. After he stopped the bleeding, he gave you some fluids and stitched you up. We still need to get you to a hospital, though."

"It really hurts."

The doctor approached with a vial and syringe and pushed some meds into the IV tubing. Within seconds, a rush of euphoria unlike anything she'd ever felt washed through her. She grinned drunkenly. "What did you give me?"

"A small dose of Fentanyl." His voice sounded far away.

She licked her parched lips. When Jericho reached for a water bottle, he moved in slow motion.

"Hold up," the doctor said. "The IV will hydrate her over time. You can wet her lips, but don't let her drink it. It could make her vomit."

Jericho popped off the cap and dribbled water across her lips.

"How's the pain now?" the doctor asked.

"What pain?" She was numb and tingly. Her own voice sounded like an audio tape played at half-speed, and it made her giggle.

Jericho adjusted the pillows she was lying on. "Are you comfortable?"

She nodded. She was better than comfortable.

"Maybe a little lower dose next time, Doc," Jericho said.

The doctor nodded. "Just keep an eye on her breathing. If it gets too slow, we'll give her some Narcan."

Jericho sat quietly beside her while she enjoyed the intoxicating effects of the drug. She'd used the term loopy for patients in the past, but this was the first time she truly understood what it meant. It could have been two hours or two days before she felt alert enough to focus.

"How do you feel?" Jericho asked again.

The pain in her back was still there, but it was dull and a little numb. "Better."

He smiled. "I wanna show you somethin'. Do you feel up to it?"

She nodded weakly.

He went to the desk and adjusted the monitor so she could see. "These hard drives are amazing. They're full of congressmen and senators and businessmen doin' stuff you wouldn't believe. This place is a blackmailer's dream. But I've found one you'll especially appreciate."

He clicked play on a black-and-white video of what appeared to be a meeting room with a long conference table in the background. Bernard Henderson was on the screen. His hair was fuller and darker, and he appeared younger than when Christine had met him. Just seeing him turned her stomach. He was animated and talking to someone off screen.

Jericho turned up the volume.

"It's a bunch of bullshit. That's what this is."

"Keep it down," a man off screen answered in a thick Italian accent. "He'll be here any minute. I for one think it's a great idea."

Bernard gritted his teeth and breathed through his nose. "Stop primping, Pietro. No one gives a shit how you look." He paused and his eyes narrowed. "Wait a minute. You're not recording this, are you?"

Pietro snorted. The back of his head moved into view close to the camera. "Are you crazy? You know what would happen if I got caught recording our meetings?"

Bernard rubbed the back of his neck. "I guess. But I still can't believe this is happening. I'm just getting everything up and running."

"Let's just see what he has to say before you get all upset."

"I know what he's gonna say. He's gonna want money. This is a regular shakedown."

There was a sound like a creaking door, and Pietro and Bernard turned toward it. Pietro bowed. "Senator."

A younger Senator Wooten stepped into camera view. He flashed his now famous politician smile and greeted them by shaking their hands and grasping their forearms. An attractive woman accompanied him, and Christine recognized her as a younger Maxine from the Dog Park.

Christine glanced at Jericho. "This is nothing. I already knew Wooten is a werg and was paid off by the WereHouse."

Jericho shook his head, still grinning. "It's much deeper than that. Just watch."

Senator Wooten cleared his throat. "Let's get to business. I'm taking a stake in the WereHouse. I'd like to operate as a secret board member with overriding authority of the others. I will take twenty percent of proceeds from all entities. That's the WereHouse, WereHunt Inc., and the Dog Parks. I'm still going to allow you to run the companies how you see fit, but I will have a say in the overall operations."

Bernard shook his head. "I don't think so."

"Excuse me?"

"We can vote on it, but I can't promise anything."

Wooten glared at him. "There's no voting, Bernard. This is happening."

Bernard took a deep breath through a grimace. "With all due respect, sir, I started this business from nothing. I was the one who acquired all the funding. I was with the mercenaries in Sandalio risking my life for this opportunity. I even gave you the werg virus at your request. I've done everything you've asked of me."

"And it's all been greatly appreciated. What's that have to do with what we're talking about now?"

"I just thought we were square. This is my company, sir. I built it from scratch. We're getting ready to have an ad during the Super Bowl, for God's sake. It's about to blow up."

"Bernard, my friend. You're looking at this all wrong. I'm still letting you have complete control of the day-to-day operations. You'll still be rich beyond your wildest dreams. I'm just going to be more in the loop and helping with the major decisions from here on out."

"And why would I allow this?"

Pietro stood quietly off to the side, his eyes wide and jaw slightly slack.

"*Allow* this?" Wooten's face hardened. "Listen, Bernard. People pay a lot of money to have a senator running interference for their company, especially a company as much on the fringe as yours. Plus, I'm going to be president one day. How much is that worth to you? Remember, *Bernie*—"

Christine smirked. She knew how much Bernard hated to be called Bernie.

"—if I don't join, I'll be forced to suggest some policy changes at the WOC that'll run your business into the ground. And if that's not enough for you, some conversations with the right people will have you spending the rest of your life in prison. And I don't mean some cushy, country club resort prison. I mean federal, bust-your-cherry prison."

There was something about watching Bernard squirm that made Christine feel a little better. But as incriminating as the video was, Wooten could easily deny ever knowing how the werepets were created.

That, after all, was where the real crime was. "This is small potatoes. He'll get a slap on the wrist at most."

Jericho grinned and gestured to the monitor. "Just keep watchin'. It's not over yet."

Wooten paced with his hands clasped behind his back. "As for the sales number, I think we need to start thinking much larger."

Bernard rolled his eyes. "Of course, we do. But it's not easy getting lifers out of the penitentiaries without anyone asking where they've gone. We only have three wardens on our payroll in the entire country. Where else can we get people to make into pets?"

"You ever thought about using the homeless? No one will even miss them."

Bernard cocked his head. "That's actually a pretty good idea."

"Of course, it is, Bern. That's the kind of outside-the-box thinking you'll get with me on the board."

Christine's stomach twisted and bile rose up her throat. She knew Wooten was corrupt, but she never would have guessed he was as much of a monster as Bernard. What were the chances these two psychopaths would find each other?

Wooten let out a disconcerting chuckle. "Hell, maybe I'll make cleaning up the streets one of my campaign promises."

"Makes my skin wanna crawl right off my body," Jericho muttered. Christine agreed.

Wooten clapped his hands. "So, it's settled?"

Pietro nodded. Bernard scowled.

Wooten turned to leave, but Pietro stopped him. "Sir?"

He rolled his eyes. "What is it now?"

"One other matter."

"I'm listening."

"About the problem I mentioned when I talked to you on the phone?"

"Refresh my memory."

"You know that Saudi official who participated in our last hunt? He's demanding a hundred werepets or he's going to expose the Island."

"Oh yeah. I'll take care of it now that I'm a part of the company. Send his name to my secure email. We might just have to have a little drone party for him. As long as his name sounds terroristy enough, I don't think it'll be a problem."

Christine mentally added overt racism to Wooten's list of depravities. How could the American people vote for such an all-around terrible person?

Once Wooten and Maxine were gone, Bernard kicked over a chair. "This is bullshit."

Pietro bobbed his hands timidly. "Calm down. It's not that bad."

"Not that bad? Are you shitting me? This is my business. He just took twenty percent. I'm just getting it off the ground. We should have gotten rid of him right when he found out what we were doing."

Pietro looked like he nearly shit himself. "*Bernard.* Don't say that," he whispered. "He's a senator, for God's sake."

"Senators have been known to have accidents, too."

"Stop it. That's enough. I want nothing more to do with talk like that. Just give him a chance. He might be good for the company. Keep the heat off."

Bernard rubbed his face. "We'll have to raise our fucking premiums."

"See, now you're thinking. We have no competition. We can charge whatever we want."

The video cut off and switched to a recording of an old breaking news story about a Saudi millionaire targeted by a US military drone. Groggy from the pain meds or not, Christine fully understood what the video meant.

Jericho closed the video window and grinned at her again. "Well? What'd I tell you? There's so much more here, too. I've barely scratched the surface. It's unbelievable. Hell, there's an entire drawer just labeled Wooten."

"We need to take that hard drive with us." She tried to sit up, but winced and fell back on the pillows.

"You need to rest," he said.

She shook her head. "There's no time. We have to find Aiden."

"Aiden? What do you mean?"

"I saw him. He's alive. He's the one who took down the plane."

Jericho balked. "Impossible."

"It was him. Trust me."

"Well, you can't go anywhere right now."

Adam cleared his throat and waved Jericho over to the doorway. They had a quiet but heated conversation.

Jericho returned to Christine's side. "I wanted to give you time to rest, but the boat won't wait forever. And if you say Aiden's out there, we need to get movin' if we wanna find him in time." He turned to the doctor. "What do we need to do so she can travel?"

"Right now?" the doctor asked.

"Yeah."

"She could rip her stitches if she does too much."

"And what happens then?"

"She could bleed. And have a lot of pain."

"We'll try to keep her from straining. And you can give her somethin' for pain."

The doctor squinted. "It could get infected."

"We'll get her antibiotics on the mainland. Anything else?"

"She'll fatigue quickly and—"

"I'll carry her if I have to."

He shrugged. "I don't know then. Give it a try, I guess."

Jericho filled a duffel bag with hard drives, including the Wooten one. "Do you think you can walk?" he asked her.

She reluctantly nodded.

The doctor knelt beside her. "Your IV bag's getting low. I think we can do away with it." He pulled the catheter from her vein, tossed it aside, and covered her arm with a folded gauze pad. She bent her elbow, pinching the pad tight over the trickle of blood.

Jericho helped her up and wrapped his good arm around her. She tried not to show how much pain she was in, but couldn't hold back a grimace. They joined Adam and the doctor in the hall where Sammy's body lay. Adam also held a full duffel bag.

"What else is in there?" she asked. It was a lot fuller than when it had just held clothes.

He smiled and partially unzipped it. A dart gun sat on top of a first-aid kit.

Christine was winded just going down the stairs, forcing Jericho to practically carry her with his one working arm. Adam poked his head out the front door and then gave them the all-clear.

They stood on the front stoop, overlooking a battlefield of dead gargoyles and soldiers. When

Christine looked past the cells to the field leading to the jungle, Jericho asked, "Are you up for this?"

She struggled to take in a deep breath. "I'll have to be."

They started down the stairs with the doctor in tow.

TOO FAR GONE

29

Christine had broken into a cold sweat and was struggling by the time they reached the jungle. Jericho made her take a break. Though she didn't want to stop, he was right. She rested against a crooked tree while the doctor took her pulse and evaluated her pupils.

Adam explored ahead and returned after a few minutes. "The plane's still smoldering. I can smell it. It's not far."

Jericho dabbed Christine's clammy forehead with a dressing from the first-aid kit. "You okay to keep goin'?"

She nodded and pushed herself away from the tree. Again, Jericho supported her weight as they walked. Adam led the way.

Eventually, they reached a piece of an airplane wing surrounded by broken tree branches. A little farther along, they found a debris field of metal and charred wreckage, some of which still smoldered.

While Christine rested again, Adam checked the plane's obliterated passenger compartment. "Pilot's dead. I don't see anyone else." He climbed down and dusted off his hands. Then he sniffed the air. "Hey. Do you guys smell tha—"

A werg exploded from behind the wreckage, swatting Adam hard into a tree. The werg turned toward Jericho.

Christine's heart squeezed painfully. "Aiden?"

He spun toward her voice, demonic eyes blazing. Blood-tinged drool dripped from his mouth.

"It's me. Christine. You're okay now. I'm here."

Aiden bared his teeth at her.

Jericho stepped between them. "Are you sure it's him?"

"Yes," Christine cried.

"Then you'd better get back. He's lost his mind." Jericho slowly removed his sling and shirt.

Aiden lowered his head between his shoulders, ready to pounce. His eyes were full of rage.

Christine grabbed Jericho's good arm. "No. Don't hurt him."

Aiden growled.

"Him?" Jericho snapped back. "It's not him I'm worried about." He slipped off his shoes, eyes still fixed on Aiden. "Back up, Christine. He's gone mad."

Aiden rose to his full height and released a weak, gurgling roar.

"What have they done to you?" she moaned.

His ears perked as if something might have gotten through to him. Then that sliver of clarity just as quickly vanished.

"Take it easy, friend," Jericho said.

Aiden charged.

Jericho shoved Christine back as he shifted and met Aiden with teeth and claws. The two wergs hit the ground, slashing and snapping at each other.

"*Stop*," Christine pleaded. She'd have better luck stopping an avalanche.

Aiden clamped down on Jericho's already damaged shoulder and Jericho yowled. In a panic, he slashed Aiden's face, but Aiden's rage was unbreakable.

The only way Christine could help was as a werg. She let the color drain from her sight, despite knowing the change would rip out her stitches. But before she could shift, a dart punched Aiden in the neck. He yelped and disengaged. His wide, terrified eyes flicked between Jericho and Adam, who stood near the wreckage reloading the tranquilizer gun.

Christine held out her hand. "Aiden? Wait. Don't run."

He turned and fled.

Adam ran to Jericho and helped him to his feet.

"We've gotta find him," Christine shouted.

"We will," Adam said. "He won't get far." He helped Jericho to the first-aid kit and shoved a new bandage over his shoulder. "Where's the doctor?"

Everyone looked around, but there was no sign of him.

Jericho leaned on a tree, shifted back to human form, and slowly redressed. He shoved his limp arm back in the sling with a groan.

Adam shook his head. "That shoulder's taken quite the beating, huh?"

Jericho grunted. Christine pulled the dressing away for a peek. If his shoulder hadn't been completely wrecked before, it was now. "You need a hospital."

"That makes both of us."

Adam casually walked by. "Not me," he gloated.

She gave him a disgusted look and turned back to Jericho. "I'm so sorry."

He shook his head. "You know, I'm not gettin' the best first impression of your friend? How bad would it be if he fell off the boat on the way back?"

She didn't know whether to laugh or cry. "I need to go find Aiden."

"You need to rest," Adam insisted. "You look like hell."

"There's no time. He can't shift back to burn off the drug if he's got a chip, and it might be too high a dosage." Though she was weak and tired, she grabbed the first-aid kit and then sniffed out Aiden's trail.

"Be careful, Christine," Adam called. "We'll be right behind you."

She found Aiden lying unconscious in the weeds not far away. She cradled his head on her lap and wriggled out the dart. "I'm here, Aiden," she whispered. His eyelids fluttered.

Like a good medic, she assessed his many injuries, from his swollen forearm to his crusty and burnt fur and the festering wound on his side. He had two more injuries around his chest that looked like bullet wounds. While looking for exit wounds, she found a scabbed-over brand on his lower back that said PREY. She shuddered. A red tag pierced one of his ears and she pried it off. *How dare those bastards?*

She found staples covering an incision on his neck, retrieved forceps from the first-aid kit, and pulled them out. The laceration held together, and for once she cursed the fact that wergs healed faster than regular people.

"I'm so sorry I have to do this." She grabbed a scalpel and went to work reopening the wound. Meticulous in every move, she mimicked Aiden's technique until she held the bloody chip. Then she pinched the wound together with one hand and fumbled for a syringe of Narcan.

After injecting it into Aiden's arm, she waited. His breathing was so deep that he snored. She looked up to find Adam watching from not far away.

"Did you get it?" he asked.

She nodded. "Where's Jericho?"

"He's coming."

"Is he okay?"

Adam walked over. "His shoulder's pretty fucked. Other than that, he'll be right as snow."

Aiden's snoring settled into deep breaths, telling her the Narcan was starting to work.

"Come on, Aiden," she whispered. "Shift for me. Please."

As if he heard her, the fur around his snout sucked into his pores. His head jerked slightly. She continued whispering encouragement as his bones popped and snapped. While waiting for his transformation to finish, she stretched butterfly strips across the incision site on his neck. As his greyish-pale werg skin pinked, she noticed the charred side of his body was red with blisters and welts. She cradled his head on her lap and waited.

His eyes blasted open, fear and confusion swirling in them. He tried to push her away, but she held him tight. "It's okay, Aiden." Tears blurred her vision.

The black ink returned to the whites of his eyes and his upper lip curled. A low growl rose in his throat.

"Aiden? It's me. Chris. You're safe now." She caressed his cheek.

Then, as if all the tension had instantly lifted from him, Aiden's shoulders relaxed, and he sighed deeply. "Chris?" His voice was scratchy and weak.

She bobbed her head.

He winced, rolled to his side, and pulled his knees to his chest. "Everything hurts," he gasped.

"I know." As she held him, her eyes drifted to where Jericho now stood. He looked away.

Adam tossed Christine the duffel bag of clothes and she helped Aiden put on a pair of sweatpants.

"Why do I feel like I've been in a war?" he asked.

"You've been through a lot. We're going to get you to a hospital."

"How did you even find me?"

Christine let out a half-laugh, half-sob. "It's a long story. But you're safe now. We just need to get to the boat." She still couldn't believe he was here. Alive. With her.

He tried to stand, but pain sat him back down. Adam hurried over and ducked under his arm. "Let me help you, pal." He lifted him to his feet, and Aiden doubled over with a groan. "Take it easy, big fella. I gotcha."

"Who are you?" Aiden asked.

"I'm Adam. I'm pretty much the entire reason you've been rescued."

Jericho led the way while Adam practically carried Aiden. Christine struggled to bring up the rear. It took them three times as long to get back to the shore, but they made it just as the boat captain was getting ready to pull away.

Christine held Aiden's head on her lap as he slept at the back of the boat. She was unable to take her eyes off him, overwhelmed with emotion. She caressed his cheek. "I missed you, Aiden," she whispered. And it was at that moment, looking at him so vulnerable and innocent, that she realized she never wanted to be without him again. Over the last year, he was the one who had been there whenever she'd had a nightmare about the WereHouse. He was the one who had comforted her every time her dad had let her down. And he was the one who was worth fighting every subconscious urge she had to sabotage what they were building.

She lifted her eyes to Jericho, standing at the boat rail and looking out over the water. She needed to talk to him.

Adam sat down next to her. "Is he gonna be all right?"

"He needs a hospital."

"We'll be on the mainland soon."

"Will you do me a favor and sit with him for a minute?"

Adam shrugged. "I guess. I'm not gonna hold his head on my lap and pat his cheek, though."

"Whatever."

He stuffed a wadded-up towel under Aiden's head as Christine slipped away.

She stepped beside Jericho. "Hey," she said, unsure of what her follow-up would be.

"Hey."

She landed on, "Can we talk?"

He nodded.

She started to say something, but he blurted out, "Before you say anything, I know I was wrong to kiss you. That wasn't fair."

She shook her head. "Don't say that. It was crazy back there."

"Just the same, I shouldn't have put you in that position. I don't know what came over me."

"Please, don't apologize. I'd be lying if I said I didn't have some of the same feelings. Even though I just met you, you already mean the world to me. And if I lived a thousand more years, I could never express how thankful I am for who you are and what you've done."

He lowered his head. "What kind of man would I be if I didn't help you?"

She touched his chin and guided his head back up so she could look into his eyes. "I care about you, Jericho. I really do." He shifted uncomfortably and tried to look away, but she followed him. "Listen to me. If this was another life and I wasn't with Aiden, it might have been different. But it's not."

"I can't help how I feel about you, Chris."

She couldn't help how she felt about him either. She took his hand and gave it a comforting squeeze, wishing he wouldn't make it so hard for her. "I know I'm making it sound like this is easy, but trust me, it's far from it. There's a part of me that wants to grab you and never let go. But as much as I've grown to care about you in this short time, I really care about Aiden, too. In fact, I … I love him." She paused, surprised she'd actually said the "L" word about a man.

Jericho bowed his head again. "I understand."

She leaned in and kissed his cheek. Then she left him to go sit with Aiden. He turned his back to her and watched the water.

TWENTY-
TWOS

30

Christine reclined in her hospital bed, listlessly watching Costa Rican television and trying not to go insane. The mystery doctor on Sandalio had done a decent job stitching her up, but she still had to stay a few days for observation. She ached to be at Aiden's side in the ICU. She hadn't seen much of Adam, her only source of information, but at least he'd managed to get her a private room. She hadn't seen Jericho at all and she was dying for news.

As if they'd heard her thoughts, Adam knocked on the door and he and Jericho came in. He sat in the only chair and set a duffel bag at his feet.

Jericho stood near the foot of the bed, dressed in street clothes with his arm in a new sling. "Hi, Chris."

She smiled. "Discharged already? How's the arm?"

"Doc says I need to see a specialist, but …" He shook his head.

Her heart broke for him and a heavy weight settled on her as she realized he'd likely sacrificed his dream to help her save Aiden.

Adam leaned in close. "We need to make a plan for the hard drives," he whispered. "I'm a nervous wreck hauling them around with me."

"What should we do?" she asked.

"Jericho and I were talking about that. I think we should upload those bastards right to the Internet."

Christine sat a little straighter. "That sounds like a great idea. Can you do that from the hotel?"

"Yes and no. It looks like you're going to be in here for a few days, and Aiden's gonna be stuck here even longer."

"And?"

"If we upload them here in Costa Rica, Wooten might be able to trace the IP address straight to us. I don't like our chances if that happens."

"Good point. So, what are you thinking?"

"We bought some equipment and made copies of the drives." He tapped the duffel bag with his foot. "We thought we could leave the originals with you and then fly back to the states and upload the videos there, and then use the plane to get the hell out."

"How would *we* get back, then?"

"Commercial. Your passports should hold up fine. I'll leave you twenty grand. Use it to put a down payment on your hospital bills and buy two tickets back to Columbus. By then, the heat should be all over Wooten."

"I don't know. What if they're already looking for you?"

"They probably don't even know who we are. I'll have the videos all over YouTube before they even know what hit 'em." He winked. "Besides, we can take care of ourselves."

Christine couldn't think of any better ideas. "Don't stay in any one place for too long until Wooten is in cuffs."

"Of course not. Don't worry about me." He stood up. "We'll fly out tonight. When this is all over, I'll find you."

"Be careful."

Jericho cleared his throat, opened his mouth, shut it, and sighed through his nose. "Good luck, Chris," he said gruffly.

"Jericho?" She stretched a hand toward him.

He silently followed Adam out of the room.

Nearly a week later, Aiden was finally cleared to travel and they caught a flight back to the States. The first sign that something wasn't right was the lack of any major news coverage on any of the channels. She rented a locker under her fake name at Columbus International Airport and stuffed the duffel bag of hard drives into it. Her next priority was finding a payphone to call Willie. If anyone had heard anything, it would be him. He was a bit of a news junkie.

But instead of Willie, a stranger answered.

"Who's this?" Christine asked.

"My name's Sergeant Collins with CPD."

"Sergeant, I'm a firefighter. Where's the guy who owns this phone?"

His pause weighed a million tons. "I'm afraid there's been an accident."

"What kind of accident?"

"There was a fire earlier today and the roof collapsed. Willie ..."

"Willie what? What happened?"

She could almost hear the struggle in his voice when he said, "Maybe you should just head down to your station. They'll be able to give you more information there. I really can't say anything else over the phone." He didn't have to. She dropped the receiver.

Aiden rushed over from the airport chairs where he had been sitting and keeping watch. "What's wrong?"

She couldn't speak. All she could do was picture Willie's family getting the news that every firefighter family dreaded and suddenly needed to vomit. She raced to a trash can and dry-heaved into it.

Aiden rubbed her back. "What happened, Chris? Talk to me."

"It's ... It's Willie. There was a fire."

"Oh no." He pulled her close.

"We have to go. I need to be with my crew. They're my family."

Aiden led her outside and hailed a cab. The ride to Twenty-twos seemed to take forever.

Christine was out of the taxi before it had even pulled to a stop in the parking lot. She sprinted through the back door, a lead weight sitting in her stomach.

The front bay doors were open, and all the trucks were in quarters as if it was just another firehouse afternoon. She smelled hamburger grease from the kitchen and ripped open the door.

Mick, Junior, Dave, Jed, and Alex looked up from the two tables. They were eating Willie's famous double-thick hamburgers for dinner.

"Hey, Chris," Alex said. "You're back? Where have you been?"

Christine stood stunned in the doorway. "Wh-where's Willie?"

The door to the attached TV room swung open and Willie strolled in. "Hey, homeslice. Where ya been?"

"What? I ... Willie?" She felt faint.

Alex helped her to a chair. "Chris, what's wrong?"

"Why would ...?"

"Why would what?" he asked.

"Willie, I called your phone."

Willie's face brightened. "You talked to someone?"

"Yeah. He said you—"

"Did you tell that sonovabitch to bring it back? Whoever it was stole the damn thing right outta my center console at the gas station yesterday. I've been calling it all day. Someone took Lieu's phone this morning, too. Crazy. Can't have nuttin' anymore."

Christine scanned the room in a daze as everyone stared back in confusion.

"Get her something to drink, Willie," Alex said.

Willie went to the cabinet for a glass.

"What's going on, Chris?" Alex asked.

"I ... I don't know."

"Did you see your dad?"

She shook her head.

"He was just here. He checks in every evening to see if you're back. He's worried sick."

Yeah, right.

Aiden stepped in from the bay and stopped short. "Willie?"

Willie nodded. "That's me, cornbread."

Christine tried to put the pieces together. If Willie was fine, who had his phone? And then the answer hit her like a freight train.

"What's going on, Chris?" Mick asked. "Does it have anything to do with that guy who called us out on a bogus call the other day?"

"What guy?"

"He didn't say his name. Had a bad arm in a sling."

"Oh God. What'd he say?"

"He asked us to give you a note." He looked around. "Hey, Willie. Where's that note for Chris from that guy?"

"It's hangin' in the food pantry."

Christine rushed over. An envelope with her name on it was taped to the inside of the door where they put all the joke memes about firefighters assigned to the station. She tore it open.

Christine. If you're reading this, get out of there. Wooten knows. He ambushed us after we landed in Tennessee. They got Adam and the hard drives. I barely escaped. I don't know where they're holding him. You need to hide. I'll find you. Jericho

The letter dangled from her limp hand. "Aiden. They know."

"Know what?" Willie asked.

Christine didn't answer.

Aiden pushed the door open and scanned the bay.

"Chris? Are you okay?" Alex asked as he steadied her. "You'd better sit back down."

Willie extended the glass of water.

She swatted it away. "It's a trap. I've put you all in danger."

"What are you talking about?" Alex patted her hand. "Tell us what's going on."

She pulled away. "I'm sorry. I have to go."

Aiden bolted into the bay, and she followed. She wadded up the note and tossed it into the trash on the way. They plowed through the back door.

A black van was already stopped by the firefighters' vehicles and a man was climbing out. He started across the lot. "Christine Alt?" he shouted. Another man stepped from the back of the van and stood at the rear bumper. He held a tranquilizer rifle.

Christine shook her head and backed away.

The man coming toward her stopped. "My name's Agent Byrne with the Federal Bureau of Werg Registration and Welfare. You need to come with us."

The man at the back of the van lifted the rifle to his shoulder.

Christine kept backing away. If she went with them, she was done.

Aiden ripped open the station door behind her. "Come on, Chris."

Agent Byrne threw up his hand. "Now, Rick," he shouted.

The other agent fired. A dart slammed into Christine's shoulder. Agent Byrne charged. But before he got farther than a few feet, he froze and looked back at Rick.

Steven came at Rick out of nowhere, shifting as he ran. Rick dropped his empty dart gun and reached for a pistol. Steven shredded him with his claws before he could get off a shot. Then he turned to Agent Byrne, who stood exposed in the center of the lot. Rick collapsed in a heap behind him.

Aiden grabbed Christine and shouted, "Come on, Chris."

She pulled away as Steven charged Byrne. "*No*," she screamed.

Byrne drew a 9MM. Steven pounced. Three gunshots sent three jolts through Christine's soul.

Steven slashed Byrne's throat and then rose to his feet. His eyes met Christine's and she could see the fear in them. He lifted a hand to his chest where blood leaked from three bullet holes.

"Steven," she whispered.

He dropped to all fours, turned, and fled into someone's back yard behind the lot. Another van stopped on the road and the side door slid open.

Aiden ripped the dart from Christine's shoulder. "We gotta go, Chris."

She wobbled, suddenly groggy. He pulled her into the station, locked the door, and hit the buttons on the wall to close the front bay doors.

"What's going on?" Mick asked, coming up beside the fire engine.

Christine slumped into Aiden's arms.

"Narcan, Mick," Aiden barked. "Lots of it."

The other firefighters poured from the kitchen as Aiden lowered her to the floor. Mick grabbed the kits off the medic. As the world faded, two figures ran past the bay door windows.

Aiden took off his shirt. "Help her and tell her to run. I'll find her."

"Don't go," Christine whispered. Her eyelids fell heavily. Then her lights went out.

When she opened her eyes, the entire fire crew surrounded her. An IV ran into her arm and nearly a dozen empty Narcan boxes lay scattered around.

"Someone's breaking in the front door, Chris," Alex shouted.

Christine sat up and yanked the IV from her arm. "Where's Aiden?"

"He turned into a werewolf, went out front, and fought with whoever's out there. I don't know where he went after."

"Okay. Get down to the basement until this is over." They hesitated. "Do it now," she screamed. They reluctantly did as she said.

She got to her feet, ripped her shirt open, and shifted with a roar.

Two hissing canisters slid across the bay floor in front of the ladder truck. Agents wearing gas masks followed. As the bay filled with sleeping gas, she plowed through the back door, catching two agents off guard. They barely had time to react before she swatted them hard against the station's brick wall.

She tore off past the firefighters' cars and toward the back yard where Steven had fled. She quickly found his scent and tracked him to where he lay face-down in the grass next to a swing set. She dropped beside him and rolled him over. His chest sizzled. She shoved her hand over the holes, but blood oozed between her fingers. She ran her hand along his back in search of exit wounds and only found one.

As Steven lay dying, his snout drew back into his face and the fur sucked into his pores. Her eyes locked on his. It might have been the first time since she was a child that she didn't see an alcoholic staring back.

"I'm sorry, Chris," he whispered, and then coughed with a wince. Blood leaked past the corners of lips so swollen they looked like he'd been stung by bees. Red welts covered his neck and chest. Her thoughts went to the Epinephrine in the medic truck, and she started to stand, but he pulled her back down.

"Don't go. It's ..." He strained to get each word out. "... too late ... to do anything ... for me."

A look at his wounds told her he was right, but she still tried to object.

He shook his head. "Stay ... with me." He tried to swallow and twisted his face in pain.

No, no, no, she silently pleaded. She cradled his head in her lap.

He winced again, almost forgetting to breathe. "I wanna ... see your face ... one more time."

She nodded, tears filling her eyes as the color returned to the world.

He smiled despite another coughing fit. His teeth chattered from the cold, and she realized hers were chattering too, but she didn't care.

"I really am sorry, Chris. You deserved ..." He squeezed his eyes closed as he was racked with pain.

"Don't say anything else."

He lifted his hand toward her face, and she leaned into his icy touch. "Please, don't go, Dad." Tears streaked her cheeks.

He grimaced. His muscles tightened and he gurgled the same devastating death rattle she had heard from patients many times in her career. His grip weakened before his hand went limp in hers. She never wanted to let go.

"Please," she sobbed. She watched his life leave him through wet eyes. "It's not fair." She lowered Steven's hand to his chest, pressed her forehead to his cheek, and sobbed.

"Don't move."

The unfamiliar voice sent a spike of fear into her belly. She smelled gunpowder and multiple people approaching from behind. She stood up, too tired to fight anymore. Her eyes locked on her father, knowing it would be the last time she'd ever see him.

Agents flanked her. "Don't do anything stupid," one of them shouted. "Hands up."

She lifted her hands.

An agent rushed over and clamped a razor collar around her neck. Another one handed her a set of hospital scrubs and allowed her a moment to dress. The neck opening was just wide enough to slip over the collar.

The agent who appeared to be in charge spoke into a walkie-talkie. "We've got the package." Then he zip-tied her hands in front of her.

They marched her around the house toward where another black van had pulled up. She left part of her heart behind.

Police sirens approached from all directions. The van's side door slid open, and a man jumped out. "What did you tell your firefighter friends about the president-elect?" he shouted.

"Nothing."

"Are you sure?"

"Yes."

He took a deep breath. "We can't take any chances." He held a walkie to his mouth. "Blow it."

Her eyes filled with panic. "What?" She spun back toward where the fire station sat beyond the neighborhood houses.

A fireball rose above the rooftops and kissed the sky, followed by an ear-shattering, devastating boom. Her stomach dropped to her feet. "Noooo," she cried.

She lunged forward, but the agents caught her and shoved her into the van. Before she could right herself, they closed the door and banged three times on the side. The van lurched forward. She jerked the latch, but it was locked. She screamed at the top of her lungs.

Then she caught Aiden's scent and whipped her head around. He sat against the back door in a pair of fire department uniform pants with a blanket over his shoulders. He also wore a razor collar.

She scurried to him and threw her bound hands over his head, squeezing him tight. His hands were secured behind his back.

"I couldn't get away," he sighed. "There were too many of them."

She pulled back, openly sobbing. "They blew up the firehouse. All my friends ..."

"Oh, Chris. I'm sorry."

"They killed my dad, too. I couldn't help him." She leaned on his chest, and he rested his cheek on her head. She was a wreck, overwhelmed with worry for Willie, Mick, Alex, and the others, on top of being unimaginably sad over losing Steven before they could reconcile in any meaningful way. If anyone had told her yesterday that his death would hurt so deeply, she'd have laughed in their face and called them a liar. It felt like an elephant sitting on her chest. Even getting stabbed was nothing compared to this kind of pain.

She couldn't stop the memories from flooding back. As they played out in unorganized, fragmented clips, one particular memory kept coming to the surface. When she was a little girl and Steven hadn't yet left for the military, he had taken her and her mom to the zoo on a beautiful afternoon. As the day passed, her little legs grew tired, and Steven carried her on his shoulders for the rest of the afternoon. His shirt was drenched in sweat by the time they returned to the car, but he never complained.

At bedtime that same night, she had pretended to be asleep when Steven arrived to tuck her in. He still read her an entire story and kissed he forehead before he left.

Regret flooded in as she realized how long it had been since she'd told him she loved him. Even when he was dying in her arms, she hadn't thought to say it. What kind of person was she? Her heart broke a thousand more times as the van carried her and Aiden to certain death.

"I'm so sorry, Chris," Aiden said again. He sat with her quietly as her tears flowed.

"I loved him," she whispered.

"I know you did. And *he* knew it, too."

She desperately wanted to believe him.

"I love you, Chris," he whispered.

It was the first time he'd said it to her, and it brought her the tiniest bit of comfort.

The van pulled to a stop and the side door slid open. The first thing she saw was the fountain outside Wooten's residence.

Two Secret Service agents stepped into view. "Let's go, sweethearts. The boss is waiting."

BIG
FISH

31

The agents led Aiden and Christine into Wooten's house and up the stairs to his loft. She had never expected to step into that room again. Aiden moved slowly, his injuries from Sandalio not yet completely healed. He put on a tough exterior, but she could tell he was hurting.

Wooten sat at the bar with his back to them. Without looking, he said, "Christine. Aiden. How good of you to join me."

"Not like we had much choice," she answered. She noticed something sitting beside his barstool and her legs nearly gave out. Adam's open duffel bag spilled over with hard drives.

Wooten turned around and smirked at her. "Surprised, Chris?" He picked up the bag and gave it to one of his men. "Destroy these."

"Right away, sir." The man carried it down the stairs, leaving two agents in the loft.

Wooten turned back to the bar and pointed a remote at the only security monitor that wasn't on in the row of six monitors above the alcohol rack. The others showed different views of the property. When the sixth one warmed up, it revealed a grainy, black-and-white image of a man sitting on a bench seat in a cell. She couldn't make out who it was at first, but when he lifted his head, she saw it was Adam.

Wooten's smirk broadened. "I can't believe you were really going to tattle on me, Chris. And after everything we've been through."

Christine's head dropped forward. "How'd you find him?"

"It was quite simple, actually. It didn't take long to get information about Slater's plane after we took control of his farm. All we had to do was wait until it showed up somewhere. We caught up to young Adam there at a small airport in Tennessee. We expected to find you with him and were quite surprised that we didn't. We had a little … altercation. And his friend got away." He studied her briefly. "Who was with him, by the way?"

If he thought she would give up Jericho, he was crazier than she imagined. She shrugged.

"That's how I thought you'd react." He took a deep breath and sighed. "So, no use keeping secrets now. Where have you been hiding for the last week? We've been looking everywhere."

"Why didn't you ask Adam?"

"Oh, believe me, we did. But he's not an easy one to crack. He can take a helluva beating. He even had us wasting our time searching in Mexico." He shook his head. "I don't like him much."

"We were in a hospital in Costa Rica."

Wooten snapped his fingers. "Ahh. Of course. Why didn't I think of that? You're okay, though?"

"As if you care."

"Well, you got me there. I wanted to kill that sonuvabitch, but those hard drives …" He shook his head and his lip curled slightly. "That damn Pietro. I could kill him for recording that shit."

"I think I might've already taken care of that for you," Aiden said.

"That's what I hear. But about those hard drives—"

"You have them," Christine cut in. "You just had them destroyed. Remember?"

"Those? No, no, no. We both know those weren't the only set. You must have made copies, and I want them."

"There're no copies."

"Riiight." He turned his attention to Aiden. "You look like shit, pal."

Aiden scowled back.

Wooten shook his head. "I don't know how you survived Sandalio. You know you killed a congressman, don't you?"

"I don't give a shit. I hope he was your friend."

"Eh. He was a suckass. But he defended me like a pit bull in the media, and that's important in politics." He flicked a hand at the couch. "You can wait over there. You'll get your chance to talk in a minute." He tapped the barstool next to his. "Chris, why don't you come over and have a seat?"

One of the Secret Service agents nudged her from behind while the other one escorted Aiden to the couch.

Wooten took a sip of whiskey. He smiled and set his glass on the bar. He pursed his lips and shook his head again. "You sure are something else, Chris. I must admit, I'm impressed you made it this far."

"It wasn't far enough." She glared icicles at him.

He held up his glass. "Drink?"

Anything to buy herself some time to figure out what to do. "From an unopened bottle."

He gave her a sly smile and retrieved one from behind the bar. "Vodka okay?"

She nodded.

He set the bottle and a glass in front of her. "Ice?"

She shook her head, poured a drink, and sat down. "I never wanted to be a part of any of this. I just wanted to live my life."

"I understand. But let's be honest here. You and Aiden have been interfering ever since we made our deal. It was only a matter of time before our paths crossed again."

"We were just trying to help wergs. We didn't know you were behind everything."

"I believe you. Really, I do. I guess things got a little out of hand. The cleanup's always the messiest part."

"You're going to kill us, aren't you?"

He sighed, poured another shot, and took another swig. "What other choice do I have? I mean, Christ, Christine. You were going to upload all my darkest secrets to the Internet, for God's sake."

Christine took a gulp from her glass, followed by an unavoidable wince. She could use about ten more gulps. "You took Aiden to that island. What was I—"

"Wait a minute. That wasn't me. I had no idea Pietro was even looking for him. And as for you, I didn't even know you were involved until I heard about the mess you made at the Dog Park. You gave Maxine quite the scare." He shook his head. "I was disappointed she spilled her guts just to keep from drowning." Then he let out a sick chuckle. "Lot of good it did her in the end."

"You didn't."

He grinned and nodded toward the hot tub on the deck. "Right over there, actually. You didn't expect me to reward disloyalty, did you?"

"You're a monster."

"Don't pretend you feel bad for her."

"I don't. But that doesn't mean you're not a monster."

He shrugged. "Eh. Maybe. I could understand going to save your little boyfriend over there, but the hard drives, Chris. Damn it. Why'd you have to get so big for your britches?"

She hated every fiber of him. "You were killing people. What else could I do?"

"Wergs. Not people."

"It's the same thing."

He shrugged again. "I guess. It's a messy world, Chris."

"But *you're* a werg."

"It's really not that difficult to understand. It all comes down to money and power. It always has. I'm about to become President of the United States." He paused as if he enjoyed hearing it. "I really couldn't have done it without Bernard's company and finances."

She poured another drink. "So, now what? Why are we still alive?"

"I need those drives and whoever you might have spoken to about them. We'll go into the other room and I'll ask you first. Then I'll ask Aiden. If either of your stories differ ..." He made a pained face and ran his thumb across his throat.

"I'm not telling you shit."

"Very well." He reached behind the bar and picked up a walkie. He keyed it and said, "Go ahead and kill him."

Christine's eyes shot to the monitor as Adam's cell door was flung open. Adam sprang to his feet and lifted his hands in surrender. A Secret Service agent entered the cell with a rifle.

"Wait," Christine shouted.

Wooten called them off. "Getting you to talk is the only reason he's still alive, so you'd better get to it."

"If I tell you where they are, then you'll let Aiden and Adam go?"

"I'm sure you understand I can't do that."

"Then why would we tell you anything?"

"Because you'll get to live. Otherwise, you're all going to die."

"You'll let us live, but you won't let us go? How's that work?"

He smirked. "You'd have to undergo a slight process at our new and improved Underground facility, of course."

"So, we'll just be hunted again? Or fight to the death in the pits?"

"I was thinking more along the lines of becoming pets. In fact, I might just keep you for myself. But, hey, at least you'd be alive."

"You're disgusting."

"Maybe so. But that's how it is. That's your only chance at life. I'm getting tired of this game. Shall we proceed?"

Panic rose to the surface. "I didn't tell anyone. I swear."

"You're telling me you've known all this about me for a week and haven't told anyone? A nurse? Your fireman friends who you forced me to blow up today?"

She shook her head. "I had no reason to tell anyone. As far as I knew, Adam had uploaded the hard drives to YouTube, and we were going to return home to find you behind bars."

Wooten chuckled again. "I'm about to be the president, Chris. It doesn't work that easily."

"You have to believe me. I swear. If you let them go, I'll take you to the other set of hard drives."

"So, there is another set. That's what I thought. But that's not how this is going to work. Let's go talk in the other room. We're going to—"

His walkie crackled. "Boss, someone's coming down the lane pretty fast."

Wooten looked to the monitor that showed the front of the house. A set of headlights sped toward it.

Wooten keyed the walkie. "What are you waiting for?"

The Secret Service opened fire as the car roared past, diving out of the way at the last second. The bullet-riddled car hopped the front steps and crashed into the foyer, its horn blaring.

Wooten and one of his agents ran to the top of the stairs while the other stayed guarding Aiden. "Who is it?" Wooten screamed over the horn. The Secret Service agents around the car fiddled with it until the horn went silent.

Christine glanced at the monitors again and saw a werg burst out of the forest at the side of Wooten's house, one arm dangling limply at his side. He downed a perimeter guard before any shots could be fired.

She glanced at Aiden to make sure he'd seen it as well. The agent next to him drifted closer to the open sliding door, preoccupied with the fresh commotion downstairs. "We need to get you into your panic room, sir," he shouted.

Wooten blew him off with a wave.

An agent in the foyer looked up at him. "There's no one in it, sir."

Christine locked eyes with Aiden. He mouthed, "One. Two. Three." Then he sprang to his feet and charged the agent by the sliding doors. With his hands still bound behind his back, he lowered his shoulder. The impact drove the agent through the open sliding door, across the deck, and over the railing.

Christine shot toward the steps and bowled into both Wooten and the agent beside him, sending them tumbling down the stairs. She bounced up and ran back to the bar, grabbed her whiskey glass, and shattered it on the floor. She snatched up a shard and cut the zip tie from her wrists. Then she joined Aiden on the deck and freed his hands as well. He crumpled a bit and grimaced, but quickly sucked it up and stood straight.

"Are you good?" she asked.

"I'll be fine."

They raced down the deck stairs. The agent Aiden had knocked over the rail lay motionless with his neck twisted awkwardly. Aiden squatted and dug through his pockets. He found a key to the razor collars and freed himself and Christine.

Before they could run, another agent rounded the side of the house with his weapon drawn. He had them in his sights.

But another werg barreled into him from behind. It was Cole. More gunfire erupted from the front of the house and Cole raced toward it.

"They came for us," Christine said, so surprised she'd frozen on the spot.

"Get to the forest," Aiden shouted.

She followed his terrified gaze to see one of the gargoyle-like creatures from Sandalio perching on the deck rail above them. It dropped toward her and lunged for her head with its clawed feet. She fell to her back just out of reach and shifted as it circled around for another pass.

Aiden shifted an instant before a second creature slammed into him from behind, sending them both to the ground. Claws and teeth and spit flew as they rolled and thrashed, trying to get at each other's throats.

She moved to help him, but the first creature dove at her like an eagle, its wings pinned to its back. She swatted blindly as it neared, but it veered away in a stunning display of agility. Its claw raked her face as it passed. Fire erupted in her snout. Before she could react, it had sliced open her arm, too. She stumbled forward. The beast pounced on her back and drove its claws into her shoulders. The impact slammed her face hard into the grass. The claws dug into her flesh and clamped around her shoulder blades. The gargoyle started to bat its wings. She knew what was coming.

Christine panicked and flailed, but its claws had sunk in too deep. Her feet left the ground. She looked to Aiden, who was still fighting for his own life.

She thrashed in the creature's grip, causing its claws to sink deeper. The gargoyle flapped its wings harder, lifting her past the deck.

Jericho careened around the side of the house in a full sprint. Even one-armed, he swiftly scaled one of the deck posts to the top of the railing and leaped at the creature as it lifted Christine past. He sank his claws into the creature's side.

The gargoyle dropped Christine to deal with Jericho. It grasped his shoulders and lifted him skyward as Christine hit the ground.

Let go, she silently pleaded. And then, to her horror, it did. She turned away an instant before Jericho struck the ground in the high grass near the back edge of the property. The sound of his impact, even from so far away, would fill her nightmares for years. She turned back to Aiden.

The gargoyle was straddling his chest. Both its greenish skin and Aiden's fur were drenched in blood. She started for them, but the other gargoyle dove at her again. This time she rolled to her back and showed the creature her claws. And once again, it easily avoided them. But that was exactly what she wanted. Just that subtle shift of its weight exposed it for her real attack. She kicked into its gut and thrust her feet outward, just like she had done to Sammy. The gargoyle grunted as its entrails splashed across her chest. It crashed in a heap next to her. She bounced to her feet and wiped rank gargoyle guts from her matted fur, almost gagging.

She turned to Aiden in time to see the gargoyle drive its teeth toward his throat. She gasped. Aiden swatted the creature aside, knocking it off balance enough to expose its own neck. And then he locked his teeth around its throat and ripped it away. The creature's gurgling wail was drowned out by Aiden's victorious roar.

He got up gingerly and hurried over to her. Gunfire ripped up the grass around them. Secret Service agents had finally made it onto the deck. Aiden grabbed her arm and pulled her toward the forest.

They cut left and right until the gunfire halted. She glanced back to see dozens of men wearing SWAT-style uniforms with weapons drawn in a standoff with Wooten's men. The back of one of the newcomer's coats had FBI on it in yellow block letters. They shouted back and forth over who had jurisdiction and who was to put down their weapons. Several of the FBI agents had started across the field toward her and Aiden.

Christine glanced to where Jericho had fallen, but couldn't see him in the high grass. She prayed he'd survived and gotten away. She followed Aiden into the forest, remembering the path to freedom from the last time they had escaped from Wooten's house a year ago.

They weren't far in when Aiden stopped abruptly, holding his still-mending side, and sniffed the air. He released a low, beastly growl. Christine caught the same scent milliseconds before Wooten in werg form rocketed into Aiden with the force of a car wreck.

Aiden bounced off a tree and landed face-down. Wooten spun to Christine. He was a muscular werg, oozing with power and ferocity. Thick, frothy slobber leaked from his jowls.

He charged.

Christine stood her ground.

He swung at her head. She caught his wrist, jumped, and drove both feet at his gut. Instead of her claws meeting his flesh, he swatted her legs away and slammed her to the ground. The impact took the wind out of her. She rolled to her side, trying to suck in a breath. He strutted around her as if playing with his prey. Then he kicked her in the stomach.

When she doubled over, he squatted, wrapped his arms around her from behind, and yanked her to her feet. His grip was strong. She winced, waiting for his teeth to clamp around her neck and finish the job. She felt his hot breath.

Aiden groaned and stirred. Wooten spun to face him, still holding her tight to his chest. Aiden got to all fours, wobbled, and shook the cobwebs from his head.

Wooten's grip loosened slightly. Christine used that mistake to spin violently and face him. She clutched his left arm at the elbow, dug the claws of her other hand into the flesh above his right pec, and drove her hip into his waist like Jericho had shown her.

Wooten's legs whipped over his head and he landed on his rear with a thud. Grabbing him from behind, she clamped her teeth on the side of his neck. Wooten froze in her grip. She didn't immediately bite down. Though he deserved to die more than anyone in the world and she wanted desperately to be the one to kill him, she resisted.

"Stop right there," someone shouted.

Christine spun toward the voice, dragging Wooten around to keep him between the guns and her. With her teeth still pressing into his neck, she lifted her eyes to see half a dozen FBI agents with their guns drawn. She assumed they were loaded with silver.

The agent in front held his pistol up in surrender. "I'm Agent Cabotage with the FBI. Let him go. It's over. No one else needs to get hurt."

A man in a dark suit stepped forward. "Don't you hurt him," he shouted.

"Stand down, Lamar," Agent Cabotage snapped. "FBI has jurisdiction, not Secret Service."

Lamar ignored him and took another step forward.

Christine gave Wooten's neck a slight squeeze and felt the pulsation of his artery against her teeth. She wanted to cry. If she let him go, no wergs would ever be safe again.

Cabotage held out his hands. "We'll work this out, Christine."

Her stomach dropped. How did he know her name?

"It's okay. We know what's going on."

She narrowed her eyes, but she knew she had no other options. She slowly loosened her jaw enough for Wooten to yank free and scurry out of reach.

He shifted back to human form and stood up and wiped his mouth. "Kill her," he shouted.

"No one's killing anyone else," Cabotage answered.

Wooten turned to Lamar. "Lamar, do something. You run the Secret Service. She tried to kill me."

Lamar shook his head. "I can't, sir. It's over." He took off his coat and gave it to Wooten to wrap around his waist.

"Why are you even here?" Wooten asked, ignoring the FBI. "Where's Clayton? He's in charge of my detail."

"And I'm in charge of the entire organization. Clayton is now in custody at the house with the other agents assigned to you. From what I'm seeing, you've used my men to facilitate some pretty awful things and may have completely destroyed the organization I've worked my entire career to make better. We may never regain the trust of the American people again. I suggest you keep your mouth shut and let your lawyers do the talking from here on out."

"Lawyers? This is ridiculous." He released a nervous chuckle as he looked at the FBI agents. Then he changed tactics and put on his famous politician smile. "All right, everyone. Calm down. There's been a huge misunderstanding." He made puppy eyes at Lamar. "Come on, man. Clayton's a good man. Anything you think we've done can be explained."

"I don't think so, sir. Every Secret Service agent who has been on your detail will be brought in and questioned and, if necessary, punished according to the strictest measures of the law."

An FBI agent handed Cabotage a razor collar. Lamar stepped between him and Wooten. "I told you that the Secret Service will handle the president-elect's surrender."

"We can't trust the Secret Service anymore, Lamar. You understand that."

"But you know me, Jim. You trust me. At the very least, let me finish this. If you do, I will see to it myself that every member of the Secret Service cooperates fully with your investigation. And when this is over, I'll hand in my resignation."

Cabotage weighed his words and then stepped aside. Lamar took the razor collar and extended it toward Wooten's neck.

Wooten took a step back. "I'm not wearing that." The whites of his eyes blackened and about a half-dozen rifles shifted in his direction.

"You have to do this, sir," Lamar said. He cautiously reached out with the collar again. This time, Wooten stood motionless while Lamar clamped the collar around his neck. "I'll see you at the house, Jim."

Cabotage sent two FBI agents to escort them out of the forest.

Another agent passed them, carrying blankets and towels. He tossed them to Aiden and Christine.

Cabotage smiled. "Let's clean you up and get you some medical help. No more fighting today, okay, Christine?" He directed his men to turn away so she and Aiden could shift, wipe down, and wrap themselves in the blankets.

The agents handcuffed them and led them from the forest toward the front of Wooten's house. As they walked, Christine asked, "I don't understand. How did you even know to come here?"

"We received an anonymous phone call. The caller gave us an unbelievable story about what Wooten's been up to and told us he was about to attack the president-elect's house to free you. Before he hung up, we heard a shit-ton of gunfire. We scrambled to get out here, and you know the rest."

"And Adam?"

"Who, ma'am?"

"He's a friend. Wooten has him in a cell somewhere. They were going to kill him."

"We're looking into everything right now. We'll add that to the list. In the meantime, we'll have some agents escort you and Aiden to the hospital for evaluation. I'm sure you understand that we're gonna need to detain you until we can figure out what's going on."

She nodded. She didn't know if she was more relieved, scared, or happy, and she couldn't believe it was over. She looked at him through wet lashes and asked, "How are my friends from the fire department?"

"That's an ongoing scene and we don't know much at this point. I assume that was Wooten, too?"

"He used the Dog Catchers to do it. I mean the Federal Bureau of—"

"I know what you mean." He pursed his lips and shook his head. "The terrorist attack narrative that's being pushed is pretty flimsy, but damn. How many agencies has he corrupted?"

"What about my friends?"

"I don't know their conditions, but I can tell you a bunch of them have been transported to the hospital.

Somehow, they were all in the basement when the place blew. That saved their lives."

As they rounded the front of the building, she looked for Trey and Cole, but they were nowhere to be found. Secret Service agents were cuffed and on their knees in the driveway.

Agents were helping Wooten into his limo. He pulled away and gave Christine a deadened glare. "Don't think you've won anything here, little lady," he shouted. "I'll deal with this, and you'll spend the rest of your life in prison. That, I can promise. I'm the fucking president-elect."

She smirked. "*Were* the president-elect," she retorted.

His face boiled red as the agents pushed him into the car.

COMING CLEAN

32

Christine spent two days at the hospital with FBI agents standing guard during her treatment. No one would tell her the conditions of her firefighter friends other than that they were all alive. After being released to the FBI's custody, she was transported to an interrogation room on the second floor of their headquarters in Columbus.

She sat at a table in a mostly empty room with a large white-faced clock on the wall. Her public defender, John, sat beside her and offered her a cup of coffee. When she reached for it, the ninety stitches in her shoulders tugged at her skin. She made a mental note not to extend her arms so far next time.

"What's going to happen?" she asked.

"They're going to want information."

"What kind of information?"

"Anything you have."

"Should I give it to them?"

"We'll have to work something out. They already know you used fake passports and that you're an unregistered werg. They also know about a car you stole after breaking into someone's house."

Christine panicked. "I was running for my life. I had to hide. I—"

"It's okay. I get it. I'm going to try and get you the best deal I can. It'll all depend on how valuable they see you."

"Any deal I make will have to include my friends."

"We'll see what they offer and work something out."

John and Christine talked for about an hour before Agent Cabotage and his partner, a woman who introduced herself as Agent Ullom, entered the room and sat down.

"Before we start, can I ask you something?" Christine asked.

Ullom shrugged. "Sure."

"Where's Aiden?"

Cabotage took out a recorder and placed it on the table. "He's giving his statement in another room. You can see him after everything's finished here."

Christine sipped the cold coffee. "Can you tell me how my friends from the firehouse are doing?"

"Of course." Cabotage cleared his throat, put on a pair of reading glasses, and opened a manila folder. "That whole situation's a mess all its own, huh?" He rifled through a few pages. "Let's see." He stopped and followed the lines with a finger. "It looks like Alexander Brooks is pretty banged up but will live. Same with David Martin and Jed Fisher. Anthony Owens is in the ICU listed as stable."

She held her breath with each name. "And Willie and Mick? What about them?"

He dragged his finger down the page. "Uh … It looks like William Hayes has already been released and …" He stopped before he got to Mick.

"What is it? Is Mick okay?" She almost didn't want the answer, fearing the worst.

"It looks like it's touch and go with him. He's in a medically induced coma with a head injury from the partial basement collapse."

Christine's stomach turned. "Is he going to live?"

"I'm sorry, I don't know that. Sounds pretty bad, though."

Christine's eyes burned with unshed tears as she pictured her friend lying in a hospital bed because of her. "What about Adam? Did you find him?"

He scanned a couple more pages. "Yes. He was in a cell in a different building near Wooten's home, actually. He's a little beat up, but overall in good condition. We've been talking to him today, too. He's quite the character. When we asked him to tell the truth, he said he was an open magazine. I don't think he quite gets idioms."

She snorted.

Cabotage flipped the page. "Oh, and we also discovered the body of a man in a back yard near your station. His name was Steven Alt. Was he a relative?"

She lowered her head and whispered, "He was my dad."

"Oh. I'm sorry."

"Thank you."

Cabotage gave her a few seconds to collect her thoughts.

A tall, thin woman wearing a pants suit with her curly hair pulled into a bun entered the room. She extended her hand. "My name is Trish Clark. I'm one of the prosecutors assigned to this."

Christine shook her hand.

Trish nodded to the public defender. "John. Good to see you."

"Likewise," he answered.

Trish politely nodded to Cabotage and Ullom, too, and pulled up a seat. "Let's get started. I'm not going to beat around the bush. We're hearing there were some hard drives with compromising information about the president-elect, but he destroyed them. We are very curious whether you happened to make copies."

So they didn't know about the originals she had hidden at the airport. She had already told John about them, however.

"If my client can help you get these valuable hard drives you think she might have, we would need some kind of assurance that certain crimes she and her friends may have committed during the course of the last few weeks will be handled in a way beneficial to them."

"If you have access to those hard drives, we would be very open to working out a deal."

Christine looked at John, and he nodded.

Trish smiled. "We would also need your cooperation throughout this investigation and willingness to testify against Wooten if needed at a later trial."

John nodded again.

"Perfect. Let me get something drawn up." Trish excused herself from the room. The FBI agents followed.

When they returned over an hour later, Trish handed John a packet of papers. He quickly skimmed through them, and recommended Christine sign. She told them where to find the hard drives at the airport.

She leaned back in her chair, trying to find a more comfortable position. She was going to be here awhile. "What else do you want to know?"

"Let's start at the beginning," Ullom suggested. "How did you become a werg?"

Christine took a deep breath and sipped at her second coffee. For the first time since she had met Bernard Henderson, she felt like she could tell the world the truth about what had happened to her. She started at the beginning, concentrating on not leaving out any important details, including her conversation with Wooten in the hospital after the WereHouse's fall.

Ullom and Cabotage couldn't write fast enough. They only stopped her occasionally to clarify something before encouraging her to go on.

Trish quietly listened with her arms crossed. "Tell us more about the farm you stayed at," she said.

"A guy had set it up for wergs who wanted to stay unregistered and not be hassled by the Dog Catchers."

"With what we've been uncovering about Wooten's WOC, and especially the Dog Catchers, I can see why. Was this guy's name Slater?"

She nodded.

"We found his body on a bench at a small airport. What can you tell us about that?"

She told them about the attack on the farm and how he had been shot trying to rescue his friends.

Trish checked her notes. "What do you know about a man named Jericho Bennet?"

It saddened Christine to hear his name. The sight of him hitting the ground at Wooten's was still fresh in her memory. "Not much. He was a really nice guy who risked everything to help me rescue Aiden. Did you find his body?"

"No. Actually, we've received a call from him."

Christine nearly fell out of her chair. "A call? He's alive?"

"Sounds like it. He wouldn't tell us where he was, but agreed to turn himself in. We gave him until the end of tomorrow before we put out a warrant."

Christine couldn't believe he had survived that fall. She sighed in relief. "He's part of our deal." she said.

Trish nodded.

The judge approved the deal so quickly that Christine wondered if someone high up was pulling strings. She was released from custody and ordered not to leave town. That was fine with her. She was too beaten down to go anywhere. She thought she would rather sit in a warm bath for the next week.

The agents led her out to a waiting room where she stood before a large window overlooking the parking lot. They told her Aiden would be out shortly.

As she waited for him, watching the cars come and go, someone standing on the sidewalk near the intersection caught her eye. He wore a ball cap and a long coat with an empty sleeve.

When he checked both ways before crossing, she saw the side of his face. It was Jericho. Her knees nearly gave out. She pounded on the window several times to get his attention. He casually turned toward her, smiled, and tipped his hat.

She held up her finger and mouthed, "Wait," before rushing to the elevator. She pressed the button a dozen times, but it took too long so she found a staircase and raced down. She burst out of the front of the building and scanned the intersection, but there was no sign of him in the bustling crowd.

Aiden came up behind her. "Hey, Chris. What're you doin' out here in the cold?"

"Nothing. I just thought I saw someone I knew." She practically tackled him in a hug despite her stitches. "It's really over, isn't it?"

"Yeah. I think it is."

She bit her lower lip and gave him a look.

"What?"

"I've had some time to think, and I realized why I've been pushing you away. I'm going to work on that. So I thought maybe we could stop by the store and get a key made."

"A key? For what?"

"You'll need one if you're moving in with me."

He smiled and gently put his arm around her shoulders. "Where to after that?"

"I wanna go to the hospital and be with Mick when he wakes up."

"That sounds like a good plan. Let me go call us a cab." He went back inside.

Christine's eyes lingered on the corner where she had seen Jericho. She smiled just knowing he was alive and well and hoped to see him again someday.

Aiden returned and took her hand as they stood on the sidewalk waiting for the cab to arrive. She pulled him close and hugged his arm, happy to feel his touch again.

He kissed her cheek. "I love you, Christine."

Hearing him say that warmed her heart in a way she'd never imagined possible. With him by her side, she was convinced there was nothing in the world she couldn't do.

She whispered, "I love you, too," and was surprised at how easy it was to say.

VENDETTA

EPILOGUE

The rain sent a chill through the werg's tired and damaged body as he crouched near a stream. His latest kill—a jaguar that had put up a hell of a fight—lay bleeding in the water.

Constantly on alert for any other potential predators, he squatted and awkwardly tore at the meat with his teeth. Attacking a jaguar had been a risky choice, but it was old and slow, and he was starving, having been unable to eat anything solid for weeks after a nasty fight that had left his jaw busted, half his throat ripped out, and something terribly wrong with his left eye. Though each bite caused tremendous pain to his still healing jaw, it was necessary to keep up what little strength he had left.

He stripped the jaguar to the bone and washed it down with water from the stream. With his stomach full for the first time in weeks, he felt invigorated enough for the long walk home.

It was just after dawn when he reached the outer edge of the soggy field leading to his mansion. Since the authorities had long finished their investigation and cleared out, he felt it safe to return. He crossed the field to his bashed-in front door and pulled the black and yellow crime scene tape from the opening. The air inside smelled stagnant. No one had been there for a while. He gave a full-body shake to dry his fur and then, for the first time since fleeing the mansion weeks before, shifted back to human form.

The floor was littered with papers and overturned furniture. Broken glass and splintered frames were strewn across the marble tiles. None of his priceless artworks had been left on the walls and sledgehammer holes in the drywall had replaced them. He wondered if that was just the investigators being dicks.

He staggered through the foyer and into the downstairs half-bath and turned on the light.

His long, dark hair draped down over his face, and he brushed it back. The mirror reflected a horrific sight. A monster stared back at him. He recoiled and whispered, "My face." A cavernous hole replaced his left eye and the skin around it looked mangled and discolored. "It can't be. This isn't me."

His hand reached up to touch the damage. The area around his empty eye socket was numb and the scarring felt calloused to the touch. A tear blurred his intact eye. He wiped it away.

He lifted his chin. A raw, purplish scar ran the width of his throat, the jagged skin a stark reminder of the torture he'd endured.

He lowered his hand to grip the rim of the sink and stared into the mirror that had somehow become his enemy. He gritted his teeth, ignoring the pain in his jaw.

Sadness and anger surged into his fist. The mirror was no match. He pulled his knuckles away, leaving shards and a bloody smear.

One of the shards landed in the sink, its sharp edges promising an end to his torment. He stared down at it for a moment, lamenting how bad a turn his life had taken. He couldn't live with such a disfigured face. He picked up the shard and pressed the edge to his wrist. A drop of blood welled up at its point.

It wasn't fair. He'd been so handsome and rich and powerful. He had had everything before they arrived. But now it was all gone. Because of *them*.

The sorrow and despair slowly gave way to the blood-boiling heat of unimaginable rage. They had made him a victim, and he'd never been a victim before. It was suddenly clear what he needed to do.

He looked up, and the shattered mirror returned a dozen ghastly reflections. But this time, instead of giving him a reason to die, it gave him a reason for something far more satisfying.

Vengeance.

He tossed the shard aside and ran cold water over his bloody knuckles, turning the porcelain momentarily red.

The mirror had shown him enough. With blood and water dripping from his hand, he reached back and flipped off the light switch, leaving a bloody streak on the wall.

He stepped back into the foyer to the empty space where his stuffed werg had once stood before the authorities had hauled it away. He knew exactly who should take its place. The road to vengeance would be long one, measured in years, perhaps. Though it would be difficult, if he had enough patience and resolve, it could be done.

He made a fist at his side. The color drained from the world. As he stood in his foyer overlooking the ruins of his life's work, he whispered through clenched teeth, "La vendetta sará mia, Aiden Talik and Christine Alt. I will come for you. And when I do, I will destroy everything you love before I rip out your hearts."

Pietro had found a reason to smile again.

If you've enjoyed my *Werepets Unleashed* world, be sure to sign up for my newsletter at www.epertasepublishing.com and keep up to date with our latest developments. How else will you know when Book Three (tentatively titled *Prey*) will drop?

Also, I humbly ask that if you like any of my work, please share it on social media and help me get the word out. How awesome would it be to see *Tamed* one day on the big screen? The best way to do that is to sell so many copies that we can't be ignored.

As an added bonus, I have included my short story, *Snowflake,* from the *Werepets Unleashed* world. Read on and enjoy.

SNOWFLAKE

A WEREPET SHORT STORY

DOUGLAS R. BROWN

Epertase Publishing

SNOWFLAKE- A WEREPET SHORT STORY

Douglas R. Brown
Published by Epertase Publishing

Copyright ©2023 by Douglas R. Brown
ISBN 978-1-7368820-9-2
Edited by Rebecca Brown
Cover art by Steve Murphy

Haldon played his Nintendo Gameboy in the back seat of his parents' SUV as trees whipped past the windows. The Gameboy was new, a birthday present from when he'd turned eight a couple of weeks earlier, and he couldn't get enough of it. His dad had turned him on to an old game called *Tetris* and Haldon had spent the last two weeks trying to beat his high score without success. It turned out his dad was pretty good at games.

Haldon was completely absorbed until he heard a groan from the front seat.

"You talk to him, Elise. He's not listening to me," his dad said.

His mom craned her head around. "Did you hear your father?" she asked.

Haldon shook his head.

"He said that whatever it is that the Martins have to show us tonight is Top Secret. We're not allowed to tell anyone about it. Not even your friends at school. Do you understand?"

Haldon nodded.

Keeping his eyes on the road, his dad asked, "Did you hear your mother?"

Elise put her hand on his arm. "He heard me, Kerry." Then she reached back and brushed Haldon's cheek with her knuckle. "I love you, my little squirrel."

He rolled his eyes. "I know, Mom. You tell me all the time."

As she turned back to the front, she said, "Put your game away now. We're almost there."

Haldon set his Gameboy aside as Kerry drove through the entrance of a swinging wrought-iron gate and continued up a long driveway to a gigantic mansion.

Haldon enjoyed visiting the Martins because they had fun stuff for kids to do, even though they didn't have any kids of their own. Mr. Martin loved games and his finished basement had a pool table, dart board, and a row of old-fashion arcade games like *Pac Man* and *Galaga*. Haldon's favorite was *Dig Dug*.

Haldon joined his parents as they headed for the front door. While waiting for the Martins to answer the bell, his mom glanced down at him and snorted. She licked her finger and scrubbed the side of his mouth.

Haldon pulled away. "Stop it."

"Whatever did you get into?" she asked.

He thought back to the cherry Popsicle he had sneaked before they'd left and tried to look innocent.

She pressed her lips together. "I swear I'm done buying Popsicles if you don't stay out of them."

Mr. Martin answered the door. He was a big man with a gentle face. He wore a huge smile, which was nothing new. "Elise. Kerry. So good to see you." He kissed Elise's cheek. "Come on in." Then he stopped and cocked his head at Haldon. "Well now, who's this young man?"

Haldon giggled. "It's me, Mr. Martin. Haldon."

Mr. Martin thrust out his hand. "Well, put 'er there, buddy. You're growing more and more every time I see you. What are you now? Six-foot-two?"

Haldon snorted as Mr. Martin pumped his hand up and down.

Mrs. Martin was in the kitchen, a plume of steam engulfing her as she dumped a pot of spaghetti into a strainer. She invited them to sit at the table and then asked her husband to put out the silverware.

Mr. Martin gathered place settings and organized them around the table while his wife followed behind him, serving chicken parmesan, spaghetti, and some of the best garlic bread Haldon had ever tasted. Elise had to reel him in after he asked for a third piece.

As the meal wound down, the adults' small talk made Haldon wish he had brought his Gameboy inside. It wasn't until the end of the meal that things got interesting.

Kerry put down his napkin and asked what Haldon had been dying to know all evening. "So, Gabe. What's the big surprise?"

If they were outside, Gabe Martin's smile could have been seen from the moon. He wiggled his eyebrows and glanced eagerly at Mrs. Martin.

She sighed. "Go ahead. I'll clean up."

Gabe bounced from his seat. "Come on," he said.

Haldon was quick to join him, but Kerry called him back. "Your plate, young man."

Haldon raced his plate to the sink and then caught up to Gabe as his parents lagged behind. Gabe led them to the basement stairs and flipped on the light. Haldon expected to see a new video game, or maybe the electronic dartboard Gabe had been thinking about buying.

When they reached the bottom, all Haldon saw was the pool table and same old arcade games. There was a new pinball machine in the corner, but he didn't like pinball. It was the biggest letdown ever.

But Gabe didn't even glance at the pinball machine. "Wait here," he said, and went to the door that led to the media room. He opened it and stepped aside.

Haldon strained to see past him.

"Well?" Kerry asked.

Gabe made a kissing sound and said, "Come on, girl."

Haldon watched intently, ready to meet a new puppy or kitten. That would be far better than an old pinball machine, but still kind of a letdown. A new pet wasn't exactly Top Secret stuff.

And then something much bigger than a dog or cat moved in the darkness. In fact, it was big enough to be a bear. The creature stepped into the light.

Haldon took a stunned step backward. He couldn't take his eyes off it. The creature sniffed the air, hesitant to come closer.

"Is that a …?" Kerry asked, eyes also plastered on it.

Gabe nodded. "Um-hm," he said. "Her name's Snowflake."

Snowflake rose to her hind legs. She was taller than Kerry and Gabe and every other man Haldon had seen in person. Her fur was a cloud of white. She had a wolf's head with a bright pink nose, and at the tips of her fingers she had pale daggers for nails. Her thick chest flowed into a skinny waist and muscular thighs.

Haldon backed into Kerry's leg. He lifted wide eyes to his dad.

"Holy shit," Kerry said. "That's a real-life …" He trailed off again.

Gabe chuckled. "Heh. Yep. It's a werepet all right. A rare albino female."

Elise struggled to find words. "I-I thought werepets were illegal now."

"It's illegal to buy them. The government's still trying to decide how to handle people who already own them. That's why you can't tell anyone."

Kerry's forehead crinkled. "Do you think it's a good idea?"

"Sure. Up until last month people were buying them everywhere. Now all of a sudden it's a bad idea? I don't see why. It's just a pet."

"There must be a reason. People are turning in their werepets left and right."

Gabe brushed off Kerry's concern with a wave. "Remember when your insurance company told you that you couldn't have your Doberman anymore because they'd re-categorized them as dangerous?"

"Sure, but—"

"It's the same thing. People have been owning these things for years now. They're safe as long as you keep up on 'em."

"Where did you get her? I thought that company closed down. What was it called again? The Were-something?"

"The WereHouse. I was in the process of buying one when they closed up shop. I think their director got into some trouble. Probably embezzling or something. Anyways, we were super disappointed. But then, a few weeks later, someone contacted us and said they could still get us one from the black market."

"I bet she cost a fortune."

"No kiddin'. Let's just say, I'm not buying a yacht anytime soon. But she's worth every penny. She's been awesome. We love having her."

While Kerry and Haldon stared in awe, Elise found the courage to creep forward.

The magnificent beast ducked under the doorframe as she stepped into the room. She looked to Gabe for direction.

He nodded. "It's okay," he assured her.

She lowered herself back to all fours with her ears tucked tight to her head.

Elise glanced back. "May I …?"

Gabe nodded. "Feel free. She's completely docile."

Elise touched Snowflake's forearm and the creature flinched. "She's beautiful."

"She's the only known albino werg in the world," Mrs. Martin said as she came down the basement stairs.

Haldon inched forward, fascinated. Snowflake lowered her snout and sniffed the air. Haldon offered her the back of his hand the way his dad had taught him for meeting strange dogs.

"I gotta tell you, Gabe," Kerry said. "She's awesome and everything, but it seems like a helluva risk. That senator guy who runs the oversight committee is really cracking down on people who own these."

Gabe scoffed. "Other than you guys, no one else even knows she's here. Besides, Senator Wooten's too busy gearing up for his presidential run. Worst case scenario is he finds out and makes me register her. Maybe they'll fine me or something. As long as he doesn't know I bought her after the crackdown, we'll be fine." He nudged Kerry with his elbow. "I can get you the guy's name if you wanna look into getting one."

Haldon's ears perked.

Kerry threw a wet blanket on the idea. "Nah. We don't need one. Besides, you can't take her outside, can ya?"

"I can't take her in public. But we go jogging in the woods. I used to carry bear spray on my runs, but now I don't even think I'd need it."

"You think she'd fight a bear?"

He shrugged. "Probably. She's loyal. It'd be a helluva fight, too. They've been known to take down bears in the past."

"What's she eat?"

"A lot of meat. But I've got a guy at the Walmart who gives me the expired stuff for cheap. She only has to eat a few times a week. It's not that bad. I put the rest in a freezer in the garage."

"Sounds like a hassle."

"Well worth it, I assure you. She's like having a dog, only way cooler."

As the adults talked, Haldon looked into Snowflake's dark eyes and noticed a hint of green. Though he didn't understand why, something about her gaze made him sad.

"Hi, Snowflake," he whispered. He reached for her hand and carefully traced a nail.

"I've got a million more questions," Kerry said as Elise finished petting the werg and joined him.

Gabe chuckled. "I'm sure you do. Come on upstairs. We'll have some drinks and I'll tell you all about her."

Elise called Haldon over, but he hesitated. "Can I stay down here?" he asked. "Pleeeease?"

Elise gave Gabe an unsure look. "I don't think that's a good idea. I—"

Gabe interrupted, "You can stay with her while we get dinner cleaned up and set up the card table, and then you can bring her upstairs. She's a bit of a counter grazer still, so you'll have to watch her. How would that be, Haldie?"

Haldon agreed enthusiastically, but Elise still looked uncertain. "You mind if I stay down here with them until you're ready?"

Gabe grinned. "You're welcome to do whatever you'd like, but I assure you Haldie will be safe alone with her. Right, Julia?"

"Safe as a kid in a car seat," Mrs. Martin confirmed.

Elise smiled. "Just the same ..."

Gabe shrugged. "Suit yourself." He joined Kerry and Julia as they headed upstairs.

With the others gone, Snowflake seemed to loosen up a pinch and meandered around the basement. Elise sat at a bar table while Haldon followed Snowflake around. Snowflake quickly warmed up to him and practically plastered herself to his side.

Haldon taught her how to play a rudimentary game of hide and seek, though he got tired of it pretty quickly. Her sniffer made him lose every time. They switched to playfully wrestling, which was a lot more fun. Even though she could have tossed him across the room, she was very gentle with him. He was giving her a good scratch when his hand brushed over a rough area on her lower back. Taking a closer look made his face turn sour.

"What is it?" Elise asked.

He shrugged. "Come look."

She walked over and parted Snowflake's fur where he pointed.

"What is it, Mom?" he asked.

She studied the rough scar that looked like letters. Then her eyes narrowed. "I think it's a brand." She continued examining the scar. "It says 'PET'."

Haldon swallowed hard. "What do you mean a brand? Like what they do to cows?"

"I think so."

"Do you think it hurt?"

She nodded slightly. "Probably, bud."

Haldon's face crumpled a little. He hugged Snowflake's neck.

Elise rubbed his back. "She doesn't seem bothered by it now, buddy. You're probably more upset about it than she is at this point."

Julia called down that they were ready for their card game, and Haldon led Snowflake upstairs. While the adults played cards, he requested some treats and used them to teach Snowflake how to play dead. She was a quick learner.

Hours passed. He couldn't get enough of her.

When Kerry announced it was time to leave, Haldon gave Snowflake the biggest hug possible. He would have moved in with the Martins if he was allowed. He followed his parents to the car, his gaze lingering behind.

Snowflake stood on the porch until Gabe gestured to the car and gave a command. She ran to Haldon's window.

He lowered the glass and touched the side of her snout. "I'll come back and play with you again soon. I promise."

She cocked her head as if she understood.

As Kerry pulled away, Haldon watched through the back window until they reached the gate and he couldn't see Snowflake anymore. His only thought on the way home was to heck with Bobby Tolliver. He'd just found his new best friend.

After meeting Snowflake, Haldon was desperate to get back to the Martins' house. His next chance came about three weeks later when his parents scheduled another Saturday night of cards.

In the week leading up to the visit, he could barely focus on school, toys, or even his favorite TV show. The hardest part about meeting Snowflake, besides the wait to see her again, had been not telling anyone about her, especially Bobby Tolliver. Bobby would have been so jealous.

When Saturday arrived, Haldon was in the SUV a half-hour before it was time to leave. He didn't even take his Gameboy along.

"Excited?" Kerry asked with a chuckle when he opened the driver's door.

Wide-eyed, Haldon bobbed his head.

"You were quite taken by Snowflake, huh?"

Obviously, Kerry hadn't seen Haldon's notebook full of werepet sketches.

The long drive over was torturous. At the Martins' house, Haldon hurried through the pleasantries with his eyes locked on the basement door. Gabe laughed out loud when he asked Haldon how he'd been and, without looking back, Haldon answered, "I'm eight."

Kerry gave him a light smack on his shoulder to get his attention.

"I'm sorry, Mr. Martin," Haldon answered. "What'd you say?"

Gabe chuckled. "It's okay. I completely understand. Will you do me a favor when you go down?"

Haldon would do anything as long as it didn't take time away from Snowflake. He nodded.

"I didn't get a chance to take her outside today. You think maybe you could take her out and play? She needs a good run."

That sounded fantastic. "Yessir."

"Perfect. She shouldn't go far, but keep an eye on her. I had to put up an invisible fence and get her a new collar to keep her from wandering off the property. She's quite curious and has been getting a little loose with her boundaries. She's already been zapped a couple times and doesn't like it much. You'll see the flags. Sound good?"

It sounded perfectly reasonable. That was the same way Kerry had trained their Doberman to stay on their property. It'd be terrible if Snowflake wandered off and got lost. Or hit by a car.

Gabe stopped him before he reached the door. "One more thing," he said. "Stay away from the forest. I think a bear got into my trash the other day. Snowflake was having a fit downstairs. When I looked outside, I thought I saw one running away."

Elise looked alarmed. "Maybe he shouldn't be outside, then."

Gabe put up a hand. "It's entirely up to you, but I don't think there's any issues. I jog in the woods a lot and haven't seen any signs of it. It was probably just passing through. I'm more concerned about Snowflake getting overly curious than I am Haldie getting hurt."

Elise looked to Kerry, who gave her a comforting nod. "It's the same forest out back of our neighborhood, Elise. He knows to keep close." Then he turned to Haldon. "Did you hear Mr. Martin, Haldie? Stay away from the woods."

Haldon nodded.

After being excused, Haldon raced downstairs and opened the door to the media-room-turned-werepet-den.

Snowflake's eyes brightened when she saw him, and she sniffed the air before coming out. Her new collar had a large, black box nestled in the fur on her throat. A green light flashed intermittently.

Haldon hugged her and scratched the side of her neck. She leaned into his hand. After pulling back, he asked, "You wanna go outside?" Then he opened the sliding door of the walkout basement and stepped onto the brick patio beneath the deck.

She froze at the door.

"What's wrong?" he asked. Then he tapped his thigh. "Come on, girl." He backed up to give her room.

She didn't move, crouching with her ears tucked and her head scrunched below her shoulders. She trembled.

Haldon took her hand and gave a slight tug. "It's okay," he encouraged.

She pulled away.

He cocked his head. "What's wrong?"

She lifted her head and touched the collar with her other hand.

And then it hit him. "Oh," he said. "You're afraid of getting shocked." He guessed Mr. Martin probably didn't know the proper way to train her and she had no idea why she'd been zapped. He gave her a comforting smile. "I won't let you get hurt again. I promise. Let me show you." He took her hand again and gave it another tug. This time she followed.

Once outside, she loosened up and investigated around the deck posts, sniffing one more intently than the others.

He gave her another pull. "Come on. I'll show you how to not get hurt."

Together, they walked until they could see the first line of white flags. It was the farthest he'd ever been on the Martins' property. Though there weren't any neighboring houses within sight, there was one under construction in the distance. Between the flags and the construction site was the end of the Martins' property line, marked by their wrought-iron fence. He imagined Snowflake could easily jump it, hence the addition of the invisible fence.

Haldon pointed to the flags. "See those?"

Her eyes followed his finger.

"That's where the zaps happen. Let me show you." A few feet beyond was a fresh line of dirt where the fence wires had recently been buried. He knew as long as he didn't let her get close to that, she'd be okay.

He spent the next half-hour or so teaching her that she couldn't cross the flags. He brought her close enough to the boundary to make her collar give a warning beep, and then he backed her off.

She caught on pretty quickly, but he wanted to make sure she wouldn't forget. He kept at it even though she was obviously getting bored. When she'd finally had enough, she gave him an ornery look and moved about fifty yards away. He cocked his head as she dropped to all fours and crouched, ready to spring.

"What in the world are you doing?"

Then she exploded into a full sprint heading straight for him. Haldon took a nervous step backward. He knew running away was pointless as she was faster than anything he'd ever seen.

She was closing fast. Haldon cringed and closed his eyes in anticipation of being plowed into the dirt. He barely heard a sound as his hair puffed backward in a rush of air. He opened his eyes. She had barreled past, missing him by inches. He spun to see her as she made a wide turn and charged again.

This time he tried to keep his eyes open, though he still flinched before she veered at the last possible second. Her reflexes were amazing. Then she made another turn and blazed toward him again. It was as if she was playing a game. If he moved an inch, he'd be mush. This time he stood firm. By her fifth pass, he was giggling uncontrollably and she seemed to be having as much fun as he was.

He could have played like that all evening, but she soon tired, panting heavily. He led her back to the house where she went straight for the water dish and drank it dry.

Gabe gave him a five-dollar bill and thanked him for playing with her. If Haldon had brought five dollars of his own, he'd have paid Gabe for the opportunity.

He was already imagining his next play date with Snowflake before he was back in his parents' SUV.

His parents' occasional card games with the Martins just weren't enough to give Haldon a proper Snowflake fix, but he was at their mercy and all he could do was wait for the next one. At least their visits started to come more frequently.

Sometimes Haldon and Snowflake would play and run outside, while other times he would just sit and talk to her about eight-year-old life as if she understood. But recently she'd become less playful and didn't always seem as happy to see him. It had been a month since they'd played the charge and veer game that he loved so much. He wished she could tell him what was bothering her.

Like each visit before, Haldon was the first one to the front door. This time when Gabe answered, he was winded and in a bit of a foul mood. His usual smile was gone.

"Hey, Haldon," he said brusquely. Gone were the handshakes that exaggerated Haldon's strength and the "how tall are you getting" jokes.

"Where's Snowflake?" Haldon asked.

"She's downstairs," Gabe replied with a limp wave to the basement door. "She's been acting a little off lately. Maybe you can figure out what's gotten into her."

Haldon crowded past him and raced to the basement. Before he closed the door behind him, he heard Elise ask, "What's wrong, Gabe?"

Haldon paused to listen.

"Ehhh. Snowflake's not been obeying very well lately. When I give her a command, sometimes she seems to think about it first instead of just doing it like she's supposed to. They told me this might happen. They said females are the hardest to keep tame, and she would need to be reeducated on occasion, but the number they gave me to call isn't working anymore. I guess I should have expected something like this."

"Oh," Elise said. "Is it all right for Haldie to be alone with her today?"

Haldon didn't wait for the answer and rushed downstairs where Snowflake was curled up on an oversized dog bed next to the pool table. Usually when she saw him, she'd stand up tall and give him a playful snarl. But this time she didn't even get up.

"Snowflake?" he whispered.

She lifted sad and distant eyes to his face.

"What's wrong?" he asked as he knelt beside her. He petted her back and she flinched away from his touch. "Did that hurt?" he asked.

She looked away.

"What happened?" He inspected her back, gently parting the fur.

She winced again, but since she trusted him, she let him continue. As he carefully examined the skin beneath her fur, he found lines of red welts. He stood up, confused and worried. "Does Mr. Martin know you're hurt?" he asked. He turned for the stairs. "I'll get him."

But Snowflake scrambled to her feet and cut him off. She trembled and refused to look in his eyes.

"Y-You don't want me to tell him?"

She shook her head so slightly that he wasn't sure if it was an answer or a coincidence. He cupped her snout in his hands and turned her head toward him. "I don't understand," he whispered.

She brushed her snout against his waist, nudging him off balance. He steadied himself and she did it again.

"What?" he asked.

At that moment, his eyes fell on something wadded up in the corner of the room next to the pinball machine. "What's that?" he asked as he walked over and picked it up. It was a leather strap. It looked like a … His eyes went to his waistband, and then to Snowflake. His stomach turned as the pieces came together.

When he approached her with the strap dangling by his side, she retreated to the back wall, trembling and shielding her face with her arms.

Haldon froze and looked at the belt. "Snowflake? Did Mr. Martin hit you with this?"

She turned away.

Horrified, he threw the belt aside. His knees buckled before he found the strength to run to her. He was crying as he wrapped his arms around her neck.

"Why?" he sobbed. "Why did he do it?"

She gently nudged him with her snout as if he was the one who'd been hurt. The sadness faded from her gaze, replaced by a look of empathy. He plopped beside her with his cheek pressed against her side and struggled to call back the tears. Crying wasn't helping her. He couldn't believe Gabe would do such a thing.

Snowflake sat with him while his mind raced. Then he got an idea of how to help her. "Wait here," he said, and hurried to the basement's half bath. He wet a towel with cool water and ran back to gently dab at her injuries. She was tense at first, but then melted into his touch. That night they didn't play games or go outside or do anything they normally did. Instead, he just sat with her and tended to her wounds until Elise called down that it was time to leave.

He didn't want to go. "I'll tell my dad what happened," he whispered. "He'll help you."

She stared back, defeated.

He started for the stairs, watching over his shoulder as she crawled to her den and closed the door. He hurried upstairs.

For the first time in his life, he saw Gabe in a sinister light. When he left, he gave Gabe a subtle glare and didn't say goodbye. He was fully prepared to accept whatever punishment came with his rudeness. His slight went unnoticed.

Haldon was especially quiet on the way home, to a degree that Kerry asked, "What's up, Haldie? Did you have fun tonight?" He lifted his eyes to the rearview mirror.

Haldon nodded, fighting an internal battle over what he should say and when. Finally, when they turned into his neighborhood, he swallowed hard and blurted, "Mr. Martin is hurting Snowflake."

Elise's head spun around.

Kerry's eyes lifted to the mirror again. "What do you mean?"

"He's beating her with a belt."

Kerry's face twisted. "What are you talking about?"

"She was afraid of me today."

"You heard Gabe. He said she hadn't been acting right lately."

"She had welts on her back ... And ... And ... There was a belt down there. She was afraid of it."

They pulled into their driveway, but no one got out. Kerry turned to better see him and gave a half-smile. "Gabe's not like that, son. I'm sure you're mistaken." He sounded like he might be trying to convince himself as much as Haldon.

Haldon shook his head vehemently. "She told me, Dad."

Kerry scoffed. "Told you? You mean she speaks now?"

"Well ... I mean ... Not like that. She—"

"Listen, kiddo. She probably hurt herself playing in the woods. You just let your imagination get a little wild today. I assure you Gabe isn't hurting Snowflake."

"But she's not allowed in the woods. And you said he had a bad temper when you were kids. That he fought a lot."

"Yeah, but that was a long time ago. I haven't seen that side of him since high school. And I've never seen him hurt an animal."

Haldon continued shaking his head. "But I—"

"Listen, son. I'll tell you what. I'll talk to him and get to the bottom of this."

Haldon panicked. "No, no, no. Please don't talk to him, Dad. I promised Snowflake I wouldn't tell him."

"Then what do you want me to do?"

"Is there someone we can call? That place you call for stray dogs or something?" He felt a rush of anxiety when he considered his dad might talk to Gabe anyway. He never should have told him. "Mom?" he cried.

She reached back and touched his cheek. "It's okay, buddy. Your dad won't say anything. We'll just keep a closer eye on things from now on. You know if your dad saw something that wasn't right, he'd speak up. Wouldn't you, Kerry?"

"Of course."

Haldon knew he wasn't getting anywhere. He felt trapped in a box. Maybe he needed to get his mom alone later and try to convince her that Snowflake was in real trouble.

"You all right, bud?" Kerry asked.

Haldon reluctantly nodded.

"Let's get inside. It's getting late."

Elise held Haldon's hand as they walked up the sidewalk. He got ready for bed on autopilot, trying to figure out how to convince her. When she tucked him in and started to leave, he took his shot. "Mom?"

She stopped at the light switch.

"I promise Snowflake is being hurt."

"I know you believe that. We're gonna look into it. Now get some sleep. We'll talk more tomorrow." She flipped off the lights and left.

He stared at the dark ceiling, unable to sleep.

Still awake at 11:30, Haldon decided to sneak downstairs for a Popsicle. He peeked into the dark and quiet hallway before tiptoeing to the top of the stairs.

That's when he heard voices from his parents' bedroom.

"I don't know *what* we should do," Kerry said.

Haldon crept closer to listen.

"This ain't right, Kerry," Elise answered.

"They're our best friends," Kerry said.

"It doesn't make it okay. Maybe Haldie was right. Maybe Gabe isn't who we think he is. Maybe—"

"Even if he *did* hit Snowflake, this is an entirely different level of evil. I just can't believe he would do such a thing."

"Do you think maybe he doesn't know? We didn't."

"That's all I can hope for. If he knew and still bought her ... I-I don't even know where to go from here. I can't believe I'm even saying this. We've known the Martins for years. There's no way Gabe would have bought a werepet if there was any chance he knew she was a ..."

A what? Haldon wondered. *What is she?*

Elise sniffled. "If he didn't know when he bought her, he surely knows now. Right? It's all over the news."

"I don't know."

"What should we do?"

"We should talk to them. Gabe's my closest friend. I owe him that much."

"Okay. We'll go see them tomorrow. What should we tell Haldie? He loves her. He'd never understand."

"What *can* we tell him? That the creature we've been letting him play with is really a person? That someone took her from her family and turned her into a ... a ... a monster?"

A strangled noise escaped Haldon's throat.

"Haldie?" Elise called out.

He raced back to his room, climbed under the covers, and pretended to be asleep. He thought he might throw up. It wasn't possible. His dad must be lying. How could Snowflake be a person? It didn't make sense.

He needed to see her right away.

Haldon lay awake throughout the night, his mind racing. His parents' go-to babysitter, Sharron from down the street, was already in the foyer when Haldon rushed downstairs the next morning. Sharron was nineteen, dressed in all black, and wore way too much eyeshadow. She was cool to kids, but shy and quiet around adults.

"Where are you guys going, Mom?" he asked in his best attempt at playing dumb.

"We need to run a few errands this morning. We'll be back in a little bit. Sharron's gonna stay with you."

Sharron gave a cute wave, smiled, and said, "Hey, squirt."

Haldon thought fast. "Hi, Sharron. Um … I'm … uh … gonna play in my room for a while. I'll be down in a little bit." He started up the stairs.

Elise called after him, "Wait. Are you hungry? I made pancakes."

He shook his head, continued to the top, and hid around the corner. When his parents walked Sharron into the kitchen, he ran back downstairs, snuck through the front door, and hid in the back of the SUV.

A few minutes later, Elise and Kerry climbed into the car and backed out of the garage.

Haldon barely breathed for fear it would be too loud.

"What are you gonna say?" Elise asked.

"I'm gonna flat-out ask him if he knew," Kerry answered.

"And what if he says yes?"

"I … I just can't imagine that. If he says yes, I guess I'll have to call someone. I don't know."

"And what about Snowflake? Do we just leave her there?"

Haldon shook his head.

Kerry sighed. "I just don't know. Let's see what he says first."

"I can't believe this."

"I know."

A tense quiet accompanied the rest of the ride.

At the Martins, Kerry entered the gate code and pulled up the driveway. He took a deep breath before getting out. Elise went with him to the front porch. Haldon peeked out the window as Gabe answered the door. He appeared surprised.

Haldon dreaded what he had to do next. But it was for Snowflake. He gathered the courage, flung the door open, and ran to his parents.

They watched him approach with confusion clouding their faces.

"Haldie?" Elise asked. "What are you doing here?"

"Mom, I'm sorry. I wanna see Snowflake."

Kerry's eyes narrowed. "You hid in the car?"

"I'm sorry, Dad." He wilted under his father's glare.

"You're in some serious trouble when we get home," Kerry said. Then he turned to Elise. "You'd better call Sharron and tell her he's here."

"What's going on, guys?" Gabe asked.

"We need to talk. Can we come in?"

"Of course." Gabe stepped aside.

Julia was in a robe in the kitchen, cooking breakfast. When the surprise of seeing their unexpected guests wore off, she offered them coffee. Kerry accepted a mug while Elise waved it off.

Haldon took his shot. "Mr. Martin, can I play with Snowflake?" he asked.

Gabe's forehead creased. "I guess. If your parents don't mind, that is. What's going on, Kerry?"

Kerry sipped at the hot coffee. "I'd rather not talk about it in front of Haldie."

Gabe gestured toward the basement door. "You know where she is, kid."

Haldon pulled the door closed behind him, waited on the stairs, and listened.

After Kerry assumed Haldon was out of earshot, he asked, "Did you see the news?"

"Yeah," Gabe answered solemnly.

"She's a person, Gabe."

"I know."

"Is that the first you heard such a thing?"

Gabe didn't answer, but he must have nodded because Kerry said, "You really didn't know?"

"What kind of person do you think I am?"

"But now that you know, what're you gonna do?"

"What do you mean?"

"She's a person. You've gotta turn her in."

"You mean to Senator Wooten and the Werewolf Oversight Committee? That's crazy. They'll put me in jail."

"You said it was just a fine."

"That was all bullshit. After the WereHouse fiasco, it became a felony to own a werepet in any way. We just didn't know why until last night."

Kerry groaned. "Well, you're just gonna have to suck it up and do what's right."

"I can't do that."

"What do you mean you can't? She's a person, for God's sake. You have to turn her in and take the consequences."

"I don't know, Kerry. Maybe I can just … you know … get rid of her."

"What?" Elise blurted. "Tell me you didn't just say that, Gabe."

"Elise, you don't understand. If I turn her in, I'll lose everything."

"I can't believe what I'm hearing," she said.

"That's not good enough," Kerry snapped. He had used the same stern, you're-in-trouble voice that always gave Haldon goosebumps.

"I don't know what else to do. If she just disappears, everything will go back to normal."

"That's insane."

"I'm not going to jail, Kerry."

"Let us take her, then," Kerry said. "We'll turn her in and say we found her somewhere."

That sounded like a great idea to Haldon. He didn't hear Gabe's answer, but it really upset his dad.

"What do you mean no?" Kerry shouted.

Gabe's voice lowered and his tone darkened. "Maybe you guys should just leave."

"What? Wait a minute," Kerry said.

"You need to worry about your own family, Kerry, and I'll worry about mine. Go get Haldon and go home. I'll handle this."

"Gabe, you can't. It's not a wounded deer you're putting out of its misery. It's a—"

"I know exactly what it is. No one will miss her."

That was all Haldon needed to hear. He finally knew what he needed to do. He raced downstairs and ripped open the door to Snowflake's den.

Surprised, she lifted her head from her dog bed. He hugged her like he always did. Then he whispered, "I know what you are and what they've done to you."

She leaned back and cocked her head.

He led her out, opened the sliding door, and motioned her outside. "You shouldn't be here," he said. "You're not an animal. You're a person … Like me."

Her eyes twisted shut for a moment.

He waved her down to his level, unfastened her collar, and threw it into the yard. "You're free now. You have to run. You don't have much time."

But she didn't move.

He looked inside and then back to her. "We really don't have time." He took her hand and pulled her toward the yard. "Come with me." Knowing she wouldn't cross the perimeter without him, he led her toward the forest. She hesitated at the flags.

He shook his head. "Snowflake, you don't have to stop this time. You're free." His eyes filled with tears. "If you stay here, I don't know what they'll do to you. They ... They ..." He couldn't finish, his tears now free-flowing.

She cocked her head.

"I wish I could make you a person again, but I don't know how. I'm so sorry." He pointed to the trees. "You have to go," he cried. "Get outta here."

When she didn't listen, he ran past the flags and faced her. "Snowflake. Come on," he pleaded.

She inched closer, her head tucked beneath her shoulders. Trust was a wonderful thing.

"That's it," he cried. "You can do it. Keep coming."

When she reached the flags and nothing happened, she continued past, her confidence building. She stopped beside him, already beyond the invisible fence.

He pushed her from behind. "Go, Snowflake," he shouted. "Be free. Don't ever come back here."

She stared back at him, vacant-eyed and scared. It wasn't working.

He knew what he had to do, and he hated himself for doing it. He dragged his fingers through the grass and found a fist-sized rock. With tears streaming down his face, he threw it hard at her feet, careful not to hit her.

She flinched.

He screamed, "*Go*. Get outta here." His heart broke as betrayal filled her face, and he wished he could make her understand why he was doing it. He found another rock and threw it closer. It could have just as easily been his heart.

That one got her attention. She took a step backward and snarled. Haldon raised his hands above his head and screamed, "Get outta here. Go. I hate you." It was the most painful thing he'd ever said.

She rose to her hind legs and sniffed the air.

He picked up another rock and shouted again, "Please, go."

She dropped to all fours, head lowered and ears back. Her sad eyes fixated on his as she turned away. Devastated, he did the same. His first step toward the house was the hardest one he'd ever taken. When he finally glanced back halfway across the yard, she was gone. That made him as sad as it did happy. He dragged his sleeve across his raining eyes.

Gabe and Kerry were stepping out onto the patio. Gabe looked agitated, pacing and glaring. "Where is she?" he shouted.

Haldon bowed his head as he walked to them.

"Answer me, Haldon."

Haldon was too afraid to speak.

Gabe scowled at Kerry. "Get him to tell me where she is."

Kerry pursed his lips. "You're on your own on this one, Gabe. We're not helping you."

Haldon's head shot up. He had already mentally conceded his Gameboy to the punishment pile for life, but that wasn't the vibe he was getting from his dad.

Gabe opened his mouth to say something else when he noticed the collar in the yard. He ran to it and snatched it up. Then he looked to the forest and grabbed his chest. "You don't know what you just did to us, kid. If someone traces her back to me, I'm in deep shit." He stormed into the house as Julia and Elise stepped outside.

Haldon's lower lip quivered. "I-I-I'm sorry, Dad. I had to do it."

Kerry rested his hand on Haldon's shoulder. "It's okay."

An engine revved from the side of the house, and Gabe shot into the back yard on a quad runner. He had the handle grip in one hand and a rifle cocked against his hip in the other.

Haldon panicked. "Dad?"

"Go with your mom and get in the car."

"But …"

A seriousness Haldon had rarely seen crossed Kerry's face. "I said go with your mom." His tone left no room to argue.

Elise took his hand. "Come on, buddy."

She pushed past Julia without so much as an "Excuse me" and escorted Haldon through the house.

Inside the SUV, Haldon started crying again as Elise held him close. She said, "I'm very proud of you. This is more than any little guy should have to go through."

"Am I in trouble?" he asked.

She gave him her special smile that always made things better. "We'll get through it. Though you're still in trouble for sneaking around and hiding in the car, your father and I understand why you did it."

Haldon sniffled. "I'm sorry, Mom. I just wanted her to be okay."

"I know."

As she held him and caressed his head, a gunshot from the woods sent a jolt through both of them. Haldon pulled away, terror filling his gut. "Mom?"

She looked just as nervous as him and didn't know what to say. While she strained to see into the forest through the driver's window, Haldon flung the passenger door open and jumped out.

"Haldon," she shouted, making a futile grab for him.

He sprinted around the house toward the forest. She might have chased him, but he didn't look back to see. He was faster than her anyway.

It wasn't until he reached the forest that he realized he didn't know where to go next. But since he had gone that far, he figured there was no reason to stop and stormed past the tree line. By nothing short of luck, he stumbled upon Gabe's abandoned four-wheeler.

"Dad?" he shouted. "Gabe?"

Just then someone hissed "Shh" from behind and Haldon spun to find Kerry hiding behind a tree.

"Dad? Where's—"

Kerry shoved his finger against his lips and frantically waved him over. "Be quiet." His face was tense and serious. When Haldon was within reach, Kerry grabbed his wrist and yanked him closer.

"What's wrong, Dad?" Haldon whispered.

"There's a bear nearby."

Seeing the naked fear on Kerry's face told Haldon how dangerous the situation had become.

Kerry's ringtone of "Another One Bites the Dust" startled them both and Kerry fumbled for his phone.

"What?" he snapped into it.

Elise's voice was loud enough for Haldon to hear. "Haldon just ran into the woods. I couldn't catch h—"

"He's with me," Kerry interrupted. "We'll be out in a …" He trailed off and lowered the phone as something caught his eye. He pressed "End" and put it back into his pocket.

"What?" Haldon asked as he followed his gaze. Kerry gently nudged him behind his leg. "There it is," he whispered.

"Where?" Haldon leaned around him for a peek. And that's when he saw a mass of black fur, rippling with each step. The creature's cold, calculating eyes dragged past them. Blood soaked its left shoulder, reminding Haldon of the gunshot he had heard. The creature paced back and forth, slowly moving closer with each pass, almost like it was trying to creep up on them while pretending not to see them.

"What's it doing, Dad?"

"You need to get back to the car."

"What about you?"

"Remember what I taught you. If a bear is brown get down. If a bear is black, attack."

"I don't understand what that means."

"It means I have to scare it away."

Haldon's eyes blasted wide.

Kerry stepped from behind the tree and threw his hands high above his head. "Get outta here," he shouted. Then he added some loud gibberish as he jumped up and down.

The bear side-eyed him as it continued stalking.

It wasn't working. Haldon felt the blood drain from his face.

The bear paused.

Kerry whispered, "Oh, shit."

Then it charged, closing the distance in a flash. Instead of Kerry, it aimed for Haldon. Haldon's legs suddenly wouldn't work.

Kerry jumped between them and shoved Haldon hard from the bear's path. From the ground, Haldon looked up in time to see the bear slash Kerry's chest and then trample him.

"Run, Haldon," Kerry shouted between grunts.

Haldon scurried to his feet. "Dad," he cried.

Distracted by Kerry, the bear lunged for his chest. Kerry pushed its snout with both hands, but the bear was too strong. Kerry squirmed as the bear clamped its teeth onto his forearm. Haldon had never heard his dad scream like he did when his bone loudly snapped.

Instead of running, Haldon found a rock and hurled the luckiest throw ever, striking the bear square on its head. It barely acknowledged the impact.

"I told you to run," Kerry shouted.

In a rage, the bear smothered him again, latching on to his shoulder and violently shaking its head like a dog with a toy. Kerry flailed at it with impotent punches as blood soaked his clothing.

The bear's growls and snorts were deafening. The sounds of Kerry's screams were horrific. Haldon realized he was watching his dad die and there was nothing he could do about it.

And then the bear stopped and lifted its soulless, merciless eyes past Haldon. Red tinted the brown fur of its snout.

Kerry cried weakly, "Please, Haldon. Run."

Haldon slowly turned his head.

Standing in the brush, not more than twenty feet away, was the most beautiful white werepet in the world.

"Snowflake?" he whispered.

Snowflake grunted and then charged straight for Haldon. He didn't even flinch or close his eyes as she blew past, missing him by inches. It was the deadliest game of charge and veer they'd ever played.

The bear rose to its hind legs, matching Snowflake's height. Broken and bleeding, Kerry dragged himself toward Haldon.

Haldon hurried to him and knelt down. His dad was covered in blood and too weak to get up. "I won't leave you, Dad."

Snowflake and the bear roared at each other in a primal language that only they understood. They collided in a violent blur of claws and teeth. The fresh blood contrasting so starkly with Snowflake's brilliant white fur gave the impression she was initially losing, but her unabated ferocity showed she was still in the fight.

The bear lunged at her. She avoided its attack and clamped her teeth onto the side of its thick neck. The bear yowled and shook free, swatting her to the ground in the process. It must have outweighed her by three hundred pounds. That weight advantage seemed insurmountable as the bear easily knocked her off her feet a second time. It clubbed her face with a paw and pinned her down while going for her gut with its teeth.

She drew lines of blood from its side with her deadly nails, but to no avail. The bear was relentless—a professional killer. She wailed helplessly as it ripped at her flesh.

"Snowflake," Haldon screamed.

Then a sudden and tremendous boom jolted him to his core and popped his eardrums. He spun to find Gabe standing behind him with a rifle held against his shoulder.

The bear yelped, spun toward the newest threat, and then retreated a few steps with a fresh hole pouring blood from its side. It roared.

Snowflake used the distraction to attack again and dug her claws into the blubber of its back. She was caught up in a bloodlust and clamped her teeth onto the back of the bear's neck. She tore a mouthful of flesh away with a jerk of her head.

The bear bucked and thrashed, throwing her free. Then it dropped to all fours and galloped into the brush.

Snowflake held her head up long enough to watch the bear disappear, and then slumped to the ground.

"Haldie?" Kerry whispered.

"Yeah, Dad?"

"Get my phone." He groaned and stopped to catch his breath. "Call for help."

Haldon dug into Kerry's pocket, found his cell phone, and called 9-1-1. He told them he needed the police and an ambulance. After Kerry fed him Gabe's address for the dispatcher, he hung up.

His thoughts returned to Snowflake as she lay on the ground. Out of the corner of his eye, he saw Gabe lift his rifle toward her and reposition it against his shoulder.

Haldon panicked. "What are you doing?" he cried.

Gabe closed one eye and trained the barrel on her.

She was helpless in his sights. Haldon knew what he needed to do. He took off toward her.

Gabe moved his finger to the trigger. He didn't see Haldon, his focus locked on his prey.

"Gabe, no," Kerry shouted.

Haldon closed his eyes and dove between Gabe and Snowflake. The rifle recoiled with another deafening boom that echoed throughout the forest.

Haldon lay motionless against Snowflake, afraid to open his eyes, but more afraid to not. He squinted, wondering when the pain would begin.

Gabe stared back, his face as white as Snowflake's fur. Kerry lay at his feet, clutching his pantleg. He had thrown off Gabe's shot at the last possible second.

Gabe's rifle fell to the ground. "Oh, God," he cried, and fell to his knees. "I'm so sorry, Haldie. I almost shot you." He covered his face with his hands and sobbed.

Kerry rolled to his back and sighed.

Haldon turned his attention to Snowflake and caressed her neck as she opened her eyes. "You'll be okay," he said as he buried his face in her fur.

She lifted her hand to the back of his head and caressed it like a caring mother might. He pulled back and looked into her eyes. They no longer looked sad, and that made him smile. She had hope for the first time.

Sirens wailed in the distance.

"You have to go now, Snowflake," he said. "They're coming."

This time she understood and struggled to all fours. She pressed her snout to Haldon's cheek and held it there. Haldon squeezed her tightly before prying himself away. "I love you, Snowflake."

Snowflake rose to her hind legs, her left arm held tight against her gut wound, and sniffed the air.

Haldon nodded. "That's it, girl. Be free. Don't ever let them catch you."

She turned, paused to look over her shoulder, and then limped away. Haldon watched until he couldn't see her any longer. Then he ran past Gabe to his dad.

The sirens closed in.

"Show 'em where we are," Kerry whispered.

Haldon ran to the edge of the woods where he could see Elise, a police officer, and two paramedics crossing the yard with a stretcher.

"This way," he shouted and waved his arms.

Elise nearly broke his ribs hugging him as the paramedics went to work on Kerry.

After Gabe regained his composure, he approached the police officer.

"What happened here?" the officer asked.

"We were attacked by a bear," Gabe answered. "Ain't that right, Haldon?"

As much as Haldon wanted to spill the beans on Gabe, the truth meant the police would send people looking for Snowflake. Her only chance to be free was if no one knew she'd ever been there.

The officer seemed content with the bear story and stepped away to call it in. Haldon went to his dad. The paramedics reported that Kerry had a broken arm and needed a whole lot of stitches, but that he should be okay. They loaded him onto the stretcher.

Kerry held out his hand for Haldon to take.

"I'll be all right, bud," he said. "You were very brave today." Then he let go so the medics could carry him to their truck.

Elise and Haldon followed them to the hospital.

For the sake of Snowflake, Kerry, Elise, and Haldon kept Gabe's dark secret, but they never spoke to the Martins again.

Douglas R. Brown is a fantasy and horror writer living in Pataskala, Ohio. He began writing as a cathartic way of dealing with the day-to-day stresses of life as a firefighter/paramedic in Columbus, Ohio. Now he focuses his writing on fantasy and horror, where he can draw from his lifelong love of the genres. He has been married since 1996 and has a son and some dogs.

Books By the Author

Legends Reborn: The Light of Epertase Book 1

A Kingdom's Fall: The Light of Epertase Book 2

The Rise of Cridon: The Light of Epertase Book 3

Tamed

Death of the Grinderfish

A Firefighter Christmas Carol and Other Stories

A Wicked Line

www.ingramcontent.com/pod-product-compliance
Lightning Source LLC
Chambersburg PA
CBHW030548020726
47494CB00005B/1526